CW01379004

Crime Files

Series Editor
Clive Bloom
Middlesex University
London, UK

Since its invention in the nineteenth century, detective fiction has never been more popular. In novels, short stories and films, on the radio, on television and now in computer games, private detectives and psychopaths, poisoners and overworked cops, tommy gun gangsters and cocaine criminals are the very stuff of modern imagination, and their creators a mainstay of popular consciousness. Crime Files is a ground-breaking series offering scholars, students and discerning readers a comprehensive set of guides to the world of crime and detective fiction. Every aspect of crime writing, from detective fiction to the gangster movie, true-crime exposé, police procedural and post-colonial investigation, is explored through clear and informative texts offering comprehensive coverage and theoretical sophistication.

More information about this series at
http://www.palgrave.com/gp/series/14927

Esme Miskimmin
Editor

100 British Crime Writers

palgrave
macmillan

Editor
Esme Miskimmin
University of Liverpool
Liverpool, UK

Crime Files
ISBN 978-0-230-20364-8   ISBN 978-1-137-31902-9 (eBook)
https://doi.org/10.1057/978-1-137-31902-9

© The Editor(s) (if applicable) and The Author(s), under exclusive licence to Springer Nature Limited 2020
This work is subject to copyright. All rights are solely and exclusively licensed by the Publisher, whether the whole or part of the material is concerned, specifically the rights of translation, reprinting, reuse of illustrations, recitation, broadcasting, reproduction on microfilms or in any other physical way, and transmission or information storage and retrieval, electronic adaptation, computer software, or by similar or dissimilar methodology now known or hereafter developed.
The use of general descriptive names, registered names, trademarks, service marks, etc. in this publication does not imply, even in the absence of a specific statement, that such names are exempt from the relevant protective laws and regulations and therefore free for general use.
The publisher, the authors and the editors are safe to assume that the advice and information in this book are believed to be true and accurate at the date of publication. Neither the publisher nor the authors or the editors give a warranty, expressed or implied, with respect to the material contained herein or for any errors or omissions that may have been made. The publisher remains neutral with regard to jurisdictional claims in published maps and institutional affiliations.

Cover Illustration: Deborah Slater Getty Images

This Palgrave Macmillan imprint is published by the registered company Springer Nature Limited
The registered company address is: The Campus, 4 Crinan Street, London, N1 9XW, United Kingdom

For William George Lightening, who likes a good story, with all of my love.

Foreword: How Many Narratives of Crime? Stephen Knight, Melbourne, Australia, 2014

Much-favoured among commentators on crime fiction is the argument offered by a Bulgarian structuralist revelling in the name Tzvetan Todorov, who proposed that a classic crime story comprises two narratives, one being the illusion generated by the murderer with false clues, misplaced suspicions, invalid miscarriages of injustice, and the other a second narrative which the detective, standing in for the modest author and the aspirant reader, slowly disinters and finally reveals as a statement of assertive detective authority as well as what passes in this novel as truth.

Hard as it is to disagree with anyone whose first name begins with t and z and v, other analysts might see yet further narratives, including ones with sociocultural content: that Christie offers a mode of fantasy security which depends on entirely domestic and female-linked forms of knowing and inquiry, which she embodies in her own favourite, Miss Marple; or that Sherlock Holmes, for all the delights of deduction and reading a person's biography from his jacket-elbows, actually realises a system of close attention to detail and an awareness of human weakness all too familiar for the anxious white-collar workers who bought *Strand Magazine*, and very likely changed trains at Baker Street on their way to work in the city.

Equipped in that intoxicatingly interpretive spirit as more than mere toadies of Todorov, we are in a good position to read (at varied levels), and mark (quite high) and inwardly digest (very nourishingly) the crime fiction encyclopedia entitled *A Hundred British Crime Writers*. The patterns that it provides themselves produce intriguing narratives. Statistics are always an excellent standby, as when Poirot counts the spills in *The Mysterious Affair at Styles*. And, still with him, gender is a good opening narrative focus. Noting that this century of British brutality falls into three zones of editorial import, it is curious to note a gender/number imbalance. Of the fifty-four who are on the shortest side, twenty-three are women (plus half of G. D. H. and M. Cole). In the medium-length category the distaff side is a good deal less potent, with a mere seven out of twenty-seven. But then among the longer-distance murderators, no less than eleven of the nineteen major hits started life as a miss.

The fact that of the British criminographical heavyweights a clear majority are women suggests a good deal, and not just a fair deal. Just as the Gothic was in many ways a woman's form, for both reader and writer, and the sensation novels remained much the same, even allowing for Wilkie Collins (who did have tiny feet), so the 1860s fictional assertion of female detectives when there were none at Scotland Yard and the surge into the mystery novel and short story by women writers in the later nineteenth century all suggest that this form has all the time had some underlying tendency towards the allegedly tender gender.

After gender, as the bible narrates, comes time. Of course there can be scholarly disputes on dates. Why else would we have scholarship? This analysis allots authors to the periods of their prime reputation-establishment, so Conan Doyle belongs to the nineteenth century like his hero Walter Scott, though three-quarters of his famed work occurred in the twentieth. Graham Greene is allotted to the pre-1940 period which might well annoy him for its naivety compared to his fit with wary post-war loucheness: Christie too is between-war identified, which she probably would have preferred. Michael Innes, with three widely read books by 1939 is also classed pre-war, and probably happy there. Both Michael Gilbert and Edmund Crispin, who might have liked to be thirtyesque, are here attached to the following period, when their impacts actually emerged. The casual commentator, free from the agonies of expertise, may feel these decisions all even out in the end, though real scholars, like real detectives, would hate such generalistically bland optimism, but if we accept our percentages as being near enough, none of our authors may perhaps be too uncomfortable in their occasionally disputable temporal locations.

Deep within these enthralling chronometrics there lurks the content-related narrative, the matter of subgenres. The Brits have primarily hovered between on one hand the true amateur, whether accidental like Baroness Orczy's old man in the corner or gentlemanly autistic (please put the violin down Sherlock), and on the other the essentially amateur improbably located among the police, like the Tolstoy of the railway-timetable, Freeman Wills Crofts' Inspector French. Even though Sergeant Cuff, that handy detective, was in fact employed privately by the languid Lady Verinder, the Anglos have never tuned in to the private eye. Though there could be more to the British story: a manly tear might be shed for the absence here of James Hadley Chase the king of the bodice-ripper rip-off and Peter Cheyney, in his time the out-seller of Dame Christie– and what other nation could boast the like of Hazell PI, the London tough guy co-authored by soccer international and Chelsea gent, Terry Venables.

But if period, origin and detective profession suggest a British preference for the antique amateur, against them flicker delightfully almost-forgotten figures: Ernest Bramah with his para-Chinese fables; E. W. Hornung, whose outlaw detective stories of Raffles are an eerie reflex of his brother-in-law's Holmesian security-fables; H. C. Bailey's unfairly lost Reggie Fortune, a Wimsey without the almost-concealed arrogance; C. L. Pirkis, the 1890s working woman's inquirer of recessively remorseless power. If the past can count such quietist achievers, there are also modern *amuse-gueules* for the over-stimulated palate: 'Bill James', master of ironic near-floridity is Welshman Jim Tucker, who wins high praise in America; Denise Mina, a high-thinking and sometimes low-punching virago from Glasgow; as well as well-mannered but also exotic identities like Enid Blyton with her rampant child inquirers or Ellis Peters and her magisterially medieval monk.

Considering how the major writers, whether recognised or recondite, actually worked their compulsive spells will beckon us back towards the theorists. You never hear the last of Todorov and his ilk. For Freudians, the crime story is classically a repetition compulsion: the more often you read it the more you will need to re-read it. The process of the consolation mechanism itself reactivates the crisis of anxiety that it temporarily contains. Like Sherlock's violin playing it is both relaxing and incoherent. And, anyway, it operated to reveal and also conceal the disturbances of our own times. That often-quoted Dorothy Sayers/Régis Messac stuff about

Oedipus Rex, the Book of Daniel or Voltaire's Zadig as the first detective stories is just a set of well-read herrings: crime fiction is the infant of modernity as personal rational inquiry confronts the anonymity and alienation of urban society.

Experts as they have been at inventing forms of relaxation, from the gin and tonic to the rules of football, the British were the great initiators of the psychic dynamics of crime fiction. Once Caleb Williams just couldn't keep his nose out of Mr. Falkland's trunk, British popular culture and its engagement with the threatening new cities generated the mystery story as a central and also crucial entertainment with aspirations of security. From France came both enlightenment instincts and urban surveillance, and from Germany the Hoffmanesque fabular form, and, with the New World explorations of Brockden Brown and the frontier elisions of Cooper behind him, Poe initiated an authoritative deployment of intellectual empiricism whose arias of analysis reverberated through readers' heads as mass literacy and international publishing in both book sales and magazine reading made crime fiction by 1900 the übergenre for the urban generation.

In our own time the world has re-asserted itself from Barcelona to Stockholm, and with dynamic modes of crime fiction notable in Central and South America, India, Japan, South Africa and Australia. Some is surely neo-colonial/tourist crime fiction like Leon and Dibdin, but some is clearly progressive, its colonialism more past than post – for sharp new voices try Vikram Chandra for the Mumbai version or Nicole Watson from indigenous Brisbane. While film and television keep offering the same dull mix of techno-violence and tacky glamour, the novel thrives in energetic variations of current sociopersonal conflict – an instance is the range of Northern Irish material, here only the edgy best, but they sit atop a huge pile of troubles thrillers debating and obscuring the local situation, much as the Spanish mystery has in the last ten years been a prime mode of reflecting on, and reassigning blame over, a half-century of rightist oppression.

English cricketers – and the amateur was long-favoured there too – tend to relax when they get to a century. Nicholas Blake, himself a Poet Laureate to be, liked to see the crime puzzle as mirroring the mix of high convention and potential violence of that game. But crime fiction should be seen now as a world game, like soccer. There are penalties for those who really break the rules, there is plenty of speed and skill and trickery and coherence – the goals are achieved in spectacular form and with mass applause. The game of crime fiction, a game of two halves, and many more than two narratives, is thriving, is very rewarding for writers and readers, and its rules are constantly evolving in the hands of its practitioners. Even making the narrator a murderer won't put you offside and you can exhibit your national achievements very widely – you can even encyclopedia the world with your narrative of all those narratives.

Acknowledgements

A huge and wholehearted thank you goes to my family for their support and encouragement: first and foremost, and with so much love, to Dan and William. Thank you also to my dad, Stewart, for introducing me to crime fiction, especially my all-time heroine Modesty Blaise, and to my mum, Paula, for suggesting the 100th author when her daughter's maths got the better of her (again). Christine Lightening, much loved and missed, always offered support. Special thanks are due to Martin, my father-in-law and partner-in-crime (reading). Aside from writing his entries, he has always shown an unfailing interest in this project that made it seem worthwhile – thanks, M. B.

Many colleagues at Liverpool have lent a kindly ear and timely advice throughout, especially Jill Rudd. Chris Routledge involved me in this project in its early stages, and the immortal words of Oliver Hardy spring to mind; I thank him for his kind support and splendid contributions. A huge 'thank you', in fact, goes to all of the contributors, for their hard work and extraordinary patience over the amount of time it has taken me to complete this. Thanks in particular to Heather Worthington for all of her suggestions, entries and extra contributors (her excellent students, who each brought their specific expertise to the book, and who are probably all professors by now). Also thank you very much to the DLSS stalwarts, Jasmine Simeone and Christine Simpson, who were incredibly kind when the going got tough. Stephen Knight's contributions and suggestions have been immensely helpful, and I'm very grateful to him for preparing his splendid foreword.

Thanks are due to the Crime Files Series Editor, Clive Bloom, for his suggestions for improvement and development. Medals for patience go to the various editorial assistants at Palgrave Macmillan, especially Vicky Bates and Rachel Jacobe, who have guided, cajoled and wished this project to its end, and who have all probably been ready to murder me, appropriately enough.

Esme Miskimmin

General Introduction: Even More 'Murder For Pleasure'

One of the first books I ever read *about* crime fiction, as opposed to the stories themselves, was Howard Haycraft's *Murder for Pleasure: the Life and Times of the Detective Story* (1941), which I bought in a second-hand bookshop when I was an undergraduate. My copy is actually the 1942 British edition with Nicholas Blake's introduction, now a seminal essay for students and critics of crime writing, but Haycraft's whole book is a key text in early critical responses to the genre. Its year of publication marked a century of crime writing since Poe's 'Murders in the Rue Morgue', widely credited with being the first 'proper' detective story and the starting point for Haycraft's discussion. Chapter by chapter, alternating between British and American writing, Haycraft carefully plots the progress of the detective story and discusses individual writers and works and their contribution to the development of the genre in the context of historical and biographical details. Many of the observations or definitions he makes have become fundamental to later discussions of crime writing: coining the term 'Golden Age' in relation to a genre, for example, or positing that 'there could be no detective *stories* (and there were none) until there were *detectives*'. (Haycraft's italics).

In writing for and editing *100 British Crime Writers*, I have drawn on Haycraft's work as both inspiration and model, discussing his ideas in my introductions to the first two sections of this book – those dealing with the Victorians to World War One and The Golden Age and World War Two – and then continuing where he left off in 1941, working through even more 'murder for pleasure' until 2015 (we had to stop somewhere). The obvious differences must be that I have focused only on his 'English' sections (for a similar survey of American crime writing see Steven Powell's *100 American Crime Writers*) and that *Murder for Pleasure* is more purist in its approach, focusing solely on detective fiction, which Haycraft establishes as distinct from other branches of crime writing in as much that it deals specifically with the 'professional detection of crime'. The remit of this book is much wider: *100 British Crime Writers* extends to a large and slightly unwieldy collection of authors and texts – from classic detective fiction in which crime is uncovered and resolved, to stories in which the criminal is the hero, or is an organisation rather than an individual, or in which the notion of crime is nebulous or morally complex or in which the presence of crime is really only the incidental generator of the narrative. Thus this list extends to thrillers and spy writing, which often invoke criminal activity or deal with the presence or discovery of crime even if it is not central to the plot, or the identity of the perpetrator is known or indeed irrelevant. There are detectives, spies, policemen, amateurs, heroes, villains, master criminals and petty thieves. I suspect that some of the choices might be seen to stretch the definitions of 'crime writing', but I believe that the provocation of such debate can only be productive. And you are, after all, free to write your own list.

Having discussed the parameters of the term 'crime writing', I should also say something about the other titular definition 'British'. This also proved a little more elastic than first intended. In the end, however, the writers included have been born in the British Isles or the British Commonwealth as such a time when their place of birth belonged to either institution, or, having been born elsewhere, have lived a significant part of their lives in Britain. I hope that none of them would, or do, take offence at their inclusion.

Overall, the general aims of this book are similar to Haycraft's, in terms of its being a survey of the progress of crime writing, focusing on specific authors as a way to do this and placing them within the discursive context of their peers as well as providing both biographical and bibliographical information. In so far as one can in a multi-voiced, semi-academic text, I have also tried to draw on a key element of Haycraft's style: the personal response within his discussions. Haycraft makes it clear what he enjoys and does not, and the reader is left to respond with equal passion. Blake expresses 'surprise' for example, that Haycraft has not included C. H. B. Kitchin's *Death of My Aunt* (1929; I haven't included it either, on the grounds that it hasn't really stood the test of time in the way that other books and authors of that era have). For my own part, I agree with Blake that Haycraft needed to mention Elizabeth Ferrars (who is included in this volume), but applaud his splendidly cursory approach to Dickens, as he observes that *Bleak House* (1853) and the uncompleted *Mystery of Edwin Drood* (1870) 'will not detain us long', as both were 'indirect and casual contributions' to the genre. I have followed suit: there is no entry in this volume on Charles Dickens. I feel that my individual contributors often reveal their enthusiasm for the authors they have chosen or offered to write about, and also their pleasure in reading their works. I would furthermore argue that it is this element of the personal in the readership that is a key feature of the genre of crime writing.

As Haycraft's title suggests, the notion of enjoyment is intrinsic to reading crime stories; in his introduction Blake writes of the 'men and women who took pleasure in their craft and gave pleasure by it'. This idea of pleasure from crime stories is admittedly a slightly odd notion when scrutinised: how can we take pleasure in reading about acts of violence and brutality? It is not the intention of this text to discuss in detail the functions of crime fiction; many theories have been put forward concerning its enduring appeal and the apparently complex nature of humans who derive gratification from tales of murder, but I would suggest that our reasons for reading are a varied and personal as the stories themselves. There is, of course, the indulgence of pure escapism: the possibility that we can in our imaginations at least become experts in ratiocination, super-cool super-sleuths, or suave spies. It could also be that crime writing allows us a vicarious indulgence of our baser instincts. Blake, talking specifically of the detective story, comments that 'democratic civilisation does not encourage us to indulge our instinct for cruelty' and that 'blood-lust' can potentially be 'sublimated' by reading about fictional murders. He also offers the suggestion that it provides 'an outlet for the sense of guilt in men's hearts in an increasingly secularised society'. This notion of reading crime or detection for cathartic purposes had already been discussed in some detail by Dorothy L. Sayers in her 1935 address 'Aristotle on Detective Fiction', and W. H. Auden would also go into the matter in his 1948 essay 'The Guilty Vicarage'. In *Women's Fiction of the Second World War: Gender, Power and Resistance* (1996), Gill Plain discusses how 'fears of social disorder can be vicariously controlled through the resolution of crime fiction', moving the functions of reading about crime away from the personal and towards the social or collective. These are just some of the reasons offered since people starting discussing and analysing crime writing in addition to reading it. Personally, I would put my own love of crime fiction down to a passion for 'stories' – really good yarns – and also to the same impulse in me that likes Sudoku and alphabetises pretty much everything. It's the reason I'm a Golden-Ager: I like the reassurance of order.

Regardless of why we read it, the processes of listing, ranking and rating crime or detective fiction also seem to be a significant pastime; this is not the first, and will not be the last, of such projects. Many of them have been undertaken by those involved in the writing or publishing of such stories: in 1957, Julian Symons produced a list of 'The 100 Best Crime and Mystery Books' for the *Sunday Times*, in 1987 H. R. F. Keating published his *Crime and Mystery: The 100 Best Books*, and both the Crime Writers Association and the Mystery Writers of America have published list of the 100 best novels (*The Top 100 Crime Novels of All Time*, 1990, and *The Top 100 Mystery Novels of All Time*, 1995, respectively). Since *Murder for Pleasure* there have also been some excellent critical works detailing the genre's history and evolution and which have become essential reading to the student of the genre. This volume does not claim a place alongside any of the aforementioned works, to list 'the best' one hundred crime writers (in my own or anyone else's opinion), or to be a definitive history of the genre – instead it aims to give a representative selection of British crime writers over the last one hundred and sixty years, and, aside from providing some useful information on each author, to place them in discourse with each other, trying to establish some relationships between the beginnings and the present day, and between writers who can apparently belong within the same genre, but seemingly have little to do with each other. The order of authors in the book is according to their first significant publication in the crime genre. Unless indicated otherwise this is usually their first novel or short story. The first of Ian Fleming's James Bond stories *Casino Royale*, for example, was published in 1953, the same year that Agatha Christie published *A Pocket Full of Rye*, a fairly archetypal country house detective story. The personal backgrounds, experiences and genders of the two writers obviously contribute to the two very different novels, but what is interesting is that these novels are arguably the product of the same national zeitgeist, and viewing them as such can bring something new to our readings of both.

Compiling a list of 100 British crime writers might sound a simple or relatively pleasant activity. Blake talks of how 'just as the devotee of cricket will spend happy winter evenings compiling imaginary teams of the greatest ever, so will the detection-addict set himself up as a one-man selection committee to choose the classics of his kind'. It is, in fact, very difficult and fraught with complications, some of which I have outlined above with regard to definitions, and made even more so by its being a collaborative project (although I would argue that this also makes it more interesting; not for me Blake's solitary fireside). Nearly everyone has an opinion, or a suggestion, or reacts with incredulity at the fact that you've never read R. D. Herring's *Murder in the Cypress Building*. In his foreword, Stephen Knight laments the absence of James Hadley Chase and Peter Cheyney and I apologise to him for this. It is important to say that I was not the only complier of this list – not as a get-out clause, but as a significant point about this book's ethos as a collective, discursive, project. It started out as a joint endeavour, and Christopher Routledge's valuable initial input shaped the first of many lists. Then I felt that there were too many male authors, and then someone suggested that maybe there were too many Golden Age writers. Individual authors came under close scrutiny, often for entirely arbitrary and personal reasons – I wrote off Dickens and wavered over Wilkie Collins. One of the later changes to the book was the deliberate inclusion of some Welsh, Scottish and Northern Irish crime writers due to the emergence of some specifically national crime literature in the last couple of decades.

Then contributors started making suggestions, and I was more than happy to make further changes, as I wanted to include writers that people felt strongly enough about to want to write on them and show other people why they should read their work. This could be because the contributor felt that the writer changed the direction of British crime writing, or because the innovative plotting was not to be missed, or possibly because the author's narrative style deconstructed the familiar with regard to the classical detective story. But, first and foremost, it was because someone thought that they were a really good read, that is, a book that they enjoyed and would recommend to others for whatever reason. Crime writing as a genre should be taken seriously and afforded careful academic and critical consideration. But it is also about murder for pleasure.

Esme Miskimmin

Works Cited

Auden, W. H., 'The Guilty Vicarage', in *Detective Fiction: A Collection of Critical Essays*, ed. by Robin W. Winks (New York: Foul Play Press, 1988), pp. 15–24.

Day Lewis, Cecil, writing as Nicholas Blake, 'Introduction' in Haycraft, Howard, *Murder for Pleasure: The Life and Times of the Detective Story* (1941; repr. London: Peter Davies, 1942), pp. xv–xxvii.

Haycraft, Howard, *Murder for Pleasure: The Life and Times of the Detective Story* (1941; repr. London: Peter Davies, 1942).

Keating H. R. F., *Crime and Mystery: The 100 Best Books* (New York: Carroll and Graf, 1987).

Moody, Susan, ed., *The Top 100 Crime Novels of All Time* (London: Hatchards, 1990).

Plain, Gill, *Women's Fiction of the Second World War: Gender, Power and Resistance* (Edinburgh: Edinburgh University Press, 1996).

Penzler, Otto, and Micky Friedman, eds, *The Top 100 Mystery Novels of All Time* (London: Random House, 1995).

Powell, Steven, *100 American Crime Writers* (Basingstoke: Palgrave Macmillan, 2012).

Sayers, Dorothy L., 'Aristotle on Detective Fiction', in *Unpopular Opinions* (London: Gollancz, 1946), pp. 178–190.

100 British Crime Writers, In Order Of Appearance

As outlined in the introduction, the entries are arranged chronologically, in order of first significant publication. Where there is more than one in the same year, they are then arranged alphabetically. This has, of course, created some interesting juxtapositions and a couple of seeming anomalies, such as those suggested by Stephen Knight in the foreword and myself in the introduction, but the overall result is an interesting one and hopefully even suggests a re-assessment of some writers in the light of unexpected contemporaries.

Contents

Part I The Victorians, Edwardians, and World War One, 1855–1918

1   Caroline Clive (1801–1873), 1855: *Paul Ferroll* 7
    Adrienne E. Gavin

2   Wilkie Collins (1824–1889), 1860: *The Woman in White* 9
    Adrienne E. Gavin

3   Mrs. Henry Wood (1814–1887), 1861: *East Lynne* 13
    Anne-Marie Beller

4   Mary Elizabeth Braddon (1835–1915), 1862: *Lady Audley's Secret* 19
    Adrienne E. Gavin

5   Arthur Conan Doyle (1859–1930), 1887: *A Study in Scarlet* 27
    Adrienne E. Gavin

6	George R. Sims (1847–1922), 1890: *The Case of George Candlemas* Esme Miskimmin	35
7	C. L. Pirkis (1839–1910), 1893: First Publication of the 'Loveday Brooke' Stories in *the Ludgate Monthly* Adrienne E. Gavin	37
8	Arthur Morrison (1863–1945), 1894: First Publication of the 'Martin Hewitt' Stories in *The Strand* Magazine Nick Freeman	41
9	E. Phillips Oppenheim (Also Wrote as Antony Partridge, 1866–1946), 1898: *The Mysterious Mr. Sabin* Alexandra Phillips	45
10	E. W. Hornung (1866–1921), 1899: *The Amateur Cracksman* Suzanne Bray	47
11	Baroness Orczy (1865–1947), 1901: First Publication of Six 'The Old Man in the Corner' Stories in *The Royal Magazine* Greg Rees	49
12	Erskine Childers (1870–1922), 1903: *The Riddle of the Sands* Christopher Routledge	53
13	Edgar Wallace (1875–1932), 1905: *The Four Just Men* Stephen Knight	57

14	R. Austin Freeman (1862–1943), 1907: *The Red Thumb Mark* (First Novel in the 'Dr. Thorndyke' Series) Nick Freeman	63
15	G. K. Chesterton (1874–1936), 1908: *The Man Who Was Thursday* Christopher Routledge	71
16	Edwy Searles Brooks (1889–1965), 1912: First Contribution to the 'Sexton Blake' Series in the *Union Jack* Story Paper Lucy Andrew	79
17	Sax Rohmer (1883–1959), 1912: First 'Fu Manchu' Story, 'The Zayat Kiss', in *The Story-Teller* Magazine Steven Powell	81
18	E. C. Bentley (1875–1956), 1913: *Trent's Last Case* Suzanne Bray	83
19	Ernest Bramah (1868–1942), 1914: *Max Carrados* Nick Freeman	87
20	John William Bobin (Also Wrote as Adelie Ascott, John Ascott, Katherine Greenalgh, Gertrude Nelson, Victor Nelson, and Isabelle Norton, 1889–1935), 1915: First Contribution to the *Sexton Blake Library* Lucy Andrew	89
21	John Buchan (1875–1940), 1915: *The Thirty-Nine Steps* Alexandra Phillips	91

Part II The Golden Age and World War Two 1919–1945

22 H. C. Bailey (1878–1961), 1920: *Call Mr. Fortune* 103
Megan Hoffman

23 Agatha Christie (1890–1976), 1920: US Publication of *The Mysterious Affair at Styles* (UK 1921) 107
Delphine Cingal

24 Freeman Wills Crofts (1879–1957), 1920: *The Cask* 115
Diana Powell

25 H. C. McNeile (a.k.a. Sapper, 1888–1937), 1920: *Bulldog Drummond* 119
Alexandra Phillips

26 G. D. H. Cole (1889–1959) writing with Margaret Cole (1893–1980), 1923: *The Brooklyn Murders* 121
Victoria Stewart

27 Dorothy L. Sayers (1893–1957), 1923: *Whose Body?* 123
Esme Miskimmin

28 Patricia Wentworth (Pseudonym of Dora Amy Elles, 1878–1961), 1923: *The Astonishing Case of Jane Smith* 129
Delphine Cingal

29 Philip MacDonald (Also Wrote as Oliver Fleming, Anthony Lawless and Martin Porlock, 1899–1981), 1924: *The Rasp* (Published Anonymously) 133
Alexandra Phillips

CONTENTS xxvii

30 Anthony Berkeley (Also Wrote as Frances Iles and A. Monmouth Platts, 1893–1971), 1925: *The Layton Court Mystery* 135
    Christine R. Simpson

31 Margery Allingham (1904–1966), 1928: *The White Cottage Mystery* Serialised in the *Daily Express* Newspaper 139
    Jasmine Simeone

32 Graham Greene (1904–1991), 1929: *The Man Within* 147
    Steven Powell

33 Gladys Mitchell (Also Write as Stephen Hickaby and Malcolm Torrie, 1901–1983), 1929: *Speedy Death* 153
    Christine R. Simpson

34 Josephine Tey (Pseudonym of Elizabeth Mackintosh, Also Wrote as Gordon Daviot, 1896–1952), 1929: *The Man in the Queue* (Writing as Gordon Daviot) 157
    Christine R. Simpson

35 Elizabeth Ferrars (Pseudonym of Morna Doris McTaggart, later Brown, Published as E. X. Ferrars in USA, 1907–1995), 1932: *Turn Single* (writing as Morna McTaggart) 161
    Victoria Stewart

36 Georgette Heyer (1902–1974), 1932: *Footsteps in the Dark* 165
    Greg Rees

37 C. P. Snow (1905–1980), 1932: *Death Under Sail* 167
    Christine R. Simpson

38 Ngaio Marsh (1895–1982), 1934: *A Man Lay Dead* 169
    Kate Watson

39 Eric Ambler (1909–1998), 1935: *The Dark
    Frontier* 175
    Steven Powell

40 Nicholas Blake (Pseudonym of Cecil Day-Lewis,
    1904–1972), 1935: *A Question of Proof* 179
    Esme Miskimmin

41 Daphne du Maurier (1907–1989), 1936: *Jamaica
    Inn* 183
    Megan Hoffman

42 Michael Innes (Pseudonym of J. I. M. Stewart,
    1906–1994), 1936: *Death at the President's Lodging* 185
    Christopher Routledge

43 John Creasey (Also Wrote as Anthony Morton
    and J. J. Marric, among other pseudonyms,
    1908–1973), 1937: *Meet the Baron* (Writing
    as Anthony Morton) 189
    Martin Lightening

44 Francis Durbridge (1912–1998), 1938: First
    Broadcast of the 'Paul Temple' Serial, *Send for Paul
    Temple* 193
    Victoria Stewart

45 Enid Blyton (1897–1968), 1942: *Five on a Treasure
    Island* 197
    Lucy Andrew

46	Edmund Crispin (Pseudonym of Robert Bruce Montgomery, 1921–1978), 1944: *The Case of the Gilded Fly* Malcah Effron	205
47	Julian Symons (1912–1994), 1945: *The Immaterial Murder Case*, and 1972: *Bloody Murder: From the Detective Story to the Crime Novel* (critical work) Christopher Routledge	209

Part III   Post-War and Cold War, 1946–1989

48	Michael Gilbert (1912–2006), 1947: *Close Quarters* Christopher Routledge	219
49	Ellis Peters (Pseudonym of Edith Mary Pargeter, also wrote as Jolyon Carr, 1913–1995), 1951: *Fallen into the Pit* Suzanne Bray	223
50	Ian Fleming (1908–1964), 1953: *Casino Royale* Christopher Routledge	231
51	H. R. F. Keating (1926–2011), 1959: *Death and the Visiting Firemen* Christopher Routledge	237
52	John le Carré (Pseudonym of David John Moore Cornwell, b. 1931), 1961: *A Call for the Dead* Steven Powell	241
53	Dick Francis (1920–2010), 1962: *Dead Cert* Malcah Effron	247
54	P. D. James (1920–2014), 1962: *Cover Her Face* Delphine Cingal	253

55	Simon Nash (Pseudonym of Raymond Chapman, 1924–2013), 1962: *Dead of a Counterplot* Christopher Routledge	259
56	Peter O'Donnell (1920–2010), 1963: *Modesty Blaise* (comic strip) Esme Miskimmin	261
57	Joyce Porter (Also wrote as Deborah Joyce and Deborah Bryan, 1924–1999), 1964: *Dover One* Heather Worthington	265
58	Ruth Rendell (Also wrote as Barbara Vine, 1930–2015), 1964: *From Doon with Death* Anne-Marie Beller	269
59	Catherine Aird (Pseudonym of Kinn Hamilton McIntosh, b. 1930), 1966: *The Religious Body* Jasmine Simeone	275
60	Reginald Hill (Also wrote as Patrick Ruell, Dick Morland and Charles Underhill, 1936–2012), 1970: *A Clubbable Woman* Malcah Effron	277
61	Frederick Forsyth (b. 1938), 1971: *The Day of the Jackal* Christopher Routledge	285
62	Robert Barnard (1936–2013), 1974: *Death of an Old Goat* Stephen Knight	289
63	Simon Brett (b. 1945), 1975: *Cast, in Order of Disappearance* Jasmine Simeone	293

64	Colin Dexter (1930–2017), 1975: *Last Bus to Woodstock* Susan Massey	297
65	John Mortimer (1923–2009), 1975: First Broadcast of *Rumpole of the Bailey* Television Series Diana Powell	305
66	John Harvey (b. 1938), 1976: *Amphetamines and Pearls* Delphine Cingal	309
67	Antonia Fraser (b. 1932), 1977: *Quiet as a Nun* Suzanne Bray	313
68	Anne Perry (Pseudonym of Juliet Hulme, b. 1938), 1979: *The Cater Street Hangman* Delphine Cingal	315
69	Dorothy Simpson (b. 1933), 1981: *The Night She Died* (First 'Inspector Thanet' Novel) Christine R. Simpson	321
70	Linda La Plante (b. 1943), 1983: First Broadcast of *Widows* Television Series Anne-Marie Beller	323
71	R. D. Wingfield (1928–2007), 1984: *Frost at Christmas* Steven Powell	329
72	Bill James (Pseudonym of James Tucker, also Writes as David Craig, b. 1929), 1985: *You'd Better Believe It* (First 'Harpur and Iles' Novel) Catherine Phelps	331

73 Anthony Horowitz (b. 1956), 1986: *The Falcon's Malteser* (First 'Diamond Brothers' Novel)   333
Lucy Andrew

74 Val McDermid (b. 1955), 1987: *Report for Murder*   337
Susan Massey

75 Ian Rankin (Also writes as Jack Harvey, b. 1960), 1987: *Knots and Crosses* (First 'Rebus' Novel)   345
Christopher Routledge

76 Peter Robinson (b. 1950), 1987: *Gallows View*   353
Greg Rees

77 Lindsey Davis (b. 1949), 1989: *The Silver Pigs*   355
Heather Worthington

Part IV To the Millennium and Beyond, 1990–2015

78 Martin Edwards (b. 1955), 1991: *All the Lonely People*   365
Christine R. Simpson

79 D. M. Greenwood (b. 1939), 1991: *Clerical Errors*   367
Suzanne Bray

80 Patricia Hall (Pseudonym of Maureen O'Connor, b. 1940), 1991: *The Poison Pool*   369
Steven Powell

81 Martina Cole (b. 1959), 1992: *Dangerous Lady*   371
Esme Miskimmin

82 Minette Walters (b. 1949), 1992: *The Ice House*   373
Heather Worthington

83	Malcolm Rose (b. 1953), 1993: *The Smoking Gun* (First contribution to the *Point Crime* Series) Lucy Andrew	379
84	Veronica Stallwood (Has also written as Kate Ivory, b. 1939), 1993: *Death and the Oxford Box* (First novel in the 'Kate Ivory' Series) Megan Hoffman	381
85	Stella Duffy (b. 1963), 1994: *Calendar Girl* Susan Massey	383
86	Alison Taylor (Birth Date Unknown), 1995: *Simeon's Bride* Catherine Phelps	385
87	Christopher Brookmyre (b. 1968), 1996: *Quite Ugly One Morning* Christopher Routledge	387
88	Susanna Gregory (Pseudonym of Elizabeth Cruwys, b. 1958), 1996: *A Plague on Both Your Houses* Steven Powell	391
89	Denise Mina (b. 1966), 1998: *Garnethill* Esme Miskimmin	395
90	Alexander McCall Smith (b. 1948), 1999: *The No. 1 Ladies' Detective Agency* Susan Massey	399
91	John Williams (b. 1961), 1999: *Five Pubs, Two Bars and a Nightclub* Catherine Phelps	401

92	Malcolm Pryce (b. 1960), 2001: *Aberystwyth Mon Amour* Catherine Phelps	403
93	Lindsay Ashford (b. 1959), 2003: *Frozen* Catherine Phelps	405
94	Adrian McKinty (b. 1968), 2003: *Dead I May Well Be* Gerard Brennan	407
95	Justin Richards (b. 1961), 2003: *The Paranormal Puppet Show* (First Novel in the 'The Invisible Detective' Series) Lucy Andrew	411
96	C. J. Sansom (b. 1952), 2003: *Dissolution* Martin Lightening	413
97	Dreda Say Mitchell (Pseudonym of Louise Emma Joseph, b. 1965), 2004: *Running Hot* Esme Miskimmin	415
98	Brian McGilloway (b. 1974), 2007: *Borderlands* Gerard Brennan	419
99	Stuart Neville (b. 1972), 2010: *The Twelve* Steven Powell	423
100	Gerard Brennan (b. 1979), 2011: *The Point* Esme Miskimmin	425
Index		429

NOTES ON CONTRIBUTORS

Lucy Andrew is a lecturer in English Literature at the University of Chester, based at the University Centre Shrewsbury. Her primary research interests are in children's and young adult literature and crime fiction and her publications include *Crime Fiction in the City: Capital Crimes* (University of Wales Press, 2013), co-edited with Catherine Phelps, and *The Boy Detective in Early British Children's Literature: Patrolling the Borders between Boyhood and Manhood* (Palgrave Macmillan, 2017).

Anne-Marie Beller is Senior Lecturer in English Literature at Loughborough University. She is the author of *Mary Elizabeth Braddon: A Companion to the Mystery Fiction* (McFarland, 2012), *Mary Elizabeth Braddon: Writing in the Margins* (Routledge, forthcoming 2017), and co-editor of *Rediscovering Victorian Women Sensation Writers* (Routledge, 2014). Anne-Marie has published articles on Braddon, Wilkie Collins, Ellen Wood, and Amelia Edwards, including essays for Blackwell's *A Companion to Sensation Fiction* and *The Cambridge Companion to Sensation Fiction*.

Suzanne Bray is Professor of British Literature and Civilisation at Lille Catholic University. She specialises in the history of ideas in Britain in the twentieth century and, in particular, in the communication of religious ideas in popular literature. She has published extensively in English and in French about authors such as C. S. Lewis, Dorothy L. Sayers and Charles

Williams. Her latest work, *Dimensions of Madeleine L'Engle*, was published by McFarland in December 2016.

Gerard Brennan recently earned his Ph.D. in English (Creative Writing) from Queen's University Belfast. His publishing credits include Undercover (2014), Wee Rockets (2012) and The Point (2011); winner of the Spinetingler Award for Best Novella in 2012.

Delphine Cingal is an Assistant Professor at Paris 2-Panthéon-Assas University. Her research subject is detective fiction and her Ph.D. thesis was on P.D. James. She is one of the organizers of the Neuilly Plaisance detective fiction festival. She is also a Chevalier des Arts et des Lettres.

Malcah Effron (Ph.D., Newcastle University) is a Lecturer in the Writing, Rhetoric, and Professional Communication program at MIT. Her work appears in journals such as *Narrative* and *Women & Language*, as well as in several edited collections, including her own *The Millennial Detective: Essays on Trends in Crime Fiction, Film, and Television, 1990-2010* (McFarland, 2011) and co-edited with Brian Johnson, *The Function of Evil across Disciplinary Contexts* (Lexington Books, 2017).

Nick Freeman is Reader in Late Victorian Literature at Loughborough University. He has published widely on the literature and culture of the *fin de siècle*, and is the author of two books, *Conceiving the City: London, Literature and Art 1870-1914* (2007) and *1895: Drama, Disaster and Disgrace in Late-Victorian Britain* (2011, paperback 2013). Both demonstrate his interest in Victorian crime, as do essays on writers such as G.K. Chesterton and Richard Marsh, and the serial poisoner and Ripper suspect, 'George Chapman'.

Adrienne E. Gavin is Emeritus Professor of English Literature and Co-founder and Honorary Director of the International Centre for Victorian Women Writers (ICVWW), Canterbury Christ Church University, UK. She is also an Honorary Academic at the University of Auckland, New Zealand where she teaches Law and Literature. Her publications include Dark Horse: A Life of Anna Sewell (2004), critical editions of Paul Ferroll, The Blue Lagoon, Black Beauty, and The Experiences of Loveday Brooke, Lady Detective and a range of edited collections.

Megan Hoffman holds a Ph.D. in English Literature from the University of St Andrews, UK. She is the author of *Women Writing Women:*

Gender and Representation in British 'Golden Age' Crime Fiction (Palgrave Macmillan, 2016).

Stephen Knight has taught English Literature in Australian and British universities and is now in retirement Honorary Research Professor in Literature at the University of Melbourne. He has worked extensively on medieval and popular literature, notably on Robin Hood, and has written about crime fiction since *Form and Ideology in Crime Fiction* (1980)— his latest is *Towards Sherlock Holmes*, McFarland, 2017, and they will next year publish his *A History of Australian Crime Fiction*.

Martin Lightening is a freelance documentary cameraman who has been a fan of detective fiction since his schooldays. Filming the police and private detectives in the real world hasn't diminished his enjoyment of reading about their many fictional counterparts. He also contributed to *100 American Crime Writers* (2012).

Susan Massey received her Ph.D. from the University of St Andrews for a thesis called 'The Uncocked Gun', which explored masculinity in contemporary crime fiction. She works at Queen's University and lives in Belfast.

Esme Miskimmin is a Senior Lecturer at the University of Liverpool. She has research interests in crime fiction and Shakespeare and occasionally combines the two. Her recent work includes some entries for Steven Powell's *100 American Crime Writers* (2012), the chapter on Dorothy L. Sayers in the Wiley-Blackwell *Companion to Crime Fiction* (2010) and an article, 'The Act of Murder: Renaissance Tragedy and the Detective Novel' for *Reinventing the Renaissance: Shakespeare and his Contemporaries in Adaptation and Performance* (2013).

Catherine Phelps lectures at Cardiff University. Her Ph.D. researched Welsh crime fiction written in English and her publications include articles on Welsh writing in English, crime fiction, and gender and genre.

Alexandra Phillips is an Associate Lecturer at the Open University in Wales. She gained her Ph.D. at Cardiff University, submitting a thesis entitled 'In the Wake of Conrad: Ships and Sailors in Early Twentieth-Century Maritime Fiction'. Published articles include 'The Changing Portrayal of Pirates in Children's Literature' for *The New Review of Children's Literature and Librarianship* (2011), a book review of Margaret Cohen's *The Novel and the Sea* in *Comparative Literature* (2013).

Diana Powell is the Curriculum Manager for Study Skills and Tutorials at Liverpool International College, and a lecturer for the University of Liverpool's continuing education programme in the areas of Victorian and crime fiction.

Steven Powell is the author of *James Ellroy: Demon Dog of Crime Fiction* (2015) published by Palgrave Macmillan. He has edited the anthologies *100 American Crime Writers* (2012) for Palgrave, and *Conversations with James Ellroy* (2012) for University Press of Mississippi, and the forthcoming *The Big Somewhere: Essays on James Ellroy's Noir World* for Bloomsbury.

Greg Rees is a graduate of Cardiff University, and has worked for many years in the publishing industry, including editing several series of crime novels. He is a fan of a wide variety of crime fiction, with particular favourites being Ruth Rendell, Caroline Graham, Dashiell Hammett, and Magdalen Nabb.

Christopher Routledge is a freelance writer, photographer, and academic. His Ph.D. thesis was on modernity in Raymond Chandler. He is currently working on a collection of photographs and poems with poet Rebecca Goss, and is writing about a whaling voyage to the east coast of Greenland in 1822.

Jasmine Simeone retired as an English teacher some years ago, although she continues to teach, mostly 1:1 English to secondary school students, three days a week. She is secretary of the Dorothy L Sayers Society and Bulletin Editor and also a member of the Margery Allingham Society. She has given several talks for the DLSS and published a number of papers in *Sidelights on Sayers*, their long-running journal.

Christine R. Simpson is a retired librarian and teacher, and has been an avid reader of detective fiction since her early teens. Membership of the Dorothy L. Sayers Society led her to start writing articles on aspects of the author for "Sidelights on Sayers". Since then she has written on a variety of authors for CADS and contributed to *The Oxford Companion to Crime & Mystery Writing (1999)* and *British Crime Writing: An Encyclopedia* (2008).

Victoria Stewart is Reader in Modern and Contemporary Literature at the University of Leicester. She is the author of *Women's Autobiography: War and Trauma* (2003), *Narratives of Memory: British Writing of the*

1940s (2006), *The Second World War in Contemporary British Fiction: Secret Histories* (2011) and *Crime Writing in Interwar Britain: Fact and Fiction in the Golden Age* (2017).

Kate Watson researches in the areas of crime fiction, nineteenth-century writing, and women's writing. Her recent work examines tattoos in crime and detective narratives.

Heather Worthington was Reader in English Literature at Cardiff University. Her research interests are nineteenth and twentieth-century crime narrative, sensation fiction and children's literature. Publications include *The Rise of the Detective in Early Nineteenth-Century Popular Fiction* (2005), *Key Concepts in Crime Fiction* (2011) and contributions to, among others, A *Companion to Crime Fiction* (2010), *The Oxford History of the Novel in English Vol II: The Nineteenth-Century Novel* (2012), *Roald Dahl: New Casebooks* (2012) and *Roald Dahl: Wales of the Unexpected* (2016). She is on the Editorial Board of *Clues: A Journal of Detection* and of *Studies in Crime Writing*.

PART I

The Victorians, Edwardians, and World War One, 1855–1918

Introduction

Popular perceptions of crime writing from this period, particularly in terms of the Victorians, tend to focus on the particular genre of detective fiction and the often-used and now mythologized narrations of super-ratiocination in foggy London streets. This is not really surprising, given that British detective fiction proper essentially begins with *A Study in Scarlet* (1887), in which we are introduced to Conan Doyle's most famous of detectives, Sherlock Holmes. During the period covered in this first part there were a significant number of crime stories in the Holmes mould, but as the following entries from Caroline Clive to John Buchan show, there is in fact a diverse range of crime writing in this era, including some genres which we perhaps might think of as more modern in their inception, such as the spy thriller (represented in this part by E. Phillips Oppenheim, Erskine Childers and John Buchan) or tales of forensic investigation, such as Austen Freeman's Thorndyke stories – arguably the very first in this field. We also find an early example of a work *on* the crime genre: Chesterton's 1902 'A Defence of Detective Stories', which foreshadows the continuing self-reflexive nature of the crime genre, and the need to make it the focus of critical discussion.

From the very earliest examples of crime writing explored here, we can see many of the issues and themes raised that preoccupy the genre and its critics over the next one hundred and sixty years, such as its explorations of justice and morality, gender, violence, the urban world and its overwhelming self-consciousness of genre and narrative. It should be remembered that, as with Haycraft's discussions in *Murder for Pleasure*, the entries in this collection are about more than the writers' works: they are about their lives and times as well. As will be demonstrated throughout this entire collection, these two factors are often linked, and we see the influence of the lives the writers lead on the fiction they write. Sometimes, it has to be said, it seems as though the lives of the writers make even more exciting reading than their stories: the biographical elements detailed below include bigamy, illegitimacy, some minor felonies and more than a few tragic endings, such as that of Caroline Clive, who is the subject of the first entry in this collection.

It is interesting to learn that contemporary responses to Clive's first novel, *Paul Ferroll* (1855), expressed anxiety about the morality of this novel, with Clive being forced to rewrite an ending in which the guilty Ferroll dies. He dies, however, unrepentant of his crimes and due to illness rather than any force of human justice, a fact that serves to illustrate that the crime genre in its various forms has always raised challenging ethical questions and explored the ambiguity of justice as a concept. In fact, crime writing often becomes a discourse on the nature of crime and punishment from both a legal and spiritual perspective and, sometimes, the tensions arising between these two; a theme made explicit in the 'Father Brown' stories of G. K. Chesterton, discussed by Christopher Routledge in the entry below, where the dual roles of priest and detective raise some complex issues.

Caroline Clive is one of the four authors in this part that pre-date Doyle. As mentioned in the general introduction, Haycraft's argument was that there could be no detective stories until there were detectives, and therefore his discussion of the British detective story begins with Arthur Conan Doyle. Holmes was not, technically, the first literary detective: accounts of Newgate crimes and the Bow Street Runners had been around some time, and writers such as Godwin and Andrew Forrester had produced crime and detective stories, but according to Haycraft, the advent of Sherlock Holmes marks 'the creation of a really great detective character, the writing of full length detective stories concerned with detection and nothing else'. Haycraft does, however, preface this discussion of the Holmes stories with a chapter entitled 'The In-Between Years' (that is, in between Poe and Doyle), in which he discusses various authors who concern themselves with crimes in their narratives, but in which the detection of the crime 'is the plum in the pudding, but it is by no means the entire pudding.'

The four pre-Doyle authors here, Caroline Clive, Wilkie Collins, Mrs Henry Wood and Mary Elizabeth Braddon, are all writers of the 'sensation fiction' popular at the time, in which lurid crimes are committed, usually within an apparently safe middle-class milieu. In his assessment of 'The In-Between Years', Haycraft discusses Collins, commenting on his lack of success in trying to write 'polemic and reformist novels', but also of his triumphs in imaginative plotting, humourous writing and quality of characterisation. However, Haycraft mentions none of the female writers listed below; indeed, Clive and Wood have been largely neglected in most critical responses to the literature of the period until recently. This has inevitably to do with gender; not least because, as Adrienne E. Gavin argues in her entry on Braddon, the subject matter of such novels was not considered suitable material for a woman as writer or reader. Gavin also points out the importance of Braddon's writing in challenging traditional roles of women in crime fiction, long before the advent of specifically feminist crime writing such as Tart Noir, and moving women away from the sole function of victim into the roles of detectives and criminals.

There are actually quite a few female detectives and crime fighters in the selection below, although the numbers are in no way even, and there are sadly no female criminal masterminds to rank alongside E. W. Hornung's Raffles or R. Austen Freeman's Romney Pringle. On the side of the good, Collins gives us Anne Rodway and Marian Halcome, and in the *Law and the Lady*, the first pregnant investigator: Valeria Brinton/Woodvill. There are also several women who have made detection their career, such as George R. Sim's Dorcas Dene and C. L. Pirkis' Loveday Brooke, advertised as a 'female Sherlock Holmes', both examples of the 'lady detective' (or, as Haycraft would have it, of 'feminine sleuths'). In her entry on Pirkis, Adrienne E. Gavin highlights some interesting differences between male-authored creations such as Dene and Pirkis' Brooke, in as much that unlike Dorcas Dene, the female-authored Loveday Brooke is unmarried, independent and not portrayed in terms of her physical or feminine qualities. Later on in this period comes Baroness Orczy's Lady Molly of the Yard, first appearing in 1910, and who, as Greg Rees points out, comes with her own proto-feminist female narrator.

A significant proportion of the works in the Victorian and Edwardian period, such as the Loveday Brooke stories, or Arthur Morrison's Martin Hewitt narratives, were originally published in serial form or as individual short stories in journals and magazines, which has an inevitable influence on them in terms of content and style; short pieces of popular fiction must rely on recognisable tropes of character and place and the conventions of genre to convey things swiftly to their readers, so potentially a full development of many narrative elements is impossible. Serialised stories can also place more emphasis on moving the plot along, and the need for a 'cliffhanger' to encourage the reader to continue in the next volume can lead to some awkward plot 'spikes' when the story is collated into novel form. That is not to say that any of these stories are lacking in originality or stylistic dexterity, or are without interest to those concerned with an analysis of the genre: their appeal can lie, in part, in these publishing origins. As we move closer to the end of this era we see several examples of experimentation with form and style, such as Freeman's collection of short stories *The Singing Bone* (1912), in which he describes the crime being committed before moving on to the process of deception. This is a device which Nick Freeman rightly describes as pioneering in its form, but which Haycraft, with some heat, described as 'a rather dangerous departure' from the norm, and even 'perilous' in its premise.

The appearance of much early crime fiction in serialised magazines and periodicals is also perhaps indicative of the genre both in relation to concepts of 'literature', and also of its readership; crime fiction is by and large 'middlebrow' writing. In her entry on Mrs Henry Wood, Anne-Marie Beller comments on her use of 'provincial and predominantly middle-class' settings, and Wood is not the only writer to locate her stories within these geographical and sociological spaces. The provinces are not utilised as much as London – the main home of crime writing in this period – but they are there, as are the suburbs of the capital; seemingly respectable middle-class worlds that are in fact as crime-filled and subversive as the rookeries of Holmes' London. One of the key features of much British crime writing established during this period is that we cannot identify the criminal by his or her otherness, such as social class or physical appearance: crime exists in every area of society. This idea, perhaps best illustrated by Conan Doyle's short story 'The Man with the Twisted Lip' (1891), must surely contribute to the vicarious frisson of the crime story: as I discuss in the general introduction, part of the appeal is that the escapism generated is paradoxically accompanied by the reader's imagined participation, for which a recognisable milieu is essential. Although London features most frequently as a setting there are always counter-spaces: the provinces and the suburbs, but also the British colonies, such as in Collin's *The Moonstone* with its Indian backstory, or the 'Sanders of the River' stories of Edgar Wallace (first appearing in 1911), set in the Belgian Congo and in which, as Stephen Knight observes, Sanders is 'a sort of colonial Sherlock Holmes'. Europe likewise is an increasingly significant setting, especially in the late nineteenth and early twentieth centuries with society's increasing concerns about German militarism.

These particular political and military circumstances contributed to the emergence of spy and adventure writing, and in this part Alexandra Phillips discusses Oppenheim's *The Mysterious Mr Sabin* (1898) as arguably the first ever spy thriller. Haycraft refers to Oppenheim as a 'border-liner', whose 'countless spy-and-intrigue novels [...] occasionally approach detection' and as such can do no more with him in a discussion of the pure detective story. Here, however, Phillips establishes his significance in terms of the crime writing genre as a response to social and political Zeitgeist and shows us that Oppenheim's own experiences had a direct influence on his novels that 'articulate anxieties about a possible German invasion'. Similarly, the personal, political and military experiences of Erskine Childers and John Buchan had an impact on the other spy stories discussed below, including Childers' seminal *The Riddle of the Sands* (1903), and Buchan's *The Thirty-Nine Steps* (1915). These gripping adventures also have a counterpart for younger readers in this era: the end of this period also sees the emergence of crime stories for juvenile readers, discussed by Lucy Andrew in her entries on Edwy Searles Brooks and John William Bobin, both of whom contributed to the 'Sexton Blake' adventure series.

Later, in the 1920s, Bobin was also to introduce the figure of the 'girl detective' to children's crime fiction, and he is not the only writer included in this part who inevitably went on writing after World War One. Some of these, such as Chesterton, continued with their established characters and style, and others, such as Freeman, adapted their writing more to the newly popular puzzle-mystery genre. In many of the later entries in this section we can see elements of style and content that are to characterise the period to follow. Although we try to give some order to the history of the form, and make use of designated eras as a way of doing this, we cannot just cut off one period and begin another afresh, even when provided with a major historical hiatus such as World War One. The best example of this is probably E. C. Bentley's *Trent's Last Case* (1913), later hailed by other writers and critics as one of the finest examples of the detective story ever written. Chronologically, Bentley belongs here, in this first part, and this is where I have placed him before neatly slicing through time in 1918. Stylistically, he probably belongs later and indeed Haycraft deliberately includes Bentley as his first entry in his 'Golden Age', rather than the last in his 'England 1890–1914'. Below, Suzanne Bray is in agreement with Haycraft, arguing that Trent is 'a model for all the gentlemen amateur detectives of the Golden Age'. This then, clearly demonstrates the diverse and constantly evolving nature of crime writing, from the early romantic and sensational novels of Clive to the detective stories of Bentley, frustrating our attempts to produce clear definitions of genre. But, as Haycraft observes: 'History often refuses to be neat and tidy – to the infinite annoyance of those who deal in chronological categories'.

Esme Miskimmin

Works Cited

Haycraft, Howard, *Murder for Pleasure: The Life and Times of the Detective Story*, (1941; repr. London: Peter Davies, 1942).

CHAPTER 1

Caroline Clive (1801–1873), 1855: *Paul Ferroll*

Adrienne E. Gavin

Best known for her 1855 crime novel *Paul Ferroll*, Clive is an important yet neglected contributor to the development of British crime writing. Born Caroline Wigley on 30 June 1801 in London, Clive was the third of five children of barrister and MP Edmund Wigley and Anna Maria Meysey. Permanently lamed by polio aged two and moving to Shakenhurst, a Worcestershire estate, when she was around ten (at which time her surname became Meysey-Wigley), she regarded her youth as comparatively unhappy and lonely. In 1829 she became lady of the house for her brother at Malvern Hall near Solihull and on his death in 1833 inherited nearby Olton Hall, and further property on her mother's death in 1836. Her desire for poetic recognition was fulfilled when her *IX Poems by V* (1840) received praise in the *Quarterly Review*. In 1840 she married the Reverend Archer Clive, Rector of Solihull. Her marriage brought her great happiness and two children: Charles (b.1842) and Alice (b.1843). In 1847 the Clives moved from Solihull Rectory to Whitfield in Herefordshire, where Archer became a country squire and Clive produced four novels.

A. E. Gavin (✉)
Canterbury Christ Church University, Canterbury, UK

© The Author(s) 2020
E. Miskimmin (ed.), *100 British Crime Writers*, Crime Files,
https://doi.org/10.1057/978-1-137-31902-9_1

Praised as 'powerful', 'remarkable' and 'original', *Paul Ferroll: A Tale* is the story of an admired gentleman who stabs his first wife to death as she lies sleeping and shoots dead a labourer he had previously helped. It was condemned for its subject matter and lack of moral comment on Ferroll, who enjoys a life of pleasure with his second wife without regret, guilt or punishment for his crimes. Arguably one of the earliest sensation novels, which flourished in the 1860s, the novel leaves judgement on its enigmatic protagonist to the reader. In December 1855, probably in response to criticism of the novel's amorality, Clive added an extra chapter to the third edition in which Ferroll dies from an illness, still unrepentant. Clive's popular prequel, *Why Paul Ferroll Killed His Wife* (1860), a less original work, reveals how Ferroll was tricked into marrying his first wife. Like Clive's other novels, *Year After Year: A Tale* (1858) and *John Greswold* (1864), the prequel is not a crime novel.

A carriage accident in 1863 resulted in Clive permanently using a wheelchair, and two years later a stroke affected her voice and caused partial paralysis. She died on 12 July 1873 after her dress caught fire at Whitfield.

Suggested Reading/Works Cited

Clive, Mary, ed., *From the Diary and Family Papers of Mrs. Archer Clive (1801–1873)* (London: The Bodley Head, 1949).

Edwards, P. D., 'Clive, Caroline (1801–1873)', in *Oxford Dictionary of National Biography* (Oxford: Oxford University Press, 2004; online edn, May 2010).

Gavin, Adrienne E., '"Deepen[ing] the Power and Horror of the Original": Caroline Clive's *Paul Ferroll* as Descendant of *Jane Eyre*', *La Revue LISA*, 7:4 (2009), 64–86.

——, 'Introduction', in *Paul Ferroll*, ed. by Caroline Clive and Adrienne E. Gavin (Kansas City: Valancourt Books, 2008), pp. vii–xxxii.

Mitchell, Charlotte, *Caroline Clive 1801–1873: A Bibliography* (Brisbane: Victorian Fiction Research Unit, Department of English, University of Queensland, 1999).

CHAPTER 2

Wilkie Collins (1824–1889), 1860: *The Woman in White*

Adrienne E. Gavin

A leading sensation novelist of the 1860s, Collins is best known for *The Woman in White* (1860), which is generally seen as the first significant sensation novels and *The Moonstone* (1868), which is often termed the first English detective novel.

Born on 8 January 1824 in St Marylebone, London, William Collins was the elder of two sons of Harriet and William Collins. His father was a painter as was his godfather, Sir David Wilkie, after whom he was given the middle name that in adulthood he used in preference to his first. Initially educated by his ex-governess mother, he started attending day school aged eleven, and at twelve moved with the family to Italy and France for two years. On their return to London in 1838 he went to boarding school which he disliked, but where he used storytelling to avoid being bullied. As he grew older he rejected his parents' evangelical Christianity.

Undecided about a career, Collins tried painting, worked from 1841 to 1846 as a tea merchant's clerk, and wrote fiction. His first short story, 'The Last Stage Coachman', was published in 1843. His first novel,

---

A. E. Gavin (✉)
Canterbury Christ Church University, Canterbury, UK

© The Author(s) 2020
E. Miskimmin (ed.), *100 British Crime Writers*, Crime Files,
https://doi.org/10.1057/978-1-137-31902-9_2

Iolani, set in Tahiti, was written in 1844 but rejected by publishers (finally published by Princeton University Press in 1999). In 1846, with his father's approval, he left clerking to commence legal training at Lincoln's Inn. Following his father's death in 1847, Collins' *Memoirs of the Life of William Collins, Esq., RA* (1848), became his first published book. Although he exhibited a painting at the Royal Academy in 1849, the positive reviews he received for *Antonina* (1850), a novel set in ancient Rome, confirmed Collins on a literary rather than artistic career.

In 1851 Collins published *Rambles Beyond Railways*, an account of a walking tour in Cornwall. In the same year, he met Charles Dickens, becoming involved in Dickens' amateur acting troupe. Although their relationship later cooled, during the 1850s Dickens and Collins were close friends and travel companions. Dickens became Collins' literary advisor, and Collins contributed regularly to, and from 1856 to 1861 served on the staff of, Dickens' journal *Household Words* and its successor *All the Year Round*. They also co-wrote plays including *The Lighthouse* (1855), *The Frozen Deep* (1857), and *No Thoroughfare* (1867), and the travel piece 'The Lazy Tour of Two Idle Apprentices' (1857).

Called to the bar in 1852, Collins never practised law, but his legal interests influenced his fiction. Although his novel *Basil* (1852) was attacked for its sexual content, his mystery *Hide and Seek* (1854) was well-reviewed, and his short story 'Anne Rodway [Taken from her Diary]' (1856), features one of fiction's earliest female amateur detectives. Collins followed these with the short story collection *After Dark* (1856), novella *A Rogue's Life* (1856), Cornwall-set mystery novel *The Dead Secret* (1857), and another volume of short stories, *The Queen of Hearts* (1859).

Collins' best known and most enduring works were published in the 1860s. Although the genre had forerunners in Caroline Clive's *Paul Ferroll* (1855) and his own *Basil*, Collins' *The Women in White* (1860) is widely regarded as the first sensation novel. Highly popular during its serialisation in *All the Year Round* (November 1859 to August 1860), its three-volume publication made it the bestseller of 1860 and ushered in the great decade of sensation writing. The novel established characteristics of the genre: secrets, mystery, false identity, sensational incidents, fast-paced plots, and crimes committed by unexpected characters in the contemporary, domestic environment of the English home. 'To Mr Collins belongs the credit of having introduced into fiction those most mysterious of mysteries, the mysteries that are at our own doors', wrote Henry James. Adept at intricate plotting, Collins was inspired by listening

2 WILKIE COLLINS (1824–1889), 1860: *THE WOMAN IN WHITE* 11

to witness statements in court to use multiple narratives—including documents, diary entries, sworn testimony, even an epitaph—to structure a story which the reader jury has to piece together.

The Woman in White also contains one of the most memorable criminals in Victorian fiction: 'Napoleon of crime' Count Fosco, a villain Collins made fat rather than traditionally thin. A proto-detective duo also appear: Marian Halcombe of the womanly figure but masculine face, and drawing master Walter Hartright, who together save Marian's half-sister Laura Fairlie from Fosco and his criminal accomplice Sir Percival Glyde. The novel brought Collins international fame, but coincided with a worsening of physical complaints, including rheumatic gout, which he had suffered since the early 1850s. To relieve his pain he became heavily reliant on laudanum for the rest of his life.

In *No Name* (1862) Collins criticised laws which prevented illegitimate children from inheriting. In the complexly plotted *Armadale* (1866) he delved into the psychological aspects of crime and created the beautiful but dastardly Lydia Gwilt who schemes, steals, forges and murders. His personal life contained sensational elements of its own. From 1859 he lived, unmarried, with widow Caroline Graves and her daughter Harriet whom he treated as his child. In the mid-1860s he met servant Martha Rudd with whom—using the name William Dawson—he instigated a long-term relationship. In 1868 Caroline Graves married another man, but two years later returned to live with Collins for the rest of his life. Neither living with nor marrying Martha Rudd, Collins continued his relationship with her, too, and they had three children together: Marian in 1869, Constance in 1871, and William in 1874.

In 1868 Collins' mother died, and due to his own poor health he started to use an amanuensis in producing the novel that, with *The Woman in White*, is his best known and most enduring. Serialised in *All the Year Round* (January to August 1868) and published in July the same year as a three-volume novel, *The Moonstone* again uses multiple narrators and prefigures British 'Golden Age' crime fiction of the 1930s in being a country house whodunit wherein various characters are suspected of stealing a valuable diamond. Described by T. S. Eliot as 'the first, the longest, and the best of modern English detective novels', it features rose-loving Sergeant Cuff of the London police. Not the first detective in British fiction, Cuff nevertheless displays the superior investigative powers and analytical, professional attention to detail echoed by later fictional detectives. He does not, however, solve the case; it takes other characters in the grip of 'detective-fever', especially unofficial sleuth scientist Ezra Jennings, to do so.

Stage adaptations of *The Woman in White* in 1871 and *The Moonstone* in 1877 were very successful, but new dramas Collins attempted were not. His novels of the 1870s and 1880s had didactic elements and are less remembered today. *Man And Wife* (1870) attacked British marriage laws as did *Miss or Mrs?* (1871). *Poor Miss Finch* (1872) featured a blind protagonist exemplifying Collins' frequent use of characters with disabilities. *The New Magdalen* (1873) depicted the poor treatment of fallen women. In *The Law and the Lady* (1875), however, he portrayed a character still rare in crime fiction: a pregnant sleuth, who investigates the truth about her husband who had received the Scottish verdict, 'not proven' when tried for the murder of his first wife. *The Two Destinies* (1876) involves telepathy. *The Haunted Hotel* (1879) is a ghost story with detective elements, and *The Fallen Leaves* (1879) tells of an ex-prostitute and a socialist. *Jezebel's Daughters* (1880) criticises insane asylum conditions. The anti-Jesuit *The Black Robe* (1881) was followed by anti-vivisection novel *Heart and Science* (1883), *The Evil Genius* (1886) about divorce, and *The Legacy of Cain* (1889) which features two protagonists, one of whose mothers was a murderer.

Increasingly ill with arthritis and angina, Collins' later life was comparatively secluded. He had a carriage accident in 1888 and in 1889 suffered a stroke, dying later that year, on 23 September, at his home in Wimpole Street, London. Fulfilling Collins' request, his friend Walter Besant completed his final novel *Blind Love* (1890). Collins' will left equal amounts to Caroline Graves and Martha Rudd and to his stepdaughter and three birth children.

Suggested Reading/Works Cited

Baker, William, Andrew Gasson, Graham Law, and Paul Lewis, eds, *The Public Face of Wilkie Collins: The Collected Letters* (London: Pickering and Chatto, 2005).

Peters, Catherine, 'Collins, (William) Wilkie (1824–1889)', in *Oxford Dictionary of National Biography* (Oxford: Oxford University Press, 2004; online edn, May 2009).

———, *The King of Inventors: A Life of Wilkie Collins* (London: Minerva, 1992).

Pykett, Lyn, *Wilkie Collins* (Oxford: Oxford University Press, 2005).

CHAPTER 3

Mrs. Henry Wood (1814–1887), 1861: *East Lynne*

Anne-Marie Beller

Along with Wilkie Collins and Mary Elizabeth Braddon, Mrs. Henry Wood (Ellen Wood, née Price) was one of the most famous sensation novelists of the mid-Victorian period. She is known chiefly for her bestselling novel *East Lynne*, published in 1861 which, together with Collins' *The Woman in White* (1860) and Braddon's *Lady Audley's Secret* (1862), was instrumental in establishing the vogue for sensation fiction during that decade. Wood's important contribution to the development of detective fiction has been largely overlooked until relatively recently and, indeed, there is still virtually no work on her 'Johnny Ludlow' short stories. This series comprises in the region of a hundred tales, many of which feature crime, mystery and detection.

Ellen Price was the eldest daughter of a successful Worcester glovemaker, Thomas Price, and his wife Elizabeth. During early childhood she lived with her paternal grandparents, returning to her parents' home in 1821 when her grandfather died. In a memorial essay on his mother, Charles Wood writes of the young Ellen as a 'peculiarly imaginative, sensitive, and impressionable' child with a precocious aptitude for learning and

A.-M. Beller (✉)
Loughborough University, Loughborough, UK

© The Author(s) 2020
E. Miskimmin (ed.), *100 British Crime Writers*, Crime Files,
https://doi.org/10.1057/978-1-137-31902-9_3

a love of reading. The memoir relates Wood's account of her own hysterical reaction on being shown the body of her dead grandfather and the lasting impression this episode made upon her. In light of Wood's later fascination in her fiction with death and sickness, this early experience is suggestive. The rather morbid preoccupation with illness and dying may also be linked to the fact that Wood had a variety of health problems during her childhood. At the age of thirteen she was diagnosed with a curvature of the spine, a condition that meant that for the next few years Wood was forced to spend long periods of time lying on a board or a couch. When she turned seventeen, the doctors declared an improvement and Wood was able to resume a normal life. The enforced inactivity of four years, though, produced a permanent delicacy of health, and Wood was to some extent a semi-invalid for the rest of her life. Charles Wood claimed that 'with [his] mother the frailty of the body was so pronounced that every word of 'East Lynne' was written in a reclining chair with her manuscript paper upon her knees'.

In 1836 she married Henry Wood, a banker and head of a shipping firm, who had also spent some time in the consular service. The couple spent the first twenty years of their marriage abroad, primarily in France, where Wood gave birth to five children, one of whom died in infancy after contracting scarlet fever. Little is known about Henry Wood, but at some point in the 1850s he retired from business, possibly due to mental health problems, and the family suffered some financial losses. From 1851, Wood's writing career had begun, with regular contributions to *Bentley's Miscellany* and the *New Monthly Magazine*. Having returned to England in 1856, and perhaps motivated by the altered financial circumstances of the family, Wood approached the editor of the *New Monthly*, Harrison Ainsworth, about writing a full-length novel for the magazine. Ainsworth initially declined, but in 1860 she won £100 in a competition to write a novel promoting temperance. Her entry (and first novel) *Danesbury House* remained in print throughout the nineteenth century, although Wood never received a penny from the sales, other than her prize money.

After this success, Ainsworth agreed to serialise a novel by Wood in his magazine and she began *East Lynne*. This story of a wife's adultery and subsequent loss of status, children, and home, incorporated a murder subplot centering on the villainous Francis Levinson, all delivered in a melodramatic and exciting narrative that Victorian readers found irresistible. The serial was successful, but both Chapman and Hall and Smith and Elder turned down the manuscript. Richard Bentley, however, agreed to publish *East Lynne* in three volumes and it became a phenomenon, going through five editions before 1862 and selling approximately 400,000 copies by 1895. Critics were less inclined to praise Wood's success and several were overtly hostile. One significant exception was a lengthy review in *The Times* on 25 January 1862, which declared it 'the best novel of the season' and praised the author for a plot which 'retains us in the proper mood of suspense'. Despite admitting the novel's shortcomings, the reviewer was generally enthusiastic, and concluded that 'with all its artistic defects *East Lynne* is a first-rate story'.

Wood consolidated the success of *East Lynne* with a string of successful novels through the next two decades, often at the rate of two books per year. Like *East Lynne*, with its subplot of murder and deception, most contained a significant element of crime or mystery, usually within provincial and predominantly middle-class settings. Fraud and theft are favoured offences, though there are plots involving murder in *Lord Oakburn's Daughters* (1864), *St. Martin's Eve* (1866), *Lady Adelaide's Oath* (1867) and others. Even Wood's less sensational domestic sagas, such as *Mrs. Halliburton's Troubles* (1862) and *The Channings* (1862), contain elements of mystery and theft.

In 1866 Wood's husband and mother died. Wood became the proprietor and editor of the *Argosy* in 1867, which became the main vehicle for her own subsequent fiction. Besides her novels, she also published her series of 'Johnny Ludlow' tales in this journal. These were initially published anonymously, and began with ten separate stories in 1868. Prolific like many of her contemporaries, Wood published over thirty novels and more than a hundred short stories during her career.

In a preface to the fifth edition of the first series of the Johnny Ludlow papers, Wood issued a statement declaring her authorship and explaining that the anonymity had been retained in order to aid the illusion that the stories had been written by a young boy. However, as in the case of her rival, Mary Braddon, who edited *Belgravia*, Wood wrote much of the material for each issue of the magazine she conducted, and the adoption of the 'Johnny Ludlow' pseudonym was most likely designed to disguise this fact.

Although many of Johnny Ludlow's tales may be read separately, some of the stories are continued in the next. For example, 'Hester Reed's Pills' is a rather melancholy tale of twin infants being poisoned when their mother administers pills doctored with arsenic. This story ends with the inquest and is taken up from the same point by the next tale, 'Abel Crew', in which the philanthropic herbalist suspected of the crime is cleared of any responsibility for the babies' deaths.

Not all of the 'Johnny Ludlow' tales feature crime. Indeed one of the most remarkable characteristics of the stories is their extreme variety and their resistance to strict generic classification. Several focus on a love story, while others narrate Johnny's adventures at school, and there are even a small number of tales with a supernatural element. However, the majority rely on crime, mystery, suspense, and a significant degree of detection, making Wood's series an important precursor to the detective short story form, which achieved such popularity in the final decades of the nineteenth century.

In 1873, Wood became seriously ill after contracting diphtheria. She recovered, though the convalescence was protracted and her productivity never again matched that of the period prior to her illness. In the subsequent year, the first series of Johnny Ludlow stories were collected and published in book form. A second and third series followed in 1880 and 1885, respectively. The fourth and fifth series were published three years after Wood's death. *The Story of Charles Strange* and *The House of Halliwell* were also published posthumously, as were some short stories. The sixth series of 'Johnny Ludlow', in 1899, was the last new book to appear. Mrs. Wood died on February 10, 1887 of heart failure and was buried at Highgate cemetery.

Adeline Sergeant, assessing Wood's legacy at the end of the nineteenth-century praised her skill as a storyteller, but also stated that 'it is impossible to claim for her any lofty literary position; she is emphatically un-literary and middle-class'. As Emma Liggins and Andrew Maunder observe in their introduction to a special Mrs. Wood edition of the journal *Women's Writing*, '[t]he fact of Wood being so obviously middlebrow proved helpful to her sales in her own day but has hindered her subsequent reputation'. Nevertheless, over the last few decades there has been renewed interest in Wood as a writer, and her contribution to the evolution of crime fiction is one of several areas in which her importance has been belatedly recognised.

SUGGESTED READING/WORKS CITED

Flowers, Michael, 'The Johnny Ludlow Stories: A Brief Introduction (2001–2006).' http://www.mrshenrywood.co.uk/ludlow.html.

Liggins, Emma and Andrew Maunder, eds, Special Edition on Mrs. Henry Wood, *Women's Writing*, 15:2 (2008).

Mangham, Andrew, 'Mrs. Henry Wood', in *A Companion to Sensation Fiction*, ed. by Pamela K. Gilbert (Oxford: Blackwell, 2011), pp. 244–256.

Sergeant, A., 'Mrs. Henry Wood', in *Women Novelists of Queen Victoria's Reign*, ed. by Mrs. Oliphant (London: Hurst & Blackett, 1897), pp. 174–192.

Wood, Charles W., 'Mrs. Henry Wood: In Memoriam', Parts 1 & 2, *Argosy*, XLIII (April 1887 & May 1887), 251–270; 334–353.

CHAPTER 4

Mary Elizabeth Braddon (1835–1915), 1862: *Lady Audley's Secret*

Adrienne E. Gavin

Best known for *Lady Audley's Secret* (1862), Braddon was a prolific and popular writer, producing more than eighty books during a literary career that spanned over half a century. A leading sensation novelist, she helped establish the characteristics and popularity of the sensation genre in the 1860s and notably subverted Victorian stereotypes of female crime.

Born on October 4, 1835 in Soho, London, Braddon was the third and youngest child of Fanny and Henry Braddon who separated when she was four due to her solicitor father's infidelity and irresponsible business practices. She then moved with her mother to St. Leonards-On-Sea, Sussex, for a few years. Returning to London they lived variously in Kensington, Hampstead, Hammersmith, and Camberwell. Although she had some periods at school, Braddon was largely educated at home.

Around 1852 Braddon became an actress, a then disreputable profession for a middle-class woman, but one which enabled her to help support herself and her mother. Until 1860 she acted in London and provincial theatres under the stage name Mary Seyton, her mother travelling with her. During her acting years she also began writing, and in about 1859

A. E. Gavin (✉)
Canterbury Christ Church University, Canterbury, UK

© The Author(s) 2020
E. Miskimmin (ed.), *100 British Crime Writers*, Crime Files,
https://doi.org/10.1057/978-1-137-31902-9_4

wealthy admirer John Gilby provided her with money so that she could write instead of act and assisted her in establishing a literary career. A year later their relationship ended badly, with Gilby accusing Braddon of being dishonest with him. By then her first novel, *Three Times Dead* (1860), had been published and her first play, *The Loves of Arcadia* (1860), performed. She had also been publishing poetry and stories in popular penny dreadful magazines produced by Irish publisher John Maxwell whom she met in 1860.

Maxwell was not free to marry as he had a wife who was said to be in an Irish insane asylum, but in 1861 Braddon moved in with him. They represented themselves to the world as if married, and Braddon became stepmother to Maxwell's then six surviving children (one subsequently dying) with whom she developed a close relationship although they were often away at boarding school She also engaged in a prodigious literary career, writing furiously not only from literary desire but to support the family and help pay Maxwell's substantial debts. Her mother, Fanny, lived with them and herself took on a role editing two of Maxwell's journals.

Braddon's most famous novel, *Lady Audley's Secret*, began serialising in Maxwell's journal *Robin Goodfellow* in July 1861 until the journal failed in September. It was then completely serialised in Maxwell's *Sixpenny Magazine* from January to December 1862 and published by Tinsley Brothers in three-volume form in October 1862. Running through eight editions within three months, volume sales were phenomenal and William Tinsley later built a house, Audley Lodge, out of his profits.

Published after Wilkie Collins' *The Woman in White* (1860), *Lady Audley's Secret* was not the first sensation novel, but it was one of the most successful and sensational in the genre. Unsettling conventional views about who might be a criminal, it included elements that became characteristic of the genre: secrets, mystery, bigamy, arson, concealed identity and madness assumed or real. Like other sensation works, it depicted crime not in the slums and dens of big cities or in distant locales, but in the contemporary domestic world of British upper-class country houses or middle-class homes.

Braddon's most enduring contribution to crime fiction is Lady Audley herself. Blue-eyed, golden-haired and childlike, Lady Audley is a cold-hearted criminal who deserts her own child in order to pursue wealth and position. Using her innocent-seeming beauty to marry bigamously into the aristocracy, she appears to be the ideal 'Angel in the House', but her angelic appearance masks ruthless criminality. To gain and maintain her luxurious lifestyle she commits crime after crime including pushing her first husband down a well and setting fire to an inn. A new type of criminal character, Lady Audley subverted mid-Victorian expectations about women, physical appearance, and criminality and was regarded by some as a dangerous development in fiction. As contemporary novelist and critic of sensation fiction Margaret Oliphant put it, Braddon had created, 'the fair haired demon of modern fiction'.

Lady Audley's Secret not only challenged perceptions about criminal characters, but also portrayed proto-detective Robert Audley, an indolent young lawyer who is spurred to investigate when his school friend, Lady Audley's first husband, goes missing. One of the earliest amateur detectives in English literature, he discovers that Lady Audley, now bigamously married to his uncle, is guilty. Like later detectives taking justice into his own hands, he sends her to a Belgian insane asylum rather than bring shame upon the Audley name through a public trial.

One of the bestselling novels of the nineteenth century, *Lady Audley's Secret* inspired multiple stage adaptations and several parodies. It established Braddon as a bestselling novelist and a leading exponent of the suspenseful, fast-paced sensation fiction which had its heyday in the 1860s. Her second best-known novel, *Aurora Floyd*, also a 'bigamy novel', was serialised monthly from January 1862 to January 1863 with volume publication in January 1863. Introducing dark-haired, passionate horsewoman Aurora Floyd who horse-whips a groom, the novel sets up expectations that, like Lady Audley, Aurora will also be revealed as criminal. Although unintentionally bigamously married, blackmailed, and suspected of murdering her first husband, she is exonerated when the real killer is revealed. The novel features in a minor role Scotland Yard detective Joseph Grimstone who does not successfully solve the case, yet gets credit and payment for it. Like *Lady Audley's Secret*, the novel shows the influence of Braddon's stage melodrama past by including a character thought dead who turns up alive.

The early years of Braddon's writing career produced her most enduring work but were also productive in other ways. Her first child Gerald was born in March 1862, followed by son Francis in January 1863, and daughter Fanny at the end of 1863. In the same year she published *John Marchmont's Legacy*, a novel of romantic intrigue in which Olivia Arundel conspires to kidnap a woman married to the man she loves, and *Eleanor's Victory* which focuses on amateur detective Eleanor Vane as she seeks to solve and avenge her father's death. *Henry Dunbar* (1864) contains both a professional detective and a more successful amateur female sleuth, Margaret Wilmot, who, like Vane, tracks a man who has wronged her father.

Braddon produced around two novels a year in addition to short stories, plays and poetry. She often worked on more than one novel at a time and constantly felt the pressures of time. Her friend and literary advisor, novelist Edward Bulwer Lytton, often urged her to write more slowly, but stories are told of the printer's boy standing in her doorway while Braddon finished work, which she passed to him immediately without time for revision.

She interspersed her sensation novel work with anonymous or pseudonymous serial fiction for Maxwell's penny and half-penny periodicals. Intended for the working classes, these portrayed extreme events thought too shocking for more respectable readers. The sensation novels she wrote under her own name which appeared in volume form after serialisation were generally intended for a middle-class readership. She also wrote more literary works of social fiction, including *The Doctor's Wife* (1864), which was heavily influenced by Gustave Flaubert's *Madame Bovary* (1857).

It was for her sensation novels that she was most famous, and the popularity of these with library readers meant that she was soon dubbed 'Queen of the Circulating Libraries'. Avidly read by many, sensation fiction was attacked by others as immoral, unrealistic, degenerate, and excessively focused on sensational incidents and crime. Sensation novels' exciting, page-turning plots that played on readers' nerves were condemned as overly stimulating and even physiologically dangerous for young female readers. The Archbishop of York preached a sermon against sensation fiction, terming it 'one of the abominations of the age', and *Lady Audley's Secret* was described by an anti-sensation reviewer as 'one of the most noxious books of modern times'. Sensation writing was attacked, too, for unsettling class expectations about readership. Clearing ground for modern detective fiction to develop, it turned penny-press plots of crime, violence and high passion into three-volume novels. As a reviewer famously wrote, Braddon 'succeeded in making the literature of the Kitchen the favourite reading of the Drawing-room'.

Women writers of sensation fiction, especially Braddon, received extra criticism for writing about matters regarded as unseemly from a female pen at a time when woman were expected to represent and raise society's moral standards. Although some commentators saw sensation fiction as impure and inappropriate for female writers and readers, sensation novelists like Braddon significantly moved female characters' position in crime fiction beyond victimhood into roles as criminals and detectives. Braddon created independent heroines of passion and dedication to (sometimes nefarious) task: women who refuse to be held back by social propriety, moral expectations, or legal restrictions and who dare to pursue their own desires.

As her fame increased, Braddon's desire to keep her private life private became more difficult to maintain. Secrets and protection of family reputations often lie at the heart of her plots, and she feared that revelation of her own secrets, even to extended family, could damage her reputation. She managed to keep her past as an actress reasonably quiet, and gave all her children the surname Maxwell which she used herself in private life, but that she was not married to Maxwell became suspected. In 1864 Maxwell published a newspaper notice announcing their recent marriage, but this was publicly denied by his first wife's brother-in-law causing reviewers to make sly and sometimes overt attacks on the immorality of Braddon's living situation. This did not seem to affect her popularity, and her literary success enabled her to buy Lichfield House in Richmond, Surrey in 1866. In the same year her second son Francis died, her fourth child William was born, and Braddon began a decade of editing Maxwell's new journal for middle-class readers *Belgravia Magazine*. The following year she produced *Birds of Prey* (1867), which features an amateur detective whose detection redeems his less reputable past.

Braddon had published over twenty novels by 1868 when her brother, who had been living in India, visited and found out she was not married to Maxwell causing a breach in their relationship. Soon after this her sister, who had married and was living in Italy, died, and just a few weeks later, in November, Braddon's mother also died suddenly. Devastated at the loss of her mother to whom she was very close, Braddon fell into a year-long nervous breakdown, exacerbated by the puerperal fever she suffered on the birth of her fifth child Winifred in December 1868. Braddon feared she would never write again, but in December 1870 her youngest child Edward was born and by 1871 she had re-established her prolific rate of production.

When Maxwell's wife died in September 1874, Braddon and Maxwell married in October. That their former union had been irregular now became public, causing all their servants to give notice and a brief scandal to erupt. The family moved to Chelsea for a year to escape notoriety.

Yellowback editions of Braddon's fiction, produced for the railway commuter market, were very popular, and many of her novels were adapted for the stage. She wrote drama in the early 1870s but this was less successful than her novels. Always a keen reader of French fiction (then regarded as more risqué than British), she often drew upon French plots in creating her own. Her interest in Émile Zola, for example, is evident in less sensational novels including *Joshua Haggard's Daughter* (1876) and *Vixen* (1879). In 1878 she also established and wrote for a Christmas annual of fiction *The Mistletoe*.

By 1880 Braddon had written over forty novels. Her popular fiction of the 1880s includes amateur detectives in *Wyllard's Weird* (1885) – which like Agatha Christie's *Murder on the Orient Express* (1934) is a story of train-passengers, one of whom has killed someone – and *The Day Will Come* (1889). Mysteries like *The Fatal Three* (1888) display her increasing interest in characters' psychology.

From 1891 Maxwell suffered health problems and Braddon's writing pace halved while she spent time caring for him until his death from influenza in March 1895. In 1894 she published *Thou Art the Man*, a murder mystery in which a man who suffers from epilepsy awakes next to a corpse with no memory of what has happened and flees to escape punishment for the murder. Ten years later the woman he had then been romantically involved with sets out to discover the truth after being given a note she believes is from the lover she thought dead. The novel also features a young amateur female sleuth.

In later life Braddon became more religious and her works were less sensational and controversial. Yet she still retained an interest in secrets, crime, and detection, and featured French-novel-reading professional detective John Faunce in both *Rough Justice* (1898) and *His Darling Sin* (1899). After a stroke in 1907 Braddon needed a cane for walking, but her writing continued, including novels *During Her Majesty's Pleasure* (1908) and *The Green Curtain* (1911). Her final works were less admired than her earlier ones, but when she died from a cerebral haemorrhage on February 4, 1915 in Richmond, she was mourned as one of the last illustrious Victorian writers. In 1916 her final novel *Mary* was published posthumously. Two of her sons, Gerald and William Maxwell, also became writers.

Suggested Reading/Works Cited

Beller, Anne-Marie, *Mary Elizabeth Braddon: A Companion to the Mystery Fiction* (Jefferson, NC: McFarland, 2012).

Carnell, Jennifer, *The Literary Lives of Mary Elizabeth Braddon: A Study of Her Life and Work* (Hastings: Sensation Press, 2000).

Mullin, Katherine, 'Braddon, Mary Elizabeth (1835–1915)', in *Oxford Dictionary of National Biography* (Oxford: Oxford University Press, 2004; online edn, May 2009).

Tromp, Marlene, Pamela Gilbert, and Aeron Haynie, eds, *Beyond Sensation: Mary Elizabeth Braddon in Context* (Albany, NY: State University of New York, 2000).

Woolf, Robert Lee, *Sensational Victorian: The Life and Fiction of Mary Elizabeth Braddon* (New York: Garland, 1979).

CHAPTER 5

Arthur Conan Doyle (1859–1930), 1887: *A Study in Scarlet*

Adrienne E. Gavin

Physician, writer and Spiritualist, Arthur Conan Doyle's name remains synonymous with the most famous fictional detective in the world, Sherlock Holmes. Holmes, along with his sidekick, Dr. John Watson, appeared in fifty-six short stories and four novels, which have since spawned a long list of film, stage and television adaptations, as well as a host of derivative works that draw on the original stories in a variety of ways. In 1934 'The Sherlock Holmes Society' (London) and the 'Baker Street Irregulars' (New York) were established, dedicated to the study and celebration of all things Sherlockian. They remain active, and there are now many similar societies in countries around the world.

Born at Picardy Place in Edinburgh on 22 May 1859, Arthur Ignatius Conan Doyle was the third child (and eldest son) of Charles Altamont Doyle, artist and draughtsman, and his Irish wife Mary. Both were Roman Catholic, the religion into which their children were baptised. Conan Doyle's childhood was overshadowed by his father's alcoholism, and he lived away from his family between the ages of five and eight. Charles

A. E. Gavin (✉)
Canterbury Christ Church University, Canterbury, UK

© The Author(s) 2020
E. Miskimmin (ed.), *100 British Crime Writers*, Crime Files,
https://doi.org/10.1057/978-1-137-31902-9_5

27

Doyle's chronic drinking and general instability meant that the family's finances were always precarious, but Arthur's uncles paid for his schooling. From 1868 he attended Hodder Place, a Catholic preparatory school in Lancashire, moving up to Stoneyhurst College in 1870. During his time at Stoneyhurst, he developed a passion for the fiction of Sir Walter Scott, and excelled as a sportsman. Conan Doyle remained a keen cricketer, footballer and golfer throughout his adult life. By the time he left Stoneyhurst in 1875, and travelled to Austria to spend a final year of schooling in Feldkirch, Conan Doyle had undergone a spiritual crisis, resulting in the rejection of his parents' Catholic faith.

In 1876 Conan Doyle entered Edinburgh University to study medicine and graduated with the degrees MB (Bachelor of Medicine) and CM (Master of Surgery) in 1881. He received his MD in 1885. During his second year at Edinburgh, Conan Doyle met Joseph Bell, the man who is typically credited with providing the inspiration for Sherlock Holmes. Bell, one of Conan Doyle's professors, for whom he worked as an outpatient clerk at the Edinburgh Royal Infirmary during the course of his studies, was renowned for his close observational skills and his ability to deduce factual information from seemingly trivial details, abilities he advocated as essential in diagnosing patients.

Establishing his own practice at this stage was impeded by lack of funds, so after a short stint as a doctor's apprentice, Conan Doyle accepted a position with the African Steam Navigation Company as medical officer in 1881. He had worked in a similar capacity the previous year, when he acted as ship's doctor on board a Greenland Whaling vessel. However, life on board the *Mayumba* proved to be a decidedly different experience to the adventurous challenges of a whaling ship, and Conan Doyle found the voyage tedious. His time at sea was later used in his fiction; he drew on both experiences in stories such as 'The Captain of the *Pole Star*' (published in *Temple Bar* in January 1883) and 'J. Habakuk Jephson's Statement' (which appeared anonymously in the *Cornhill* in 1884).

Against the advice of his mother and a number of colleagues, Conan Doyle accepted a partnership with George Turnavine Budd, a general practitioner in Plymouth. Conan Doyle had mixed feelings about Budd (a fellow student at Edinburgh), and the partnership proved unsuccessful. He left after a few months to establish a new practice of his own in Southsea, Portsmouth. His younger brother, Innes, joined him and the practice became a successful one.

5 ARTHUR CONAN DOYLE (1859–1930), 1887: *A STUDY IN SCARLET*

Conan Doyle had submitted work to journals such as *Blackwood's Edinburgh Magazine* while still at university, though with little success until 'The Mystery of Sasassa Valley' was accepted for publication by *Chamber's Journal* in 1879. At Southsea he continued to write short stories for the flourishing periodical market as a way of supplementing his income. On 6 August 1885, Conan Doyle married Louisa (Louise) Hawkins. They had two children, Mary Louise (1889) and Arthur Alleyne Kingsley (known as Kingsley, 1892), before Louisa's death from tuberculosis in 1906. Conan Doyle continued to have a close relationship with his mother, a bond he later described as 'a passionate love affair'. His father's alcoholism had worsened with devastating effects, and he was confined in mental institutions for the last twelve years of his life.

Sherlock Holmes made his first appearance in the novel, *A Study in Scarlet*, published in the *Beeton's Christmas Annual* 1887. The publishers Ward Lock had previously bought all the rights to the novel for £25, a sum which Conan Doyle considered exploitative. Holmes and Watson's first outing was moderately well-received, and a sequel was commissioned by *Lippincott's Monthly Magazine*. This second Holmes novel, *The Sign of the Four*, was published in 1890, but other work had appeared in the meantime, including *The Mystery of Cloomber* (1888), *The Firm of Girdlestone* (1890), and his first historical novel, *Micah Clarke* (1889) and two collections of the shorter fiction. After its initial serialisation in *Lippincott's*, *The Sign of the Four* was republished in various other journals, before its release in book form in October under the slightly altered title, *The Sign of Four*. However, it wasn't until the short stories began to be published in the *Strand* magazine from 1891 onwards, skilfully illustrated by Sidney Paget, that Holmes became such a phenomenally popular character.

One of the attractions of the stories was the way in which each was self-contained, yet held together by recurring characters. In his autobiography, *Memories and Adventures* (1924), Conan Doyle gives an account of striking upon this idea for a disconnected set of stories, and his sense that 'a single character running through a series, if it only engaged the attention of the reader, would bind that reader to that particular magazine [...] Looking around for my central character, I felt that Sherlock Holmes, who I had already handled in two little books, would easily lend himself to a succession of short stories'. Six stories initially appeared, beginning with 'A Scandal in Bohemia', which introduced the fascinating Irene Adler, the only woman ever to hoodwink the brilliant detective.

Though she appears in one single story, Adler is alluded to in other Holmes tales. The *Strand* commissioned six more stories, and then a further twelve as the popularity of Holmes soared. Conan Doyle had long been concerned that the success of his Holmes stories would overshadow what he considered to be his more worthwhile literary endeavours, but he had continued, enticed by the increasingly large sums of money offered by the *Strand*.

The success of Conan Doyle's stories contributed to a significant growth in detective fiction, spawning an array of imitators. Jacques Futrelle's Professor Augustus S. F. X. Van Dusen, known as 'the Thinking Machine', took Holmes' cold hard logic to the extreme, while Arthur Morrison introduced an inverted Holmes figure, the cheery and intensely ordinary Martin Hewitt. Despite a host of rival detectives, Holmes' hold over the reading public remained strong and Herbert Greenhough Smith, the editor of the *Strand* between 1891 and 1830, was determined not to lose their star attraction. However, Conan Doyle was tired of his creation and wrote to his mother: 'I must save my mind for better things [...] even if it means I must bury my pocketbook with him'. He took the decision to 'kill off' his detective and in December 1893, the *Strand* published 'The Adventure of the Final Problem' (later the concluding story in *The Memoirs of Sherlock Holmes*), in which Watson reports the death of Holmes after a struggle at the Reichenbach Falls with his arch-enemy Professor Moriarty.

In 1903 Conan Doyle was persuaded to resurrect Holmes when *Collier's Weekly*, an American magazine, made him the phenomenal offer of $5000 per story. The stories would also continue to appear in their original home, the *Strand*, at an additional fee of £100 per thousand words. Holmes duly returned in 'The Adventure of the Empty House', later collected in *The Return of Sherlock Holmes*, although readers had already enjoyed more of their favourite detective's sleuthing in *The Hound of the Baskervilles* – serialised in the *Strand* between August 1901 and April 1902, and deliberately set before the events at Reichenbach. This serialisation was estimated to have increased the *Strand*'s circulation by 30,000.

Though Conan Doyle always claimed that he had partly based the character of Holmes on Joseph Bell, the influence of Edgar Allan Poe's C. Auguste Dupin is also evident, despite being dismissed by Holmes in *A Study in Scarlet* as 'a very inferior fellow', whose displays of deduction were 'showy and superficial'. The relationship between the unemotional

Holmes and his friend, assistant, and chronicler, Dr. Watson also resembles that of Dupin and Poe's unnamed narrator in some respects, though Conan Doyle was able to develop his characters in greater detail through the fifty-six stories and four novels in which they appeared. Most of these are narrated by Watson, even those in which he himself plays no active part, such as 'The Adventure of Gloria Scott' (collected in the second book of stories, *The Memoirs of Sherlock Holmes*, 1893), where Holmes recounts the details of his very first case to Watson. There are a few exceptions: 'The Last Bow' has a third person unnamed narrator, whereas 'The Adventure of the Blanched Soldier' and 'The Adventure of the Lion's Mane' are narrated by Holmes himself.

Critical opinion tends to view the earlier collections as superior to later efforts such as *The Case-Book of Sherlock Holmes* (1927). The final book-length Holmes adventure, *The Valley of Fear*, was published in 1915. The Sherlock Holmes stories were not Conan Doyle's only mystery fiction. Notable among his non-Holmes contribution to the genre is a series entitled 'Round the Fire Stories', written between 1898 and 1899, which were published in the *Strand*, and later in book form (1908). Among the best of these stories are 'The Japanned Box' and 'The Beetle Hunter', both of which equal the finest of the Holmes tales. Conan Doyle wrote over fifty books during his career, and experimented with a variety of genres. In 1912 he turned his attention to science fiction, introducing the irascible Professor Challenger in *The Lost World*, who reappeared in four further books. Conan Doyle always believed his historical novels, particularly *The White Company* (1891) and *Sir Nigel* (1906), to be the pinnacle of his literary achievements. He claimed of *Sir Nigel*, a story of chivalry and adventure set during the Hundred Years War, that it 'represents in my opinion my high-water mark in literature'.

A year after the death of Louisa, Conan Doyle married Jean Elizabeth Leckie, a woman fourteen years his junior, with whom he had been in love for nearly a decade. Conan Doyle roundly declared that their relationship was platonic during Louisa's lifetime but, despite the lack of concrete evidence, many recent commentators and biographers have speculated that Leckie was his mistress. This second marriage produced three further children.

Conan Doyle supported Britain's controversial role in the Boer War, to the extent that he went out to South Africa as a volunteer surgeon and war correspondent. In a further attempt to justify British actions, he turned his pen to propaganda in the form of a pamphlet entitled *The War in South*

Africa: Its Cause and Conduct, which was later extended into a book, *The Great Boer War* (1900). These patriotic endeavours almost certainly played a part in securing Conan Doyle's knighthood in 1902. However, World War One had a much more complex and profound effect. Initially fired with a patriotic fervour, Conan Doyle's immediate response to the war was to turn propagandist again, with a pamphlet entitled 'To Arms'. He was too old to join the army, although he attempted to enlist, so had to content himself with travelling to various fronts and gathering material for a book about the conflict, which he believed might be his magnum opus. Yet the war brought great personal losses, the most devastating of which were his brother, Innes and his eldest son, Kingsley, who both died of pneumonia at the end of the war.

Conan Doyle embraced the Spiritualism that had interested him from as early as 1893 when he had joined the Society for Psychical Research, and which now came to dominate his life. He wrote a string of books on the subject in the last decade of his life, including *Spiritualism and Rationalism* (1920), *The Wanderings of a Spiritualist* (1921), *The Early Christian Church and Modern Spiritualism* (1925), and *The History of Spiritualism* (1926), in addition to undertaking numerous lecture tours. He eagerly accepted as truth the claims of two young Yorkshire girls, Elsie Wright and Frances Griffiths, to have seen and photographed fairies in their garden, images which are now proven to have been faked, but which led Conan Doyle to write a book on the phenomenon, *The Coming of the Fairies* (1922). Andrew Lycett has summed up the apparent conundrum represented by Conan Doyle's psychic beliefs: 'Becoming a spiritualist so soon after creating the quintessentially rational Sherlock Holmes: that is the central paradox of Arthur's life'. His last years were plagued by coronary problems, although he remained relatively active. Conan Doyle died of a heart attack on 7 July 1930, at his home in Crowborough, East Sussex.

The Sherlock Holmes stories have spawned many film and television adaptations. The earliest film was a thirty second silent short entitled *Baffled*, which was shown in coin-operated mutoscope machines in the very early years of the twentieth century. A longer silent film, *Held for Ransom* (1905), was loosely based on *The Sign of the Four*. Holmes continued to attract film-makers throughout the early years of cinema, most famously in the 1939 *The Hound of the Baskervilles* starring Basil Rathbone as Holmes and Nigel Bruce as Watson. This film was the first of fourteen Sherlock Holmes films to feature Rathbone and Bruce in the roles. Other notable names to play Holmes on screen include Douglas Wilmer, Peter Cushing, along with Jeremy Brett in the successful Granada television series (1984–1994). In 2009 Robert Downey Jr. portrayed a kinetic Holmes, supported by Jude Law as Watson in Guy Ritchie's action-orientated *Sherlock Holmes* film. The most recent incarnation is Benedict Cumberbatch's interpretation of the role in *Sherlock*, a three-part television series for the BBC. Created by Mark Gatiss and Steven Moffat, *Sherlock* updates the stories for the twenty-first century, substituting the Victorian setting for present-day London. The success of these latest adaptations speaks of the perennial fascination of Conan Doyle's most iconic creation.

SUGGESTED READING/WORKS CITED

Conan Doyle, Sir Arthur, *Memories and Adventures: An Autobiography*, ed. by David Stuart Davies (1928; repr. Ware, Hertfordshire: Wordsworth, 2007).

Edwards, Owen Dudley, 'Doyle, Sir Arthur Ignatius Conan (1859–1930)', in *Oxford Dictionary of National Biography* (Oxford: Oxford University Press, 2004; online edn, Jan 2009).

Lellenberg, John, Daniel Stashower, and Charles Foley, eds, *Arthur Conan Doyle: A Life in Letters* (London & New York: Penguin, 2007).

Lycett, Andrew, *Conan Doyle: The Man Who Created Sherlock Holmes* (London: Weidenfeld & Nicolson, 2007).

Redmond, Christopher, *Sherlock Holmes Handbook*, 2nd edn (Toronto: Dundurn Press, 2009).

CHAPTER 6

George R. Sims (1847–1922), 1890: *The Case of George Candlemas*

Esme Miskimmin

George Robert Sims was a journalist, social reformer, writer and dramatist. His first detective novel *The Case of George Candlemas* was published in 1890 and reviewed by *The Spectator* in the same year as 'a very clever and readable little book' with 'no lack of movement'. His key contribution to the crime canon, however, were the two volumes of short stories featuring the 'lady detective', Dorcas Dene (1897 and 1898).

Sims was born in London and was educated at Hanwell College (a school for army cadets) and then in France and Germany before joining his father's business. He began writing short stories and verses for *Fun* magazine to relieve the tedium, during which time a humorous open letter to Henry Irving caused him to be sued for libel. From here his journalistic career took off and he wrote for the Referee paper under the name 'Dagonet'. The *Dagonet Ballads* (1879) and the *Ballads of Babylon* (1880), collected editions of his columns, were never out of print for the next thirty years and, aside from their entertainment value, revealed Sim's highly developed social conscience. This was also clearly evident in the articles he wrote for various papers such as the *Daily News*, including 'The

E. Miskimmin (✉)
University of Liverpool, Liverpool, UK

© The Author(s) 2020
E. Miskimmin (ed.), *100 British Crime Writers*, Crime Files,
https://doi.org/10.1057/978-1-137-31902-9_6

social kaleidoscope' and 'How the poor live'. Sims' social campaigning continued throughout his life. While factual, Sim's articles reveal his flair for melodrama, and it is as a writer for the popular stage that his name is most often referred to; from his first farce, *Crutch and Toothpick* (1879) to his long-running *The Lights o' London* (1881) and his collaborations with Robert Buchanan, his plays were continually in performance. His private life often overlapped with his public one: despite being married, he had a well-publicised affair with the actress Mrs. Campbell (Sims was actually married three times, but had no children).

The influence of his theatrical career can be seen in the Dorcas Dene stories: they are narrated by a male character, the dramatist Mr. Saxon, who knew Dorcas before her marriage when she worked as an actress, and the themes of disguise and performance are recurrent. Dene herself is a somewhat dichotomous character: she is a proto-feminist figure of bravery, resourcefulness and logic, and her adventures often place her in peril (in 'The Empty House' she rescues a woman who is held caged 'like a wild animal' by breaking into a house in the dead of night), but her strengths are simultaneously underwritten and undermined by the narrator's need to assure his audience that she is a 'womanly woman', whose 'soft grey eyes [grow] moist' when she thinks about the disabled husband she is forced to support, and who only undertakes cases 'in which an angel could engage without soiling its wings'.

Sims died of liver cancer, leaving a prolific and diverse oeuvre that is not often recognised within canonical literary surveys. His popularity in his lifetime is undeniable, however, and his Dorcas Dene stories deserve their place in the history of 'the lady detective' and crime fiction in general.

Suggested Reading/Works Cited

Anonymous, 'Review: The Case of George Candlemas', *The Spectator*, 3 November 1890, p. 30.

Klein, Kathleen Gregory, *The Woman Detective: Gender and Genre*, 2nd edn (Chicago: University of Illinois Press, 1995).

Sims, G. R., *My Life: Sixty Years' Recollections of Bohemian London* (London: Eveleigh Nash Company, 1917).

Waller, Philip, 'Sims, George Robert (1847–1922)', in *Oxford Dictionary of National Biography* (Oxford: Oxford University Press, 2004; online edn, May 2010).

CHAPTER 7

C. L. Pirkis (1839–1910), 1893: First Publication of the 'Loveday Brooke' Stories in *the Ludgate Monthly*

Adrienne E. Gavin

Catherine Louisa Pirkis is best known for The Experiences of Loveday Brooke, Lady Detective (1894), a collection of seven short stories which features one of fiction's earliest female-authored women detectives, Pirkis also wrote thirteen novels and a range of short stories.

Born Catherine Louisa Lyne on 6 October 1839 in Shoreditch, London, Pirkis was the youngest daughter of Susan Lyne nèe Dixon and stockbroker Lewis Stephens Lyne. On 19 September 1872 she married Frederick Edward Pirkis, a Fleet Paymaster in the Royal Navy. The year following their marriage Fred retired from active navy service, devoting his energies to dog welfare and anti-vivisection movements in which Catherine also become involved. They had a daughter Norah in 1873, a son Frederick in 1875, and sometime after 1878 a niece and nephew also joined the household, which by 1881 was in Richmond, Surrey. They later moved to The High Elms, Nutfield, Surrey, and kept a London home in Redcliffe Square, South Kensington.

A. E. Gavin (✉)
Canterbury Christ Church University, Canterbury, UK

© The Author(s) 2020
E. Miskimmin (ed.), *100 British Crime Writers*, Crime Files,
https://doi.org/10.1057/978-1-137-31902-9_7

Pirkis' first novel, *Disappeared From Her Home* (1877) centres on the mystery of a young woman who has gone missing. Her subsequent novels and short stories are mainly romances, some containing elements of crime or mystery. Her novella, 'A Bride of a Summer's Day' (1891), for example, also centres on a missing young woman. *Di Fawcett: One Year of Her Life* (1884), includes a murder and *A Red Sister: A Story of Three Days and Three Months* (1891) contains a female murderer who is herself blackmailed.

Advertised as 'A Female Sherlock Holmes', Pirkis' female detective Loveday Brooke marked the culmination of her authorial career. Appearing initially as a series of six stories in *The Ludgate Monthly* in 1893, with a seventh added in the renamed *Ludgate Illustrated Magazine* in February 1894, the stories that comprised The Experiences of Loveday Brooke, Lady Detective were published as a collection in 1894. Employed by Ebenezer Dyer, the head of a London detective agency, Loveday Brooke is one of the earliest 'lady detectives' in British fiction. Unlike later – often male-authored – female detectives such as the protagonists of Grant Allen's *Miss Cayley's Adventures* (1899) or M. McDonnell Bodkin's *Dora Myrl, the Lady Detective* (1900), Loveday Brooke is not married off, her physical appearance is not emphasised, and she becomes a detective for financial rather than personal reasons (i.e. she does not detect to save a male relative or lover). She is independent, highly skilled and thoroughly professional.

SUGGESTED READING/WORKS CITED

Gavin, Adrienne E., "'C. L. Pirkis (not "Miss")': Public Women, Private Lives, and *The Experiences of Loveday Brooke, Lady Detective*', in *Writing Women of the Fin de Siècle: Authors of Change*, ed. by Adrienne E. Gavin and Carolyn W. de la L. Oulton (Basingstoke: Palgrave, 2011), pp. 137–150.

——, 'Introduction', in *The Experiences of Loveday Brooke, Lady Detective*, by C. L. Pirkis, ed. by A. E. Gavin (London: Pickering & Chatto, 2010), pp. ix–xxiv.

Hendrey-Seabrook, Therie, 'Reclassifying the Female Detective of the Fin de Siècle: Loveday Brooke, Vocation and Vocality', *Clues: A Journal of Detection*, 26:1 (2008), 75–88.

Kestner, Joseph A., *Sherlock's Sisters: The British Female Detective, 1864–1913* (Aldershot: Ashgate, 2003).

Miller, Elizabeth Carolyn, 'Trouble with She-Dicks: Private Eyes and Public Women in *The Adventures of Loveday Brooke, Lady Detective*', *Victorian Literature and Culture*, 33:1 (2005), 47–65.

CHAPTER 8

Arthur Morrison (1863–1945), 1894: First Publication of the 'Martin Hewitt' Stories in *The Strand* Magazine

Nick Freeman

Born in Poplar in London's East End, Morrison's life is obscure; he was evasive about his origins, his wife burned his papers after his death and it is unlikely any biography of him will ever appear. After a rudimentary education, he worked as a clerk before becoming a journalist and then a freelance writer in the early 1890s. His first significant work was the slum vignettes, *Tales of Mean Streets* (1894), a collection that was followed by well-observed novels of London low-life such as *A Child of the Jago* (1896) and *The Hole in the Wall* (1902), both of which depict juvenile crime.

Morrison's most significant contributions to crime fiction were his Martin Hewitt stories, published by *The Strand* after Sherlock Holmes' 'death' in 1893 and illustrated by Sidney Paget. Hewitt was the polar opposite of Holmes; a character whose chubby build and bland affability were deliberately 'ordinary'. The Hewitt stories were informed by Morrison's first-hand knowledge of the capital's street life; crisply written

N. Freeman (✉)
Loughborough University, Loughborough, UK

© The Author(s) 2020
E. Miskimmin (ed.), *100 British Crime Writers*, Crime Files,
https://doi.org/10.1057/978-1-137-31902-9_8

and tightly plotted, even their extravagant moments, such as the anarchist plot in 'The Case of the Lost Foreigner' (1895), or the ingenious quasi-musical cipher in 'The Case of the Flitterbat Lancers' (1896) were distinguished by well-observed London settings. Morrison recounted nineteen of Hewitt's cases in three collections (1894–96) before returning to the character in the interlinked stories of *The Red Triangle* (1903) in which Hewitt battles Mayes, a master criminal who combines the attributes of Svengali, Professor Moriarty and Guy Boothby's Dr. Nikola.

More subversive than Hewitt was the private inquiry agent, Horace Dorrington of *The Dorrington Deed-Box* (1897), a duplicitous figure motivated solely by self-interest. Although Dorrington solves crimes, he is also prepared to commit them, and will even countenance murder if the rewards are sufficiently enticing. His ruthlessness and amorality can be seen as foreshadowing hard-boiled fiction and anticipating Patricia Highsmith's Ripley. Like the Hewitt stories, these tales show Morrison's interests in the late Victorian sporting world, particularly cycling, boxing and horse-racing. Several Hewitt and Dorrington stories were adapted for ITV's series, *The Rivals of Sherlock Holmes* (1971).

Morrison also published comic stories about Spotto Bird, a London thief and pickpocket (*Divers Vanities*, 1905) and a novel, *The Green Eye of Goona* (1904), clearly indebted to Wilkie Collins' *The Moonstone*. Morrison was also an authority on Oriental art which he utilised in Dorrington's 'The Case of Mr Loftus Deacon'. Morrison largely abandoned fiction before World War One; that his estate was valued at £45,000 suggests he was highly successful as a dealer in Japanese prints and antiquities.

Suggested Reading/Works Cited

Benvenuto, Richard, 'Arthur Morrison', in *Dictionary of Literary Biography, Volume 70: British Mystery Writers 1860–1919*, ed. by Bernard Benstock and Thomas F. Staley (Detroit: Gale, 1988), pp. 212–218.

Calder, Robert, 'Arthur Morrison: A Commentary with an Annotated Bibliography of Writings About Him', *English Literature in Transition*, 28 (1985), 276–297.

Freeman, Nick, 'Double Lives, Terrible Pleasures: Oscar Wilde and Crime Fiction in *Fin de Siècle*', in *Formal Investigations*, ed. by Paul Fox and Koray Melikoğlu (Stuttgart: Ibidem, 2007), pp. 71–96.

Loughlin-Chow, M. Clare, 'Morrison, Arthur George', in *Oxford Dictionary of National Biography* (Oxford: Oxford University Press, 2004; online edn, May 2009).

Morrison, Arthur, *A Child of the Jago*, ed. by Peter Keating (London: MacGibbon & Kee, 1969).

CHAPTER 9

E. Phillips Oppenheim (Also Wrote as Antony Partridge, 1866–1946), 1898: *The Mysterious Mr. Sabin*

Alexandra Phillips

Edward Phillips Oppenheim was one of the first authors to write in the spy fiction genre and he is known today for his pre-war novels articulating anxieties about a possible German invasion. Oppenheim was born in London on 22 October 1866 and moved to Leicester as a boy, entering Wyggeston Grammar School in 1877. He left school aged sixteen and worked in his father's leather business until, aged forty, he sold the business and commenced writing full time. In 1891 he travelled to the United States with his father, where he met and married Elsie Hopkins after a whirlwind romance. They returned to the UK and settled in Evington, near Leicester, where their daughter was born. They moved to Norfolk in 1905 and stayed there until 1918, during which time Oppenheim wrote propaganda for the war effort. After the war, Oppenheim bought a yacht and a villa in Cagnes sur Mer. His autobiography is short on facts but is filled with anecdotes about high society on the French Riviera, with guests and residents including Admiral Jellicoe, P. G.

A. Phillips (✉)
Open University Wales, Cardiff, UK

© The Author(s) 2020
E. Miskimmin (ed.), *100 British Crime Writers*, Crime Files,
https://doi.org/10.1057/978-1-137-31902-9_9

Wodehouse and F. Tennyson Jesse. At the beginning of World War Two, Oppenheim and his family were trapped in France, but they returned to Britain in 1941. They moved to Guernsey after the war, shortly before Oppenheim died on 3 February 1946.

In his lifetime Oppenheim produced a phenomenal quantity, if not quality, of writing: some 115 novels and 39 collections of short stories. Much of his spy and mystery fiction follows a simple formula: an aristocratic Englishman is pitted against a sinister foreign villain in an attractive location, such as Monte Carlo, Sicily, London or Paris. The tales are heavily didactic and the characters undeveloped but his novels sold well, offering his readers a glamorous world of noble gentlemen, elegant women and international intrigues. *Expiation* (1886) was the first of Oppenheim's novels to be published, but it was with spy novel *The Mysterious Mr. Sabin* (1898), which features a French agent selling British secrets to the Germans, that Oppenheim started to achieve real success. His novels became increasingly popular in the years leading up to and during World War One, a period in which he embarked on what he describes as his 'crusade against the menace of German militarism, as was evidenced in four or five of [his] novels published about this time – *The Mischief Maker*, *A Maker of History*, *The Great Secret*, *The Illustrious Prince* and a few years later the *Double Traitor* and *The Great Impersonation*'. This last novel, which features an English nobleman and a German spy, is probably his most popular; it sold a million copies and inspired film adaptations in 1921, 1935 and 1942.

Suggested Reading/Works Cited

Denning, Michael, *Cover Stories: Narrative and Ideology in the British Spy Thriller* (London: Routledge & Kegan Paul, 1987).

Oppenheim, E. Phillips, *The Pool of Memory* (London: Hodder & Stoughton, 1941).

Snow, E. E., *E. Phillips Oppenheim: Storyteller, 1866–1946* (Leicester: Evington, 1985).

Standish, Robert, *The Prince of Storytellers: The Life of E. Phillips Oppenheim* (London: Peter Davies, 1957).

CHAPTER 10

E. W. Hornung (1866–1921), 1899: *The Amateur Cracksman*

Suzanne Bray

Best known as the creator of Raffles, a gentleman burglar in late Victorian London, Ernest William ('Willie') Hornung was born in Middleborough, the third son of John Peter Hornung, an Hungarian immigrant and Harriet (Armstrong) Hornung. He attended Uppingham School, developing a lifelong interest in cricket, but in 1883 he moved to Australia for the milder climate. Traces of his Australian experience appear in many of his writings but he stayed only two years before returning to England.

Hornung lived most of his life in London where his friends included well-known writers such as George Gissing, Rudyard Kipling and J. M. Barrie. Although he began as a journalist, often writing about crime or social issues, his short stories quickly started appearing in many popular literary magazines. His first novel, *A Bride from the Bush*, was published in 1890.

Hornung's most famous creation, Arthur J. Raffles, cricketer, burglar and master of disguise, first appeared in *The Amateur Cracksman* (1899), which was later adapted into a play. The model for Raffles is said to have been George Ives, a Cambridge-educated criminologist. Raffles and his

S. Bray (✉)
Lille Catholic University, Lille, France

© The Author(s) 2020
E. Miskimmin (ed.), *100 British Crime Writers*, Crime Files,
https://doi.org/10.1057/978-1-137-31902-9_10

sidekick, Bunny Manders, are well-educated, impecunious men-about-town. Amateurs at both cricket and crime, they commit a series of spectacular burglaries, often with unusual motives. In one story Raffles steals a gold cup from the British Museum and then sends it as a Diamond Jubilee present to Queen Victoria. This period ends in their being uncovered following a theft aboard ship. Raffles jumps overboard while Bunny is arrested.

The series continues with a professional period for Bunny and Raffles, in which they are social outcasts, and which starts when Bunny applies for a job as valet to an elderly invalid who turns out to be Raffles in disguise. These crimes, narrated in *The Black Mask* (1901), are more complex because Raffles has to conceal his identity and the atmosphere is darker than before. In the same way as Raffles' French counterpart, Arsène Lupin, wipes out his sins by enlisting in the Foreign Legion, Raffles and Bunny volunteer to fight in the Boer War where Raffles dies a hero's death after exposing an enemy spy. Hornung later published another volume of stories about the early Raffles, *A Thief in the Night* (1905), and a full-length novel, *Mr. Justice Raffles* (1909), in which a cynical Raffles defeats an unpleasant East End moneylender.

After the death of his son in action in July 1915, Hornung joined the anti-aircraft corps and also served at the YMCA canteen in Arras until the end of the war. He died and was buried in St. Jean de Luz, France.

Suggested Reading/Works Cited

Orwell, George, 'Raffles and Miss Blandish', *Horizon*, 10 (1944), 232–244.
Rowland, Peter, *Raffles and His Creator: The Life and Works of E. W. Hornung* (London: Nekta Publications, 1999).

CHAPTER 11

Baroness Orczy (1865–1947), 1901: First Publication of Six 'The Old Man in the Corner' Stories in *The Royal Magazine*

Greg Rees

Baroness Emma Magdolna Rozália Mária Jozefa Borbála Orczy de Orczi, known as Baroness Emmuska Orczy, was a Hungarian noblewoman, artist and writer best known for her *Scarlet Pimpernel* and *Old Man in the Corner* series.

Born in 1865 to a family of Hungarian nobility, Baroness Orczy was raised in various parts of Europe before her family settled in London in 1880. She was to spend most of the rest of her life in England. Orczy met her husband, Montague Barstow, while at art school; they married in 1894 and they had one son, the writer John Blakeney (who took his nom de plume from his mother's *Pimpernel* character). The Scarlet Pimpernel novels are perhaps Orczy's most famous works. Set during the time of the French Revolution, they feature the English aristocrat Sir Percy Blakeney, who becomes embroiled in adventures and scandals set against the bloodshed of the Terror and its aftermath.

G. Rees (✉)
Cardiff University, Cardiff, UK

© The Author(s) 2020
E. Miskimmin (ed.), *100 British Crime Writers*, Crime Files,
https://doi.org/10.1057/978-1-137-31902-9_11

Orczy wrote a substantial number of crime fiction works. One of her most acclaimed creations is the Old Man in the Corner. This series, first published between 1901 and 1909, featured an intellectual detective (the eponymous 'Old Man') in the mould of Sherlock Holmes. Rzepka notes that, similar to Holmes, the Old Man is a 'strictly 'consulting' detective [...] solving cases entirely by brain-power while sitting in a tea-room'. The Old Man differs from the Holmesian archetype in that he does not actually help apprehend the criminals: it is enough that he solves their ingenious crimes, admiring their 'artistic or strategic skill' as Kayman puts it. It could be argued that, unlike Holmes, the Old Man is a 'different sort of intellectual': a more accessible character, happy working in the open, public space of cafes instead of 'inhabiting the masculine chambers of other cerebral detectives'. The *Old Man* stories have been dramatised a number of times: in the 1920s, in the 1970s by Thames TV, and in the late 1990s for BBC Radio 4.

Orczy's *Lady Molly of Scotland Yard* (1910) is considered a milestone in the advancement of the female protagonist in detective fiction. As Kestner points out, Orczy's narrator is a woman, Mary Granard (who plays the 'Watson' to her aristocratic friend), reflecting 'the influence of the suffrage movement and the need for women as sisters to bond together'. Additionally, many of the criminals in *Lady Molly* are also women, thus women 'occupy both the subject and object positions': a stark contrast to the typical crime fiction of the period. Lady Molly is an amateur detective from the upper echelons of society, who is very assured of her place there; Orczy's own conservative position on many issues reflected her traditional aristocratic background, and Lady Molly's 'supercilious attitudes towards the lower classes [reflect] much of the Baroness' own aristocratic prejudices'.

Baroness Orczy authored over fifty novels in total (including many historical novels), plus several plays and short story collections, as well as translating native Hungarian tales into English. She enjoyed great acclaim and financial success through her writing, enabling her to travel widely and to purchase a number of properties including an estate in Monte Carlo.

With her Lady Molly and Old Man stories, Orczy provided a highly significant addition to the crime fiction canon, helping to define and widen the concepts of both the female detective and the intellectual-outsider detective in popular crime fiction.

Suggested Reading/Works Cited

Kayman, Martin, 'The Short Story from Poe to Chesterton', in *The Cambridge Companion to Crime Fiction*, ed. by Martin Priestman (Cambridge: Cambridge University Press, 2003), pp. 41-58.

Kestner, Joseph A., *Sherlock's Sisters: The British Female Detective 1864–1913* (Aldershot: Ashgate, 2003).

Lehman, David, *The Perfect Murder: A Study in Detection* (Ann Arbor: University of Michigan Press, 2000).

Rzepka, Charles, *Detective Fiction* (Cambridge: Polity Press, 2005).

CHAPTER 12

Erskine Childers (1870–1922), 1903: *The Riddle of the Sands*

Christopher Routledge

Childers is best known for *The Riddle of the Sands: A Record of Secret Service* (1903), an early spy novel which became hugely popular in Britain during the years leading up to the beginning of World War One. Its basic premise, that a German invasion of the British Isles was imminent, made it highly topical, placing it at the centre of a national debate about Britain's international position and its imperial decline. *The Riddle of the Sands* was also a milestone in the development of the spy thriller, since its blend of fiction with verifiable details made it a precursor to the work of espionage writers later in the twentieth century, including Graham Greene, Ian Fleming and Len Deighton. Childers is often credited as the originator of the modern spy story, which Julian Symons describes, in reference to Joseph Conrad, as the 'political detective story'.

Robert Erskine Childers was born in Mayfair, London. His father, Robert Caesar Childers, was a translator who specialised in Oriental languages, and his mother, Anna, came from the wealthy, protestant, Barton family, who owned Glendalough House in County Wicklow, Ireland. Both Childers' parents were dead by the time he was twelve

C. Routledge (✉)
Freelance Writer and Photographer, NW England, UK

© The Author(s) 2020
E. Miskimmin (ed.), *100 British Crime Writers*, Crime Files,
https://doi.org/10.1057/978-1-137-31902-9_12

years old, and he and his four siblings were sent to Ireland, where they lived comfortably at Glendalough. Childers was educated at Haileybury College, a boarding school in Hertfordshire, and later at Trinity College, Cambridge, where he studied law and edited the university magazine the *Cambridge Review*.

Childers was a keen sailor and during school and university vacations he spent much of his time sailing off the Wicklow coast. After graduation, in 1895, he took a job as a House of Commons clerk, partly because he was at that time a British patriot, but also with the idea that he could spend the long parliamentary recesses sailing. Interestingly, while his cousin, Hugh Childers, MP, campaigned for Irish Home Rule, Erskine Childers was in this period firmly against Irish independence, although he later became an Irish Nationalist.

By the late 1890s Childers was an experienced sailor, with his own yacht, a thirty-foot sloop, *Vixen*, which he sailed to the North Sea coast of Germany and to Scandinavia. Information and material gathered on these voyages would later provide detail for *Riddle of the Sands*. However, as Brett F. Woods explains in his essay 'Pen and Sword: The Enigma of Erskine Childers,' the beginning of the Boer War in South Africa brought a temporary halt to Childers' sailing adventures, and proved to be a turning point in his life.

Childers volunteered for the Army, and served in South Africa until a foot infection forced him to leave. Woods speculates that it was conversations with Boer prisoners that first made him doubt the validity of British imperial rule. Later, on his return to Britain, and his job in the Commons, his doubts became more concrete.

The Riddle of the Sands can be seen as being part of a Victorian tradition of adventure stories that included writers such as Rider Haggard, but the addition of the spy plot was new. The story concerns two men, Davies and Carruthers, who embark on a yachting holiday to the German Frisian islands. There they find a hidden German naval base, which turns out to be part of a plan to invade England. The story is further complicated by the revelation that the base is being run by an Englishman. When Davies falls in love with the traitor's daughter, the situation becomes even more difficult. Both characters change with their experiences, Davies emerging as a practical man of action, while Carruthers is transformed from a deskbound civil servant into a plausible secret agent. Julian Symons sums it up thus: '[T]he whole story has immense charm, vivacity, and an underlying idealism that takes for granted the way in which an honourable man must behave.'

However, the book also appealed to a growing xenophobia in Britain in the early years of the twentieth century, and to a prevailing sense of Britain being under threat from unscrupulous foreigners and hidden traitors. It is a celebration of Britain and the moral qualities that apparently underpinned the Empire, but it is also conscious of the ease with which empires come and go, and of the conflicting viewpoints of occupier and occupied.

Childers' sailing experience plays a significant part in the novel, much of which is concerned with the details of navigating the Frisian coast, and sailing a small boat in difficult, rock-strewn waters. This combination of factual description with fictional adventure is arguably the novel's most lasting legacy. It helped shape both the spy novel, and crime fiction more widely, over the following century and beyond. The novel has been adapted for film on two occasions, in 1979 and 1987.

By 1914 Childers had given up the idea of standing for election as an MP in the British parliament. He was by then a well-known supporter of Irish home rule, and, just two weeks before the war began, used his yacht, *Asgard*, to smuggle German guns into Ireland, where they were used, in 1916 Easter Rising, against British soldiers. Nevertheless, Childers spent the war working for British Naval Intelligence and received the Distinguished Service Cross (D. S. C.) in 1916. He was later recruited as a navigator and observer in naval air reconnaissance missions and was one of the earliest recruits to the Royal Air Force when it was formed in 1918.

When the war ended Childers committed himself to the cause of Irish independence, and was elected as Sinn Fein representative for County Wicklow in 1921. He was a senior secretary to the Irish delegation that negotiated the Anglo-Irish Treaty in 1921, though he favoured full independence rather than the Free State. Already a traitor in England, he joined the Irish Republican Army and was arrested at Glendalough carrying an unauthorised firearm, a capital crime under martial law. He was court-martialled and executed by firing squad on 24 November 1922. His son, Erskine Hamilton Childers, served as President of the Irish Republic from 1973 until his death in 1974.

Suggested Reading/Works Cited

Price, Leonard, *The Tragedy of Erskine Childers* (London: Hambledon Continuum, 2007).
Ring, Jim, *Erskine Childers: A Biography* (London: John Murray, 1997).
Seed, David, 'Spy Fiction', in *The Cambridge Companion to Crime Fiction*, ed. by Martin Priestman (Cambridge: Cambridge University Press, 2003), pp. 115–134.
Symons, Julian, *Bloody Murder: From the Detective Story to the Crime Novel*, rev. edn (London: Faber, 1985).
Woods, Brett F, 'Pen and Sword: The Enigma of Erskine Childers', in *Richmond Review* http://www.richmondreview.co.uk/library/pen__and_sword.html.

CHAPTER 13

Edgar Wallace (1875–1932), 1905: *The Four Just Men*

Stephen Knight

Commentators seem unable to avoid using the term 'phenomenon' to describe Edgar Richard Horatio Wallace, referring usually to his enormous popularity in Britain, America and Germany, and his extraordinary productivity. In crime fiction he produced at least 158 novels and story collections (though titles were often changed, and there may be overlaps), and he could be astonishingly prolific: his finest year was 1929 when he produced twenty-three titles, nearly matched by 1926 (eighteen) and 1927 (fourteen). But the commentators always seem to be using 'phenomenal' in a slightly derogatory way, as if he were the cause of some embarrassment: Dorothy L. Sayers was cool about his 'thrillers' in the introduction to her influential 1928 anthology, *Great Short Stories of Detection, Mystery and Horror*.

Wallace is certainly different from the acknowledged mainstream crime writers, but in many ways he is close to the normality of very successful popular writing, being multi-generic. His first novel, *The Four Just Men* (1905), is essentially crime fiction, in the international adventure thriller mode that was then popular, from Guy Boothby and William Le Queux.

S. Knight (✉)
University of Melbourne, Melbourne, VIC, Australia

© The Author(s) 2020
E. Miskimmin (ed.), *100 British Crime Writers*, Crime Files,
https://doi.org/10.1057/978-1-137-31902-9_13

But this novel actually lost him money: a self-publisher, he spent too much on publicity and too many people claimed the prize he offered for solving the final puzzle. He struggled on, writing for magazines, but, turning to a topic familiar to him as a *Daily Mail* reporter in the Belgian Congo, he achieved real success with his stories about 'Sanders of the River', starting in 1911. This generated five collections, and with the assistance of fiction editor Isabel Thorne (she earned a dedication), he elevated the minor figure of 'Bones', a junior colonial officer, to be central to four books. Starting in 1915, the Sanders and Bones stories deployed vivid context, rapid action and remorseless white supremacy. Sanders is a sort of colonial Sherlock Holmes and Bones is, even less acceptably, an imperially located Bertie Wooster. With these figures as foci of post-Conrad stories shorn of irony and complicity, Wallace first made his name and his success.

He had come a long way to achieve that position. Born on April 1, 1875, illegitimate son of an actor and actress, Richard Horatio Edgar and Polly Richards, he was first fathered onto another man, Polly's husband the comedian Walter Wallace, and then fostered with the family of a London fish-market worker – an origin that characters never suffer in any of the fiction. The young man inherited the adaptability of the actors' trade and after some mistakes – working on a trawler was the biggest – he joined the army, was rapidly, like another crime writer Eugène Sue, transferred to the medical corps and by 1896 found himself in military South Africa, tending towards writing as a career. His technical skill and courage – or perhaps just cheek – led him to scoop the Boer War peace treaty for the *Daily Mail*, and receive official sanctions; but his respect for authority led him to imitate Kipling in his non-fiction *The Mission that Failed* (1898). His mix of assertiveness and aspiration led him to persevere in journalism, and he returned to Britain in 1902 to work for Harmsworth at the *Daily Mail*, but also hatch his ambitious *The Four Just Men*.

Its mix of direct action, cynicism and relentless mystery make it seem very modern, and in his introduction to the 1995 Oxford edition, David Glover links its 'crisp demotic prose' with the new style the *Daily Mail* introduced. Wallace never again matched the intensity of this book, perhaps through haste, perhaps through increasingly easy popularity. The Four are international Avengers; they turn on the illiberal arrogance of the London government, and bring off their crime with a panache and mystery only matched by Wallace's presentation, ending with a locked-room mystery to match Zangwill's in *The Big Bow Mystery* (1891) and before Gaston Leroux's *Le Mystère de la Chambre Jaune* (1907): commentators usually forget Wallace's shaping contribution to this crime fiction holy grail, and few recall his firm-minded anti-racist standpoint. After this, penniless, out of work at the *Mail* – his less-than-careful reporting had cost Harmsworth libel pay-outs – Wallace resorted to the magazine publishing that would eventually lead to new success in the imperial platitudes of Sanders and Bones.

It might have seemed that his crime fiction activity was a one-novel sport, but by the end of the war he, like Christie and Sayers, was attracted by the evident success of the form, largely in hands now forgotten like J. S. Fletcher, Baroness Orczy, A. E. W. Mason, and the Americans Carolyn Wells and Mary Roberts Rinehart. Wallace began to produce crime novels, and their titles show the influence of these unassuming writers.

The Clue of the Twisted Candle (1918) adapts the low-toned clue-puzzle to his favoured active mode, with a mystery writer being set up on a murder charge by an Albanian adventurer: a lovely woman is frightened, the writer kills his enemy, and the CID let him off. The equally tame-sounding *The Daffodil Mystery* (1920) is another frame-up – Wallace, never really on the side of law, liked them as much as brilliant and triumphant criminals – and provides his characteristic sensational ending. As always, it bears a moral message, but also is an intriguing variant of the classic mystery, with multiple activity at the death scene and much misleading evidence.

Wallace was also continuing with his own non-Golden-Age style: *The Man Who Bought London* (1915) is the criminal-business-romance fantasy which the Americans would soon call a tough guy story, and that highly improbable mix of heroic action, fine women, fearful betrayals and hyper-active climaxes remained Wallace's dominant mode. By 1921 he was linked to the ambitious popular publisher Hodder and Stoughton, who established the Wallace brand and named him the 'King of Thrillers'. Producing books rapidly – *The Crimson Circle* (1922) *The Sinister Man* (1924), *The Daughters of the Night* (1925) – he soon settled on a code-word titling style for a set of very successful novels: *The Joker* (1926), *The Forger* (1927), *The Squeaker* (1927), *The Avenger* (1927), *The Twister* (1928), *The Gunner* (1928). The titles made male action central – US titles could oddly reduce this effect as in *Gunman's Bluff* (*The Gunner*) and *The Clever One* (*The Forger*) – but the plots varied. *The Joker* (also known as *The Colossus*) is in fact one of the 'Inspector Elk' police series that Wallace produced intermittently, though it is still a thriller with a substitution/impersonation core. *The Forger* is a melodrama with corrupt police, an unpunished criminal and a strong sense of melodrama.

Perhaps genetically, theatre was a recurrent interest for Wallace (he wrote over twenty plays and ten screenplays) and one of his greatest successes was turning his novel *The Gaunt Stranger* (1925) into a play with the series-linked name, *The Ringer*. It opened in 1926 as the Great Strike began, and was a huge success. An Australian master criminal and even more masterful impersonator is in Britain for vengeance (much like one of the Just Men): the police cannot find him. In a brilliant double denouement his identity is revealed in a splendid 'least-likely' surprise and at the final moment he, with his beautiful wife, eludes the police yet again. As both play and novel, *The Ringer* has the condensed clarity of *The Four Just Men*, probably because the great actor Gerald du Maurier reworked the plot as he directed it for the stage – though he did not, contrary to some reports, play the Ringer: that was Leslie Faber.

The criminal adventure continued to fascinate Wallace. *The India Rubber Men* (1927) is a surprisingly comical one, with Inspector Elk in the background, but some of the work from this period treads water: *The Flying Squad* (1928) is routine London crime and duplicity; *The Big Fix* (1929) offers mechanically surprising short stories about crime in high European places. Other novels move on. *On the Spot* (1931) is set in Chicago, which Wallace had visited in 1929, and published in New York. His action style suited America, but he also moved towards sadomasochism – presumably he had read Hammett's *Red Harvest*. *When the Gangs Came to London* (1932) is a violent account of the Americanisation of London crime, with the usual grey-eyed beauty: Peter Cheyney would do much with this pattern. It was in America that Wallace died in 1932, from diabetes and pneumonia, when working on the film that was to be *King Kong*.

Wallace was never a uniform or monochrome figure. His writing could be opportunist – he liked follow-ups like *The Three Just Men* (1925) and *Again the Ringer* (1929); but he could work across a whole range of subgenres and showed himself at times as genuinely inventive. If he appropriated the locked-room mystery and the Golden Age style before Christie was published, he also in a way surpassed it in the still popular story collection *The Mind of Mr. J. G. Reeder* (1925). A quiet investigator, Reeder looks into puzzling events and generates subtle forms of rough justice.

A petit-bourgeois Father Brown (Wallace clearly read everything with his journalist's appetite), Reeder supervises the opposite of what his author usually stands for: brash, rapid, melodrama.

It was his action mode that made Wallace very successful in Germany: by 1931 he is described by Cicely Hamilton in *Modern Germany* as that country's 'dominant English author'. Perhaps like Byron and Christie, his emphasis on content rather than style made him operate better in translation, but his German public had been loyal: in 1959 an 'Edgar Wallace Series' started there and would publish 23 titles.

In many ways Wallace was the opposite of the traditional recessive crime writer. He behaved with assertive flashiness – cars, parties, horses, houses; he treated writing like an industry – he was said to plan six novels at a time, and once took and won a bet that he could dictate a novel over a weekend. Much about him and his work proclaims the novelist as journalist. Like the *Daily Mail* then and now he sought sudden sensation, apparent innovation, all within a frame of conventionality and conservatism. And yet his deviances, his devices, his plots and his resolutions are remarkably close to the work of the honoured Golden Age writers, especially Christie and Sayers. Wallace's work was the tabloid version of the clue-puzzle broadsheet, and his energy, his tricksterish variety and his assertive self-construction all realised a new twentieth-century figure, the industrial, populist writer about crime – a true phenomenon.

SUGGESTED READING/WORKS CITED

Adrian, Jack, 'Edgar Wallace', in *St. James Guide to Mystery and Crime Writing*, 4th edn, ed. by Jay P. Pederson (Detroit: St. James, 1996), pp. 1019–1023.

Bleiler, Richard, 'Edgar Wallace', in *Mystery and Suspense Writers: The Literature of Crime, Detection, and Espionage*, Vol. 2, ed. by Robin Winks and Maureen Corrigan (New York: Scribner, 1998), pp. 943–955.

Cox, J. Randolph, 'Edgar Wallace', in *Dictionary of Literary Biography, Volume 70: British Mystery Writers, 1860–1919*, ed. by Bernard Benstock and Thomas F. Staley (Detroit: Gale, 1988), pp. 290–302.

'Edgar Wallace', in *Contemporary Authors*, Vol. 218, ed. by Jenai A. Mynott (Detroit: Gale, 2004), pp. 421–427.

'Edgar Wallace', *Twentieth-Century Literary Criticism*, Vol. 57, ed. by Joann Cerrito (Detroit: Gale, 1995), pp. 393–409.

Glover, David, 'Edgar Wallace', in *Oxford Dictionary of National Biography*, ed. by H. C. G. Matthew and Brian Harrison (Oxford: Oxford University Press, 2004), pp. 928–930.

Lane, Margaret, *Edgar Wallace: The Biography of a Phenomenon* (1938; repr. London: Hamilton, 1964).
Wallace, Penelope, 'Introduction', in *The British Bibliography of Edgar Wallace*, ed. by W. O. G. Lofts and Derek Adley (London: Baker, 1969).

CHAPTER 14

R. Austin Freeman (1862–1943), 1907: *The Red Thumb Mark* (First Novel in the 'Dr. Thorndyke' Series)

Nick Freeman

Freeman was a doctor, novelist and short story writer who created the medical sleuth, Dr. John Thorndyke. The son of an alcoholic tailor, Richard Austin Freeman was born in London in 1862. He was educated at what he described as 'a boarding school in North London' – this may have been a board school – was apprenticed as an apothecary and then trained at Middlesex Hospital, becoming a licensed apothecary in 1886. His obvious talents for medicine led him to become first house physician at Middlesex and then the head surgeon in its ear and throat department. During this time, he immersed himself in the work of Alfred Swaine Taylor, whose *Principles and Practice of Medical Jurisprudence* (1865) would help shape Dr. Thorndyke in years to come. Freeman passed the entry examinations for the Royal College of Physicians and the Royal College of Surgeons, but like Arthur Conan Doyle, he harboured literary as well as medical ambitions. His interweaving of the two would

N. Freeman (✉)
Loughborough University, Loughborough, UK

© The Author(s) 2020
E. Miskimmin (ed.), *100 British Crime Writers*, Crime Files,
https://doi.org/10.1057/978-1-137-31902-9_14

eventually lead to the creation of Thorndyke, scientist and criminologist, Freeman's lasting contribution to detective literature.

Freeman registered as a medical practitioner in 1887 and secured a job as an assistant colonial surgeon in what is now Ghana. His role was wide-ranging; in 1889, he was part of the mission that took over Ashanti and Jaman as Imperial protectorates, acting as a geographer and mapper as well as a botanist, zoologist and topographer. He was then made a member of the Anglo-German Boundary Commission for Togoland, but was stricken with blackwater fever and almost died before returning to England, his health permanently impaired. To add insult to injury, he was denied a pension since his colonial service was two months short of the required duration. He wrote of his African experiences in *Travels and Life in Ashanti and Jaman* (1898), used them as the basis for his novel, *The Golden Pool* (1905) and revisited them later in life as background for the Thorndyke story, *The Magic Casket* (1927).

Freeman's poor health undermined his attempts to work as a specialist physician, and, having failed to establish himself in private practice, he worked briefly at the Westminster Ophthalmic Hospital before securing the less-than-prestigious post of assistant medical officer at Holloway Prison. This did however have a very significant consequence. Freeman and his family (he had married in 1887; his sons were born in 1893 and 1897) lodged with his superior, John James Pitcairn, and the two men began to collaborate on literary projects, working under the pseudonym 'Clifford Ashdown'. The fruit of this partnership was Romney Pringle, a gentleman rogue who appeared in *Cassell's Magazine* in 1902.

Aimed at the burgeoning market for charismatic fictional criminals dominated by Hornung's Raffles, Romney Pringle poses as a literary agent (an obvious joke about the proliferation of such figures during the 1890s) but he is essentially a trickster who lives on his wits, or, as Stephen Knight has it, 'a fraud about town'. Like Arthur Morrison's Dorrington, he often preys on other criminals, a habit which sees him swindling the swindlers behind a patent medicine racket in 'The Assyrian Rejuvenator' and which draws him into a dangerous battle of wits with a professional burglar known as The Toff. Other Pringle adventures saw him caught up in the espionage surrounding the Anglo-French naval rivalry of the time ('The Submarine Boat') and the illicit diamond buying Raffles had encountered in 'A Costume Piece' ('The Kimberley Fugitive'). Six stories made up *The Adventures of Romney Pringle* (1902), and another six were subsequently collected in his *Further Adventures* (published posthumously in 1969), concluding with an exciting escape from Pentonville Prison ('The House of Detention'). Unfortunately, despite considerable wit and flair absent from much of Freeman's subsequent work (an exception being the late novel, *The Stoneware Monkey*, 1938), the character was not popular with the reading public. The collaborators turned instead to Dr. Wilkinson, a travelling medical detective, but he was no more successful and the partnership broke up, with Pitcairn returning to medicine and Freeman moving to Gravesend in Kent to become a full-time writer. Freeman remained interested in literary rogues and published *The Exploits of Danby Croker* in 1916. If anything Croker was even less popular than Pringle had been, but by 1916, Freeman's name was already synonymous with a far more significant creation.

A man of diverse talents, Freeman's hobbies included modelling in wax and clay, painting, book-binding and engraving. He built a laboratory in his attic, conducting experiments to determine the accuracy of his fiction's scientific content (in this respect he was a far cry from Conan Doyle), and the magazine appearances of a number of the Thorndyke stories were accompanied by photographs of microscope slides Freeman had made of crucial 'evidence'. At the outbreak of World War Two, Freeman even designed his own air raid shelter (an improvement on Government issue) for his garden, and used it as a makeshift workroom when writing *Mr. Polton Explains* (1940). His many skills would be significant in the series of novels and the forty short stories he wrote between 1907 and 1942 that featured Dr. John Evelyn Thorndyke, barrister, medical jurist and finally professor of medical jurisprudence at St. Margaret's Hospital Medical School. The antithesis of the flamboyant Sherlock Holmes, Thorndyke, helped by Nathaniel Polton, his devoted servant and laboratory assistant and his frequent sidekick Dr. Jervis, works in both official and unofficial capacities, assisting the baffled police with their inquiries while also solving mysteries on his own account. Though the books lack the sparkle of the Pringle stories, and can be given to a solipsistic interest in the details of forensic detection (the discussion of the gutta-percha shoes in *Mr. Pottermack's Oversight* [1930] is one of the most tedious episodes in any detective novel), they are ingeniously plotted, convincingly characterised (Polton is especially well drawn) and show remarkably well sustained narrative invention. The doctor's method is well illustrated in *Dr. Thorndyke Intervenes* (1923), where he announces: 'Now, in the criminal department of my practice, I have been in the habit, from the first, of using what I may call a synthetic method. In investigating a known or suspected crime, my custom has been to put myself in the criminal's place and ask myself what are the possible methods of committing that crime, and, of the possible methods, which would be the best; how, in fact, I should go about committing that crime, myself. Having worked out in detail the most suitable procedure, I then change over from the synthetic to the analytic method and consider all the inherent weaknesses and defects of the method, and the means by which it would be possible to detect the crime'.

Thorndyke made his debut in *The Red Thumb Mark* (1907). The Fingerprint Branch at Scotland Yard had only been established in 1901, and here, as elsewhere, Freeman was quick to exploit new ideas, theories and technology for narrative purposes. As John McAleer points out, the author was certainly well enough informed to create a villain able to make a fingerprint-forging device: Freeman had already made a gelatine stamp to copy his own prints. British publishers were not yet ready for Thorndyke however, and Freeman apparently paid for *The Red Thumb Mark*'s publication with the unheralded firm of Collingwood. The reading public however quickly seized on the character, and prompted by the success of the novel, Chatto and Windus snapped up Freeman's collection of short stories, *John Thorndyke's Cases* (1909), based on pieces which had appeared in *Pearson's Magazine* the year before.

Freeman made sure he was always up to date with forensic technology, with X-rays playing a significant role in *The Eye of Osiris* (1911). Subtitled 'a detective romance', perhaps in homage to the 'scientific romances' of H. G. Wells, the book's methods were scrupulously accurate and exploited the contemporary vogue for Egyptology while being a little ahead of their time. Thorndyke's portable laboratory allows on-the-spot forensic work, and he is keen to make sure that investigating officers do not accidentally damage the evidence: it would not be until 1924 that the forensic pathologist, Sir Bernard Spilsbury, identified the need for police to take a 'murder bag' to the scenes of crime. According to McAleer, the French Sûreté used Thorndyke's equipment as the basis of its own laboratories.

The Singing Bone, Freeman's influential 1912 collection, pioneered the 'inverted' detective story by showing the crime being committed and then, in the second half of the tale, explaining how it was solved. Later the basis of the US television series, *Columbo* (1968–2003), the inverted story replaced mystery with technical expertise, though it could also prompt entertaining battles of wits between suspects and detectives and generate considerable suspense. *The Singing Bone* contained a quartet of such stories, the first of which was 'The Case of Oscar Brodski' in which a diamond merchant is killed on a train during the course of a robbery. The story was unusual in that Freeman rarely drew upon real-life crimes in his work, and professed not to read detective fiction (McAleer suggests that this was something of a blind, since individual stories are influenced by Poe, Chesterton, Sayers, Willis Crofts and van Dine). Here however he revisited the world's first railway murder, the killing of the London bank-clerk, Thomas Briggs, by Franz Müller in July 1864, although as Freeman had acquired a dislike of capital punishment during his years at Holloway, he had his murderer drown after falling overboard from the ship bringing him to justice, whereas Müller was hanged at Newgate in November 1864.

The Silent Witness (1914) was Thorndyke's last adventure before Freeman joined the Royal Army Medical Corps in 1915. The book was notable for a painstaking account of the laboratory analysis of ash and bone fragments, which developed the similarly detailed analysis of various forms of dust central to 'A Wastrel's Romance' in *The Singing Bone*. The novel showed Freeman trying to balance the competing claims of narrative, characterisation, psychological realism and accurate scientific procedures: that he was not able to mix a wholly successful cocktail of them may explain why he reworked the novel's plot in *The D'Arblay Mystery* (1926), a story much admired by T. S. Eliot. His perfectionism in producing believable scientific solutions to narrative puzzles also prompted 1912's 'The Dead Hand' to become the longer and more detailed *The Shadow of the Wolf* thirteen years later.

Freeman's poor health meant that he could not join the RAMC in France although he volunteered to do so (his older son, Jack, was badly wounded there in 1917). As a captain in the RAMC, he was based in Maidstone: he was therefore able to remain living at home in Gravesend which may explain how he found time to write not only the 'Danby Croker' stories but also several Thorndyke adventures, two of which appeared in his 1918 collection *The Great Portrait Mystery*. He finally left the army in 1919 and resumed work on the Thorndyke series.

Although the Thorndyke novels were popular, Freeman's ambitions extended beyond detective fiction and into more serious matters. Interested in genetics and heredity and eager to investigate whether scientific rationalism could be used to prevent a repeat of the 1914–18 catastrophe, he published *Social Decay and Regeneration* in 1921, its title a riposte to the pessimism of Max Nordau's *Degeneration* (1892, English translation 1895), a work that had been influential before the war. *Social Decay and Regeneration*, which boasted a foreword by Havelock Ellis, advocated a system of eugenics in which 'the voluntary segregation of the fit' would be part of a wider programme of socio-political change. It also singled out what Freeman termed 'the sub-man' as a 'bad citizen' and concomitant social menace. However, while *Social Decay* considered notions of 'social pathology', few of Freeman's fictional criminals could be classed as 'sub-men': the types of crime they committed did not merit Thorndyke's attention and were perhaps too close to real life to entertain a readership hoping for escapism.

Thorndyke continued to be the mainstay of Freeman's fiction during the 1920s, although the extent to which the doctor appears varies from one novel to another: he may be involved in mysteries from the beginning or be called in by a younger, less experienced or worldly friend or colleague. Repetitive in many ways (if comforting for their fans), the series did occasionally strike off in surprisingly directions, as in *Helen Vardon's Confession* (1922), for instance, in which the narrator is Helen herself or Freeman's rewrite of Dickens' unfinished final novel, *The Mystery of Edwin Drood* (1870), *The Mystery of Angelina Frood* (1924). Here cross-dressing is a major aspect of the plot, and leads to a perhaps unintentionally amusing courtroom scene in which Thorndyke summarises some obvious differences between male and female bodies without perhaps being obvious enough. Also noteworthy in his work was a willingness to understand rather than simply condemn criminals. The cunningly plotted *As a Thief in the Night* (1928) shows Thorndyke's unrivalled knowledge of toxicology in tracking down an arsenic poisoner, while at the same time providing an emotionally involving storyline that prompts sympathy for both the perpetrator and their victims. *Mr. Pottermack's Oversight* went further still in Thorndyke's refusal to arrest the blackmailed protagonist, an amateur scientist not unlike Freeman himself, who killed his tormentor.

Perhaps Freeman's most significant work of the 1920s was his essay, 'The Art of the Detective Story' (1924) which took pains to discriminate between the 'intellectual satisfaction', 'logical analysis' and 'subtle and acute reasoning' offered by 'the good detective story' and the thriller's 'crude and pungent sensationalism': it is hard to imagine Freeman enjoying Bulldog Drummond or Sexton Blake. Superior detective fiction, he argued, 'arouses the enthusiasm of men of intellect and culture' and enriches its readers. Thrillers and films however debase theirs through the law of diminishing returns prompting a need for ever greater, ever more vulgar stimulus.

Freeman's late novels showed his strengths and weaknesses in equal measure. His detractors (notably Dorothy L. Sayers) disliked and disbelieved the range of Thorndyke's accomplishments which seemed to violate the canons of fair play. They also found his explanations laborious and thought his prose at best workmanlike. His admirers however pointed to his continued interest in technological developments (*Mr. Pottermack* involves a telephoto camera) and the variety of his plots: *For the Defence: Dr. Thorndyke* (1934) involves identity theft, while *The Penrose Mystery* (1936) has an archaeologist murdered and concealed in an ancient burial mound.

Suggested Reading/Works Cited

Donaldson, Norman, *In Search of Dr. Thorndyke* (Bowling Green, OH: Popular Press, 1971).

Glover, David, 'The Writers Who Knew Too Much: Populism and Paradox in Detective Fiction's Golden Age', in *The Art of Detective Fiction*, ed. by Warren Chernaik and Robert Vilain (Basingstoke: Macmillan, 2000), pp. 36–49.

Knight, Stephen, *Crime Fiction 1800–2000: Detection, Death, Diversity* (Basingstoke: Palgrave Macmillan, 2004).

Mayo, Oliver, *R. Austin Freeman: The Anthropologist at Large* (Hawthorndene, SA: Investigator Press, 1980).

McAleer, John, 'R. Austin Freeman', in *Dictionary of Literary Biography, Volume 70: British Mystery Writers 1860–1919*, ed. by Bernard Benstock and Thomas F. Staley (Detroit: Gale, 1988), pp. 143–153.

CHAPTER 15

G. K. Chesterton (1874–1936), 1908: *The Man Who Was Thursday*

Christopher Routledge

The creator of Father Brown, a Catholic priest with a talent for detection, Chesterton was a Catholic convert whose vast output of writing includes poetry, essays, novels, stories, reviews and journalism. His series detective Father Brown ranks alongside Sherlock Holmes and Hercule Poirot as one of the best-known British detectives, featuring in fifty-two stories. Father Brown stands out among these deductive geniuses by solving mysteries primarily using intuition and a priestly insight into human corruption. However, while Chesterton is well known for his fascination with mysticism and paradox, Father Brown is not opposed to rationality; on the contrary, he considers faith itself a rational process. Beyond the Father Brown stories Chesterton's best-known novel of detection is *The Man Who Was Thursday* (1908); he also wrote several popular biographical studies of famous writers including *Charles Dickens: A Critical Study* (1906).

Gilbert Keith Chesterton was born in Kensington, London and educated at St. Paul's School. There he met E. C. Bentley, author of *Trent's Last Case* (1913) and inventor of the 'clerihew', a form of

---

C. Routledge (✉)
Freelance Writer and Photographer, NW England, UK

© The Author(s) 2020
E. Miskimmin (ed.), *100 British Crime Writers*, Crime Files,
https://doi.org/10.1057/978-1-137-31902-9_15

humorous biographical poem four lines in length. They remained friends until Chesterton's death. Chesterton went on to study art at the Slade School of Art, and also studied literature at University College, London, but he began a career in publishing in 1896 and did not graduate. The same year he met Frances Bogg, but although he claimed to have fallen in love at first sight, they did not marry until 1901 because Chesterton's parents did not approve of the match and Chesterton did not earn enough to support her until then.

Chesterton was a gregarious and popular conversationalist and enjoyed the social side of literary London. Close friends included Hilaire Belloc, and George Bernard Shaw, but while he shared religious and political attitudes with Belloc (Shaw referred to them as ChesterBelloc), he was often at odds with Shaw, whose atheism, teetotalism, vegetarianism and Socialism made him an intellectual opposite. Despite the astringency of some of his views Chesterton was influential on writers such as Dorothy L. Sayers, C. S. Lewis, J. R. R. Tolkien, H. G. Wells and the Catholic priest and crime writer Ronald Knox. Sayers claimed that his book *Orthodoxy* (1908) helped revive her religious faith. After their marriage Chesterton and his wife moved to Beaconsfield in Buckinghamshire and remained there for the rest of his life.

Chesterton was a prolific writer in many different forms and genres. A well-known literary critic, essayist, poet and popular philosopher, his output covers a huge range of subjects. He had strong, complex and often contradictory political views, some of which, including his supposed anti-semitism, were controversial even in his own time. In *What's Wrong with the World* (1910), a little book with a characteristically ambitious title, Chesterton argues for a form of 'distributism', a political and economic philosophy which aimed, as its name suggests, to distribute wealth and power more fairly, not by concentrating it in the state, but by creating what he called a 'peasant proprietorship'. He condemned as failures both Capitalism as it existed at the time, and Socialism, both of which, in one of his analogies, were 'trying to abolish hair rather than abolishing lice'. Distributism reached the height of its popularity in the United States in the 1930s, where Chesterton published essays on the subject in the *American Review*. However Chesterton is most famously a Roman Catholic convert and it is his devout religious beliefs and his fascination with paradox that permeate most deeply into his work.

Chesterton began early as a writer, reputedly dictating original stories from the age of three. Besides hundreds of poems, short stories and over eighty books, he wrote articles and reviews for several newspapers and contributed to publications such as the *Encyclopaedia Britannica*; he wrote regularly for the *Illustrated London News* for over thirty years. While Chesterton's religious, philosophical and political writings were significant in their own time, he is best known as a writer of detective stories and in particular for his stories featuring Father Brown.

As a writer of detective fiction Chesterton ranks with Sir Arthur Conan Doyle and Edgar Allan Poe as one of the great distinctive voices in the genre. While Poe helped establish the idea of the rational detective hero, and Doyle created its archetype in Sherlock Holmes, Chesterton was interested in an abstract and perhaps also a more metaphysical notion of truth, theorising in his 1902 essay 'A Defence of Detective Stories' that 'it is the earliest and only form of popular literature in which is expressed some sense of the poetry of modern life'.

Chesterton's paradoxes and unexplained mysteries can be placed in a line of development that includes Jorge Luis Borges, Umberto Eco and Paul Auster, practitioners of what has become known as the 'metaphysical detective story', and in which there are no solutions, or at least none with clear meaning. As I argue in 'The Chevalier and the Priest: Deductive Method in Poe, Chesterton and Borges' (2001), where Poe's mysteries have unexpected solutions, Chesterton problematises the genre by revealing mysteries impervious to deduction and the usual approaches of the police. Patricia Merivale, in her essay on 'Postmodern and Metaphysical Detection' in the Blackwell *Companion to Crime Fiction* (2010) goes further, placing Chesterton in a tradition of metaphysical detection: where Chesterton fears the maze with no centre, 'Borges rejoices in the centerlessness of the maze, or its paradoxically empty center, or its center with something 'wrong' in it'.

Chesterton's famous defence of the detective story as an expression of the poetry of the modern world is carried through in his fiction. In 1904 he made his first deliberate attempt at detective fiction in *The Club of Queer Trades*, a collection of six stories in which, as John C. Tibbetts explains in 'The Case of the Forgotten Detectives' (1995), we meet two detectives who represent the best and worst forms of detection: one, Rupert Grant, is a private detective who collects clues and 'is cut from the standard mold'; the other, his brother Basil, who 'scorns a dependence on mere data' to work with intuition and 'atmosphere'. It is the latter approach that Chesterton favours.

The Man Who Was Thursday, published in 1908, has been described by Adam Gopnik in the *New Yorker* as a 'hidden hinge' in twentieth-century literature, forming a link between the Victorian tradition of nonsense and fantasy and the alienation and horror which often features in modernist writing. The novel's subtitle 'A Nightmare' is suggestive of the later existential horror of Kafka and Borges.

The Man Who Was Thursday is essentially a spy story, its central character, Syme, being a Scotland Yard detective whose mission is to infiltrate and undermine a secretive, and violent anarchist group. Befriending a poet, Lucien Gregory, who aims to be elected to the high anarchist council, Syme finds himself drawn into an organisation in which, with one exception, nobody is as they seem. The exception is the openly and sincerely anarchist Gregory whose openness about his beliefs has, paradoxically, made him seem harmless to the authorities. It is Syme, rather than Gregory, who is elected to the council, the members of which are all named for days of the week. Syme, who takes the place of 'Thursday', discovers after a series of twists that those he had thought he was against are actually on the same side and that what he thought was evil, is in fact good.

The many plot twists, paradoxes and mysteries in *The Man Who Was Thursday* anticipate the later 'Father Brown' stories, while its chase scenes, in which pursuing detectives traverse a dream-like and fantastical London, support the view of Chesterton as a poet of modernity and the city. These chase scenes are a madcap re-enactment of Baudelaire's wanderings around Paris, or Poe's 'Man of the Crowd' being followed by his obsessive pursuer. Here the detective, as Chesterton himself argued in 1902, is an 'is the original and poetic figure, while the burglars and footpads are merely placid old cosmic conservatives'.

The novel is partly an expression of Chesterton's developing Christianity and his own struggle with metaphysics, but it is also representative of his flamboyant and playful style, and his tendency to social criticism. For example, Syme describes himself as 'a poet of law, a poet of order' in contrast with Gregory's anarchism; describing another character, Renard, and anticipating Chesterton's later advocacy of Distributism, he says: "'He's rationalistic, and, what's worse, he's rich. When duty and religion are really destroyed, it will be by the rich'".

While *The Man Who Was Thursday* is arguably Chesterton's finest sustained piece of fiction writing, it is for Father Brown, the little Catholic priest who appears in fifty-two short stories, that he is most widely known.

Father Brown first appeared in the story 'The Blue Cross' in *The Storyteller* magazine in 1910, but in this story, uniquely, the narrative focuses on French police prefect Valentin, rather than the priest. Most of the stories in which he features were first published in magazines, but they were also included in five collections: *The Innocence of Father Brown* (1911), *The Wisdom of Father Brown* (1914), *The Incredulity of Father Brown* (1926), *The Secret of Father Brown* (1927) and *The Scandal of Father Brown* (1935).

The character of Father Brown was based on Father John O'Connor, the Catholic priest who offered theological guidance to Chesterton in the years leading up to his conversion to Catholicism in 1922. 'The Blue Cross' contains an apparent portrait of the two friends in the characters of Flambeau, the career jewel thief, and Father Brown. Flambeau, like Chesterton, is very tall and large, while Father Brown, like O'Connor, is small. In the story Valentin pursues two priests, one tall and one short, who turn out to be Flambeau, in disguise, and Father Brown himself. The flamboyant criminal contrasts with the unassuming and apparently withdrawn Father Brown, who uses his quiet priestly demeanour to appear unthreatening and disengaged while he watches, draws his conclusions and guides the criminal to redemption.

As Julian Symons notes in his book *Bloody Murder*, the Father Brown stories were controversial: 'Logicians of the detective story complained with some bitterness that Chesterton outraged all the rules they had drawn up'. In the Father Brown stories, Symons points out, Chesterton 'leaves out everything extraneous to the theme he wants to develop', abandoning the idea established in the work of Poe, and especially Doyle, that the solution to the mystery must be derived from clues revealed in the story. Father Brown's attitude to the police is good-humoured scepticism. Not only do policemen sometimes turn out to be corrupt, but their bureaucratic approach to solving crime is both ineffectual and a threat to truth and justice.

Father Brown's method is no less rational than Holmes', but it is more dependent on a particular world view, on intuition and an ability to unpick paradox. In 'The Blue Cross' the priest explains to Flambeau that despite appearances, his experience in the confessional has revealed to him the full extent of human evil. He sees through Flambeau's disguise as a priest because 'You attacked reason. It's bad theology'.

Elsewhere, in 'The Honour of Israel Gow', Father Brown concludes that the crime was committed not out of evil but from a 'strange and crooked honesty'. He sees anomalies and deceptions where they hide most effectively: in full view. Symons concludes that these stories, with their paradoxes, social criticism and strange premises, are 'a diet too rich' for every day, but admits that the best—he lists 'The Queer Feet', 'The Secret Garden' and 'The Man in the Passage', among others—are 'among the finest short crime stories ever written'.

Chesterton was a popular and celebrated writer, journalist, lecturer, broadcaster and humorist, the breadth of whose output on religion, politics, economics, the arts, morality and ethics as well as his novels, short stories and poems, made him one of the most influential public figures of his time. His writings on religion, philosophy and economics remain pertinent in the twentieth century, but it is his detective fiction that has had the most lasting influence, both on the genre itself, and on popular culture more generally. The Father Brown stories have been remade for radio, television and film, and most have been in print since they were first published, but many other stories and collections are concerned with detection in some form or other, including *Manalive* (1912), *The Man Who Knew Too Much* (1919) and *Four Faultless Felons* (1930).

Chesterton was an optimistic and hopeful man whose work reflects his own powerful belief in the possibility of redemption and the miraculousness of the universe. He completed his autobiography shortly before he died. Famously, his coffin was too large to be taken down the stairs and out of the front door, so it had to be lowered out of the window.

Suggested Reading/Works Cited

Chesterton, G. K., 'A Defence of Detective Stories (1902)', in *The Art of the Mystery Story*, ed. by Howard Haycraft (New York: Simon and Schuster, 1946), pp. 3–6.

Gopnik, Adam, 'A Critic at Large, "The Back of the World"', *The New Yorker*, 7 July (2008), p. 52.

Merivale, Patricia, 'Postmodern and Metaphysical Detection', in *A Companion to Crime Fiction*, ed. by Charles Rzepka and Lee Horsley (London: Blackwell, 2010), pp. 308–320.

Routledge, Christopher, 'The Chevalier and the Priest: Deductive Method in Poe, Chesterton and Borges', *Clues: A Journal of Detection*, 22:1 (2001), 1–11.

Symons, Julian, *Bloody Murder: From the Detective Story to the Crime Novel*, rev. edn (London: Faber, 1985).

The Chesterton Society Website http://www.gkchesterton.org.uk/.

Tibbetts, John C., 'The Case of the Forgotten Detectives: The Unknown Crime Fiction of G. K. Chesterton', *The Armchair Detective: A Quarterly Journal Devoted to the Appreciation of Mystery, Detective, and Suspense Fiction*, 28:4 (1995), 388–393.

Ward, Maisie, *Gilbert Keith Chesterton* (London: Sheed and Ward, 1943).

CHAPTER 16

Edwy Searles Brooks (1889–1965), 1912: First Contribution to the 'Sexton Blake' Series in the *Union Jack* Story Paper

Lucy Andrew

Edwy Searles Brooks was a prolific writer of juvenile story paper fiction, particularly detective stories. He began his writing career in 1907 with the publication of 'Mr Dorien's Missing £2000' in *Yes or No* magazine. By the time of his marriage in 1918, he had established himself as a competent and constant writer of story paper fiction and his wife Frances played an active role in the preparation of his manuscripts. Though Brooks cannot be credited with creating many original detective protagonists, the quantity of titles produced and the popularity of the detective series to which he contributed secures his status as an influential writer of children's detective fiction.

He began writing *Sexton Blake* stories for the *Union Jack* in 1912, continuing the already established, multi-author series about the hero-detective and adventurer, but it was in the *Sexton Blake Library* that he made his most significant contribution to the series through the creation of Waldo the Wonder Man in 1918. On his first appearance, Waldo,

L. Andrew (✉)
University of Chester, Chester, UK

an escaped convict with superhuman strength, is established as a serial enemy to Sexton Blake, but later Brooks toned down Waldo's criminal traits, allowing him to occasional to become Blake's ally. Writing under the pseudonym of Berkeley Gray, Brooks later reinvented the character of Waldo as the eponymous hero of his *Norman Conquest* series.

Brooks wrote for the *Nelson Lee Library* from its launch in 1915 and, within months, became a lead writer of the series. By 1917 he was its sole author and was responsible for transferring Nelson Lee and his young assistant, Nipper, to St Frank's school. The *St. Frank's* stories, which Brooks wrote regularly for sixteen years, contributed significantly to the establishment of the detective-school story hybrid, a subgenre that dominated British juvenile detective and mystery fiction in the early twentieth century. Brooks is credited with writing 26 *Dixon Hawke* stories between 1923 and 1937 although, since the stories were published anonymously, the true extent of his contribution remains uncertain. Among his other detective series for child readers are his *Clive Derring* stories for *Cheer Boys Cheer* (1912) and the *Falcon Swift* stories for the *Boy's Magazine* (1931–33).

In the late 1930s, after several of the children's detective series folded, Brooks turned his attention towards adult crime fiction, publishing his first *Beeke and Cavendish* police story in 1935. Stories of his gentleman thief, Norman Conquest, appeared in *The Thriller* in 1937 and were reproduced and revised a year later as adult hardback novels. Similarly, his Scotland Yard detective Ironsides Cromwell made his debut in *The Thriller* in 1939 and, later that year, appeared hardback novel format. Brooks' output waned towards the end of his career and he produced very little original material, frequently revising or rewriting his old detective stories to accommodate another detective character.

Suggested Reading/Works Cited

Blythe, Robert C., *The Nelson Lee Library and Bibliography of the Writings of Edwy Searles Brooks*, 3rd edn, revised by Mark Caldicott (Leeds: Happy Hours, 1995).

Turner, E. S., *Boys Will Be Boys: Sexton Blake, Billy Bunter, Dick Barton, et al* (London: Michael Joseph, 1975).

CHAPTER 17

Sax Rohmer (1883–1959), 1912: First 'Fu Manchu' Story, 'The Zayat Kiss', in *The Story-Teller* Magazine

Steven Powell

Rohmer is often credited with the success of the 'Yellow Peril' school of mystery thrillers due to his most famous creation, the evil genius Fu Manchu. Rohmer was born as Arthur Henry Ward in Birmingham. His mother was an alcoholic whose deranged ramblings often included the claim that she was descended from the seventeenth-century Irish general Patrick Sarsfield. Rohmer later added the name Sarsfield to his own. In 1905 he met Rose Elizabeth Knox, and they married in 1909, staying together for the next fifty years. From an early age he discovered he was temperamentally unsuited to a job with set hours, and he resolved to be a writer. His early efforts were met with a slew of rejection slips, which, undeterred, he would use to paper a wall in his room. His first piece of fiction to sell was the short story 'The Mysterious Mummy' (*Pearson's Weekly*, 1903) and reflected his interest in Egyptology and the Near East. At his wife's insistence, he adopted the pseudonym Sax Rohmer and would later use it in personal life.

S. Powell (✉)
University of Liverpool, Liverpool, United Kingdom

© The Author(s) 2020
E. Miskimmin (ed.), *100 British Crime Writers*, Crime Files,
https://doi.org/10.1057/978-1-137-31902-9_17

Fu Manchu made his first appearance in 'The Zayat Kiss' published in *The Story-Teller* in 1912. The character was inspired by Rohmer's research into the mysterious 'Mr King', criminal boss in London's Limehouse 'Chinatown'. The first stories were serialised and then also published in book form. They followed the same formula of a battle of wits between Fu Manchu and the Holmesian Dennis Nayland Smith. *Daughter of Fu Manchu* (1931) introduced Fah Lo Suee, as much a devious mastermind as her father. *President Fu Manchu* (1936) and *The Drums of Fu Manchu* (1939) adapt the turbulent politics of the 1930s into the narrative. The stories were fantastical, but Rohmer excelled in detail: 'rather than an invading army from the East, the reader was invited to shudder at a more personal menace: a paralysing drug, a deadly insect searching out its prey, Dacoit with his weird cry and strangler's kerchief'. The series may seem xenophobic by contemporary standards reflecting Britain's curious but suspicious attitude towards the Orient at the time, but this is more than offset by Fu Manchu's qualities: his remarkable intellect and dignified, aristocratic manner. In the later stories, his ethnicity became less important. One of Rohmer's best novels outside the Fu Manchu series was *The Moon is Red* (1954), a murder mystery set in Florida. In 1950, Rohmer began another series character with the novel *Sins of Sumuru*, Sumuru being a female super-villain very similar to Fu Manchu, although of no specified ethnicity. Four more Sumuru novels followed. Despite his writing success, Rohmer was never financially comfortable. He squandered much of his money on frivolities and was defrauded by his first literary agent. By the end of his life, Rohmer was living in virtual poverty in a small apartment in New York City. His last works were a return to his most famous creation, *Re-enter Dr. Fu Manchu* (1957) and *Emperor Fu Manchu* (1959); both novels carried a distinctly anti-communist theme.

SUGGESTED READING/WORKS CITED

Briney, R. E., 'Rohmer, Sax', in *Twentieth Century Crime and Mystery Writers*, ed. by John M. Reilly (New York: St. Martin's Press, 1985), pp. 772–775.

van Ash, Kay and Elizabeth Sax Rohmer, *Master of Villainy: A Biography of Sax Rohmer* (Bowling Green: Bowling Green University Press, 1972).

CHAPTER 18

E. C. Bentley (1875–1956), 1913: *Trent's Last Case*

Suzanne Bray

A well-known illustrator and author of several thrillers, Edmund Clerihew Bentley is best known as the inventor of the clerihew, a form of humorous verse and as the author of the influential detective novel, *Trent's Last Case* (1913). John Carter called him 'the father of the contemporary detective novel'.

E. C. Bentley was born in Shepherd's Bush in 1875. His father was an official in the Lord Chancellor's Department. He was educated at St Paul's School and later claimed in his autobiography, *Those Days* (1940), that 'the supreme importance to me of my schooldays lies in the fact that they were the time when I saw the most of Gilbert Keith Chesterton'. Bentley, Chesterton and several friends founded a literary club called the Junior Debating Society and edited an unofficial magazine, *The Debater*, which published their earliest literary and journalistic efforts. In 1894, Bentley won a history scholarship to Merton College, Oxford. He became president of the Oxford Union and got a creditable degree in spite of spending six afternoons a week rowing. In 1898 Bentley graduated from Oxford and went to London to study Law at the Inner Temple. He was

S. Bray (✉)
Lille Catholic University, Lille, France

© The Author(s) 2020
E. Miskimmin (ed.), *100 British Crime Writers*, Crime Files,
https://doi.org/10.1057/978-1-137-31902-9_18

called to the Bar in 1902 after working for two years in William Hansell's chambers. During this period Bentley had already started to write articles for various newspapers and magazines.

As Bentley wished to be financially independent and to marry as soon as possible, he abandoned the Law for Fleet Street, obtaining a staff appointment on *The Daily News* in the autumn of 1902. He stayed there for ten years before transferring to the more conservative *Daily Telegraph*. During this period he acquired a certain celebrity through the publication of a book of comic verses or 'clerihews', *Biography for Beginners* (1905) under the transparent pseudonym 'E. Clerihew'. The clerihew has been defined as a humorous pseudo-biographical quatrain, rhymed as two couplets. The name of the subject is usually found in the first line and the humour is gentle and inoffensive. G. K. Chesterton provided the illustrations to the first volumes of clerihews, while the final volume was illustrated by the author's son, Nicolas.

In 1910 Bentley decided to write a full-length detective novel. Troubled by 'the extreme seriousness of Holmes, and the equal seriousness of his imitators', he thought that it must be possible 'to write a detective story in which the detective was recognisable as a human being and was not quite so much the heavy sleuth'. The result of his efforts, *Trent's Last Case*, was published in 1913 and dedicated to Chesterton in return for *The Man Who Was Thursday*, which his friend had dedicated to him five years earlier. It is the story of a most unpleasant murdered millionaire, Sigsbee Manderson, and of the generally amiable people who are suspected of killing him. The novel was unexpectedly successful and much admired by critics of the genre. For Agatha Christie, it was 'one of the three best detective stories ever written', Howard Haycraft was struck by Bentley's relaxed, low-key approach, and Dorothy L. Sayers stated that 'It is the one detective story of the present century which I am certain will go down to posterity as a classic. It is a masterpiece'. Sayers was particularly impressed by the way Bentley managed to make the love interest, the detective's love for the widowed Mabel Manderson, into an integral part of the plot and also by the quality of his writing. For George Grella, *Trent's Last Case* is 'the most influential source for the comedy of manners which came to dominate the formal detective novel'.

Bentley's detective, Philip Trent, is certainly less spectacular than Sherlock Holmes and is in many ways the model for all the gentlemen amateur detectives of the Golden Age. His ability to understand the situation comes in part from his familiarity with the social context and his sensitivity to cultural nuances. He has a family, a job and friends, and is both likeable and fallible. In fact, his carefully constructed solution to the actual crime turns out to be completely wrong, even though he manages to unravel many of the minor mysteries. Bentley himself considered that the novel was 'not so much a detective story as an exposure of detective stories', but acknowledged that this fact did 'not seem to have been generally noticed'. *Trent's Last Case* has three times been adapted for the cinema. Orson Welles and Margaret Lockwood successfully portrayed the Mandersons in the last of these adaptations (1952).

In spite of the success of *Trent's Last Case*, Bentley merely wrote a few short stories with Trent as hero until he retired from journalism in 1934. He then collaborated with H. Warner Allen to produce a second Trent novel, entitled *Trent's Own Case* (1936). Allen's own wine detective, William Clerihew, named in honour of Bentley, also makes a cameo appearance. Although Trent still has the same engaging character, the novel is less tightly focused than *Trent's Last Case*, and wanders off into various complex subplots. Once again the victim is an unendearing rich man, whose loss is hard to regret, and Trent's success comes in part from his familiarity with the social context. However, the dual authorship does nothing for the style of the prose.

The final volume of Trent's adventures, *Trent Intervenes*, a volume of short stories, was published in 1938. The earliest story in the book, 'The Clever Cockatoo' dates from 1914, but most of the stories were written in the late 1930s. Many of the tales include the description of a cunning crime, which Trent has to detect. Although justice is always done to Trent's satisfaction, the reader detects a certain admiration for some of the more ingenious schemes and sympathy for the criminals. However, there is nothing but scorn for the domestic tyrant who beats his wife and makes her life hell before being murdered. Here, as in several other cases, Trent feels no need to reveal his murderer's identity to the police. In all these stories, we return to the relaxed style of *Trent's Last Case*, making the whole collection very agreeable to read. One final Trent story, 'The Ministering Angel' (*The Strand*, 1938), was not included in the collection. Bentley also edited an anthology of detective fiction, *A Second Century of Detective Stories*, the same year. During this period he also edited and wrote introductions to several volumes of short stories by the American writer Damon Runyon, the best known being *More than Somewhat* (1937). For thirteen years Bentley was the second president of the famous Detection Club, taking over from G. K. Chesterton when he died suddenly in 1936. He also contributed to the Detection Club radio serials *The Scoop* and *Behind the Screen*, which were finally published in 1983. He enjoyed the atmosphere of the club and got on well with his fellow writers. A parody of Dorothy L. Sayers' fiction, called *Greedy Night* (1936), was written for their mutual amusement.

In 1940, as many of his former colleagues joined the armed forces, Bentley returned to journalism, replacing Harold Nicholson as chief literary critic at *The Daily Telegraph*. The same year he published *Those Days*, which contains both autobiographical elements and reflections on the international situation and the world before World War One. Bentley retired again, permanently this time, in 1947. His wife died two years later and Bentley moved to a London hotel where he spent his final years writing. His last novel, a thriller called *Elephant's Work* and dedicated to his friend John Buchan, was published in 1950, but did not catch the public's imagination.

Suggested Reading/Works Cited

Bentley, E. C., *Those Days* (1940; repr. Looe: House of Stratus, 2001).

Grella, George, 'Murder and Manners: The Formal Detective Novel', *NOVEL: A Forum on Fiction*, 4:1 (1970), 30–48.

Silet, Charles L. P., 'E. C. Bentley and the Contemporary Crime Novel', *The Strand*, 2 (1999), 45–47.

Witchard, Anne, 'Detective Fiction', *English Literature in Transition 1880–1920*, 51:4 (2008), 447–451.

CHAPTER 19

Ernest Bramah (1868–1942), 1914: *Max Carrados*

Nick Freeman

Bramah worked in a variety of genres but his best-known crime fiction is his series of stories featuring the blind detective, Max Carrados, published between 1914 and 1934.

Born Ernest Brammah Smith in Manchester in 1868 and educated at Manchester Grammar School, Bramah began his adult life as a farmer, an occupation for which he was thoroughly unsuited. A newspaper column about his failures paid rather better and suggested a career in journalism. He moved to London and, supported by a parental allowance, became one of Jerome K. Jerome's secretarial assistants on *To-Day* in 1892. By 1895 he was editing the *Minister*, although he left this in late 1897 to become a full-time author. Bramah published on topics as diverse as farming and coin collecting before achieving considerable popularity with the first of his Kai Lung short stories, collected in *The Wallet of Kai Lung* (1900). Kai Lung, an impeccably formal Chinese itinerant storyteller, was an exotic creation who proved surprisingly popular with the public. Bramah was still writing Kai Lung tales in the year of his death

N. Freeman (✉)
Loughborough University, Loughborough, UK

© The Author(s) 2020
E. Miskimmin (ed.), *100 British Crime Writers*, Crime Files,
https://doi.org/10.1057/978-1-137-31902-9_19

87

and had a considerable following when he published the eight stories comprising *Max Carrados* in 1914.

Carrados was as unlikely a figure as Kai Lung. Max Wynn, a gentleman bachelor from the Home Counties, inherits a fortune from an American cousin on condition that he changes his name to Carrados. He spends his days enjoying music, numismatics, boxing, fishing and punting until, blinded in a freak riding accident, he becomes a detective. This allows him to make use of his highly trained remaining senses. While Bramah was at pains to assure the public that most of Carrados' achievements had precedents in real life, it is nonetheless surprising to read how his keen sense of smell allows him to detect a false moustache worn by a sweating suspect or how his sensitive fingertips can read newspaper headlines and identify their typefaces. Aided by his secretary, Greatorex, and his resourceful valet, Parkinson, Carrados tackles Sinn Fein plotters, apparently impossible burglaries, mysterious disappearances, a husband who plans to kill his wife by feigning a lightning strike and, in 'The Game Played in the Dark' (1914), outwits the villainous Dompierre and his accomplices by trapping them in a blacked-out room. Later stories collected in *The Eyes of Max Carrados* (1924) and *The Specimen Case* (1924, which also included Kai Lung tales) saw Carrados take on German spies and, in 'The Missing Witness Sensation', escape from a cellar in circumstances of singular if highly entertaining improbability. Only in his sole Carrados novel, *The Bravo of London* (1934) did Bramah's invention flag, though Joolby, a criminal antique dealer, makes for a memorable villain.

Bramah was an intensely private man, and it was sometimes suggested that he did not exist, being instead a front for a writing syndicate. He certainly shunned publicity throughout his career, dying in Weston-Super-Mare in the summer of 1942.

Suggested Reading/Works Cited

Oxbury, H. F., 'Smith, Ernest Brammah', *Oxford Dictionary of National Biography* (Oxford: Oxford University Press, 2004; online edn, 2013).

Seay, Joan, 'Ernest Bramah', in *Dictionary of Literary Biography, Volume 70: British Mystery Writers 1860–1919*, ed. Bernard Benstock and Thomas F. Staley (Detroit: Gale, 1988), pp. 45–50.

Wilson, Aubrey, *The Search for Ernest Bramah* (London: Creighton & Read, 2007).

CHAPTER 20

John William Bobin (Also Wrote as Adelie Ascott, John Ascott, Katherine Greenalgh, Gertrude Nelson, Victor Nelson, and Isabelle Norton, 1889–1935), 1915: First Contribution to the *Sexton Blake Library*

Lucy Andrew

John William Bobin is known primarily for his mystery and detective output in early twentieth-century juvenile story papers. His first detective title was for the *Sexton Blake Library* in 1915, a series to which he contributed regularly until 1931. He was the primary writer of the *Derrick Brent* detective series (1916–17) and the pseudo-detective and mystery series, *Don Darrel/'Bulldog' Holdfast* (1922–26), published in the *Boys' Friend* under the pseudonym 'Victor Nelson'. He also produced a serial for the *Nelson Lee Library* in 1933, writing as 'John Ascott'.

His most valuable contribution to juvenile detective fiction, however, was his development of the girl-detective figure. Mystery was a common theme in girls' story papers in the early twentieth century and, as

L. Andrew (✉)
University of Chester, Chester, UK

© The Author(s) 2020
E. Miskimmin (ed.), *100 British Crime Writers*, Crime Files,
https://doi.org/10.1057/978-1-137-31902-9_20

'Gertrude Nelson', Bobin wrote a number of mystery stories for the *Schoolgirls' Own*, the *School Girl* and *Schoolgirls' Weekly* from 1922 to his death in 1935. In 1932 he created a pseudo-detective serial for *Schoolgirls' Weekly* that featured the Silent Six, a secret society of schoolgirls whose purpose was to solve mysteries and right injustices at Highcroft School. Yet Bobin's real breakthrough was with the character Sylvia Silence, who is credited as being the first girl-detective protagonist in British children's literature. As 'Katherine Greenhalgh', Bobin introduced fifteen-year-old girl sleuth Sylvia Silence in the first issue of *Schoolgirls' Weekly* in October 1922. With the encouragement of her detective father, Sylvia solves mysteries with her sidekicks, Jacko the monkey, and Wolf the Alsatian. Bobin created a similar character, schoolgirl-detective Lila Lisle, in a short serial for the *Schoolgirls' Own* in 1930. Yet, while both Sylvia Silence and Lila Lyle are defined as detectives, their characterisation as such is underdeveloped: the resolution of their cases often relies upon coincidence or feminine intuition rather than any discernable detective skills or methods.

In 1933, under the pseudonym 'Adelie Ascott', Bobin created his most sophisticated girl-detective character, eighteen-year-old Valerie Drew, for *Schoolgirls' Weekly*. Like Bobin's earlier girl sleuths, Valerie has an animal assistant, an Alsatian called Flash, whose almost-human qualities lead him to solve his first mystery in a story entitled 'Detective Flash' in April 1934. All three of Bobin's girl detectives become involved in sleuthing through their fathers' professions, but Valerie, like her American counterpart Nancy Drew, soon proves herself capable of independent detective work. After Bobin's death in 1935 the series continued anonymously in *Schoolgirls' Weekly* until July 1937 when the stories were credited to 'Isabel Norton'. The last original *Valerie Drew* titles appeared in the *Popular Book of Girls' Stories* in 1941.

Suggested Reading/Works Cited

British Juvenile Story Papers and Pocket Libraries Index Website http://www.phi lsp.com/homeville/bjsp/s106.htm.

Craig, Patricia and Mary Cadogan, *The Lady Investigates: Women Detectives and Spies in Fiction* (London: Victor Gollancz, 1981).

———, *You're a Brick Angela! A New Look at Girls' Fiction from 1839 to 1975* (London: Victor Gollancz, 1976).

Drotner, Kirsten, 'Schoolgirls, Madcaps, and Air Aces: English Girls and Their Magazine Reading Between the Wars', *Feminist Studies*, 9 (1983), 33–52.

CHAPTER 21

John Buchan (1875–1940), 1915: *The Thirty-Nine Steps*

Alexandra Phillips

John Buchan was an industrious writer, editor, publisher and politician, producing over seventy works of fiction and non-fiction from novels to biographies and histories, plus a number of short stories, essays and articles. Today he is best known as the author of spy thriller *The Thirty-Nine Steps* (1915), but he achieved many notable appointments in his life, including that of Governor-General of Canada.

Buchan was born in Perth, Scotland, the eldest of four children to Helen and Reverend John Buchan of the Knox Free Church. His religious upbringing is evident in works such as *Mr. Standfast* (1919), in which numerous references are made to Bunyan's *The Pilgrim's Progress* (1678). Buchan attended Hutcheson's Grammar School and won a bursary to Glasgow University in 1892, where he studied a General M. A., comprising the compulsory subjects of Latin, Greek, Mathematics, Logic, Moral Philosophy, Natural Philosophy and English Literature. During this time Buchan published articles in the Glasgow university magazine and his first full-length work of non-fiction, *Essays and Apothegms of Francis Lord Bacon* (1894).

A. Phillips (✉)
Open University Wales, Cardiff, UK

Buchan wrote his first novel *Sir Quixote of the Moors* (1895) just before going to Oxford, where he had won a scholarship to study Classics at Brasenose. While there he wrote a number of essays and published a collection entitled *Scholar Gipsies* (1896). Buchan excelled in debates and public speaking and was elected President of the Oxford Union. While at Oxford he wrote three novels, *John Burnett of Barns* (1898), *A Lost Lady of Old Years* (1899) and *The Half-Hearted* (1900), and a number of short stories, which were published in *The Yellow Book* and *Blackwood's* magazine, and later appeared in three collections: *Grey Weather* (1899), *The Watcher by the Threshold* (1902) and *The Moon Endureth* (1912). Despite achieving a First, he was passed over for a fellowship so decided to read for the bar. He was called to the bar in 1901 but in August Lord Milner, High Commissioner for South Africa, appointed him as his private secretary. During Buchan's two-year commission he travelled widely and took a keen interest in politics, publishing *The African Colony* in 1903.

South Africa provided inspiration for his fiction, particularly in novels such as *A Lodge in the Wilderness* (1906), where he envisioned a conference of world leaders debating the future of Africa and *Prester John* (1910, first serialised as 'The Black General' in juvenile monthly publication *The Captain*). This text makes uncomfortable reading because of its imperialist stance and racist stereotyping, themes that occur throughout Buchan's works. Critics have differing opinions on how to approach these issues; Dennis Butts suggests that the reader can 'adopt a historical perspective when considering Buchan's attitude to race', and Miles Donald accounts for the current demand for new editions of Buchan's novels by showing how they offer the reader a simple world where contradictions, implausibilities and inconsistencies are glossed over and the difficult issues of race and sex are avoided.

On returning to the UK, Buchan took up work as a barrister. In 1906 he became engaged to Susan Grosvenor, was offered the job of Assistant Editor of *The Spectator* and he became the chief literary advisor to publishing company Thomas Nelson. Buchan divided his time between London and Scotland, and achieved particular success with two series of affordable editions: the Nelson Sixpenny Classics (non-fiction) and the Sevenpenny Library (fiction). He married Susan in 1907 and they had four children between 1908 and 1918. His first taste of public affairs came in 1911 when he became the prospective Unionist candidate for Peebles & Selkirk. Around this time he started to publish a number of important non-fiction titles and was noted for his biographies: *Sir Walter*

Raleigh (1911) and *The Marquis of Montrose* (1913). The family lived in London until 1920 when they moved to Oxford and Buchan was appointed Director of news agency Reuters.

Prevented from joining active service in World War One by his age, and ill-health, Buchan's efforts went instead into producing volumes of 50,000 words cataloguing a running history of the war, which would eventually run to twenty-four volumes as *Nelson's History of the War* (1915–1919). He went out to the Western Front in 1915 as a correspondent for *The Times* and covered the second Battle of Ypres and the Battle of Loos. In 1916 Buchan became a lieutenant in the Intelligence Corps and worked for the Foreign Office, writing reports and propaganda. In 1917, he was recalled to become Director of Information in the Department of Information (which became the Ministry of Information in 1918), where he was appointed Lieutenant Colonel. He was promoted to Director of Intelligence in 1918.

His knowledge and experience of politics and military strategy informs much of his fiction, including *Salute to Adventurers* (1915), and the most successful books Buchan produced; the four spy novels featuring protagonist Richard Hannay, *The Thirty-Nine Steps* (1915), *Greenmantle*, (1916) *Mr. Standfast* (1919) and *The Three Hostages* (1924). There are two other novels that also feature Hannay in minor roles, *The Courts of the Morning* (1929) and *The Island of Sheep* (1936), but these are omitted from the various collected editions of the Hannay novels until 1995. *The Thirty-Nine Steps*, a military adventure set in London before World War One was serialised in Blackwood's Magazine under the pseudonym 'H de V' before being published as a novel. The ongoing popularity of *The Thirty-Nine Steps* may be due in part to several film versions of the text, most notably Alfred Hitchock's critically acclaimed 1935 adaptation.

Initially, *Greenmantle* was more popular with the reading public than *The Thirty-Nine Steps*. This novel introduces the character of Sandy Arbuthnot who, Kate McDonald proposes, is likely to be drawn from Buchan's friends Aubrey Herbert and T. E. Lawrence. The fact that this text is now eclipsed by *The Thirty-Nine Steps* may be due to the fact that the plot is more convoluted, that it has never been televised, or perhaps due to the racial stereotyping of Germans and Jews. Nonetheless, the novel remains popular due to its gripping pace and the detailed historical backdrop of the less well-known war in the Near East.

Mr. Standfast was far more didactic than Buchan's previous two Hannay novels and less popular. Hannay's mission is to join the pacifist movement and, along with agent Mary Lamington, to uncover German agitators who have infiltrated it. In this novel to even question the war is misguided at best, or cowardly and unpatriotic. Hannay, Mary and Sandy appear again in *The Three Hostages*, a novel that examines the gap between an ordered society and civilisation thrown into chaos: a tension that runs through much of Buchan's fiction. The recurrence of characters is another feature. In addition to the major players, Buchan also recycles minor characters, such as Archie Roylance, Andrew Amos and Herr Gaudian.

Before Hannay, Buchan had created Edward Leithen. The first of the Leithen novels was *The Power-House* (1916), followed by *John McNab* (1925), *The Dancing Floor* (1926), *The Gap in the Curtain* (1932) and Buchan's final novel *Sick Heart River*, published posthumously in 1941. Unlike Hannay, Leithen is more of an observer than a hero; in *The Dancing Floor* Leithen recounts the adolescence and adulthood of Vernon Milburne who is haunted by a recurring dream about a strange house. Leithen becomes more involved when a girl named Koré, a mutual acquaintance of both men, is found to be the heir to a cursed house on a remote Greek island. On visiting the house, Koré discovers that the superstitious inhabitants intend to burn her as a witch. Vernon and Leithen save her by employing the typical Buchanian devices of play-acting and disguise. Leithen also recurs briefly at the beginning of the *A Prince of the Captivity* (1933) as the defence counsel for protagonist Adam Melfort.

Another of Buchan's serial protagonists is Dickson McCunn, a wealthy retired grocer from Glasgow drawn to Romantic adventure. He first features in *Huntingtower* (1922), and his adventures continue in *Castle Gay* (1930). His story is continued in *The House of the Four Winds* (1935). These farcical parables, reminiscent of Wodehouse, show Buchan's fear of social unrest but do not play to his strengths of creating historically authentic settings.

In his authoritative biography, Lownie quotes Buchan's own summary of his life: 'Publishing is my business, writing my amusement and politics my duty'. Yet even when his roles in public office became increasingly important, Buchan still wrote prolifically. From 1927 to 1935, when he was MP for the Combined Scottish Universities, he produced two of his most acclaimed biographies: *Sir Walter Scott* (1932) and *Oliver Cromwell* (1934). Other fictional works at this time include *Witch Wood* (1927), a short story collection entitled *The Runagates Club* (1928), and *The Magic Walking-Stick* (1932), his only children's book.

Buchan was appointed High Commissioner to the General Assembly to the Church of Scotland in 1933 and 1934. In 1935, King George V created Buchan the 1st Baron Tweedsmuir of Elsfield of the County of Oxford prior to his appointment as Governor-General of Canada. Following his arrival in Canada, Buchan toured extensively, as he did in South Africa, to acquaint himself with the people and their lives. It was Buchan who authorised Canada's declaration of war in September 1939 before dying unexpectedly a few months later from a cerebral embolism.

SUGGESTED READING/WORKS CITED

Buchan, John, *Memory Hold-the-Door* (1940; repr. London: Dent, 1984).
Buchan, William, *John Buchan: A Memoir* (London: Harrap, 1985).
Butts, Dennis, 'The Hunter and the Hunted: The Suspense Novels of John Buchan', in *Spy Thrillers: From Buchan to le Carré*, ed. by Clive Bloom (Basingstoke: Macmillan, 1990), pp. 44–58.
Donald, Miles, 'John Buchan: The Reader's Trap', in *Spy Thrillers: From Buchan to le Carré*, ed. by Clive Bloom (Basingstoke: Macmillan, 1990), pp. 59–72.
Lownie, Andrew, *John Buchan: The Presbyterian Cavalier* (London: Constable, 1995).
MacDonald, Kate, *John Buchan: A Companion to the Mystery Fiction* (Jefferson: McFarland & Co., 2009).

PART II

The Golden Age and World War Two
1919–1945

INTRODUCTION

As with that from the Victorian era, crime writing from the interwar years has a clear identity in the popular imagination: the murder-mystery detective story complete with country house, limited cast of characters, idiosyncratic amateur detective and the careful construction of a series of clues and red herrings that may or may not enable the sharp-eyed reader to make their own deductions. In terms of *100 British Crime Writers*, the genre of the puzzle story certainly dominates this next section, and there are entries on some of the biggest names in British crime fiction of any era. Stephen Knight notes in his foreword that 'of the British criminographical heavyweights a clear majority are women', and below we find four of these female 'heavyweights': Agatha Christie, Dorothy L. Sayers, Margery Allingham and Ngaio Marsh, all key exponents of the murder-mystery and often collected together and designated *the* 'Queens of Crime'. They are not necessarily the only authors below who are deserving of this title: Christine Simpson, for example, rightly argues for Josephine Tey's place in the ranks of the crime writing monarchy, and Megan Hoffman strives for gender equality in placing H. C. Bailey, Freeman Wills Croft and R. Austen Freeman alongside their female counterparts.

Male or female, most of the writers in this part all produced classic 'Golden-Age' detective fiction, including various subgenres such as the academic or 'donnish' murder mystery by Innes, Nash and Crispin. The key features of the Golden Age murder mystery, such as those mentioned above, have been defined many times and I do not propose to redescribe them in detail here. What is significant, perhaps, is that as a genre it seems to have been aware of these stereotypes almost from its inception. In his introduction to *The Best Detective Stories of the Year 1928* (1929), Ronald Knox observes that: 'We know as we sit down to the book that a foul murder has almost certainly been done at a country house; that the butler will have been in the family for sixteen years; that a young male secretary will have been only recently engaged; that the chauffeur will have gone away for the night to his widowed mother [...] If I walked into the detective story house I believe I should be able to find my way about it perfectly; it is always more or less the same in design'. This is the same essay in which Knox produced his 'ten commandments' for crime writers, supposedly to ensure fair play for their readership. As we see in the entries below, both Agatha Christie and Gladys Mitchell provoked critical response when they broke with this precept: Haycraft's only criticism of Christie, in fact, is her 'not always scrupulous use of the least-likely-person motif'.

Knox's 'detective story house' also illustrates the shift from the Victorian urban to the largely rural settings that distinguish the interwar period. Whilst London and other cities still feature, the world of the interwar crime story, especially within the detection genre, is predominantly provincial and a high percentage of the stories take place in the countryside so feared by Holmes as the lawless counterpart to the Capital's policeable spaces. There are murders in fields, on riverbanks, in hunting lodges and, of course, in country houses.

Knox's account of this milieu also reveals an understanding of the stereotype by its writers, readers and critics, which suggests that all concerned were aware of the rather unrealistic nature of the genre. This awareness is often revealed by an intertextual self-consciousness on the part of the Golden Age writers; Bruce Montgomery, for example, generates dialogues between his fictional author Edmund Crispin and his detective, Gervase Fen; C. P. Snow and Dorothy L. Sayers show their characters reading each other's books at various points, and Agatha Christie's Ariadne Oliver is very much not alone as a crime-writer-amateur-detective character. There is also clear sense of a literary movement of genre, which culminated in the 'Detection Club', proposed by Anthony Berkeley and enthusiastically participated in by Dorothy L. Sayers and, it seems, everyone else; it is actually quicker to count the number of writers in this section who did not belong to this club than those who did.

Despite this apparently cheerful adherence to a type, however, it becomes clear that many of the writers discussed here have something special that distinguishes them from their peers and the contributors are keen to make those distinctions: Christine Simpson discusses the ways in which Berkeley breaks with formula, and the 'variety and innovation' of Tey's plots; Victoria Stewart observes the ways in which Elizabeth Ferrars 'eschews the comforting resolutions' of the standard Golden-Age novel; and Kate Watson discusses how Marsh plays with the conventions in a way that is 'sophisticated, witty and self-consciously ironic'. In addition to this, the 'literary' nature of some of the writing is commented on, a feature that Jasmine Simeone rightly identifies in Allingham's fiction, and which is also identified in the novels of Blake and Sayers. Given that Nicholas Blake is the pseudonym of poet C. Day Lewis this is perhaps not so surprising, but a curious number of Golden-Age writers seem to have had a literary alter ego, or to have made distinctions between their crime writing and any other literary works they may have produced. For Sayers, the attempts to marry the two were apparently exasperating, and probably resulted in her giving up on crime fiction altogether.

In the Golden Age, then, we find ourselves in a self-conscious discourse on genre, but also in a discourse on the literary 'value' of crime writing. Haycraft actually divides this period into two: 1918–1930, which he coins as 'The Golden Age', and 1930 to his time of writing in 1941, which he designates 'The Moderns', and which he sees as characterised in part by what he describes as the 'literary' detective novel. Haycraft also comments on the inevitable tensions between genre and style, observing, for example, that Margery Allingham occasionally 'commits the error [...] of becoming a little to profound and precious for her medium and audience', and praises Blake for sensing 'more than most of his fellows the dangers of being too "highbrow" in an essentially entertainment form'. In a period in which the 'brows' debate becomes a bit more heated, (Virginia Woolf threatened to 'take [her] pen' and 'stab, dead' any 'half-crushed worm' that called her middlebrow), we see the crime writers of the period directly engaging with this discourse, often paradoxically defending and deprecating their own genre at the same time.

One change that can be observed from the previous era's writing, linked perhaps to this qualitative discussion on the genre, is that there are now more novels as first texts rather than short stories or serial publications although the latter format continues to be popular. This move towards the novel form might in part be because of the advent of affordable book publications, made available through various subscription book clubs that followed *The Times Book Club* (1904), such as *The Book Society* (1929) and the advent of Penguin books in 1935. Allen Lane's affordable, mass-market paperbacks meant that lower-income readers had wider access to the book market, and that writers such as Woolf were available in the same format as those such as Christie. Ironically, all writers were similarly affected by the paper rationing imposed in 1940, which reduced both the print size and paper quality of novels published during the war, and pretty much everything to 'pulp fiction'.

The omnipresence of war in this period – past, imminent and present – manifests itself in more than just the quality of the print and paper themselves. As with the previous period, the crime fiction of this time responds to the world that generates it. The context of war perhaps seems to inspire an even more intense discourse on the moral complexities of killing and retribution both within the stories and by critics of the genre. Coming back to a point raised in the introduction, it perhaps seems odd that at a time in which violence and death predominate, the popularity of a genre that focuses on those very subjects seems to soar. In his concluding chapters, Haycraft discusses the 'accelerated demand for detective stories in the bomb shelters of London'. Detailing the Fascist party's 1939 ban on Edgar Wallace and Agatha Christie, he makes an argument for the detective story as a 'democratic institution': 'of all the democratic heritages, none has been more stubbornly defended by free peoples the world over than the right of a fair trial—the credo that no man shall be convicted of crime in the absence of *proof*, safeguarded by known, just and logical rules'. In the face of 'despotisms' and 'dictatorships', he argues, the democratic world turns to a literature that upholds its very tenets.

It is not all detective fiction in this era; as with the Victorian period there is a diversity of genre to be found and the influence of war can be seen in the range of other genres that emerge and flourish. Chief amongst these is the spy thriller, which is hardly surprising given the political zeitgeist of the time: just as the imminence of World War One inspired the writing of Oppenheim, Buchan and Childers, its aftermath and the clear likelihood of another, similarly scaled conflict in Europe meant that the spy novels, such as those of Eric Ambler, continued to develop as a genre. Ambler drew heavily on his wartime experiences to produce what Haycraft describes as 'spy-and-intrigue' writing that 'comes close to a legitimate marriage with detection'. Overlapping with the spy novel is the thriller, of which Grahame Greene's first novel, *The Man Within* (1929), is a classic early example. This has lead, perhaps somewhat contentiously, to Greene being in this part and rubbing shoulders with the likes of Agatha Christie and Gladys Mitchell, but it is for the more popular, less 'literary' aspect of his oeuvre, writing that he referred to as 'Entertainments', that he is here at all. You could even say that there are elements of the popular crime novel in Greene's often violent, often mysterious, later writing; Steven Powell's argument below for *The End of the Affair* (1951) as 'an immensely complex theological detective story' is a compelling one. It is also worth bearing in mind that Agatha Christie wrote several cracking spy thrillers, including *The Man in The Brown Suit* (1924) and *They Came to Baghdad* (1951); like many of the authors here, she was actually a multi-genre writer.

Others in this part that provide us with alternatives to the detective story are H. C. McNeile writing as 'Sapper', whose military adventure stories have their basis in McNeile's own service; Daphne du Maurier, whose chilling suspense novels perhaps find their roots in the sensation writing of the nineteenth century, and John Creasey, prolific writer of crime and thriller adventures and, more importantly, when writing as J. J. Marric, one of the key inceptors of the police procedural with his Gideon novels. If you want an illustration of the diversiform nature of crime writing, there are three unlikely companions for you.

Creasey's introduction of the police procedural is a significant genre development, as it breaks the mould of the police investigator to this point, individuals such as Collin's Cuff and Marsh's Alleyn, who are almost paid amateurs, private individuals who happen to be policemen. The police procedural instead gives us a law-enforcement department working together in the station investigation room and, as Martin Lightening observes, often working on multiple and overlapping cases rather than just one murder. After this, the police procedural became more established as an American genre with writers such as Ed McBain, but Creasey's Gideon arguably gives roots to later twentieth-century British police stories such as those by R. D. Wingfield, Reginald Hill, Colin Dexter and Ian Rankin, four of the 'heavyweights' that emerge in the period of crime writing that follows World War Two.

Howard Haycraft published *The Simple Art of Murder* in 1941, concluding his survey of British crime writing at that time with the sobering observation that Eric Ambler was 'serving in his country's armed forces at the time of the present writing'. With the future of the modern world undecided, it is interesting to consider Haycraft's last chapter, in which he contemplates the future of the detective story from 1941 onwards. One possible future he offers is that the genre, and the democracy that it represented, would be obliterated 'by the kind of external events and forces tragically prevalent in large areas of the world's surface as these paragraphs are penned'. This possibility, Haycraft observed, was not to be 'controlled or ameliorated by any efforts of authors, editors, publishers or booksellers'. Another possible future he posited was the 'self-exhaustion of the form', which could be overcome by intelligence and labour on the part of crime writers in ensuring the evolution and progress of the genre. As with the first part of this volume, the diversity of the authors listed below, from Bailey to Symons, show that this evolution is both ongoing and inevitable.

Esme Miskimmin

Works Cited

Haycraft, Howard, *Murder for Pleasure: The Life and Times of the Detective Story*. (1941; repr. London: Peter Davies, 1942).

Knox, Ronald A., 'Introduction', in *The Best Detective Stories of the Year 1928*, ed. by Ronald A. Knox and H. Harrington (London: Faber & Gwyer, 1929), pp. vii–xxiii.

Woolf, Virginia, 'Middlebrow' (letter written, but not sent, to the editor of *The New Statesman*), in *The Death of the Moth and Other Essays* (1942; repr. London: Penguin, 1961), pp. 152–160.

CHAPTER 22

H. C. Bailey (1878–1961), 1920: *Call Mr. Fortune*

Megan Hoffman

Henry Christopher Bailey is best known for creating detective character Reggie Fortune, who appears in eighty-five short stories and ten novels. Fortune is a doctor who becomes medical advisor to Scotland Yard after his skill in solving crimes comes to the attention of the police. Bailey also wrote a series of crime novels featuring Joshua Clunk, an unscrupulous lawyer who solves puzzling cases that he often profits from himself. Bailey was a founding member of the Detection Club along with other successful crime writers of the day including E. C. Bentley, G. K. Chesterton and Dorothy L. Sayers. He is considered to be one of a group of well known, bestselling British crime writers sometimes referred to as the 'Big Five' that also includes Sayers, Agatha Christie, Freeman Wills Crofts and R. Austin Freeman.

Bailey was the only child of Henry and Jane Bailey. Born in London, Bailey attended the prestigious City of London School, after which he won a scholarship to Oxford's Corpus Christi College. While at Oxford, he studied classics and joined Corpus Christi's rowing team. Bailey also found time at University to write his first novel, an historical romance

M. Hoffman (✉)
Independent Scholar, Southsea, UK

called *My Lady of Orange* (1901). After graduating from Oxford with a first-class honours degree, Bailey acquired a job as a correspondent at *The Daily Telegraph*. Coincidentally, one of Bailey's co-workers at the newspaper was fellow crime writer E. C. Bentley. While working as a journalist, Bailey would serve as war correspondent and drama critic before being promoted to writing various feature stories. For one particularly adventurous assignment, he was a passenger in the first biplane to cross the English Channel. In 1905, while on holiday in Wales, Bailey met Lydia Guest, the sister of an acquaintance. Bailey and Guest married in 1908. After their marriage, the Baileys moved to London with their two daughters, Betty (b. 1910) and Mary (b. 1913). Bailey wrote in the evenings after returning from work at *The Daily Telegraph* and continued to publish novels throughout his career as a journalist; he produced twenty-nine historical novels between 1901 and the late 1920s. In addition, Bailey published a history of the Franco-Prussian War entitled *Forty Years After: The Story of the Franco-German War, 1870* (1914). To distract himself from the stressful conditions he encountered while serving as a war correspondent during World War One, Bailey began writing short detective stories featuring plump, fresh-faced physician Mr. Reginald Fortune. Bailey's first collection of Reggie Fortune short stories, *Call Mr. Fortune*, was published in 1920.

Reggie Fortune seems at first glance to be an insouciant, boyish man who complacently enjoys his upper-middle-class lifestyle. However, Fortune resembles fellow Golden-Age sleuths such as Margery Allingham's Albert Campion and Dorothy L. Sayers' Lord Peter Wimsey in that his foolish appearance masks a sharp intellect and keen powers of observation. Educated at Oxford University, Fortune expects to succeed his father in their comfortably prosperous family medical practice. While studying to become a doctor, Fortune realises that he is particularly proficient in surgery and pathology and reluctantly decides to undertake specialist training in those areas before assuming his place as his father's assistant. During his medical training, Fortune hones skills that will serve him well when he later turns his hand to detection, retaining the 'poise, manual dexterity and diagnostic ability' of a surgeon and 'the love of investigation, the patience in scientific method and the flair' of a pathologist, as Bailey explains in the essay 'Meet Mr. Fortune: An Introduction to a Character by His Creator' (1942). After Fortune begins to display an aptitude for solving crimes related to his medical cases, Scotland Yard becomes aware of his gifts and retains him as a medical advisor. Bailey stresses that Fortune is an 'ordinary man, feeling about things and people and reacting to them in the natural way'. He goes on to state that Fortune would say 'the effective practitioner [of criminology] ... is the ordinary man who knows enough of everything to know his way about in anything and can use his mind in a scientific way'. Like Sherlock Holmes, another gentleman detective, Fortune possesses a superficial yet vast general fund of knowledge that helps him analyse small pieces of physical evidence that often prove crucial to uncovering the truth in a difficult case.

Though he had been publishing Reggie Fortune stories since 1920, Bailey did not produce a full-length crime novel until the first of his Joshua Clunk series, *Garstons*, in 1930. Clunk is featured in ten novels, though he would not prove to be as popular a character as Fortune. Unlike the amiable Fortune, the hymn-quoting Clunk is a devious criminal solicitor who tends to manipulate the law in order to achieve his own ends. Also in contrast to Fortune, Clunk does not come from a privileged background; he is a patron of the working-class Methodist Church and cultivates connections with the criminal underworld. Though he seems to have an ambiguous sense of morality, Clunk nevertheless feels compelled to help vulnerable victims, particularly children. Clunk and Fortune appear together in several books from both series, including *Clunk's Claimant* (1937), *The Great Game* (1939), *The Veron Mystery* (1939) and *The Wrong Man* (1945).

After his retirement from journalism in 1946, Bailey and his wife moved to Wales, where they lived in Bernina, the house where they had first met. Bailey wrote only three novels during his years of retirement, preferring to live quietly and pursue hobbies such as hiking and postcard collecting. Bailey's last book, *Shrouded Death*, was published in 1950.

SUGGESTED READING/WORKS CITED

Binyon, T. J., *Murder Will Out: The Detective in Fiction* (Oxford; New York: Oxford University Press, 1989).

McColley, Robert, 'H. C. Bailey', in *Critical Survey of Mystery and Detective Fiction*, Vol. 1, ed. by Carl Rollyson (Pasadena, CA: Salem Press, 2008), pp. 54–60.

Penzler, Otto and Chris Steinbrunner, 'Bailey, H(enry) C(hristopher), (1878–1961)', in *Encyclopedia of Mystery and Detection* (New York: McGraw-Hill, 1976).

Talburt, Nancy Ellen, 'H. C. (Henry Christopher) Bailey', in *Twelve Englishmen of Mystery*, ed. by Earl F. Bargainnier (Bowling Green: Bowling Green University Popular Press, 1984), pp. 30-35.

Watson, Colin, *Snobbery with Violence: English Crime Stories and Their Audience* (New York: St. Martin's Press, 1971).

CHAPTER 23

Agatha Christie (1890–1976), 1920: US Publication of *The Mysterious Affair at Styles* (UK 1921)

Delphine Cingal

Agatha Christie is one of the best-known British writers of detective fiction. She contributed to the establishment of the 'Golden Age' genre and created two of the most famous literary detectives, Hercule Poirot and Miss Marple, as well as the investigative couple Tommy and Tuppence Beresford, Ariadne Oliver, the police detective Superintendent Battle and many other detectives, amateur and professional, that feature in her stand-alone novels. Often listed with the other Golden Age 'Queens of Crime', Allingham, Sayers and Marsh, Christie arguably is Empress in terms of sheer volume and the overall phenomena generated by her work, which is comparable to that of Conan Doyle and his Sherlock Holmes stories. She wrote sixty-six novels and around 150 short stories, which appeared in various fiction magazines and journals as well as in collected editions. She also wrote six romance novels as 'Mary Westmacott', and several works of non-fiction including her autobiography *Agatha Christie: An Autobiography* (1977). She was a successful playwright, writing a total of seventeen

D. Cingal (✉)
Paris 2-Panthéon-Assas University, Paris, France

© The Author(s) 2020
E. Miskimmin (ed.), *100 British Crime Writers*, Crime Files,
https://doi.org/10.1057/978-1-137-31902-9_23

plays, a few of which were either unpublished or unperformed in her lifetime, but which for the most part were well-received, and the most famous of which *The Mousetrap* (1952), is the longest-running show in the history of British theatre. Her work has been translated into over forty languages and sold billions of copies worldwide. Many of her stories have been adapted for film, television, stage and radio as well as, more unusually, a series of graphic novels by François Rivière (1995–2002; in 2005, along with Anne Martinetti and Philippe Asset, Rivière also published a book of recipes of dishes mentioned in Christie's novels, *Crème et châtiments: recettes délicieuses et criminelles d' Agatha Christie*). Christie's own life, especially her notorious disappearance in 1926, has also become the focus of dramatic adaptation and she has appeared as a fictional character in two detective novels: Gaylord Larsen's *Dorothy and Agatha* (1990) and *The London Blitz Murders* (2004) by Max Allan Collins.

Agatha Mary Clarissa Miller was born in Ashfield House, Torquay, the youngest of three children; her sister, Margaret Frary Miller ('Madge', 1879–1950), was eleven years Agatha's senior, and her brother, Louis Montant Miller ('Monty' 1880–1929), was ten years older than herself, leading to Christie's childhood being somewhat solitary, but, she always maintained, never lonely. Her mother, Clarissa Margaret Boehmer, was British and her father, Frederick Alvah Miller, American. Christie received a very unconventional education; she taught herself to read at the age of four, but never went to school or received formal home-schooling. Her father taught her mathematics and her nanny taught her French, which she had the opportunity to improve at a series of French 'finishing schools' from the ages of fifteen to seventeen. She learned music and composition, and for a while had hopes of a career in this area. She had a large library at her disposal at Ashfield and read an eclectic range of literature, which contributed to an already vivid imagination. In her autobiography, Christie details the various imaginary narratives that she played out involving her toys and various make-believe companions. She also wrote lyrical poetry from childhood (she had two volumes of poetry published in her lifetime: *The Road of Dreams*, in 1924, and *Poems*, 1973). Her first attempt at writing prose was encouraged by her mother when Christie was in her late teens and convalescing from influenza. She produced 'The House of Beauty', the first of many short stories that, she says, she sent hopefully to various magazines and which came back 'promptly with the usual slip: "The editor regrets. . ."'. She was, however, hooked on writing and continued trying until her first detective novel, *The*

Mysterious Affair at Styles (1920) was accepted for publication, beginning a career in writing crime fiction that lasted more than five decades.

Before this, however, Christie was to meet and marry her first husband, Archibald Christie (1889–1962). She had, like many girls of her age and class, done the usual round of tennis parties, concerts, formal balls, and country house weekends that appear in many of her detective novels. In 1914, she met Archie at a dance. He had applied to be an aviator in the Royal Flying Core and when he was accepted, he asked her to marry him. At the instigation of Mrs Miller, they agreed to wait, and when war broke out Archie was sent to France. He came back at Christmas, 1914, and they were married by special licence on Christmas Eve before he returned to his duties. During the war, Christie became a V. A. D. (member of the Voluntary Aid Detachment) and served first as a wardmaid and nurse in Torquay hospital, and then in the hospital dispensary. She passed the Society of Apothecaries examination and had an excellent knowledge of drugs and poisons, which was to be useful for her later novels: *The Pharmaceutical Journal* actually gave a very favourable review of *The Mysterious Affair at Styles*. Much later, Christie also made literary use of one of the pharmacists, 'Mr. P', who she recalls as 'a strange man' who kept a lump of curare in his pocket because, he explained to her, it made him 'feel powerful'. She describes how: 'his memory remained with me so long that it was still there waiting when I first conceived the idea of writing my book *The Pale Horse* [1961] – and that must have been, I suppose, nearly fifty years later'.

Archie Christie returned home at the end of the war, and the Christies moved to London in 1919 where their only child, Rosalind, was born. In the same year, John Lane took up the manuscript for *The Mysterious Affair at Styles* and contracted Christie for five more books. *Styles* introduced Christie's first serial detective, Hercule Poirot, a former Belgian policeman who finds himself in England as a war refugee. Christie had met quite a few Belgian refugees in Devonshire during the war and had been touched by their plight. Poirot's key characteristics are established early on; he is fussy, obsessively tidy and fastidious over his appearance, all traits which make him an occasional figure of fun to both the reader and his loyal narrator, Captain Hastings, who chronicles many of Poirot's investigations. He is also, however, incredibly intelligent (although he is aware of this and boasts endlessly about his 'little grey cells'), fiercely moral and possessed of kindness and compassion for human suffering, encouraging many people to confide in 'papa Poirot'. *Styles* is one of the first classic Golden Age country house murder mysteries, and meets the now clichéd expectations of the genre in many ways. As with many of the other country house novels to follow, however, the household is fragmented by the war and by personal concerns, suggesting a new and discordant world that cannot quite recapture an idyllically remembered past. This is not the only instance of this in Christie's writing: hers is an often rural, upper-middle-class, quintessentially English domain, but change and modernity do intrude.

Christie's next novel, *The Secret Adversary* (1922) introduced another recurring duo of detectives: Tommy Beresford and Tuppence Cowley, two bright young things who meet in London in the economic aftermath of the war, searching unsuccessfully for jobs for 'ten long, weary months', before finding themselves doing some unofficial work for British Intelligence. A very different type of story from *Styles*, *The Secret Adversary* is one of Christie's forays into the spy-thriller genre, another notable example of which is the stand-alone novel, *The Man in the Brown Suit* (1924). Having become engaged at the end of *The Secret Adversary*, Tommy and Tuppence appeared in a further three novels, and a collection of short stories, *Partners in Crime* (1929), in which they take it in turns to investigate in the style of famous fictional detectives, a device which demonstrates neatly the self-reflexive nature of the Golden Age genre. The protagonists age with each book: by *Postern of Fate* (1973), they are retired with grandchildren.

After *Styles*, Christie found that she was 'tied to the detective story [and] tied to two people: Hercule Poirot and his Watson, Captain Hastings' (although several later Poirot stories dispense with the faithful narrator), and she continued to alternate Poirot stories with various stand-alone novels and short story collections for the next decade. Of these, there are two of particular note: the first, *The Murder of Roger Ackroyd* (1926) because it generated heated discussion for not playing fair according to the rules of the Golden Age, and its break with narrative convention marks it out as a significant milestone in the development of the genre; and the second, the collection of short stories *The Mysterious Mr Quin* (1930) because they mark another genre departure for Christie. The enigmatic, possibly non-human Harley Quin seems to belong more to ghost stories than crime fiction, and the narratives in which he appears are mystical, even supernatural, in quality (some later short stories by Christie are more straightforward ghost stories, such as many of those in the collection *The Hound of Death*, 1933).

During this decade, the Christies travelled considerably with Archie's job: Agatha Christie enjoyed travel her whole life, and drew on her experiences around the world for her novels. They also moved from London to Sunningdale, Berkshire, and eventually bought a house there which they renamed *Styles*. At this point, it seems, their marriage began to go wrong, and Archie met another woman, Nancy Neele. He asked Agatha for a divorce in 1926, and it was at this point that Christie became involved in her own *cause célèbre*. On 3 December, she left the house having put her daughter to bed and disappeared. Her car was found abandoned at Newlands Corner, near Guildford in Surrey, and a nationwide manhunt began. Christie was eventually found booked into a spa in Harrogate under the name of Mrs. Neele, and claimed to have no memory of the events of the previous ten days. Public response was quite negative, and many saw the whole affair as a publicity stunt, although Christie claimed to have had a breakdown. She never spoke of it again, and omits the entire episode from her autobiography. In 1979, Vanessa Redgrave played Christie in *Agatha*, a movie about her disappearance, and it continues to be the focus of speculation. Archie and Agatha divorced in 1928, and Christie found herself alone: her mother, a massive presence in her life, had died in 1926, and Rosalind was happy at boarding school. She decided to travel again, and booked herself onto the Orient Express, a journey that arguably resulted in one of her most famous novels, and another in which she departs from the 'fair play' genre, *Murder on the Orient Express* (1934).

Christie continued to write and travel, particularly in the Middle East. In 1930 she went to Ur to visit her archaeological friends, Leonard and Katherine Woolley, and here she met her second husband, Max Mallowan, an archaeologist fourteen years younger than herself. The dig at Ur gave her experiences to draw on in *Murder in Mesopotamia* (1936), in which Poirot makes a somewhat cameo appearance as detective. Max and Agatha's marriage appears to have been a happy one; they travelled together a lot and this allowed her to draw on other exotic settings for her novels, such as *Death Comes as the End* (a historical novel set in Ancient Egypt, 1944), *Death on the Nile* (an Hercule Poirot novel, 1937; probably Christie's most frequently adapted novel for film, television and radio), *Appointment with Death* (a Poirot novel set in Jerusalem, 1938) and *They Came to Baghdad* (a stand-alone spy novel, 1951). In England, they had homes in London and Christie's much-loved Devonshire, where they bought Greenway House, Galmpton. Christie often returns to the south west in her settings: 'Saint Loo' in *Peril at End House* (1932) is based on Torquay, and in *Five Little Pigs* (1942), she uses Greenway as the model for the home of artist Amyas Crale.

1930 saw another significant change for Christie: the first novel featuring her other well-known detective, Miss Jane Marple: *Murder at the Vicarage*. Miss Marple had appeared in 1927 in a series of short stories in the *Sketch Magazine* (published as *The Thirteen Problems* in 1932), and like Poirot, her character is established from the outset. Behind the 'benign and kindly' Victorian exterior of a slightly twittery, elderly, spinster lurks a mind of steel and razor-sharp intuition. Unlike Poirot, who relies on a slightly Holmesian ratiocination, Miss Marple's investigations are driven by an intrinsic understanding of human nature and a capacity to (as Christie explains it) 'expect the worst of everyone and everything.' Poirot travels all over the world; Miss Marple rarely leaves St. Mary Mead, which she argues, gives her all the insight she needs as 'there is a great deal of wickedness in village life'. Most of the Miss Marple novels are set here or similar villages: rural, Home Counties, parochial and tight-knit communities with a similar set of characters and institutions in each. Once or twice Miss Marple ventures up to London: in *At Bertram's Hotel* (1965), she stays at a hotel she stayed in as a girl, but is conscious that the idyllic past, like the innocent façade of the hotel, is an illusion, and in *A Caribbean Mystery* (1964) she finds herself on an all-expenses-paid holiday to St. Honoré. The milieu is exotic, and not to Miss Marple's tastes – 'so *many* palm trees' – but her recognition of some fundamental human traits helps her solve the crime. One of the characters she encounters in this novel forms the basis of the action for a later Miss Marple novel, *Nemesis* (1971), in which Miss Marple investigates a twenty-year-old murder while on a tour of English country houses. It is ironic that in this later example of Christie's work, the country houses of her youth and earlier stories have become preserved relics of the past, as Miss Marple tours the settings she is popularly associated with.

This self-consciousness is to be found more explicitly in the novels featuring Ariadne Oliver, crime novelist and sometime sidekick to Poirot. She also appears as one of Mr. Pyne's staff in the quirky collection of adventure stories *Parker Pyne Investigates* (1934). Much has been made of the *alter ego* aspect of Oliver, who allows Christie to explore, often with humour, the conventions in which she writes: In *Cards on the Table* (1936), Ariadne Oliver explains: '"What really matters is plenty of bodies! If the thing's getting a little dull, some more blood cheers it up"'. She adds: '"Somebody is going to tell something - and then they're killed first! That always goes down well. It comes in all my books - camouflaged different ways of course"'. Oliver also expresses the same weariness about her Finnish detective, Sven Hjerson, which Christie occasionally seems to have felt about Poirot.

Christie was a prolific writer, and some of her work perhaps suffers from over-use of certain formulas, such as the one outlined by Ariadne Oliver above, but many of her works are groundbreaking in her treatment of narrative convention, such as the aforementioned *The Murder of Roger Ackroyd* and *Murder on the Orient Express*. Her final Poirot novel, *Curtain: Poirot's Last Case* (1975) in which Poirot, an elderly and ill man, is reunited with Captain Hastings at Styles, now a guest house, is similarly challenging of conventions and was well-received critically.

Christie was honoured many times and in many capacities by her peers and her readers: she succeeded Dorothy L. Sayers as president of the Detection Club in 1957, for example, and in 1955 she was awarded the Mystery Writers of America's Grand Master Award – the first one ever. Her play *Witness for the Prosecution* received the Edgar Award by the Mystery Writers of America for Best Play, and she received countless other awards for her writing. Her achievements were also recognised on a national level: in 1956, she was made Commander of the Order of the British Empire, and 1971, she became Dame Commander of the Order of the British Empire. Her stories continue to be performed for screen and radio and she remains one of the most popular and famous British crime writers.

SUGGESTED READING/WORKS CITED

Christie, Agatha, *Agatha Christie: An Autobiography* (1977; repr. London: Collins, 1990).
Makinen, Merja, 'Agatha Christie (1890–1976)', in *A Companion to Crime Fiction*, ed. by Charles J. Rzepka and Lee Horsley (Chichester: Wiley-Blackwell, 2010), pp. 415–426.
———, *Agatha Christie: Investigating Femininity* (Basingstoke: Palgrave Macmillan, 2006).
Morgan, Janet, *Agatha Christie: A Biography*, rev. edn (London: Harper Collins, 1997).

Rowland, Susan, *From Agatha Christie to Ruth Rendell: British Women Writers in Detective and Crime Fiction* (Basingstoke: Palgrave Macmillan, 2001).

York, R. A., *Agatha Christie: Power and Illusion* (Basingstoke: Palgrave Macmillan, 2007).

CHAPTER 24

Freeman Wills Crofts (1879–1957), 1920: *The Cask*

Diana Powell

Crofts is best known for Inspector (later Chief Superintendent) Joseph French of Scotland Yard, his character who excels at dismantling solid alibis and was the focus of a series that spanned thirty years and ran to twenty-nine novels. Crofts was a popular writer in his day but his focus on intricate plotting over character development has led to him being largely forgotten by a modern audience.

Born in Dublin to English parents, Crofts' army doctor father died while serving abroad, and his mother remarried a Belfast archdeacon. Crofts' own relationship with the church was long-standing: he played the church organ and was a church choirmaster, and he wrote one religious book, *The Four Gospels in One Story* (1949). At the age of seventeen, Crofts was apprenticed as a civil engineer to his uncle, who was then Chief Engineer of the Belfast and Northern Countries Railway. Crofts began work as a Junior Assistant Engineer in 1899, graduating to District Engineer (Coleraine, 1900) and later to Chief Assistant Engineer (Belfast, 1923–1929).

D. Powell (✉)
University of Liverpool, Liverpool, UK

© The Author(s) 2020
E. Miskimmin (ed.), *100 British Crime Writers*, Crime Files,
https://doi.org/10.1057/978-1-137-31902-9_24

Crofts' first novel, *The Cask* (1920), was credited with helping launch the Golden Age of detective fiction when it appeared the same year as Agatha Christie's *The Mysterious Affair at Styles*. Crofts was a member of the Detection Club (which included Christie), and Christie parodied Inspector French in *Partners in Crime* (1929). Although Crofts' novels were an immediate success, he continued to balance working as an engineer and writing for nine years, until health problems forced his retirement from the railway. Crofts and his wife, Mary Bellas Canning (whom he married in 1912), left Belfast for Surrey in 1929 and moved to Sussex in 1953.

It was on the advice of his doctor during a long illness that Crofts began writing and *The Cask*'s dedication suggests the doctor's continued guidance: 'To Dr Adam A. C. Mathers, in appreciation of his kindly criticism and help'. Crofts' occupational training and lifelong interest in transport is apparent in the plot: set in London and Paris, *The Cask* begins in the offices of a shipping company, but soon moves to the docks, where gold pieces and a human hand are discovered in casks meant to contain wine. The whole shipping process, therefore, falls under investigation and the killer is eventually caught out by a private investigator who studies the train timetables and debunks his alibi.

Three more stand-alone novels followed: *The Ponson Case* (1921), which opens with a typically Golden Age plot of an aristocrat murdered at his country estate; *The Pit Prop Syndicate* (1922), which returns to the Anglo-French setting of *The Cask*, when an Englishman holidaying in France stumbles upon a smuggling operation; and *The Groote Park Murder* (1923), which moves from a supposed railway accident in South Africa to a Scottish setting.

Crofts' novels elaborate puzzles, yet they are psychologically straightforward; French's cases are complex and require considerable legwork, but his criminal's motives are never sympathetic. French is not infallible as an investigator, as confirmed in his first 'greatest' case where he is surprised by the identity of the murderer.

Crofts wrote fifty short stories (several for the Detection Club), thirty radio plays for the BBC and a play, *Sudden Death* (1932). He was made a fellow of the Royal Society of Arts in 1939.

Suggested Reading/Works Cited

Evans, Curtis, *Masters of the "Humdrum" Mystery: Cecil John Charles Street, Freeman Wills Crofts, Alfred Walter Stewart and the British Detective Novel, 1920–1961* (Jefferson, NC: McFarland, 2012).

CHAPTER 25

H. C. McNeile (a.k.a. Sapper, 1888–1937), 1920: *Bulldog Drummond*

Alexandra Phillips

Herman Cyril McNeile was best known by the pseudonym 'Sapper', military slang for an engineer, which derived from his career in the Royal Engineers of British Army (1907–1919). Authors in active service were only allowed to publish anonymously and it is by his pen name that McNeile has been known since. He was born in Bodmin, Cornwall, in 1888 and attended school in Eastbourne, followed by Cheltenham College and the Royal Military Academy in Woolwich. He married in 1915 and had two sons. After World War One he was awarded the Military Cross and subsequently retired at the rank of Lieutenant Colonel to pursue a full-time career as a writer. He moved to Switzerland in 1921 and then returned to the UK in 1931, settling in West Sussex.

Sapper started writing military adventure stories during the war, publishing *The Lieutenant and Others* (1915) and *Sergeant Michael Cassidy, RE* (1915), the latter selling 50,000 copies in the first nine months after publication. From 1920 to 1937, when the magazine sector was booming, Sapper started publishing his stories in *The Sovereign*, *Hutchinson's Magazine* and *The Strand*. His tales of murder and intrigue,

A. Phillips (✉)
Open University Wales, Cardiff, UK

often carrying moralistic messages about alcohol and infidelity, are based around the glamorous lifestyles of the aristocracy, and are characterised by the way they conclude with a final narrative 'twist'. Sapper produced ten short story collections in total, from *The Man in Ratcatcher* (1921) to *Ask for Ronald Standish* (1936). These collections sold hundreds of thousands of copies, leading to Gerard Fairlie's claim that Sapper was the highest-paid short story writer in Britain between the wars.

Sapper's best-known character is Bulldog Drummond, whose adventures were translated onto the stage in 1925 and formed the basis of many film adaptations from 1929 onwards. Captain Hugh Drummond, a burly and jovial ex-Army officer who speaks in public school clichés and is motivated by desire for adventure, and his adversary, Carl Peterson, first appeared in *Bulldog Drummond* (1920). The pair featured in a further three novels: *The Black Gang* (1922), where Drummond leads an anti-Communist vigilante group; *The Third Round* (1924), which involves a plan to create artificial diamonds, and *Final Count* (1927), in which Peterson is killed. Sapper wrote five more Drummond novels: *The Female of the Species* (1928), *Temple Tower* (1929), *Bulldog Drummond at Bay* (1935) and *The Return of Bulldog Drummond* (1936). After his death, another six books based on the character were ghostwritten by Gerard Fairlie. The Drummond novels have been published in new editions this century, attracting criticism for fascist and anti-Semitic content but also arousing popular and critical interest in the era they represent.

Suggested Reading/Works Cited

Adrian, Jack, 'Introduction', in Sapper, *The Best Short Stories*, ed. by Jack Adrian (London: Dent, 1984).

Bertens, Hans, 'A Society of Murderers', in *Twentieth-Century Suspense*, ed. by Clive Bloom (Basingstoke: Macmillan, 1990), pp. 51–68.

Trewin, Ion, 'Introduction', in Sapper, *The Black Gang* (London: Dent, 1983).

Watson, Colin, *Snobbery with Violence: English Crime Stories and Their Audience* (London: Eyre Methuen, 1979).

CHAPTER 26

G. D. H. Cole (1889–1959) writing with Margaret Cole (1893–1980), 1923: *The Brooklyn Murders*

Victoria Stewart

George Douglas Howard Cole was an economist with an early involvement with the Fabian Society, and a historian of the labour movement. Educated at St. Paul's School, London and Balliol College, Oxford, he became the first Reader in Economics at Oxford in 1925 and was elected Fellow of All Souls in 1944. Margaret Cole attended Roedean in Sussex and went to study classics at Girton College, Cambridge in 1911. She did not hold an academic post but published widely on social and political issues. They met when she was working in the Research Department of the Fabian Society towards the end of World War One and married in 1918. They had a son and two daughters.

The Brooklyn Murders (1923) appeared under G. D. H. Cole's name; he apparently wrote it for a bet while convalescing. Subsequent jointly authored novels, which eventually numbered almost thirty, were published as by G. D. H. and Margaret Cole. Their short fiction was collected in *A Lesson in Crime and Other Stories* (1933) and *Wilson and*

V. Stewart (✉)
University of Leicester, Leicester, UK

© The Author(s) 2020
E. Miskimmin (ed.), *100 British Crime Writers*, Crime Files,
https://doi.org/10.1057/978-1-137-31902-9_26

Some Others (1940). G. D. H. Cole was also credited as the sole author of *Death in the Tankard* (1943); Margaret Cole claimed to have run out of steam and abandoned their current joint effort half-finished at around this time, and they published no more detective fiction.

The Coles' detective protagonists include Superintendent Wilson and Inspector Fairford of the CID, with Sir Everard Blatchington, introduced in *The Blatchington Triangle* (1926), reappearing in *Death in the Quarry* (1934). Margaret Cole noted that she and her husband were fans of R. Austin Freeman's Thorndyke stories, and this influence can be seen in *End of an Ancient Mariner* (1933), which has an inverted plot. Julian Symons describes the Coles as belonging to the 'Humdrum' school, of which Freeman Wills Crofts is his exemplar, and it seems clear that the intellectual challenge of the clue-puzzle form, as much as a desire to capture and cultivate an audience, fuelled their production. However, novels such as *Murder at Crome House* (1927), in which an unsuspecting history tutor gets caught up in investigating a murder after discovering a photograph left in the pages of a library book, *Off with Her Head!* (1938), the plot of which unfolds in an Oxford college, and *Murder at the Munition Works* (1940), which makes good use of a wartime factory setting, remain interesting and unusual contributions to the genre.

SUGGESTED READING/WORKS CITED

Barzun, Jacques and Wendell Hertig Taylor, *A Catalogue of Crime* (New York: Harper & Row, 1971).

Bedell, Jean F., 'Cole, G. D. H. and Margaret Cole', in *The St. James Guide to Crime and Mystery Writers*, 4th edn, ed. by Jay J. Pederson (Detroit: St. James Press, 1996), pp. 209–214.

Cole, Margaret, *The Life of G. D. H. Cole* (London: Macmillan, 1971).

CHAPTER 27

Dorothy L. Sayers (1893–1957), 1923: *Whose Body?*

Esme Miskimmin

Dorothy L. Sayers is best known for her detective stories featuring her aristocratic sleuth, Lord Peter Wimsey, who appears in eleven of her twelve detective novels, four collections of short stories and was the focus for the televised adaptations of three of the books in 1987. Sayers was a member of the Detection Club, established in the 1920s at the height of the Golden Age and wrote a chapter of their collaborative novel *The Floating Admiral* (1931) as well as being its president from 1949 to 1957. Sayers' crime writing is a small part of a wide-ranging literary career that includes poetry, letters, essays, criticism, theological scholarship and drama.

Sayers was the only child of the Reverend Henry Sayers, headmaster of the Christchurch Choir School, Oxford, and Helen Mary Sayers (nèe Leigh). In 1897, Henry Sayers was offered the living of Bluntisham-cum-Earith, Huntingdonshire, and moved his family there. Sayers' lifelong attachment to East Anglia began; it was later to become the fictional home of Wimsey's family seat (Duke's Denver) and the setting for her

E. Miskimmin (✉)
University of Liverpool, Liverpool, UK

© The Author(s) 2020
E. Miskimmin (ed.), *100 British Crime Writers*, Crime Files,
https://doi.org/10.1057/978-1-137-31902-9_27

dark and complex detective story *The Nine Tailors* in which Sayers' evocation of fen life is bleak and often claustrophobic, despite the apparently endless horizons. Sayers was educated at home until the age of fifteen, when she was sent to Godolphin School, Salisbury, to prepare for entrance to Oxford. She went up to Oxford in 1912 to study Modern Languages at Somerville and gained a first, although like other female students she was not actually awarded her B.A. and M.A. until the university conferred degrees on women in 1920. She began writing poetry while at University and continued to do so throughout her life, often incorporating it into her other genres. Although Sayers' poetry is largely overlooked and perhaps not the most successful of her literary endeavours, she had two volumes published: *Op 1*(1916) and *Catholic Tales and Christian Songs* (1918). Both of these volumes establish the spiritual and theological themes that pervade all of her writing and clearly demonstrate a lyricism that is also evident her prose style, such as in her description of the roof of the parish church in Fenchurch St. Paul in *The Nine Tailors*: 'Incredibly aloof, flinging back the light in a dusky shimmer of bright hair and gilded outspread wings, soared the ranked angels, cherubim and seraphim, choir over choir, from corbel and hammer-beam floating face to face uplifted'.

After leaving university in 1915, Sayers took various jobs including teaching, a brief time at Blackwell's publishers, a period in France as an assistant to the head of a schools exchange scheme and, like many individuals in the post-war period of depression, periods of unemployment. In 1922 she moved to London, having secured a post as a copywriter at the advertising firm of Benson's, where she remained until 1931. Sayers showed considerable flair for this job and her most notable work was on the 'Mustard Club' campaign and on Guinness' iconic 'My Goodness My Guinness' advertising series with artist John Gilroy. This experience at Benson's later provided the background for her 1933 novel, *Murder Must Advertise*, in which a copywriter is murdered. In 1921, however, she began writing her first detective novel, *Whose Body?*, eventually published in 1923 by Gollancz, which marked the beginning of a period of prolific writing in this genre.

Despite having a secure job and the beginnings of a career as a writer of detective fiction, Sayers' personal life was less satisfactory. Following an unhappy love affair with a John Cournos, she began a relationship with a neighbour, Bill White, in 1922, which resulted in an unplanned pregnancy. White could not marry Sayers – he was already married – and did not want to acknowledge the child. Sayers decided to conceal her pregnancy from the world and in 1924 gave birth to her only child, John Anthony White (later Fleming), subsequently placing him in the care of her cousin, Ivy Shrimpton. The existence of Sayers' son remained a secret from nearly all of her family and friends, and certainly her reading public, until after her death.

In 1925, Sayers met a reporter on crime and motor-racing, Oswald Arthur 'Atherton' Fleming, known to everyone as 'Mac'. They were married on 13 April 1926 in a registry office since Mac was divorced, another instance of Sayers' personal experiences conflicting with her deeply felt Christian beliefs and upbringing. For a while, Sayers seems to have cherished hopes of her son living with them and Mac becoming his adoptive father. This never happened and as the marriage progressed it became increasingly unhappy. The situation was made worse by Mac's ill-health, a result of being gassed in the trenches of World War One, and Sayers' consequent position as the main breadwinner for them both. The physical and psychological after-effects of the war on ex-soldiers are explored in her novel *The Unpleasantness at the Bellona Club* (1928) and several biographers have drawn parallels between Mac and the character of George Fentiman, a bitter victim of Mustard Gas who must rely on his wife's income.

With the expense of supporting a child and an increasingly invalid husband, the extra money to be earned from writing popular detective fiction became more significant and, besides, it was something that Sayers enjoyed and was good at. Despite troubles in her personal life, professionally she prospered. She excelled at writing the pure 'puzzle story' of the Golden Age, of which her early works are classic examples, making use of the generic conventions of the closed environment, the limited cast of suspects, and the ubiquitous 'red herrings'. Sayers' detective fiction acknowledges these conventions and the 'puzzle' quality of the genre. There are innumerable references to other puzzle pastimes such as chess and crosswords in each of her books; there is a short story, for example, 'The Fascinating Problem of Uncle Meleager's Will' (first published in *Lord Peter Views the Body*, 1928), in which both Wimsey and the reader can arrive at the true solution through the completion of the blank grid of a crossword. Sayers' seventh novel, *Five Red Herrings* (1931) is a somewhat dry, textbook exercise in the puzzle form, revolving around timetables and alibis, a list of suspects and a process of elimination. The Golden Age rule of reader participation is observed: if, as the murder scene is described, we can deduce what Wimsey perceives to be missing (and Sayers is confident in a brief note to her readership that 'the intelligent reader will readily supply these details for himself'), then we have a clue to the identity of the murderer. Sayers' even initially suggested to her publisher, 'a sealed page' with the solution at the end of the book. Her deliberate adherence to genre with this novel is important, as it is a response to criticism of the previous novel, *Strong Poison*, which had deviated from the formula and moved towards an emotional and psychological development of the characters that was to continue in her later novels. As a result, *Five Red Herrings* was written with the intention of its being, as she put it in a letter to Victor Gollancz, a 'pure puzzle story', where her readers could play 'spot the murderer'.

By 1930 Sayers' dissatisfaction with this kind of writing was becoming more evident. The constraints of genre writing meant that more 'literary' elements appeared in her detective fiction and these either seriously compromised the detective narrative or potentially displeased her reading public. She also found that the detection got in the way of discourses on subjects such as science vs. religion, such as in *The Documents in the Case* (1930) or the education of women, for example in *Gaudy Night* (1935).

Writing about Sayers' work in his 1944 essay 'The Simple Art of Murder', Raymond Chandler identified this problem, arguing that such writing was 'an arid formula which could not even satisfy its own implications. It was second-grade literature because it was not about the things that could make first-grade literature' and that 'Dorothy Sayers' own stories show that she was annoyed by this triteness'. Sayers addressed these problems through the potentially autobiographical character of Harriet Vane, Wimsey's love interest and a writer of detective fiction. For example in *Gaudy Night* Harriet is struggling with her novel '*Death Twixt Wind and Water*' and Wimsey agrees with the concerns that she outlines, commenting that 'from a purely constructional point of view [he doesn't feel that] Wilfred's behaviour is sufficiently accounted for', and suggests that she 'make[s] Wilfred one of those morbidly conscientious people, who have been brought up to think that anything pleasant must be wrong [...] Give him a puritanical father and a hell-fire religion'. This re-creation of 'Wilfred' with a psychological dimension would obviously develop Harriet's book beyond its genre, but would involve writing '"literature", not detective fiction'. Harriet sees this and complains that if she rewrites her character, with 'violent and life-like feelings, he'll throw the whole book out of balance', to which Wimsey replies that she would 'have to abandon the jig-saw kind of story'.

Despite the considerable success of her detective fiction, Sayers seems to have done just that, concentrating instead on her theological writings, both non-fiction and drama. The collection of short stories, *In the Teeth of the Evidence* (1939) was the last of her detective writing to be published in her lifetime, and by the time it was in print she had already completed several projects entirely unrelated to the detection genre, including a religious drama for the Canterbury Festival, *The Zeal of Thy House* (1937). The beginnings of a final Wimsey novel, *Thrones Dominations*, were in existence but Sayers declared her intention to write no more detective fiction, at least until the war was over, and in fact never returned to it. The novel was completed for publication by Jill Paton Walsh in 1998. Paton Walsh has since written three other 'Wimsey' novels, one of which *A Presumption of Death* (2002) takes as its inspiration 'The Wimsey Papers' (see below).

By the outbreak of World War Two in 1939, Sayers and Mac had been living for nearly a decade in Witham, Essex, although Sayers was still making frequent visits to London for work. Sayers was becoming recognised as a theological writer and scholar: she had been invited to write several essays for publication, including 'The Greatest Drama Ever Staged' for the *Times* Passion Sunday edition and a radio nativity play for children, *He That Should Come* (1938). What was becoming clear with each of these projects was that Sayers had her own often quite dogmatic way of approaching her faith and its teachings; her aim was to communicate these views in a way that was clear and accessible. This direct approach is also evident in the wide range of essays, talks and pamphlets that she wrote in response to the war, many of which had a Christian basis. Her Christmas message to the nation, *Begin Here* (1940), which was commissioned by Gollancz, asserts that 'In 1918 we were given an opportunity to rebuild Europe on better lines. We bungled that as we have bungled other opportunities from time to time [...] There is a good deal to be said for the opinion that a sin is a sin and an error an error; that both should be examined, admitted repented of, and then put out of our thoughts'. This forthright approach is typical of Sayers, and it probably resulted in her being dropped by the Ministry of Information Authors' Planning Committee, on which she served briefly. She did write towards the war effort in a less direct and more popular format, however. From November 1939 to January 1940 she resurrected the characters of her detective novels for one last appearance in a series of fictional letters in the *Spectator* (now referred to collectively as 'The Wimsey Papers'), in which the various member of the Wimsey family discussed the war, particularly in terms of the home front with the aim of disseminating information and boosting public morale.

After the end of the war, and after Mac's death in 1950, Sayers continued to write within the public domain – essays, papers and letters – but her chief project was her translation of Dante's *Divine Comedy*, a culmination of all her intellectual, linguistic and poetic passions. She completed the first two volumes, *Hell* (1949) and *Purgatory* (1955) but left *Paradise* unfinished at her death from heart failure on 17 December 1957. It was completed by her friend, Barbara Reynolds, who was also responsible for what is considered the definitive biography of Sayers, *Dorothy L. Sayers: Her Life and Soul* (1998).

Suggested Reading/Works Cited

Chandler, Raymond, 'The Simple Art of Murder: An Essay', *The Atlantic Monthly*, 1944, repr. in *The Simple Art If Murder* (New York: Ballentine, 1972), pp. 1–21.

Downing, Crystal, *Writing Performances: The Stages of Dorothy L. Sayers* (Basingstoke: Palgrave Macmillan, 2004).

Miskimmin, Esme, 'Dorothy L. Sayers (1893–1957)', in *A Companion to Crime Fiction*, ed. by Charles J. Rzepka and Lee Horsley (Chichester: Wiley-Blackwell, 2010), pp. 438–449.

Reynolds, Barbara, *Dorothy L. Sayers: Her Life and Soul* (London: Hodder and Stoughton, 1998).

——, ed., *The Letters of Dorothy L. Sayers*, 5 vols (London: Hodder and Stoughton, 1995–2002).

Rowland, Susan, *From Agatha Christie to Ruth Rendell: British Women Writers in Detective and Crime Fiction* (Basingstoke: Palgrave Macmillan, 2001).

Sayers, Dorothy L., *Begin Here* (London: Gollancz, 1940).

CHAPTER 28

Patricia Wentworth (Pseudonym of Dora Amy Elles, 1878–1961), 1923: *The Astonishing Case of Jane Smith*

Delphine Cingal

Writing as Patricia Wentworth, Dora Elles was a prolific crime writer best known for her traditional Golden Age genre stories featuring her elderly spinster detective, Miss Silver. Elles was born in the foothills of the Himalayan range, in Mussorie, Uttarakhand, in the North of India, the daughter of a British officer. Initially privately educated, she was then sent to her grandmother's in England along with her two brothers and she studied at Blackheath High School in London. After her graduation, she returned to India where she married her first husband, Colonel George F. Dillon, in 1906. He died shortly after their marriage and she moved with her young daughter and three stepsons to England. She started writing historical novels under the name Patricia Wentworth, beginning with *A Marriage Under the Terror* (1910), a novel set in the French Revolution, which earned her the Melrose prize.

In 1920, she married Lieutenant George Oliver Turnbull; they moved to Camberley in Surrey and they had a daughter. He encouraged her

D. Cingal (✉)
Paris 2-Panthéon-Assas University, Paris, France

to write and even acted as a scribe as she dictated her novels to him. In 1923, she won the first prize in a competition organised by the *Daily Mail* for her first mystery novel, *The Astonishing Case of Jane Smith*. Eight more novels followed until the publication of the first Miss Silver novel, *Grey Mask* (1928), in which Miss Silver is called by Charles Moray to investigate the disappearance of his fiancée, Margaret Langton, who jilted him at the altar before being suspected of involvement in a kidnapping plot. The Miss Silver novels are atypical of the Golden Age style in terms of setting and character; Miss Maud Silver is a retired governess turned private detective, and is often compared to Agatha Christie's Miss Marple in as much that she is an unassuming, genteel and gossipy old lady. A distinctly 'Victorian' lady with a fondness for Tennyson and meticulous order, Miss Silver starts a new notebook for every case she has to investigate, which is her ritual for beginning on a new job. She has rather good relationships with the police and one of the secondary characters in her stories, Inspector Ernest Lamb, ended up having a small series all to himself (starting with *the Blind Side*, 1939). Miss Silver's other sidekicks are sometimes Chief Constable Randal March or Inspector Franck Abbott of Scotland Yard, both of whom she habitually corrects and upbraids.

Miss Maud Silver is the typical armchair detective of the Golden Age detective novels, in which the innocent is vindicated, the young lovers reunited, peace restored to the *status quo ante criminem* and the villain punished. Apart from solving crimes, Miss Silver often saves the lives of young innocent maidens or young men in distress (in *The Lonesome Road*, 1939, or *The Case of William Smith*, 1948, for instance) or has to protect young lovers (*Miss Silver Intervenes*, 1943; US title *Miss Silver Deals in Death*), leading to her stories often having a gently romantic element. Opinion is often divided on the literary merit of Wentworth's detective novels, but her engaging characters and well-plotted stories ensure that she remains popular.

SUGGESTED READING/WORKS CITED

Smith, Christopher, 'Patricia Wentworth (Dora Amy Elles)', in *Dictionary of Literary Biography, Volume 77: British Mystery Writers, 1920–1939*, ed. by Bernard Benstock and Thomas F. Staley (Detroit, MI: Gale, 1989), pp. 309–314.

Wynne, Nancy Blue, 'Patricia Wentworth Revisited', *Armchair Detective: A Quarterly Journal Devoted to the Appreciation of Mystery, Detective, and Suspense Fiction*, 14:1 (1981), 90–92.

CHAPTER 29

Philip MacDonald (Also Wrote as Oliver Fleming, Anthony Lawless and Martin Porlock, 1899–1981), 1924: *The Rasp* (Published Anonymously)

Alexandra Phillips

Biographical material of MacDonald is scarce but it is known that he was the grandson of poet and novelist George MacDonald and served with a British Cavalry regiment in Mesopotamia during World War One. MacDonald married novelist F. Ruth Howard in 1931 and they moved from the UK to Hollywood, where he later became a prolific screenwriter working in the mystery/detective genre.

MacDonald is best known for his detective Colonel Anthony Gethryn, introduced in his first crime novel *The Rasp* (1924). Gethryn appeared in eleven novels, including *The White Crow* (1928), *The Link* (1930), *Murder Gone Mad* (1931), *R.I.P.* (1933) and *The Nursemaid Who Disappeared* (1938). A second detective, Dr. Alcazar, appeared in 'The Green-and-Gold String' (1948) and two other short stories. MacDonald also wrote under the pseudonyms of Oliver Fleming, Anthony Lawless

A. Phillips (✉)
Open University Wales, Cardiff, UK

© The Author(s) 2020
E. Miskimmin (ed.), *100 British Crime Writers*, Crime Files,
https://doi.org/10.1057/978-1-137-31902-9_29

133

and Martin Porlock, with the majority of these novels published under the name of Porlock including *Mystery at Friar's Pardon* (1931), *Mystery at Kensington Gore* (1932) and *X. v. Rex* (1933).

Although MacDonald was considered a significant author in the 1920s and 30s, his novels and short stories are not widely studied today and critics are divided in their opinions of his work. On one hand A. E. Murch praises Macdonald as a writer, particularly how he finds 'ways of imparting information with scrupulous fairness in the midst of action and excitement'. On the other hand, Julian Symons is less effusive, describing MacDonald as a light-hearted 'farceur' and a 'restless but careless experimenter'. This experimentation is evident in *Murder Gone Mad* (1931) where MacDonald went beyond the traditional whodunit formulae to which his contemporaries subscribed by focusing instead on *how* to catch a mass murderer who informs the police prior to each crime. In the 1940s and 50s he concentrated on films rather than fiction but brought out another Gethryn mystery in 1959: *The List of Adrian Messenger*. He also wrote a number of short stories in this period, which are considered to be his best work. MacDonald published two collections: *The Man Out of the Rain and Other Stories* (1955) and *Death and Chicanery* (1962). His most successful collection, however, was *Something to Hide* (1952), for which he won the Edgar Allan Poe award from the Mystery Writers of America and was subsequently published in the UK as *Fingers of Fear* (1953).

Suggested Reading/Works Cited

Murch, A. E., *The Development of the Detective Novel*, rev. edn (London: Peter Owen, 1968).

Symons, Julian, *Bloody Murder: From the Detective Story to the Crime Novel*, 3rd edn (New York: Mysterious Press, 1993).

CHAPTER 30

Anthony Berkeley (Also Wrote as Frances Iles and A. Monmouth Platts, 1893–1971), 1925: *The Layton Court Mystery*

Christine R. Simpson

To his contemporaries, Anthony Berkeley Cox was rather a mystery. He was the son of a Hertfordshire doctor, born in Watford and educated at Sherborne School and University College, London. During World War One he served in the army and for the rest of his life he suffered from the effects of being gassed. After the war, his writing career began with journalism, with contributions to *Punch* and *The Humorist*, using the sense of humour that would enliven his novels. Berkeley dropped his surname when writing fiction featuring his amateur detective, Roger Sheringham. He wrote his psychological crime novels using the pseudonym Francis Iles, the name of one of his mother's ancestors, and for one early novel wrote as A. Monmouth Platts. *The Layton Court Mystery* (1925) appeared anonymously, as did *The Wychford Poisoning Case* (1926).

Although following the puzzle pattern of the Golden Age mystery writers of the 1920s, *The Layton Court Mystery* was not entirely formulaic. In an introductory letter to his father, Berkeley states that he 'cannot

C. R. Simpson (✉)
The Dorothy L. Sayers Society, Essex, UK

© The Author(s) 2020
E. Miskimmin (ed.), *100 British Crime Writers*, Crime Files,
https://doi.org/10.1057/978-1-137-31902-9_30

see why even a detective story should not aim at the creation of a natural atmosphere, just as any other work of lighter fiction'. He believed that a fictional detective should be as fallible as any other human and that the reader must be given every scrap of evidence (a theory adopted as a rule by the Detection Club). Roger Sheringham, the series detective, is at first portrayed as offensive and conceited, but mellows in the course of the novels and is often incorrect in his deductions. In his first appearance, he is dealing with a 'locked-room' mystery in a country house, a typical Golden Age setting. The host is found dead in his study, and Sheringham works out a logical explanation of what has happened. When travelling home he realises that he is wrong, and identifies the correct guilty party. Because he decides (as in some other cases) that justice will not be served by naming the murderer, who does not deserve to die, he keeps his conclusion from the police, although Sheringham says that the police inspector 'is no fool', unlike those in 'story books'. Similar references to the genre, typical of Berkeley's humour and gentle satire, appear in most of the novels.

In *The Wychford Poisoning Case* (1926), Berkeley refers to psychology as an element of detection, a theme he was to explore in-depth as Francis Iles. The plot of this second Sheringham novel concerns arsenic poisoning, and bears similarities to a real-life murder: the case of Florence Maybrick who was found guilty of poisoning her husband. Berkeley offers several ingenious solutions to his fictitious crime. His interest in true crime is also demonstrated in his contributions on Crippen, and the murder of 'Madame X' in *Great Unsolved Murders* (1935) and on the Rattenbury Case in *The Anatomy of Murder* (1936). Sheringham expresses again the author's views about psychology in *Roger Sheringham and the Vane Mystery* (1927; US: *The Mystery at Lovers' Cave*), when he says, 'every detective must be a psychologist, whether he knows it or not'. This may not be true of Inspector Moresby of Scotland Yard, who first appears in this novel. Working with Sheringham on a number of cases, his methods prove more successful on several occasions, as in the complex plot of *The Silk Stocking Murders* (1928). Sheringham's judgement is clouded by personal involvement with suspects, unlike Moresby, who identifies the murderer of several young women who have been hanged with their own stockings. This book was followed by the best of the Sheringham novels, *The Poisoned Chocolates Case* (1929), which was an expanded version of an excellent short story 'The Avenging Chance' (first published in *Pearson's Magazine*, 1929), in which the murder method is one of Berkeley's cleverest contrivances. In the novel, the problem is investigated by members of the Crimes Club (based on the real Detection Club), including Sheringham and Mr. Ambrose Chitterwick, who produce the correct solution.

After *The Poisoned Chocolates Case*, Mr. Chitterwick is involved in two more murders. He is quite different in character and habits from the man-about-town Sheringham, being a fussy bachelor, under the thumb of a domineering maiden aunt. In *The Piccadilly Murder* (1929) he sees, by chance, a murder committed while he is having tea in an unfashionable Piccadilly hotel. This leads him into adventure and investigation, and the final correct solution of the crime, which has eluded Inspector Moresby. The plot is clever, with many clues and twists, but the opening is too slow and there is too much emphasis on Mr. Chitterwick's bumbling. He makes his final, much briefer, appearance in *Trial and Error* (1937), which has a more unusual plot. In this, a man with a fatal medical condition decides to commit a murder before he dies to rid the world of someone who is thoroughly despicable. This he does, and enlists Mr. Chitterwick's help to prove that he is guilty when the police do not believe his confession. The book ends with one of Berkeley's best twists. Of the five remaining Sheringham novels, *The Second Shot* (1931) is most memorable for its preface on the future of the detective novel, which states that 'the puzzle element will no doubt remain but it will become a puzzle of character rather than [...] of time, place, motive and opportunity'. In *Top Storey Murder* (1931) and *Murder in the Basement* (1932), both of which have surprise endings, police investigations at murder scenes are described in realistic detail, an approach neglected in most detective fiction at that time. The final book in which he appears, *Panic Party* (1934; US: *Mr. Pidgeon's Island*), has one of the weakest plots.

In the first novel written as Francis Iles, the author puts into practice his theories on a psychological approach to crime fiction. The puzzle formula is abandoned. From the opening ironic sentence of *Malice Aforethought* (1931), the murderer's name is known. The plot holds the reader's interest by concentrating on his mental processes, his methods of committing his crimes and whether he will escape detection. The ending is masterly. *Before the Fact* (1932), followed. In this, it is a victim whose mind is explored. The interest of the plot lies in whether a besotted women, who knows that her husband is a murderer, will remain with him until he kills her. Suspense builds as she fears the approach of her own death. The outcome is not explicit. The third Iles title, *As for the*

Woman, is less satisfactory. The situation, in which a woman urges her lover to murder her husband, is approached with originality, but the characters are unappealing. It was published in 1939, in the same year as the last Berkeley novel, *Death in the House*. Set in the House of Commons, its use of suspense is good, as is the denouement. After 1939, the author published no more novels. From the 1930s, as Francis Iles, he wrote reviews of crime fiction for a number of newspapers, including *The Daily Telegraph*, *The Manchester Guardian* (later *The Guardian*) and *The Observer*.

Despite his natural reserve, it was Berkeley who, in 1928, suggested the creation of the Detection Club. Dorothy L. Sayers and others took up the idea enthusiastically. She described the club as '... a private association of writers of detective fiction in Great Britain, existing chiefly for the purpose of eating dinners together [...] and of talking illimitable shop [... with] no object but to amuse itself'. To raise funds, collaborative works were produced by members, Berkeley included. All his contributions to Club publications demonstrate his accomplishments as a writer: the ability to tell an intriguing story, imaginative plots with surprising twists, well-drawn characters, and a good writing style enlivened with humour and irony. For his introduction of the psychological approach to crime fiction, he has earned his place in the history of the genre as one of its greatest innovators.

SUGGESTED READING/WORKS CITED

Edwards, Martin, 'Anthony Berkeley.' http://www.martinedwardsbooks.com/berkeley.htm.

Turnbull, Malcolm J., *Elusion Aforethought: The Life and Writing of Anthony Berkeley Cox* (Bowling Green, OH: Bowling Green University Popular Press, 1996).

CHAPTER 31

Margery Allingham (1904–1966), 1928: *The White Cottage Mystery* Serialised in the *Daily Express* Newspaper

Jasmine Simeone

Margery Allingham is best known as the writer of the stories featuring Albert Campion, her upper-class detective, but her oeuvre includes some lesser-known juvenilia (mostly plays), as well as articles and book reviews published in national and local newspapers and journals, including *Time and Tide*. She also wrote three novels under the pseudonym Maxwell March.

Margery Louise Allingham was the eldest child of Emily (Em) and Herbert Allingham. Her parents, first cousins, have been described as 'idiosyncratically religious'. Herbert was thirty-five and Em twenty-three when they married and accounts of the marriage suggest that it did not seem to have been an especially happy one. Allingham had a close relationship with her father, but Emily seems not to have been the most natural of mothers and frequently relied on the children's maternal grandmother to take care of them. Em worked as a jobbing writer of fiction for women's magazines. Herbert initially edited the journal *The Christian*

J. Simeone (✉)
The Dorothy L. Sayers Society, Essex, UK

© The Author(s) 2020
E. Miskimmin (ed.), *100 British Crime Writers*, Crime Files,
https://doi.org/10.1057/978-1-137-31902-9_31

Globe, owned by his father, and he ran *The London Journal*, but he later gave up both for freelance story writing for children and adults enabling a move into the countryside of Essex when Allingham was five, her brother Philip was a baby and sister Joyce as yet unborn.

Allingham was initially educated at home. She delighted in persuading the family to dress up and take part in play-acting of various kinds; she also found great solace in the garden of the rented Old Rectory at Layer Bretton. It was rather a lonely childhood in which the traditional Edwardian separation between parents and children was emphasised by the shortage of other young people to whom Allingham could relate. Consequently, she was thrown more and more into her writing, in which she was encouraged by the family, and had her first story published when she was eight years old in a magazine edited by her aunt, Maud. Allingham also edited a family magazine called *The Wag-Tale* and is known to have written stories and articles continually throughout her childhood. At twelve years old she began school in Colchester, which she attended for most of World War One. She was then sent as a boarder to the Perse School in Cambridge in January 1919, where she wrote, produced and performed in a costume play, perhaps foreshadowing the 'dramatic' presences in her later detective fiction. However, she had problems all of her life with serious academia, and could not cope with people who seemed too 'headmistressy', including Dorothy L. Sayers, who invited her to join the Detection Club.

From 1921 to 1923, Allingham attended Regent Street Polytechnic, London, where she studied, with her father's assistance and approval, Speech and Drama. It is interesting to note that at this point she had ambitions of performing centre stage, whereas in later life she became retiring and found it difficult to face public speaking. However in her late teens and early twenties, she was lively, vivacious and self-confident, throwing herself into her studies, practising elocution in order to lose her stutter, writing and performing in her verse-play *Dido and Aeneas*, and in several smaller works and monologues with her fellow students. It was here that she renewed her acquaintance with her future husband Philip (Pip) Youngman Carter, fine artist and illustrator, who first assisted her with the scenery for *Dido*. He was the son of a woman for whom Allingham's father had an unfulfilled passion some years before, and though at first they believed that they (like Allingham's parents) were cousins, in fact they were not related by blood.

In 1921 when Allingham was seventeen years old, the family spent one of a number of holidays on the island of Mersea in the Thames Estuary, off the Essex coast. As a family they were all interested in the unusual and sometimes the occult (her brother Philip eventually became a cheapjack and astrologer, and expert in the circus and the language of circus folk). On these holidays the Allingham family frequently found themselves the victims of poor summer weather, and limited opportunities for entertainment outside the home, unlike in London. Allingham expressed some interest in local legends, and her first novel, *Blackkerchief Dick: A Tale of Mersea Island* (1923), grew out of this fascination and a particularly revealing session with an Ouija board on one such holiday.

Whatever the origins of this story, and whether it was pure imagination or a concoction of local legends, there is no doubt that for a first novel produced by a teenage writer, it has its merits, although the plot does not have the finesse of later works by Allingham. There are similarities to Baring Gould's *Mehalah* (1880), set on the same island, and it owes much to her teenage passion for Shakespearean language and the strangely compulsive atmosphere of bleak Mersea. In later years she was embarrassed by its presence in her lists, but it has a freshness and vibrancy that foreshadows the adult writer of the Golden Age. A lack of support, especially in the matter of appropriate editing, rather left Allingham exposed to public criticism and ridicule concerning this book, and may have contributed to her developing feelings of inadequacy.

Allingham ultimately failed her LRAM diploma at the Regent Street Polytechnic and returned home in the summer of 1923 knowing that with money worries at home again there was pressure on her to join the family writing 'firm' to play her part in raising the family fortunes. There were some false starts: a playlet with Donald Ford, which should have been the libretto for an opera and which did not succeed, and a book, *Green Corn*, based on her school days at the Perse which was not well enough received even to be published. Eventually, however, her novel, *The White Cottage Mystery* (1928) was ready for serialisation in *The Daily Express*. In the same period she announced her engagement to Pip. This was a surprise as she had not hitherto been very complimentary about him, but was a move born of the exigencies of the time; romance does not seem to have been of great importance in this relationship. However, just as her father had been an influence and support for Allingham in the writing of her first published works, Pip was invaluable in supporting her writing of the next major novel *The Crime at Black Dudley* (1929).

Allingham had arguably not yet found her stride with this novel. It has certain flaws, including a slight datedness especially in the use of humour appropriate to the world of the 1920s. However what it does do, which became of utmost importance, is provide the reader with an introduction to the character professionally known as Albert Campion. Much has been written on the subject of Allingham's use of the 'lunatic, silly ass, upper class' detective. In this novel, the first of some eighteen works with Campion as the focal point, he was intended to be a minor and somewhat supercilious character, but proved such a success with the publishers that more of the same was requested; Allingham had found her stock, serial detective. Among the best of the books featuring this detective are *Look to the Lady* (1931), *Police at the Funeral* (1931), *Flowers for the Judge* (1936), *Dancers in Mourning* (1937), *More Work for the Undertaker* (1948) and *A Cargo of Eagles* (1968).

Allingham's handling of the material in her Campion novels is careful and often clever. We are given a rounded and intriguing character in Albert Campion; small dark hints about his background and true identity are allowed to slip out to the reader in each novel, though we are never told the whole story, and when asked directly Allingham was inclined to tease the enquirer by making improbable suggestions. We are sometimes introduced to other members of his family: Valentine, his sister, in *The Fashion in Shrouds* (1938) and his brother, Herbert, in *Mystery Mile* (1930). Campion is funny and witty, loyal to his friends and perspicacious in the solving of crimes; just, in fact, as one would satisfyingly expect a Golden Age detective to be. Some of her novels, such as *The Case of the Late Pig* (1937) and *The Tiger in the Smoke* (1952), verge on the surreal in places, perhaps creating a tension between a more 'literary' style and the popular genre she is writing in, but certainly making her work stand out among many of her Golden Age contemporaries in terms of its quality. Additionally, Allingham's plots are well worked, and her characters are well-drawn.

The Tiger in the Smoke is among several of her works that reveal her deep and abiding love of London with all its quirks, and which she treats as a character in its own right throughout many of the novels. *The Fashion in Shrouds* makes use of the settings of the fashionable worlds of London theatre and haute couture, and *The Tiger in the Smoke* evokes the seedier back streets and the customary smoggy atmosphere of the immediate post-war city. She seems able to capture the essence of a place in just a few lines or a well-chosen paragraph.

Some of her characters are drawn from local life: the character of Mike Barnabas in *Flowers for the Judge*, for example, was probably drawn from a friend Leslie Cresswell ('Cressie') with whom she would sit out at dances and the more exuberant parties, which Pip sometimes persuaded her to attend and which she found very difficult. Even Allingham's minor characters are universally well-drawn and expressed with insight; they are rarely of the 'cardboard cut-out' type so beloved of some of her contemporaries. Aside from Campion, however, there is no doubt that Allingham was most fond and proud of her creation of the somewhat unlikely manservant Magersfontein Lugg, a former cat-burglar now grown too large for that career who makes a perfect counterpoint to the apparently effete Campion.

Allingham's work is usually set in London or East Anglia and although she makes reference to wartime in *Traitor's Purse* (1941) and *Coroner's Pidgin* (1945), and many of her works have a flavour of the period she is writing, she is arguably at her best when she writes of a more nebulous time when nasty events could be dealt with in comforting order, with satisfactory results achieved, loose ends tied up neatly and all against the backdrop of the great city, the theatre or the traditional country house. Her best account of World War Two is to be found in *The Oaken Heart* (1941; republished 2011), which is a non-fiction account of life in the village of Tolleshunt D'Arcy where she lived most of her adult life.

Allingham's life continued to be fraught with money worries after she was married. Pip's work as an illustrator was occasionally lucrative, but frequently he depended on her writing income to keep him and their friend Alan Joseph Gregory ('Grog') in the manner to which they wished to become accustomed. 'Grog' once 'came for tea and stayed' and Pip enjoyed a lively and exciting social life which seems to have included not a few marital infidelities. Allingham usually managed to turn a blind eye in public to these peccadilloes, but was somewhat scathing in her diaries. The shyness which Allingham had managed to overcome while at the Regent Street Polytechnic returned in paralysing force as she grew older and her dread of speaking in public never really left her. Instead she continued, through sickness and in health, to do what she did best: write.

Over the course of her life, Allingham wrote in a wide variety of genres including short stories (several collections of stories which were published posthumously), short articles and reviews for newspapers and magazines, the well-known Campion books, three Maxwell March books which are lurid thrillers, and non-fiction work such as *The Oaken Heart*. Her novels were published regularly and almost annually from *Blackkerchief Dick* in 1923 to another novel focusing on extra-sensory perception, set in a Cold War world, *The Mind Readers* (1965). Though this work now seems somewhat dated, especially in its scientific aspects, it is an indication of the way in which her work developed inexorably from the somewhat hesitant beginnings of the fledgling author before World War Two, determined to write the detective novel which more or less follows rules of clarity and order, to that of an assured and fearless post-war author writing in the same world which produced John le Carré. In her later works, she handles material with an assurance and enthusiasm. As a result her books are mostly still extremely readable nearly fifty years after her death, most are reprinted and many have not been out of print. Several have been adapted for film and radio, including a 1956 version of *Tiger in the Smoke*, starring Donald Sinden and Tony Wright (which was perhaps most notable for its omission of the character of Campion) and the BBC series 'Campion' (1988-1990) with Peter Davidson in the title role.

Allingham only outlived her mother Em by a matter of seven years. Throughout her life, she had supported her mother, husband and other family and friends as the need arose, and she was known as an inspiration and a life-enhancing friend to many people. As she grew older, she was beset by various illnesses and died of heart failure following two strokes in the summer of 1966. Pip lived for a further three years, and after completing her last book *A Cargo of Eagles* he wrote two further Campion books himself (*Mr. Campion's Farthing*, 1969, and *Mr. Campion's Falcon*, 1970). He died in 1969 leaving a further book of his own unfinished.

In her later years, Allingham expressed fears that her life would soon be forgotten and would count for nothing. There were no children of her marriage and neither her brother nor her sister had offspring. There may be no bloodlines in the human sense, but there is no doubt that her literary 'children' live on, and far from showing signs of fading, her reputation as a Golden Age detective story writer is as strong as ever.

Suggested Reading/Works Cited

Jones, Julia, '"A Fine, Sturdy Piece of Work": Margery Allingham's Book Reviews for Time and Tide', *Clues: A Journal of Detection*, 23:1 (2003), 9-18.

———, *The Adventures of Margery Allingham* (Chelmsford: Golden Duck Publishing, 2009).

Rowland, Susan, *From Agatha Christie to Ruth Rendell: British Women Writers in Detective and Crime Fiction* (Basingstoke: Palgrave Macmillan, 2001).
The Official Margery Allingham Website. http://www.margeryallingham.org.uk.
van Hoeven, Marianne, ed., *Margery Allingham: 100 Years of a Great Mystery Writer* (Thornden: Lucas, 2004).

CHAPTER 32

Graham Greene (1904–1991), 1929: *The Man Within*

Steven Powell

Although best remembered as a novelist, Henry Graham Greene was also a short story writer, playwright, screenwriter and journalist. Greene was a frequent traveller, and the settings of his novels include exotic locations such as South America, Africa and South-East Asia. Greene's novels such as *The Power and the Glory* (1940) set in Mexico, and *The Quiet American* (1955) set in Indochina now Vietnam, are noted for evoking the essence of a country, rather than communicating exact geographical descriptions. The atmospheric details in Greene's novels, including scrub and swamps, huts made of mud or tin, haggard-looking diplomats drinking pink gin and a general populace oppressed by dictators and tyrants, have been described by some critics as 'Greeneland'.

Henry Graham Greene was born in Berkhamsted, Hampshire to Charles Henry Greene and Marion Raymond Greene. His father was the headmaster of Berkhamsted School, where Greene was forced to board as a child and was subjected to severe bullying on account of being the headmaster's son. Greene attempted suicide several times at school, and in 1920 he was sent to the care of the Catholic psychiatrist Kenneth

S. Powell (✉)
University of Liverpool, Liverpool, UK

Richmond and underwent psychoanalysis. It was during this time that Greene developed a lifelong fascination with dreams and began a journal of his dreams, which were later transferred to his novels such as *A Burnt-Out Case* (1960). Greene attended Balliol College, Oxford, where his depression, fuelled by boredom (one of the main curses of his life), was counteracted by heavy drinking and playing Russian roulette with one bullet in a chamber that held six. Greene later put two bullets in the chamber to heighten the risk.

When he was fourteen, Greene read *The Viper of Milan* (1906) by Marjorie Bowen. Although he was extremely well-read, this was the book he credited with inspiring him to write. During his studies at Oxford, Greene wrote poems, stories, articles and reviews which were published in the student magazine *Oxford Outlook* and *Westminster Weekly Gazette*. His first book was a collection of verse, *Babbling April* (1925). In 1926, Greene was an unpaid writer for the *Nottingham Journal* and a salaried sub-editor for the *Times*. Greene was also a film critic for *The Spectator* and co-edited the magazine *Night and Day*, the latter of which folded in 1937 after a lawsuit from Twentieth Century Fox. Fox claimed they had been libelled by Greene in his criticism of the sexualisation of the child star Shirley Temple in his review of the film *Wee Willie Winkie* (1937). Most of Greene's novels would be adapted into films with Greene writing several screenplays himself. Greene also wrote the screenplay for one of the most famous British film noirs, *The Third Man* (1949). Greene married the devout Roman Catholic Vivien Dayrell-Browning in 1927. Greene converted to Catholicism in order to marry Vivien. Their union was not a happy one, and although they had two children together, they were separated for most of their lives as divorce was out of the question. In his lifetime, Greene had many affairs with married women and also frequented brothels.

Greene's first novel was the moderately successful thriller *The Man Within* (1929). This was followed by *The Name of Action* (1930) and *Rumour at Nightfall* (1932), which were not critically or commercially successful and Greene later suppressed their republication. Greene's first major trip abroad came when he travelled to West Africa and walked across Liberia without the benefit of a map, sleeping in seedy, rat-infested huts. His account of this trip was published in *Journey Without Maps* (1936). Greene travelled to Mexico in 1937 to investigate the religious persecution in Tabasco and Chiapas under the anti-Catholic administration of Tomas Garrido Canabal. He wrote of his experiences of this trip in *The Lawless Roads* (1939). Greene spent time in Mexico with underground churches hiding from Canabal's paramilitary organisation the Red Shirts. It was the first time that he felt a genuine spiritual connection to his Catholic faith since his conversion in 1926. After a series of successful novels, Greene became critically identified as a Catholic novelist with the publication of *Brighton Rock* in 1938. In the novel, the sociopathic teenage gangster Pinkie Brown marries a young Catholic girl in order to ensure her silence over a crime he has committed. Although Pinkie appears to be an evil character who deserves damnation, there remains a glimmer of hope that he attains salvation due to 'the appalling strangeness of the mercy of God'.

Greene challenged traditional Roman Catholic doctrines such as the existence of Hell. Greene's 'Catholic' novels are generally regarded as *Brighton Rock*, *The Power and the Glory* (1940), *The Heart of the Matter* (1948) and *The End of the Affair* (1951). Greene based *The End of the Affair* on his relationship with Catherine Walston, the wife of Henry Walston, then one of the richest men in Britain and a Labour MP. The story concerns an up and coming writer Maurice Bendrix who begins an affair with a married woman Sarah. When Sarah breaks off the relationship suddenly, Bendrix hires a private detective to find out why and later discovers that Sarah had made a promise to God that she would not see Bendrix again if He allowed Bendrix to live after a near-death experience. The narrative can be read as an immensely complex theological detective story in which God leaves a series of clues, which lead Bendrix to discover His existence, only for Bendrix to denounce Him and reject salvation in the denouement. Throughout his career, Greene labelled several of his novels as 'Entertainments', among them being his early thrillers *Stamboul Train* (1932) and *The Confidential Agent* (1939), and his witty satire on the spy genre *Our Man in Havana* (1958). Greene had direct experience of the world of espionage as he was recruited by MI6 during World War Two and was stationed in Freetown, Sierra Leone.

Greene joined the Communist party for four weeks in 1925. He later joined the Independent Labour party, but he preferred the freedom and ambiguity of not belonging to a political party, although his views can be categorised as broadly leftist. During his time with the Intelligence services, Greene developed a lifelong friendship with the British spy Kim Philby. When Philby was unmasked as a double agent and defected to the Soviet Union, Greene never lost his admiration for his friend. He began a novel titled *A Sense of Security*, which was to be partially based on Philby, with British Intelligence portrayed in an unsympathetic light. He never completed the book in that form. Returning to it years later in *The Human Factor* (1978) the lead character is an ageing intelligence officer who betrays his country for the woman he loves, a black South African. Greene developed a lifelong antipathy towards the United States: his novel *The Quiet American* (1955) concerns France's disastrous war in Indochina in the 1950s and is a prophetic warning to America that it should not become involved in the politics of the region.

Greene interviewed the Vietnamese President Ho Chi Minh, but was so nervous that he experimented with opium and turned up to the meeting stoned. Greene was also a friend and admirer of Fidel Castro, having met Castro and his band of guerrillas in the Cuban mountains before the revolution. Greene travelled to Haiti, which formed the basis of *The Comedians* (1966), a thinly veiled criticism of the brutal regime of Francois 'Papa Doc' Duvalier. Duvalier was so angered at the portrayal that he denounced Greene in a book, which he had published at his own expense. Greene turned down the opportunity to go on a promotional tour in the United States for his novel *The Honorary Consul* (1973) and instead travelled to South Africa to lend his support to anti-apartheid activists. Greene later befriended the Panamanian President General Omar Torrijos, which he related in the book, *Getting to Know the General* (1984). While visiting President Salvador Allende of Chile, Greene was believed to be under CIA surveillance. In the 1950s Greene's visa to visit the United States had been delayed under the McCarren act, due to his past membership of the Communist party. In later life, Greene moved to a small apartment in Antibes on the French Riviera. In 1982 Greene wrote the pamphlet, *J'Accuse: The Dark Side of Nice*, about organised crime in the region. As a consequence, he received death threats and he returned his Légion D'Honneur. He received very little peace in Antibes and found it difficult to sleep because of the noisy partygoers and constant stream of tourists. He would sometimes sit on his balcony and fire a water pistol at passers-by out of his extreme frustration. Greene died in Switzerland on 3 April 1991.

SUGGESTED READING/WORKS CITED

Donaghy, Henry J., *Conversations with Graham Greene* (Jackson: University of Mississippi, 1992).

Sherry, Norman, *The Life of Graham Greene: Volume One 1904–1939* (London: Viking Adult, 1989).
——, *The Life of Graham Greene: Volume Two 1939–1955* (London: Viking Adult, 1995).
——, *The Life of Graham Greene: Volume Three 1956–1991* (London: Penguin, 2004).

Gladys Mitchell (Also Write as Stephen Hickaby and Malcolm Torrie, 1901–1983), 1929: *Speedy Death*

Christine R. Simpson

Gladys Maude Winifred Mitchell was born in Cowley, Oxfordshire. During her childhood, her family moved to London, and then to Hampshire. Her father, James Mitchell, was Scottish, inspiring his daughter's later interest in his native country. He came from a poor family and had to work from an early age, so was determined that his children should benefit from a good education. From a village school, Mitchell moved to the Green School, Isleworth, then on to Goldsmith's College (University of London) where she obtained a teacher's certificate in 1921. Thereafter, she spent almost all of her working life teaching in secondary schools in Middlesex and London. She continued studying at the University of London Extra-Mural Department until she was awarded a diploma in English and European history. Her wide reading in many subjects is clearly demonstrated in her books through their backgrounds, settings and references. During her vacations she travelled widely, gathering material for books, such as *Lament for Leto* (1971), set in Greece.

C. R. Simpson (✉)
The Dorothy L. Sayers Society, Essex, UK

Mitchell is best known for sixty-six crime novels featuring her eccentric amateur detective, Mrs. (later Dame) Beatrice Adela Lestrange Bradley. She also wrote numerous short stories and some children's fiction. As Stephen Hockaby she produced five novels, and, using the pseudonym Malcolm Torrie, wrote a short series involving the detective Timothy Herring. Her first novel, *Speedy Death* (1929), placed its author firmly among the best of the Golden Age writers of detective fiction. It also demonstrates her independent, innovative style and wit, separating her work from that of more humdrum contributors to the genre. Following a well-tried pattern, the setting is a house party with a closed community of guests, but the first murder victim is far from conventional. The body of a famous male explorer turns out to be that of a woman, which creates a unique motive for her death. Mrs. Bradley makes her first appearance as one of the guests, becoming the series detective instead of the young man originally intended to fill that role. She herself is tried for a second murder and acquitted after being defended by her son, Ferdinand Lestrange, QC. Afterwards she admits her guilt, but feels the crime was justified. As in other novels, she is uninhibited by moral scruples and has ignored the forces of law and order to act as judge and jury, and, in this case, executioner.

Adela Lestrange Bradley is well qualified to investigate crime, being a trained psychoanalyst. As consultant for the Home Office she is officially involved in many cases. From her first appearance she looks old and is no beauty, frequently described as 'saurian' in appearance. Mitchell leaves the reader guessing about her age – she says that 'she might have been thirty-five ... or ... ninety' (*The Mystery of a Butcher's Shop*, 1929). She is quite different, especially with her powerful intellect, from other women detectives such as Miss Marple and Miss Silver and although, like them, she knits, her creations are amorphous garments. Her dress sense, particularly in choice of colours, is atrocious. Although appearing old and frail, she is extremely strong (perhaps due to her indulgence in hearty meals of all kinds). Her brain is keen and she is almost omniscient. During her career, she is helped by various sidekicks. Her first Watson is a rather feeble curate who narrates the story of *The Saltmarsh Murders* (1933), a chilling portrait of village feuds and hatred. He soon disappears, to be replaced later by the feisty Laura, whom Mrs. Bradley first encounters as an Amazonian student in *Laurels Are Poison* (1942). She devotes herself to her employer and detection, often at the expense of her husband, the policeman Robert Gavin, and their two children. Relatives of Mrs. Bradley appear in various roles, assisting her investigations, even if only by providing accommodation for those involved. It seems that the formidable Dame married three times, but it is not clear how many sons she has: sometimes two, sometimes three, are mentioned. Apart from Ferdinand Lestrange, her first and favourite, she says she prefers nephews to sons.

The Mystery of a Butcher's Shop, closely following *Speedy Death*, contains more indications of Mitchell's originality, with multiple motives, a macabre method of disposal of the body, and twists in the plot to bemuse the reader, including the final display of Mrs. Bradley's omniscience. The victim's skull, separate from the other body parts, is at first thought to be an archaeological relic. The head is reconstructed, an innovation in detective fiction. This technique was in its infancy, and little used in criminal investigations at the time. Mrs. Bradley gets the better of the unfortunate police officers she encounters in this complicated case. Like those in other plots, they rarely stand a chance of outwitting her.

Inevitably, with Mitchell's prolific output, producing almost one book a year until she died, not all of her works attain the high standard of her best. Some of the most successful have academic backgrounds, like the author's own favourite, *Laurels are Poison* (1942), and include *St Peter's Finger* (1938), and *Tom Brown's Body* (1949). Scenes in school classrooms and staffrooms are realistic, being based on the author's own experience. That she was interested in the latest educational theories is demonstrated by the attitude of the headmaster of the co-educational school in *Death at the Opera* (1934, US: *Death in the Wet*). His ideas on teaching and discipline are based on those of A. S. Neill, an educational pioneer in the 1920s. His relaxed approach is somewhat shaken when an unpopular mistress is murdered by drowning in a washbasin during the course of the school production of *The Mikado*. Motives and suspects abound and the denouement, when the true murderer and motive are revealed, breaks the fair play rules of most contemporary detective fiction.

During her years of teaching, Mitchell developed a sympathetic rapport with children, admirably portrayed in characters like the narrator of *The Rising of the Moon* (1945). Seen through the eyes of the child, this is one of the most powerfully atmospheric of the plots, with echoes of Jack the Ripper and a particularly gruesome method of disposal of a body. Unlike most other Golden Age writers, Mitchell did not shrink from macabre details in her plots. In *Printer's Error* (1939), various body parts turn up in a printer's workshop. *Come Away Death* (1937) includes a box of snakes in which a head has been placed. Other plots reflect the author's wide interests, among them unnatural phenomena and witchcraft: *The Devil at Saxon Wall* (1935), *When Last I Died* (1941); play productions: *Death at the Opera*; archaeological monuments: *The Whispering Knights* (1980); Scotland: *Cold, Lone and Still* (1983); folklore: *A Hearse on Mayday* (1972); and athletics and sports: *A Javelin for Jonah* (1974), *The Longer Bodies* (1930). Her delight in and wide knowledge of literature of many kinds is shown throughout her writings.

In 1933, Mitchell was accepted as a member of the Detection Club, an indication that she was well regarded by distinguished authors of detective fiction. She was sponsored by Anthony Berkeley and Helen Simpson and initiated into the club by G. K. Chesterton. That she was enthusiastic about it is evident from a piece called 'The Golden Age' that she wrote as introduction to the *Post Mortem Books Catalogue of Crime* (1981), and an unpublished letter written to a relative. In these she describes club meetings and rituals, and lists many of the authors who were members. She contributed to two of the club's joint publications: *Ask a Policeman* (1933), in which she and Helen Simpson swapped detectives (Saumarez and Bradley) to write their respective chapters, and *No Flowers by Request* (1984). It is a pity that, despite the high quality of her imaginative plots and settings and the skilled writing of her best books, she is less well-remembered than other authors of the Golden Age, most of whom she outlived. For the poet Philip Larkin, an enthusiastic admirer of her blend of eccentricity and common sense, she was 'the great Gladys'.

Suggested Reading/Works Cited

Fowler, Christopher, 'Forgotten Authors No. 10: Gladys Mitchell', *The Independent*, 19 October 2008. http://www.independent.co.uk/arts-entertainment/books/features/forgotten-authors-no-10-gladys-mitchell-963946.html.
Fuller, Nick, 'Gladys Mitchell: The 1930s', *CADS*, 46, 33–39.
———, 'Gladys Mitchell: 1940–1944', *CADS*, 46, 27–29.
Pike, B. A., 'In Praise of Gladys Mitchell', *Armchair Detective: A Quarterly Journal Devoted to the Appreciation of Mystery, Detective, and Suspense Fiction*, 9:4 (1976), 250–260.
———, 'Pen Profiles, 36: Malcolm Torrie [Pseud]—Detective: Timothy Herring', *CADS*, 47, 42–44.
The Stone House: A Gladys Mitchell Tribute Site. www.gladysmitchell.com.

CHAPTER 34

Josephine Tey (Pseudonym of Elizabeth Mackintosh, Also Wrote as Gordon Daviot, 1896–1952), 1929: *The Man in the Queue* (Writing as Gordon Daviot)

Christine R. Simpson

Born in Inverness, Elizabeth Mackintosh achieved much in a sadly curtailed life. On leaving school she chose to train as a remedial gymnast at a college of physical education rather than accept a university place. In World War One she joined the V. A. D., and suffered the loss of the man she loved at the Battle of the Somme. In 1923, she had settled happily in Kent, teaching at a High School, when another death changed her life completely as she returned to Scotland to nurse her dying mother, afterwards remaining to housekeep for her father. It was then that she began to write. Her first published work, the detective novel *The Man in the Queue* (1929) was written for a competition sponsored by Methuen Publishers. She adopted the pseudonym Gordon Daviot for this and several other non-detective novels (all subsequent detective fiction was published under the name Josephine Tey), but it was for her dramatic works that the name

C. R. Simpson (✉)
The Dorothy L. Sayers Society, Essex, UK

© The Author(s) 2020
E. Miskimmin (ed.), *100 British Crime Writers*, Crime Files,
https://doi.org/10.1057/978-1-137-31902-9_34

157

Daviot brought her the most acclaim; *Richard of Bordeaux* (1933) was an instant, and her greatest, success. Many more plays followed before she returned to writing crime fiction.

The Man in the Queue is a police murder investigation in the classic style of the Golden Age. The book introduces Inspector Alan Grant of Scotland Yard, who appears in five of the author's subsequent seven detective novels. Only the first and second plots, *The Man in the Queue*, and *A Shilling for Candles* (1936) follow the conventional pattern, with deaths, respectively, by stabbing and drowning. Two of Grant's later investigations begin when he is not on duty, and only the first takes place wholly in London. He is called into assist a county police force with an alleged case of kidnapping, in *The Franchise Affair* (1948), in which he takes little part; a local solicitor actually solves the mystery. In a plot with an extraordinary denouement, *To Love and Be Wise* (1950), he becomes involved in the disappearance, and possible murder, of a famous photographer. The investigation of his final, unofficial, case provides therapy when he is recovering from stress in the Scottish Highlands (*The Singing Sands*, published posthumously, 1953). The earlier novel, *The Daughter of Time* (1951), details Grant proving, while bored in hospital, that Richard III was not the murderer of the Princes in the Tower.

Aside from the Grant novels, *Miss Pym Disposes* (1946) has an amateur detective playing judge and jury, when she realises that the 'accidental' death of a student is actually murder, and *Brat Farrar* (1949) is a quite different crime story in which a young man impersonates a missing heir to an estate, and was based in part on an actual Victorian *cause célèbre*, the Titchbourne case of the 1860s and 70s. Tey was not content to follow the Golden Age pattern slavishly, as the variety and innovation of her plots demonstrate. She uses her own experiences to create backgrounds, particularly in *Miss Pym Disposes*, set in a college of physical education. Knowledge of the theatre is often evident, and her descriptions of places, especially Scotland, are evocative, as in *The Singing Sands*. The main characters are well developed, particularly Grant himself. The books are well written, with touches of humour. For her outstanding achievements in the genre, Josephine Tey deserves to be ranked with the other 'Queens of Crime': Sayers, Christie, Allingham and Marsh.

Suggested Reading/Works Cited

Kaplan, Cora, 'Josephine Tey and Her Descendants: Conservative Modernity and the Female Crime Novel', in *End of Empire and the English Novel Since 1945*, ed. by Rachael Gilmore and Bill Schwarz (Manchester: Manchester University Press, 2012), pp. 53–73.

Martin, Christina R., 'Josephine Tey: Scottish Detective Novelist', *Studies in Scottish Literature*, 29 (1996), 191–204.

Perriam, Geraldine, ed., *Josephine Tey: A Celebration*, consultant ed. Catherine Aird (Glasgow: Black Rock Press, 2004).

CHAPTER 35

Elizabeth Ferrars (Pseudonym of Morna Doris McTaggart, later Brown, Published as E. X. Ferrars in USA, 1907–1995), 1932: *Turn Single* (writing as Morna McTaggart)

Victoria Stewart

Ferrars was a detective novelist and short story writer; her earliest two novels (*Turn Single*, 1932 and *Broken Music*, 1934) were published under the name Morna McTaggart, but her first novel as Ferrars, *Give a Corpse a Bad Name* (1940), introduced former journalist Toby Dyke and sidekick George as investigators, and some later works saw Virginia and Felix Freer, a married but separated couple, solving crimes together. Several of her novels, beginning with *Something Wicked* (1983), featured Andrew Basnet, a retired professor of botany. Ferrars edited and introduced *Planned Departures*, a 1958 short story collection, and contributed to *Crime on the Coast and No Flowers by Request* (1984), a collaborative novel which first appeared in instalments in the British newspaper the *News Chronicle*.

V. Stewart (✉)
University of Leicester, Leicester, UK

© The Author(s) 2020
E. Miskimmin (ed.), *100 British Crime Writers*, Crime Files,
https://doi.org/10.1057/978-1-137-31902-9_35

Born in Rangoon, Burma, Ferrars was educated in Freiburg, Germany and then Bedales School, Hampshire (1918–1924) and University College, London (1925–1928). After publishing two novels as Morna McTaggart, she turned to crime writing, using her mother's maiden name. During a career spanning the years from 1940 until her death – her final novel appeared posthumously – Ferrars published over sixty novels, many of them with a village or small-town setting, but her marriage in 1945 to Robert Brown, a lecturer in botany, provided opportunities for travel, reflected in novels set in Scotland, Africa and Madeira. Her husband's occupation seems to have influenced the content not just of the Andrew Basnet novels, but of others taking academics as their protagonists, especially those working in the life sciences. *The Decayed Gentlewoman* (1963) sees a botanist tracking down a missing painting, while *Zero at the Bone* (1967) features a zoology student.

Ferrars also engages with World War Two in a number of novels published during the 1940s. In *Murder Among Friends* (1946), the London blackout is not just as a backdrop to the action but a crucial aspect of the plot, and this novel also evidences a characteristic of much of Ferrars' later works; although some of the settings and mechanics of her plots may seem superficially similar to those of the 'Golden Age' writers, she often eschews comforting resolutions. *The Lying Voices* (1954) takes the 'murder swop' plot found in Patricia Highsmith's *Strangers on a Train* (1950) and resituates it in post-war England to disarming effect.

Ferrars was one of the co-founders of the Crime Writers' Association in 1953, becoming its chair in 1977, and in 1980 was awarded a CWA Silver Dagger in recognition of her achievements.

Suggested Reading / Works Cited

Adrian, Jack, 'Obituaries: Elizabeth Ferrars', *The Independent*, 19 April 1995. http://www.independent.co.uk/news/people/obituarieselizabeth-ferrars-1616223.html.

Baker, Susan, 'E. X. Ferrars', in *And Then There Were Nine … More Women of Mystery*, ed. by Jane S. Bakerman (Bowling Green, OH: Bowling Green State University Popular Press, 1985), pp. 148–166.

Becker, Mary Helen, 'Elizabeth Ferrars (Morna Doris Brown)', in *Dictionary of Literary Biography, Volume 87: British Mystery and Thriller Writers Since 1940*, ed. by Bernard Benstock and Thomas F. Staley (Detroit: Gale, 1989), pp. 73–84.

MacDonald, Gina with Elizabeth Sanders, *E. X. Ferrars: A Companion to the Mystery Fiction* (Jefferson NC: McFarland, 2011).

CHAPTER 36

Georgette Heyer (1902–1974), 1932: *Footsteps in the Dark*

Greg Rees

Georgette Heyer was an English writer of popular fiction, most notably historical and detective novels. Born in South West London, Heyer grew up as the eldest of three siblings. The family lived in Paris for many years until World War One, at which point they returned to England, with Heyer's father serving as an officer in the British Army during the conflict.

Heyer's first published work, *The Black Moth*, was written when she was only seventeen, and was released in 1921 when Heyer was still in her teens. The novel sets the standard for many of her romantic tales, introducing themes and features that recur throughout her work: strong male characters, independent women and an historical setting.

Heyer's career was soon in its ascendancy, and she had five novels published by the time of her marriage to George Ronald Rougier, an aspiring engineer, which occurred shortly after her father's death in 1925. Her son, Richard, was born in 1931. Her 1926 novel, *These Old Shades*, was an outstanding success, selling over one hundred thousand copies

G. Rees (✉)
Cardiff University, Cardiff, UK

© The Author(s) 2020
E. Miskimmin (ed.), *100 British Crime Writers*, Crime Files,
https://doi.org/10.1057/978-1-137-31902-9_36

despite the poor economic conditions of the time. Heyer's novels regularly sold in excess of 100,000 copies: Wallace observes that Heyer was 'a consistent bestseller from 1926 until her death in 1974'.

Heyer is not as well known for her detective stories as for her historical romances, but between 1932 and 1953 she published over a dozen crime novels, beginning with *Footsteps in the Dark*. Although arguably less well-regarded as Agatha Christie's or Ngaio Marsh's work, Heyer's crime novels share many of the classic tropes of Golden Age detective fiction, often being set in genteel society and with amateur detectives playing major parts in her plots. Eight of her books featured the detectives Hannasyde and Hemingway, and a play, *Merely Murder*, was based around one of these stories in 1937. Her crime fiction is known for its wit and dialogue.

Georgette Heyer died of lung cancer at the age of 71, an age at which she was still writing regularly. Heyer's oeuvre is substantial; indeed, she wrote profusely until her death, and additional works were published posthumously. It is also weighty in terms of influence: as Diana Wallace points out, 'Heyer is important not only because her career [...] spans such a large part of the twentieth century, but because of her influence on other writers'. A. S. Byatt is one well-renowned writer who explicitly voices Heyer's influence on her own work, which arguably culminates in Byatt's *Possession: A Romance* (1990), a work which has its roots in Byatt's childhood love of Heyer's novels.

Although Heyer might not have received the levels of critical acclaim enjoyed by her crime writing contemporaries, Dorothy L. Sayers and Agatha Christie, she remains a respected and well-regarded writer of clever stories in the crime genre, as well as a huge influence on historical and romance fiction.

Further Reading/Works Cited

Fahnestock-Thomas, Mary, *Georgette Heyer: A Critical Retrospective* (Saraland, AL: Prinny World Press, 2001).
Kloester, Jennifer, *Georgette Heyer* (London: Heinemann, 2011).
Knight, Stephen, 'The Golden Age', in *The Cambridge Companion to Crime Fiction*, ed. by Martin Priestman (Cambridge: Cambridge University Press, 2003), pp. 77–94.
Wallace, Diana, *The Woman's Historical Novel* (Basingstoke: Palgrave Macmillan, 2005).

CHAPTER 37

C. P. Snow (1905–1980), 1932: *Death Under Sail*

Christine R. Simpson

Charles Percy Snow, later Sir Charles, then Baron Snow, was distinguished in several spheres. He started life as an academic and research scientist and worked in government during World War Two. These experiences provided themes for his fiction and he united the two spheres of science and the arts in his now-famous controversial lecture 'The Two Cultures and the Scientific Revolution' (1959), in which he deplored the ignorance of scientists and those with an arts background of each other's respective fields.

His first published work, *Death Under Sail* (1932), is an ingenious crime novel following the typical Golden Age pattern of murder in a closed community. The victim is the host of a disparate party of guests sailing on the Norfolk Broads. The plot is narrated by the character of Ian Capel, who discovers the body, and, like the other five in the group, is regarded as a suspect by the local police sergeant. The narrator persuades his friend Finbow to investigate, pitching the amateur detective against the police, another common motif in crime writing of this period. After some clever twists in the plot, Finbow solves the mystery, but allows the

C. R. Simpson (✉)
The Dorothy L. Sayers Society, Essex, UK

murderer to escape the justice system, generating a slightly more morally complex conclusion than the more formulaic elements of the book anticipate. Interestingly, during the course of the novel a character is presented as reading Dorothy L. Sayers' *Unnatural Death* (1927), and Sayers was later to make use of Snow's novel *The Search* (1934) in her novel *Gaudy Night* (1935), illustrating the framework of contemporary references and intertextuality that characterises much Golden Age writing.

Not all of Snow's fiction was in the crime genre, but he returned to detection in his last published novel, *A Coat of Varnish* (1979). Although its plot revolves around the brutal murder of an elderly dowager, its main focus is on character. It explores the residents of a London Square: their personalities, morals, lifestyles and sex lives. Seen through the eyes of the senior investigating officer, much of this background is relevant to motives and opportunities in the case. There are complications caused by tax evasion, financial juggling and a possibly corrupt MP. The murderer is identified, but without tangible proof, and with his refusal to confess under psychological pressure, he too escapes justice. Snow's crime fiction is a tiny part of his oeuvre, but, like all of his writing, it is intellectually engaging and observant of contemporary society.

Suggested Reading/Works Cited

Tredell, Nicholas, *C. P. Snow: The Dynamics of Hope* (Basingstoke: Palgrave Macmillan, 2012).

CHAPTER 38

Ngaio Marsh (1895–1982), 1934: *A Man Lay Dead*

Kate Watson

Ngaio Marsh divided both her career and her life between New Zealand and London, and is rightly known alongside Agatha Christie, Dorothy L. Sayers and Margery Allingham as one of the 'Queens of Crime' of the Golden Age. She was an internationally bestselling author of the form and a perennial favourite, with her detective novels all featuring the British detective, Inspector Roderick Alleyn. In addition to these popular detective novels, Marsh wrote in many forms, including short stories, travel journalism, non-fiction, plays, television scripts and articles. Marsh was also a prominent figure in and director of twentieth-century New Zealand theatre, a BBC broadcaster and a painter. Marsh's impact and significance is evidenced by her being honoured with the title of Dame Commander of the British Empire in 1966. In 1967, the Ngaio Marsh Theatre (Christchurch) was opened in her name. These, however, are just a few of her numerous accolades.

Edith Ngaio Marsh was born on 23 April 1895 in the suburb of Fendalton, Christchurch, to Rose Elizabeth Seager and Henry Edmund Marsh, a clerk in the Bank of New Zealand in Christchurch. From the

K. Watson (✉)
Cardiff University Alumni and Teacher of English, Cardiff, UK

© The Author(s) 2020
E. Miskimmin (ed.), *100 British Crime Writers*, Crime Files,
https://doi.org/10.1057/978-1-137-31902-9_38

start Marsh had connections with the policing of crime; her grandfather on her mother's side, Edward William Seager, was in the Colonial Police Force, rising to the rank of Sergeant-Major in 1858. Seager later was in charge of Lyttelton Gaol and afterwards became Asylum Supervisor at Sunnyside. He had a passion for dramatics, which was passed on to Marsh's mother and, as is evident, Marsh herself. Marsh's father also shared this interest. Inevitably, Marsh's artistic endeavours were encouraged throughout her youth. When Marsh was young, her family moved to Cashmere Hills, the country outside Christchurch, where her father had built a house. This house would provide an important base and home for Marsh for the rest of her life. In February 1910 she experienced life outside of her country home when she was enrolled at St Margaret's College, a High Anglican school. Here, two of Marsh's lifelong loves, writing and an appreciation of Shakespeare's works, came to the fore with Marsh publishing articles in the school magazine, as well as editing the first issue with W. G. Hughes. At eighteen, Marsh wrote her own play, 'The Moon Princess', which was performed in September 1913.

Marsh left school in 1913 and then joined the Canterbury College School of Art in Christchurch to pursue painting. As this work progressed, she won awards, although Marsh would struggle with or be not wholly satisfied with her painting for the rest of her life. After World War One, Marsh rented a studio in Cashel Street with her friends, where she absorbed herself in painting. It was in 1919 that her first article was published in the Christchurch *Sun* and this was followed by more paid stories, articles and poems for the same newspaper. Marsh's concentration shifted to Shakespeare and productions of Shakespeare in the wake of the visit of the Allan Wilkie Shakespeare Company in 1919–1920. This visit inspired her to write a play, 'The Medallion', and after receiving a copy Wilkie offered Marsh a position of actress in their tour of New Zealand. It was this experience that would inform her 1937 novel, *Vintage Murder*. After another theatrical tour with the Rosemary Rees Comedy Company, Marsh returned to Christchurch in 1921, aged twenty-six, where she continued to exhibit her paintings.

When Marsh was thirty-three, she travelled to Europe with her mother to visit and reside with her good friends, the Rhodes, who were based in Buckinghamshire. Marsh intertwined this independent move with self-funding via her writing, producing travel writing, 'A New Canterbury Pilgrim' articles, for New Zealand newspapers. She would continue to convey her experiences of and commentary on London through journalistic articles. In 1929 Marsh set up an interior decorating shop, 'Touch and Go', in Knightsbridge with her friend Nelly Rhodes. It was a few years after this that Marsh composed her first crime fiction novel, *A Man Lay Dead* (1934), in her basement flat in Bourne Street. Margaret Lewis details this inception: 'Chief Detective-Inspector Roderick Alleyn, CID, was born between the limp sheets of a penny exercise book in 1931'. As with Dorothy L. Sayers' Lord Peter Wimsey and others, Alleyn's characterisation is in fitting with quintessential, upper-class professional detecting figure of The Golden Age. In her essay 'Birth of a Sleuth', Marsh wrote that he was 'an attractive, civilised man with whom it would be pleasant to talk, but much less pleasant to fall out' and 'thin with an accidental elegance ... fastidious ... compassionate ... with a cockeyed sense of humour, dependent largely upon understatement but, for all his unemphatic, rather apologetic ways, he could be a formidable person of considerable authority'. With the advent of the Alleyn novels, Marsh had found her calling, and carried on writing crime fiction until her death in 1982, although her interests and experiences in theatre and painting remained intrinsic to her work.

After Marsh's mother returned to Christchurch she became ill with cancer and Marsh left England in 1932; her mother died in November. Marsh then stayed in New Zealand to care for her father. It was this return which influenced the New Zealand milieu of her detective novels between 1932 and 1937. Marsh's connections with London were not lost: they were present throughout her life, and she visited often. In New Zealand, she continued her painting, writing and producing and became heavily involved in the theatre. The onset of World War Two impeded Marsh's European visits, and she drove an ambulance for the Red Cross during World War Two. She was involved in New Zealand drama between 1943–7 and was a prominent and encouraging figure, fostering new talent. In 1948 she was both awarded an OBE for her services in drama and literature in New Zealand and appointed as Honorary Lecturer in Drama at Canterbury University College. Sadly, her father died the same year.

The genesis of the name of her famous detective has not been completely resolved, but many suggestions involve Marsh's theatrical influences; Stephen Knight has written that 'Her detective, Inspector Alleyn was named after Christopher Marlowe's lead player', whereas Margaret Lewis suggests that the name originated from the Elizabethan actor that her father's grammar school was founded by: Edward Alleyn.

Regardless, Marsh's love and knowledge of theatre and art influenced her crime writing and its contexts. She described this *melange* as 'a little cellar of experiences which would one day be served up as the table wines of detective cookery'. Marsh published thirty-two detective novels between 1934 and 1982, all of which featured Alleyn. All but four were set in England; in the four set in New Zealand, Alleyn is on secondment to the New Zealand police. Many of Marsh's novels involve the backdrop of theatres or theatrical performances, such as *Overture to Death* (1939), *Final Curtain* (1947), *Opening Night* (1951) and *Death at the Dolphin* (1967). Painting features equally as prominently: her sixth Roderick Alleyn novel is titled *Artists in Crime* (1938), in which he meets his artist wife, Agatha Troy, during the investigation into a murder at her studios. He later marries Troy, and her painting becomes intrinsic to several investigations, such as in *Clutch of Constables* (1968) and *Tied up in Tinsel* (1972). Alleyn and Troy grow older as the novels progress, from their early courtship to the birth of their son, who is fully grown and an aspiring writer by *Last Ditch* in 1977.

Marsh followed the well-established Golden Age rules, which included murder, an enclosed setting, a usually upper-middle-class and wealthy victim, a threat from within, and the detective story as a game for the reader to solve, yet she simultaneously played with these conventions. In *Bloody Murder*, Julian Symons breaks 'The Golden Age' into two sections, with Marsh in the latter: 'The Golden Age: The Thirties'. He comments that 'Margery Allingham and Ngaio Marsh used the standard formula in a way rather different from that of Christie and Sayers', conforming less to the standard tropes. A majority of Marsh's works do not conform to the 'English cosy' pattern, with an English country village setting, largely because Marsh wrote about topics and places that she knew about. An unusual twist on the 'country house' convention, for example, is her 1943 novel, *Colour Scheme*, which is set in North Island of New Zealand and involves death by steaming mud pool.

Marsh's characters and style are sophisticated, witty and self-consciously ironic. Marsh differs from Christie in her concentration on character as opposed to plot. She clearly had a command over the form, as she states in her essay 'Entertainments' that:

> It is a form that can command our aesthetic approval. It is, by its nature, shapely. It must have a beginning, a middle, and an end. The middle must be an extension and development of the beginning and the end must be

implicit in both. The writing is as good as the author can make it; nervous, taut, balanced and economic. Descriptive passages are vivid and explicit. The author is not self-indulgent. If he commands a good style, there is every reason for maintaining it.

However, when discussing the reception of her crime work in her autobiography, *Black Beech and Honeydew* (1965), Marsh wrote that her 'intellectual New Zealand friends tactfully avoid all mention of my published work and if they like me, do so, I cannot help but feel, in spite of it'. Despite this reception from her friends in New Zealand, the general reception was favourable worldwide. Marsh's detective novels featured as televised adaptations, and she is still republished today, which is a testament to the longevity of her work and its engagement and readability. In 1949, the publishers Penguin and Collins released the 'Marsh Million', which comprised of 100,000 copies each of ten of her works. She was named by the Mystery Writers of America as 'Grandmaster' in 1977 and was honoured with the 'Edgar' award in 1978.

In 1979 her essay, 'Portrait of Troy', was published in Dilys Wynn's edited *Murderess Ink: The Better Half of the Mystery* (1979). By this time, Marsh's health was ailing, and in June 1980 she suffered from a heart attack. Despite this, she kept writing, publishing *Photo Finish* in September 1980. She also started writing her last novel, *Light Thickens*, which she sent to her agents in January 1982, before dying from a brain haemorrhage on 18 February 1982, in her family home. This final book was Marsh's most popular, outselling her other titles.

In terms of personal life, Marsh never married. *Black Beech & Honeydew* was reticent and not very telling of this element of her life. Joanna Drayton, in her recent new biography of Ngaio Marsh, *Ngaio Marsh: Her Life in Crime* (2008), has suggested a new reading of Marsh's ambiguous sexuality. Drayton also, rightly, re-establishes Marsh's place in the history of New Zealand.

Suggested Reading/Works Cited

Bargainnier, Earl F., 'Ngaio Marsh', in *10 Women of Mystery*, ed. by Earl F. Bargainnier (Bowling Green, OH: Bowling Green State University Press, 1981), pp. 78–108.

Drayton, Joanna, *Ngaio Marsh: Her Life in Crime* (New Zealand: HarperCollins, 2008).

Knight, Stephen, *Crime Fiction, 1800–2000: Detection, Death, Diversity* (Basingstoke: Palgrave Macmillan, 2004).
Lewis, Margaret, *Ngaio Marsh: A Life* (London: Chatto and Windus, 1991).
Marsh, Ngaio, 'Birth of a Sleuth', in *Writing Suspense and Mystery Fiction*, ed. by A. S. Burack (Boston, MA: The Writer, Inc., 1977), pp. 123–128.
——, *Black Beech and Honeydew* (1981; repr. London: HarperCollins, 2011).
——, 'Entertainments', *Pacific Moana Quarterly*, 3:1 (1978), 27–31.
Symons, Julian, *Bloody Murder: From the Detective Story to the Crime Novel* (London: Penguin, 1985).

CHAPTER 39

Eric Ambler (1909–1998), 1935: *The Dark Frontier*

Steven Powell

Eric Clifford Ambler was an influential author of spy novels noted for bringing a new level of realism to the genre and for pioneering the sophisticated political thriller that would be further developed by authors such as Len Deighton and John le Carré. Ambler's first five novels are considered classics of the spy genre.

Ambler was born to Alfred Percy Ambler and Amy Andrews at his parents' rented terrace house in Charlton, London. His parents were entertainers who worked predominantly in music hall theatre under the stage names Reg and Amy Ambrose. Growing up in London, Ambler experienced the Zeppelin raids during World War One. He attended Sandhurst Road School before winning a scholarship to Colfe's grammar school. Ambler also won a scholarship to study for a B.Sc. in engineering at Northampton Engineering College (now City University), although he often skipped classes in order to pursue his passion for the theatre by watching plays in the West End. Ambler found work as a 'technical trainee' at the Edison Swan Electric Company, but was moved to the publicity department and worked as a copywriter alongside published

S. Powell (✉)
University of Liverpool, Liverpool, UK

© The Author(s) 2020
E. Miskimmin (ed.), *100 British Crime Writers*, Crime Files,
https://doi.org/10.1057/978-1-137-31902-9_39

novelist Cecil Maiden and future novelist Gerald Butler. In 1929, Ambler had an affair with a married woman that resulted in her pregnancy. He arranged for her to have an abortion at a cost of fifteen pounds, which he subsequently described as one of the worst experiences of his life.

Ambler joined the Territorial Army before the war and had been involved in the military policing of London during the General Strike of 1926. In the 30s, Ambler travelled through Italy and would later channel his experience of the Fascist state into his fiction. In his memoirs, wittily titled *Here Lies Eric Ambler* (1985), Ambler describes being on holiday in Marseille, France in 1934. One afternoon he was looking out of his hotel window contemplating how his position would be a good spot for a sniper. One week later, King Alexander of Yugoslavia was shot dead by Vlado Chernozemski in the same street as the hotel Ambler was staying in. Upon the outbreak of World War Two, Ambler served briefly as a Lance-Bombardier in the Royal Artillery and worked on an anti-aircraft battery tasked with defending the Prime Minister from potential Luftwaffe attacks at Chequers and at his country house in Chartwell.

The majority of Ambler's wartime service was dedicated to the production of propaganda films. Ambler co-wrote the army training film *The New Lot* (1943) with Peter Ustinov. Most instructional films had been of poor quality, but Ambler and Ustinov wrote an engaging script about five reluctant army conscripts. Carol Reed directed the film, and it was later remade by Ambler and Reed as *The Way Ahead* (1944), one of the most acclaimed British films of the war. Transferred to Italy, Ambler wrote the script for *The Battle of San Pietro* (1944), directed by John Huston, for the Psychological Warfare Division. Most of the film was re-enacted 'combat' footage from the battle of the title. One scene featured corpses being dumped in shallow graves. The US War department banned the film for several years as it was deemed too graphic and anti-war in tone. By the end of the war, Ambler had attained the rank of Lieutenant-Colonel.

Ambler first felt compelled to become a writer after viewing a performance of Luigi Pirandello's *Six Characters in Search of an Author*. Ambler wrote the play *White to Harvest* about a street-corner evangelist, but it never developed past the initial reading at his local repertory theatre, and Ambler later came to regard it as awful. Ambler's first attempt at a novel resulted in two chapters of an unfinished work he titled *The Comedians*, which was to be based on the life of his father. His first published novel, *The Dark Frontier* (1935), is a prophetic, fast-paced thriller set in a fictional Balkan state. After a car crash, the lead protagonist's personality is divided in a Jungian-influenced narrative. The novel switches to the first-person viewpoint of an American journalist halfway through. Much of the plot revolves around a fascist state developing a weapon of mass destruction. Ambler had studied the structure of the atom at college and foresaw the development of the atomic bomb. He considered most detective/thriller writing at the time to be preposterous and wanted to create realistic villains from contemporary and topical threats yet his left-wing views contributed to the largely unconvincing Utopian ending, with the victorious revolutionaries heralding a new society.

Although he held left-wing sympathies, while working for Edison Swan Ambler was forced to canvass for the Conservative candidate Winston Churchill during the 1929 General election. Ambler attended Popular Front events in the 1930s, which usually featured pro-communist speakers, a cause he sympathised with. Ambler's novels *Cause for Alarm* (1938) and *Journey into Fear* (1940) feature the charming and courageous Soviet Agent Andreas Zaleshoff and reflect Ambler's anti-Fascist views and his then belief that the Soviet Union was an effective counterweight to European fascism. Ambler's lead protagonists are often ordinary people, such as the teacher Josef Vadassy in *Epitaph for a Spy* (1938). Vadassy comes from ambiguous and confusing ethnic heritage, which makes it difficult for him to have loyalty to any one state. Vadassy begins the novel with no knowledge of espionage and suddenly finds himself plunged into a world in which he is ill-prepared to survive. In one of Ambler's most famous novels, *The Mask of Dimitrios* (1939; published in the United States as *A Coffin for Dimitrios*, which was Ambler's preferred title), a crime writer travels across Europe to uncover the story of the gangster Dimitrios. As the narrative progresses, it becomes clear that Dimitrios is more than just an evil man; he is symbolic of a greedy and ruthless societal system.

Ambler returned to writing novels after an eleven-year hiatus with *Judgment at Deltchev* (1951). The novel is based on the Eastern Bloc party show trials of the late 1940s and early 1950s. Ambler conducted most of his research with the novelist Romain Gary, who had witnessed the Bulgarian show trials as a French diplomatic observer. *Judgment at Deltchev* is generally interpreted as Ambler's final break with the far-left, and he received scathing letters from former friends about the novel. One anonymous source posted him a single piece of used toilet paper. Despite this political shift, Ambler largely avoided the Cold War as a subject in his later novels. *The Schirmer Inheritance* (1953) concerns a young attorney attempting to trace a wealthy heir who has disappeared amidst the ruins of Europe shortly after World War Two. Ambler developed the plot from the stories of a friend, Win Harle, who had been engaged in a similar investigation before she was imprisoned by the Nazis during the war. Ambler collaborated with the Australian writer Charles Rodda for five novels written under the pseudonym Eliot Reed. He claimed this was not a productive working relationship, as he only gave substantial contributions for two of the novels.

Ambler would continue to write with remarkable consistency. In the 1950s and 1960s, he also worked as a screenwriter, earning an Academy Award nomination for *The Cruel Sea* (1953). Ambler was living in Los Angeles when he co-wrote and produced the television series *Checkmate* (1960–1962), about three private investigators in San Francisco. Ambler's novels have been developed into films with varying results. Some of the more notable adaptations include *Journey into Fear* (1943), which was produced by and starred Orson Welles and several members of the Mercury Theatre, and *Topkapi* (1964), a light-hearted heist film based on his novel *The Light of Day* (1962). Notable later works include *Dr. Frigo* (1974) and *The Care of Time* (1981). At the time of his death, his work had fallen out of critical favour and was out of print, but the centenary of his birth in 2009 led to the reissuing of his first five novels. Ambler moved to Switzerland, partly for tax reasons, in 1969 and would not return to England to live until 1985. Ambler received numerous honours throughout his career: he was awarded the Edgar Award by the Mystery Writers of America in 1964 and the title of Grand Master in 1975. Ambler received a Diamond Dagger for Lifetime Achievement from the British Crime Writers' Association in 1986. In 1981, he was named an Officer of the Order of the British Empire.

SUGGESTED READING/WORKS CITED

Ambler, Eric, *Here Lies Eric Ambler* (London: Weidenfeld and Nicholson, 1985).
Ambrosetti, Ronald, *Eric Ambler* (New York: Twayne, 1994).
Lewis, Peter, *Eric Ambler* (New York: Continuum, 1990).
Wolfe, Peter, *Alarms and Epitaphs: The Art of Eric Ambler* (Bowling Green, OH: Bowling Green Popular Press, 1993).

CHAPTER 40

Nicholas Blake (Pseudonym of Cecil Day-Lewis, 1904–1972), 1935: *A Question of Proof*

Esme Miskimmin

Cecil Day-Lewis, poet, novelist, translator, critic and broadcaster was a key literary figure who came to prominence in the 1930s alongside Louis MacNeice, Stephen Spender and W. H. Auden and whose successful career led him to be appointed Poet Laureate in 1968. As Nicholas Blake, he is best known for the amateur investigator Nigel Strangeways, who features in sixteen of the twenty detective novels Day-Lewis wrote under this pseudonym.

Day-Lewis was born at Ballintubbert, Queen's County (now County Laios), the only child of Frank Cecil Day-Lewis, a Church of Ireland clergyman, and his wife Kathleen, who died when Cecil Day-Lewis was four. On Kathleen's death, Frank moved the family to London, where Day-Lewis was educated at Wilkie's preparatory school before boarding at Sherborne School, Dorset. He went up to Wadham College, Oxford, in 1923 to read classics. Day-Lewis' first volume of verse, *Beechen Vigil* appeared in 1925 and he continued to grow in significance in the literary

---

E. Miskimmin (✉)
University of Liverpool, Liverpool, UK

© The Author(s) 2020
E. Miskimmin (ed.), *100 British Crime Writers*, Crime Files,
https://doi.org/10.1057/978-1-137-31902-9_40

world until the 1960s when, despite the many honours he had achieved, his poetry fell out of fashion and critical favour.

From a crime fan's point of view, however, the key moment in Day-Lewis' career was the publication of his first Nicholas Blake novel, *A Question of Proof* (1935), featuring Nigel Strangeways. Day-Lewis appears to have taken to crime writing as a way of supplementing his income as a prep-school teacher; after Oxford, he taught first at Summer Fields School, and then moved to Larchfield School, Helensburgh, and then in 1930 to Cheltenham School in Gloucester with his first wife, Mary, and their two sons. He drew on his teaching experiences for *A Question of Proof*, which is set in 'Sudely' school and in which the murder of the headmaster's nephew is solved by Strangeways, an early-career private detective and friend of the English master.

Strangeways is the nephew of an Assistant Commissioner of Scotland Yard and is a thorough and careful investigator, characterised by what Haycraft describes as 'studied casualness and insouciance'. In the books that follow, there is always some kind of love interest in Strangeways' investigations: in the second Nicholas Blake book, *Thou Shell of Death* (1936), Strangeways meets Georgia Cavendish, explorer, who begins as a suspect and whom Strangeways eventually marries. Georgia Cavendish is actually the key protagonist in a later, less successful story, *The Smiler with the Knife* (1938) and is killed driving an ambulance in the Blitz in *Minute for Murder* (1941). After Georgia, there are various females in Strangeways' life, including Clare Massinger, who first appears in *The Whisper in the Gloom* (1954) and to whom he is later unfaithful in the final Strangeways novel *The Morning After Death* (1966). Day-Lewis' representations of women in these novels have provoked comment; Patricia Craig observes his 'unaccountable tendency to go in for generalisations on the subject of women'. Strangeways' complicated relationships perhaps mirror those of his creator: Day-Lewis was rarely faithful, he had a lengthy affair with novelist Rosamond Lehman, eventually leaving both her and Mary for actress Jill Balcon who he married in 1951, and with whom he had another two children.

The Strangeways novels are, as might be expected, literary in style, and the earlier ones are notably left-wing in their approach, in keeping with Day-Lewis' then strongly held political views (he was a member of the Communist party from 1936 to 1938). Contemporary reviews of the books were enthusiastic: in his 1936 review of *Thou Shell of Death*,

Rupert Hart-Davis says that 'with [Blake's] first book he showed outrageous promise: with his second he steps firmly into the front rank of contemporary detective novelists'. While time has perhaps removed Blake from the very 'front rank' of the Golden Age writers, the novels are still very popular and highly rated in terms of style and form.

As Nicholas Blake, Day-Lewis also made contributions to the Golden Age crime world by reviewing fellow crime writers for *The Spectator*, and writing various essays on the detective fiction genre, including his often-quoted introduction to Haycraft's *Murder for Pleasure* (1941; UK edition with an introduction by Blake, 1942).

SUGGESTED READING/WORKS CITED

Craig, Patricia, 'Blake, Nicholas', in *The Oxford Companion to Crime and Mystery Writing*, ed. by Rosemary Herbert (Oxford: Oxford University Press, 1999), pp. 40–41.

Day-Lewis, Sean, 'Lewis, Cecil Day-[Pseud. Nicholas Blake] (1904–1972)', in *Oxford Dictionary of National Biography* (Oxford: Oxford University Press, 2004; online edn, May 2013).

Hart-Davis, Rupert, 'The Poetics of Detection: *Thou Shell of Death*', *The Spectator*, 13 March 1936, p. 32.

Haycraft, Howard, *Murder for Pleasure: The Life and Times of the Detective Story* (1941; repr. London: Peter Davies, 1942).

CHAPTER 41

Daphne du Maurier (1907–1989), 1936: *Jamaica Inn*

Megan Hoffman

Daphne du Maurier is best known for her romantic suspense novel *Rebecca* (1938) and short story 'The Birds' (1952), both adapted for film by Alfred Hitchcock. Though she is often described as a 'romantic' novelist, du Maurier's work frequently includes elements of crime, gothic and sensation fiction as well as of romantic fiction. Novels such as *Jamaica Inn* (1936), *Rebecca* (1938) and *My Cousin Rachel* (1951) and short stories like 'Don't Look Now' (1971) are characteristic of du Maurier's signature blend of horror, romance, suspense and psychological realism. Such works can be closely identified with crime fiction as they explore the psychological effects of murder or death and include a 'detective' figure who uncovers disturbing truths.

Daphne du Maurier was the second of three daughters of successful actor-manager Gerald du Maurier and actress Muriel du Maurier (nee Beaumont). Born in London, England, Daphne du Maurier spent her childhood in London until the age of eighteen, when she attended finishing school in France. In 1926, the du Mauriers purchased a holiday home called Ferryside in Cornwall. Daphne du Maurier was so attracted

M. Hoffman (✉)
Independent Scholar, Southsea, UK

© The Author(s) 2020
E. Miskimmin (Ed.), *100 British Crime Writers*, Crime Files,
https://doi.org/10.1057/978-1-137-31902-9_41

183

to the house and its surroundings that she began to go there alone to work on her writing. It was at Ferryside where du Maurier produced her first novel, *The Loving Spirit* (1931), which follows the lives of four generations of a Cornish family. Her work would become known for its evocative descriptions of Cornwall's landscape and people. In 1932, du Maurier married Lieutenant-General Sir Frederick Arthur Montague Browning. Her first child, Tessa, was born in 1933, followed by another daughter, Flavia, in 1937 and a son, Christian, in 1940. While in Egypt with her husband and his regiment in 1937, du Maurier began to write *Rebecca*, which would become her most famous novel. Du Maurier was made a Dame of the British Empire in 1969.

During the course of a long and productive career, du Maurier wrote seventeen novels and thirteen volumes of short stories as well as two plays and numerous works of non-fiction, including five biographies and an autobiography, *Growing Pains: The Shaping of a Writer* (1977). Many of du Maurier's novels and stories have been adapted into well-known films, including *Jamaica Inn* (novel 1936, film 1939), *Rebecca* (novel 1938, film 1940), 'The Birds' (story 1952, film 1963) and 'Don't Look Now' (story 1971, film 1973). Du Maurier's final work, the pictorial memoir *Enchanted Cornwall* (1989), was published shortly before her death on 19 April 1989.

Suggested Reading/Works Cited

Auerbach, Nina, *Daphne du Maurier: Haunted Heiress* (Philadelphia: University of Pennsylvania Press, 1990).
Forster, Margaret, *Daphne du Maurier* (London: Chatto & Windus, 1993).
Helen Taylor, ed., *The Daphne du Maurier Companion* (London: Virago, 2007).
Horner, Avril and Sue Zlosnik, *Daphne du Maurier: Writing, Identity and the Gothic Imagination* (Basingstoke: Palgrave Macmillan, 1998).

CHAPTER 42

Michael Innes (Pseudonym of J. I. M. Stewart, 1906–1994), 1936: *Death at the President's Lodging*

Christopher Routledge

A novelist and academic whose best known stories take place in English university settings and feature Inspector Appleby, a series detective who rises through the ranks to become Police Commissioner at Scotland Yard, Innes was a pioneer of the 'donnish' detective story in the 1930s, establishing the popularity of a subgenre that has persisted into the twenty-first century. Innes' novels frequently make use of literary quotations and allusions, and have a relaxed, witty, humorous tone. Writing in 1941, Howard Haycraft described Innes as 'one of the youngest of first-rank detective-story writers […] he has one of the finest natural talents operating in the genre today'. In his academic career, J. I. M. Stewart wrote several books, including biographies of Joseph Conrad and Rudyard Kipling.

Michael Innes is the pseudonym for John Innes Mackintosh Stewart, who was born near Edinburgh. His mother was Elizabeth Clark, and his father John Stewart was an academic lawyer and later Edinburgh's Director of Education. Stewart attended the prestigious Edinburgh

---

C. Routledge (✉)
Freelance Writer and Photographer, NW England, UK

© The Author(s) 2020
E. Miskimmin (ed.), *100 British Crime Writers*, Crime Files,
https://doi.org/10.1057/978-1-137-31902-9_42

Academy and Oriel College, Oxford, where he studied English. After a year studying psychoanalysis in Vienna, Stewart became a lecturer in English at the University of Leeds in 1930, where he stayed until 1936. He married Margaret Hardwick, a doctor, in 1932 and they had three sons and two daughters.

In 1935 Stewart and his young family moved to Adelaide, South Australia, where he became Professor of English at the University of Adelaide. He drafted his first, and perhaps best known, novel, *Death at the President's Lodging* (1936; *Seven Suspects* in the United States) on the long sea voyage from Liverpool to Australia. The novel is set in the fictional St. Anthony's College, which closely resembles an Oxford College both architecturally and culturally. It takes the form of a reverse locked room mystery in that all the possible suspects had both the motivation and a key to the lodging where the murder has taken place. Appleby's job here is to unravel the alibis to find the murderer.

Innes' second novel, *Hamlet, Revenge!* appeared in 1937 and he published almost a book a year after that until 1986. Also notable is *Appleby's End* (1945), in which the detective contemplates early retirement. His main series character is Inspector John Appleby, who made his first appearance in *Death at the President's Lodging* and from then had a developing career in the police, rising eventually to become Sir John Appleby, Metropolitan Police Commissioner. Innes' second series character was the amateur detective, Charles Honeybath R. A. Honeybath is a painter who makes his first appearance in *The Mysterious Commission* (1975). Honeybath gave Innes/Stewart an excuse for demonstrating his erudition, but does not have the dynamism or interest of Appleby; he brought the two together in *Appleby and Honeybath* (1983).

Innes often used unusual settings as a backdrop for his stories, in much the same way as Sir Arthur Conan Doyle takes Sherlock Holmes to places such as Utah and the Reichenbach Falls. Apart from the familiar academic setting, Appleby solves cases in rural Australia (*The Daffodil Affair*, 1942), while other novels are set in Ireland (*The Journeying Boy*, 1949), and California (*From London Far*, 1946). Part of the comforting appeal of the novels is the way in which the erudite, educated voice prevails amid the chaos.

Literary references extend to places and even plot elements, as Innes brings strange events to mundane settings. In *The Weight of the Evidence* (1943) a meteorite is dropped on a university professor, paralleling the plot of Horace Walpole's original Gothic novel *The Castle of Otranto*

(1764), in which a giant iron helmet falls on the son of the castle's lord. In *Lament for a Maker* (1938), Innes uses as his structure Wilkie Collins' early detective novel *The Moonstone* (1868) to create what Haycraft describes as 'one of the vividly outstanding detective novels of the generation'.

Stewart's two careers, as academic and detective fiction writer, ran in parallel. In 1945 he returned to Britain and took a post at Queens University, Belfast, but moved to Oxford as a 'Student' (Fellow) of Christ Church, Oxford, where he eventually was given a professorship. He retired in 1973. During his academic career Stewart wrote several books of criticism, including *James Joyce* (1957), *Rudyard Kipling* (1966), *Joseph Conrad* (1968) and *Thomas Hardy: A Critical Biography* (1971), edited a scholarly edition of *Vanity Fair*. He also wrote a volume of the *Oxford History of English Literature*. From the early 1950s he also began to write fiction under his own name, and produced in total over 70 novels and six collections of short stories, alongside his scholarly work and teaching duties. His autobiography, *Myself and Michael Innes*, was published in 1987.

Stewart retired from his university post in 1973, but continued to write almost up to his death aged 88. His final Appleby novel *Appleby and the Ospreys*, was published in 1986, but in 2007 the rights to his work were sold by his estate to Owatonna Media; a final collection of stories was published in 2010. Notwithstanding his enormous output, Stewart is remembered principally for the remarkable novels he wrote as Michael Innes in the 1930s and 1940s, when he, along with writers such as Edmund Crispin, and Simon Nash, established what has become a significant subgenre of academic mysteries.

SUGGESTED READING/WORKS CITED

Haycraft, Howard, *Murder for Pleasure: The Life and Times of the Mystery Story* (New York: Carroll and Graf, 1941).
'Obituary', *The New York Times*, 16 November 1994. http://www.nytimes.com/1994/11/16/obituaries/j-i-m-stewart-49-wrote-mysteries-as-michael-innes.html.
Stewart, J. I. M., *Myself and Michael Innes* (London: Gollancz, 1987).

CHAPTER 43

John Creasey (Also Wrote as Anthony Morton and J. J. Marric, among other pseudonyms, 1908–1973), 1937: *Meet the Baron* (Writing as Anthony Morton)

Martin Lightening

John Creasey was a prolific and successful writer of over six hundred crime and thriller mysteries and the founder of the British Crime Writers' Association. He is probably second only to Agatha Christie in terms of the numbers of screen and radio adaptations of his work, such as John Ford's *Gideon's Day* (1958). This, combined with the recognition he received in his writing lifetime: Grand Master of the Mystery Writers of America 1969; an Edgar Award for *Gideon's Fire* (1961), makes it difficult to understand why he is often overlooked in contemporary critical discussions of crime writing.

The seventh of nine children from a poor family, Creasey left school at fourteen but remembering the encouragement of one of his teachers, he determined to earn a living as a writer. At twenty-four, while working as a postman and with nine unpublished novels behind him, he won the

M. Lightening (✉)
Freelance Cameraman and Writer, Manchester, UK

© The Author(s) 2020
E. Miskimmin (ed.), *100 British Crime Writers*, Crime Files,
https://doi.org/10.1057/978-1-137-31902-9_43

£1500 Cracksman Competition for Crime writers with *Meet The Baron* which he wrote in six days to meet the deadline. *The Baron*, written as Anthony Morton, became a series that ran for thirty-five years and was the first of many stories which he wrote under about twenty different pseudonyms. Most of his characters, such as The Baron, The Toff, Patrick Dawlish, Inspector West, Department Z, Gideon of Scotland Yard, Superintendent Folly, Dr. Palfrey and Dr. Cellini, all had their own series, and their own set of fans.

His later, major contribution to the development of crime writing was his popularising of the police-procedural novel as J. J. Marric, with a series of twenty-two novels that began with *Gideon's Day* (1955) and ran until *Gideon's Drive* (1976). Five further 'Gideon' novels were written after Creasey's death by William Vivian Butler, continuing the series until *Gideon's Fear* (1990). The series was well-received internationally and, along with Ed McBain and his *87th Precinct* series, established the 'police procedural' style that is a familiar feature of modern crime literature, film and television. Commander George Gideon became one of the most famous individual policemen in the world but, in the procedural style, he was actually the head of a team of officers and laboratory specialists at Scotland Yard all of whom had their part to play in solving a multitude of overlapping cases.

Creasey wrote entertaining page-turners and felt that the escapism that they provided was a significant function of his work, especially during World War Two. Despite their escapist nature, however, his novels all contain a sense of social and political philosophy which reflect Creasey's own strong social conscience, strengthened by his involvement in liberal politics from an early age and his later experiences travelling the world.

Unable to serve during World War Two due to the lasting effects of childhood polio, he assisted with the National Savings Movement, work which won him an MBE in 1946. He was also closely involved in charities for famine relief, road safety and campaigns for a united Europe.

Creasey had total sales worldwide of over eighty million copies in at least 5000 different editions in twenty-eight different languages. Although largely forgotten of late, there are signs of a revival of interest in Creasey's work. His son Richard has written a new Dr. Palfrey novel, *Eternity's Sunrise* (2012), and some of Creasey's own works are beginning to be republished.

SUGGESTED READING / WORKS CITED

Harvey, Deryck, 'The Best of John Creasey', *Armchair Detective: A Quarterly Journal Devoted to the Appreciation of Mystery, Detective, and Suspense Fiction*, 7 (1973), 42–43.

Lachman, Marvin S., 'John Creasey', in *British Mystery Writers, 1920–1939*, ed. by Bernard Benstock and Thomas F. Staley (Detroit, MI: Gale, 1989), pp. 87–105.

The John Creasey Online Resource. http://www.johncreasey.co.uk/.

Francis Durbridge (1912–1998), 1938: First Broadcast of the 'Paul Temple' Serial, *Send for Paul Temple*

Victoria Stewart

Best known for creating Paul Temple, a crime novelist turned investigator whose adventures were serialised on radio and television as well as appearing in novelised form, Francis Henry Durbridge was also a prolific author of other serial thrillers for television and radio and, in the 1970s, turned to writing stage plays.

Born in 1912 in Bradford, Yorkshire, Durbridge attended Bradford Grammar School and then went on to Birmingham University, graduating with a degree in English in 1933. He married Norah Lawley in 1940 and they had two sons. For a short time after graduating, he worked in a stockbroker's office, and wrote in his spare time, but he soon sold his first radio play to the BBC; this was a 'straight' drama without a mystery element called *Promotion* (broadcast 1933). The first Paul Temple serial, the eight-part *Send for Paul Temple*, was broadcast in April 1938, with Hugh Morton as Paul and Bernadette Hodgson as his wife, Steve. This met with a very positive audience response, and Durbridge continued to

V. Stewart (✉)
University of Leicester, Leicester, UK

© The Author(s) 2020
E. Miskimmin (ed.), *100 British Crime Writers*, Crime Files,
https://doi.org/10.1057/978-1-137-31902-9_44

produce Paul Temple radio serials into the 1960s. Several actors took the part of Paul over the years, but Peter Coke, who first appeared in *Paul Temple and the Gilbert Case* (1954), is probably most strongly identified with the role, not least because of the repeat broadcast of surviving serials on BBC radio and their reissue on CD since the early 2000s. Marjorie Westbury first played Steve in *Send for Paul Temple Again* (1945) and continued in this role until the series ended. Although not the original choice for signature tune, Vivian Ellis' rousing *Coronation Scot* became closely associated with the show.

The central pairing of Paul and Steve, who live with their manservant in a Mayfair flat, is key to the success of Paul Temple; Temple's reasoning and intellect are countered by Steve's intuition, a gendered division of labour that they self-consciously joke about on occasion. Their adventures take them on travels across Europe, and often involve encounters with mysterious foreigners. Each episode ends with a dramatic cliffhanger, and Durbridge used radio sound effects to their full potential, with Paul and Steve having to cope with boarding a flight on a booby-trapped plane, being run off the road by villains in stolen cars, or being swept into the sea when their launch is rammed by a motorboat. (This last incident featured in *Paul Temple and the Lawrence Affair* [1956], and presented many technical challenges, with Paul and Steve providing a performance of floundering in one studio, unable to hear the sea sound effects being created in a neighbouring room.) The Temples are habitués of nightclubs, cocktail parties and good hotels, defying post-war austerity. Traced from episode to episode, the plots reach almost Chandler-esque complexity, but each individual episode is structured so as to be of interest in itself.

Durbridge also wrote what he described as 'the first adult series for television', a thriller called *The Broken Horseshoe*, which was broadcast live in six parts between March and April 1952. This was followed by several other two, three or six-part thrillers throughout the 1950s and 1960s, including, in 1960–1961, the eighteen parts of *The World of Tim Frazer*, broadcast under the banner 'Francis Durbridge Presents'. This comprised of three separate six-part stories featuring an engineer who is recruited as an agent by a secret government department. Durbridge may have felt that Tim Frazer was better suited to television than Paul Temple at a period when 'gritty' realism was making its mark across genres. However, Paul Temple was also transferred to television in the late 1960s and early 1970s, with 64 episodes in all being produced, some as a co-production between the BBC and the German broadcaster ZDF; Temple had a strong following on continental Europe. John Bentley played Temple in the initial 12-part series, with Francis Matthews taking the role in two 26-part series of 50-minute episodes, with Ros Drinkwater as Steve. At the time, the £630,000 budget for the first of these two series was the largest ever for a BBC crime series.

The television version of 'Paul Temple' was not scripted by Durbridge, who preferred the serial form to stand alone drama when writing for this medium. The television incarnations of Paul and Steve do convey something of the glamour evoked by the radio series, with Francis Matthews' costumes foreshadowing the suede-jacket-and-cravat look favoured by Roger Moore in *The Persuaders*, and lavish use was made of location filming, with episodes shot in Malta, Spain and Germany. Perhaps inevitably, however, the hectic pacing of the radio version is slowed down and the casual banter between Paul and Steve, one of the engaging details of the radio serial, is never quite matched in the television scripts, which tend to be diffuse in their focus. The series was eventually dropped by the BBC, despite continued interest from Europe, having been deemed too commercial by Huw Wheldon, then the BBC's Managing Director.

Meanwhile, Durbridge also continued other television writing, notably *Melissa*, which was broadcast in 1964 and remade in colour in 1974. A writer – a not uncommon choice of protagonist for Durbridge – finds himself in the frame for the murder of his wife, Melissa. As he attempts to uncover what really happened, and thereby clear his name, he encounters blackmail, gambling and drug abuse among his apparently genteel London set. Another version of *Melissa*, by Alan Bleasdale, was broadcast by Channel 4 in 1997.

A novelisation of *Melissa* appeared in 1967 and this was not the only work of Durbridge's that was refashioned in this way. Many of the Paul Temple adventures also appear as novels, as did *The World of Tim Frazer* and other serials from the 1950s. A number of novels co-authored with Douglas Rutherford appeared with 'Paul Temple' as the named author, a proto-postmodern nod to the amateur detective's supposed day-job. The fact that at this period repeat screenings or broadcasts of television or radio shows were rare would have given an impetus to the production of such novelisations, which, perhaps inevitably, were dialogue-heavy. Notably some of the Paul Temple radio serials were remade during the 1950s, the originals presumably not having been recorded when first broadcast.

Four Paul Temple films co-scripted by Durbridge, were made between 1946 and 1952. A number of television serials were also remade as feature films, including *Portrait of Alison* (1955), scripted by Guy Green and Ken Hughes and directed by Guy Green. *My Friend Charles*, a 1956 serial, was filmed as *The Vicious Circle* (1957), scripted by Durbridge, directed by Gerald Thomas and starring John Mills. In a similar vein to *Melissa*, *The Vicious Circle* features a central character, in this case a doctor, who has to try to clear his name of murder when the evidence appears irrefutable. This type of plot, with its undertow of paranoia, was evidently one which appealed to Durbridge, as variations on it recur in his writing for the stage.

Durbridge's move to writing for theatre in 1971 saw him successfully transfer the thriller format to the stage in works which remain repertory theatre mainstays. Plays including *Suddenly at Home* (1971), *Touch of Danger* (1987) and *The Small Hours* (1991) operate in familiar Durbridge territory, with respectable upper-middle-class professionals, often writers, becoming entangled in blackmail and murder. It is perhaps this conjunction of comfortable lives and grubby crimes which is the constant throughout Durbridge's work from Paul Temple onwards; the plots may be fantastical but the threats menacing respectable lives lead to all-too-believable extremes of behaviour.

Not least because of the survival of many of the original radio recordings, Paul Temple is likely to remain Durbridge's most enduring creation, but the scope of his oeuvre for television was also impressive; he was a pioneer of the paranoid thriller which remains a mainstay of British television drama.

SUGGESTED READING/WORKS CITED

Barnes, Melvyn, 'Durbridge, Francis [Henry]', in *The St. James Guide to Crime and Mystery Writers*, 4th edn, ed. by Jay J. Pederson (Detroit: St. James Press, 1996), pp. 209–214.

Fowler, Christopher, 'Forgotten Authors No. 39: Francis Durbridge', *Independent*, 27 September 2009. http://www.independent.co.uk/arts-entertainment/books/features/forgotten-authors-no39-francis-durbridge-1792560.html.

'Francis Durbridge, Obituary', *The Times*, 13 April 1998, p. 23.

List of Francis Durbridge Serials (1952–1980) Website. www.whirligig-tv.co.uk.

CHAPTER 45

Enid Blyton (1897–1968), 1942: *Five on a Treasure Island*

Lucy Andrew

Enid Mary Blyton, one of Britain's most prolific children's writers, published approximately six hundred books, the most famous of which are probably her *Noddy* and *Famous Five* series, the latter of which is probably her best-known detective fiction for children. Her work has been translated into over one hundred languages, and her most popular series have prompted numerous spin-off books, films, television series and a vast range of merchandise. While her work has incited controversy among adult critics, Blyton remains incredibly popular with child readers.

Blyton was born on 11 August 1897 in East Dulwich, South London. She was the first child of Thomas Carey Blyton and Theresa Mary Blyton (nee Harrison). Her brothers, Hanly and Carey, were born in 1899 and 1902, respectively. Blyton was enrolled at St Christopher's School for Girls in 1907, where she excelled as tennis champion, lacrosse team captain and head girl. Encouraged by her father, she read and composed stories avidly as a child and, as her parents' relationship became increasingly fraught, Blyton used storytelling as a form of escapism. After Thomas Blyton left his family just before Blyton's thirteenth birthday, her

L. Andrew (✉)
University of Chester, Chester, UK

© The Author(s) 2020
E. Miskimmin (ed.), *100 British Crime Writers*, Crime Files,
https://doi.org/10.1057/978-1-137-31902-9_45

fictions began to spill over into her real-life as her mother forced her to conceal her father's absence from the family home. Later in life, Blyton constantly used this technique to erase unwanted details from her personal life, constructing a fictional biography for herself. During her school years, Blyton provided short stories for *Dab*, a magazine that she produced with her friends Mirabel Davis and Mary Attenborough. She achieved her first taste of literary success after receiving a letter from Arthur Mee in response to her entry to one of his children's poetry competitions. He informed her that he intended to publish her verses and expressed a desire to see her future writings. Following this, however, Blyton's numerous submissions to various magazines were repeatedly rejected.

Blyton received little encouragement in her initial writing endeavours. Her mother resented her consequent withdrawal from the family and abandonment of domestic chores. Her father, who taught her piano from the age of six and ensured that her tuition continued after his departure, expected her to enter Guildhall School of Music in 1916. After leaving school, however, Blyton discovered her aptitude for teaching, seeing this vocation as an opportunity to study children and continue writing. With her father's consent, she began the National Froebel Union Course in Ipswich in September 1916. By this point Blyton's relationship with her mother had deteriorated and she left home permanently. During her teacher training Blyton had three poems accepted by *Nash's Magazine*.

Leaving her first teaching job at Bickley Park School, Kent, in December 1919 after only a year, Blyton became a governess in Surbiton and soon began to teach a small class of the neighbourhood's children. It was here, in 1920, that Blyton learnt of her father's sudden death from a heart attack at the age of fifty but, despite their closeness, she did not attend his funeral. Later that year, Blyton became reacquainted with school friend Phyllis Chase, an illustrator. After deciding to collaborate, they sold a fairy story to one of Cassell's weekly magazines in 1921 and became regular contributors to *Teachers' World* from 1922. In summer 1922 their first book, *Child Whispers*, was published by J. Saville, followed by a second book of poems, *Real Fairies* in 1923. In July 1923 Blyton began writing 'From my Window', a weekly feature for *Teachers' World*.

1924 was a turning point for Blyton as, having left her position as governess, she married Hugh Pollock, an ex-army man, then editor of George Newnes' book department. His wife had left him for another man during the war and he became engaged to Blyton soon after his divorce was finalised at Easter 1924. They married on 28 August 1924 at Bromley

Register Office. Blyton's relatives were notably absent from the ceremony. Newnes, who soon became Blyton's primary publisher, released *The Enid Blyton Book of Fairies* and *The Zoo Book* in 1924 and *The Enid Blyton Book of Bunnies* the following year, when she also produced a set of 'Readers' for Thomas Nelson.

From 1926 Blyton's literary output increased significantly. She became editor of *Sunny Stories for Little Folks* (1926-1937), wrote nature books, such as *The Bird Book* (1926), *The Animal Book* (1927) and *Nature Lessons* (1929), children's plays, *A Book of Little Plays* (1927) and *The Play's the Thing!* (1927), and re-tellings of classic tales, including *Tales of Brer Rabbit: Retold* (1928), *Tales from the Arabian Nights* (1930) and *Tales of Robin Hood* (1930). In 1929 she also began to produce 'Enid Blyton's Children's Page' for *Teachers' World*.

By contrast, 1931-1933 was a quieter period in Blyton's literary career. After consulting a gynaecologist who diagnosed her with an undeveloped uterus, and taking a course of hormone injections in an attempt to rectify the problem, Blyton finally conceived in 1930 and her first daughter, Gillian Mary, was born on 15 July 1931. Blyton struggled to find time to write while looking after Gillian, though she coped better with the birth of her second daughter, Imogen Mary, born on 27 October 1935, relying upon a nanny to oversee her child's early development. In January 1937 *Sunny Stories* was released in a new weekly format and Blyton's first long serial for the magazine, *The Adventures of the Wishing Chair*, was published in book form by Newnes later that year. Similarly, her second serial for *Sunny Stories*, *The Secret Island*, was published in full by Basil Blackwell in 1938.

With Blyton's increasing literary success came the disintegration of her marriage to Hugh Pollock, who had been close to a breakdown in 1933 and, unknown to his wife, had resorted to alcohol in an attempt to cope. Blyton discovered her husband's alcoholism in 1938 when he suffered a bout of pneumonia. Their marriage recovered temporarily, yet further frictions arose when Pollock decided to rejoin the army in 1940 against Blyton's wishes. Pollock became romantically involved with another author, Ida Crowe, during the war and, at the same time, Blyton met her second husband, Kenneth Darrell Waters, a married surgeon. Blyton and Darrell Waters both divorced in 1943 and married each other on 20 October of the same year at the City of Westminster Register Office, just before Pollock married Crowe. Blyton swiftly erased her first husband from the family circle, changing her daughters' surname to Darrell Waters and denying Pollock access to them, actions which he greatly resented.

Blyton was barely affected by paper rations during the war, as she distributed her work between a number of publishers and her popularity ensured that her titles were given priority over those of lesser-known authors. In 1940 alone she produced eleven Blyton books and two more under the pseudonym 'Mary Pollock'. The war period saw the creation of most of her best known series: the *Secret* books (1938); *Amelia Jane* and *Faraway Tree* (1939); the *Naughtiest Girl* (1940); *St. Clare's* (1941); *Mary Mouse* and the *Famous Five* (1942); the *Find-Outers/Mystery* series (1943) and the *Adventure* series (1944). The first *Malory Towers* title appeared in 1946, while the *Barney Mysteries*, the *Secret Seven* and *Noddy* all made their debut in 1949. Blyton wrote play versions of her most popular series, *Noddy* and the *Famous Five*, which premiered in 1954 and 1955, respectively. The first issue of the *Enid Blyton Magazine* appeared on 18 March 1853, complete with puzzles, competitions, nature lovers' corner, serials, short stories, cartoon strips and a letter from the editor, Blyton herself. Through this magazine, Blyton established several charitable clubs, including the Famous Five Club and The Sunbeam Society, which both supported babies' homes.

Blyton was never reconciled with her mother and refused to attend her funeral when she died in 1950, nor did she renew her relationship with her estranged brothers. When Darrell Waters retired in 1957, he was anxious about his wife's health and encouraged her to downscale her writing commitments. Blyton characteristically refused, yet when she fell ill in May she became convinced, despite the doctor's diagnosis of a digestive malfunction, that, like her father, she had developed a heart condition. Her husband did not dispel her misapprehension, using her anxiety to convince her to limit her literary engagements. Yet Blyton's illness did not stop her from attending her daughter Gillian's wedding to television producer Donald Baverstock in August 1957 and she soon began to increase her workload again. Within a few years, however, Blyton's mental faculties declined and her husband began to suffer greatly from arthritis. Before Darrell Waters died in 1967, he put his wife's affairs in order, burning her early diaries. Blyton became increasingly ill after her husband's death and was admitted to a nursing home in Hampstead where she died, after three months residence, on 28 November 1968.

Blyton's most crucial contribution to mystery and detective fiction for children was her development of the juvenile detective ensemble. Though this grouping was common in detective school stories in the juvenile story papers of the early- to mid-twentieth century, and was adopted again in Erich Kästner's influential *Emil and the Detectives*, first published in Britain in 1931, Blyton's juvenile detective ensemble differs significantly. Where the school story ensembles are necessarily single-sex, and Emil's helpers are a gang of Berlin boys, Blyton prefers more diverse groupings: her detective ensembles are mixed in terms of gender, age, ability, characteristics, social class and even species – dogs, in particular, become intelligent investigators of crime with human qualities. A more crucial difference, perhaps, is the setting in which Blyton places her detective ensembles. Rather than the safe confinement of the boarding school, overseen by hawk-eyed teachers, or the bustling city of Berlin, with its ever-present adult authorities, Blyton situates crime and mysteries in abandoned country mansions, hidden caves and on treasure islands. Her children investigate in the great outdoors where, free from adult supervision, they develop into independent detective characters.

In some cases, however, exploration of new environments overwhelms the mystery or detective plot so that the stories display traits of the holiday adventure genre, which was popularised by the publication of Arthur Ransome's *Swallows and Amazons* (1930). Blyton's most famous mystery/adventure hybrid series is the *Famous Five* (1942–1963, twenty-one titles). The books follow the school holiday adventures of siblings Julian, Dick and Anne, their cousin George, and her dog Timmy, where adventure expeditions are often invaded by unsuspecting criminals whose shady activities are inevitably foiled by the Five. A similar, but lesser-known, series, the *Barney Mysteries* (1949–1959, six titles), features a more varied group: siblings Diana and Roger, their orphaned cousin, Snubby, his dog Loony, Barney the circus boy and his trained monkey, Miranda. Like the *Famous Five* books, the *Barney Mysteries* are often preoccupied with the characters' interaction with, and exploration of, their environment, but the detective ensemble in this series more obviously engage in investigative processes that the Five.

A series that can be more strongly identified with the detective genre is the *Secret Seven* (1949–1963, fifteen titles), which features a secret society of seven children Janet, Peter, George, Pam, Barbara, Colin, Jack – and Scamper the dog. Written for younger children, the language is simplistic and the characters interchangeable. Yet, since the stories are set in the Seven's home environment, they are free to focus on detection rather than exploration. Moreover, the Seven impose a conscious detective identity upon themselves and their leader, Peter, distributes investigative tasks among the group in order to efficiently solve crimes/mysteries. Blyton's most sophisticated detective series, however, is the *Find-Outers/Mystery* series (1943–1961, fifteen titles). Larry, Pip, Daisy, Bets, Fatty and his dog Buster are the 'Five Find-Outers and Dog', solving crime in their home village of Peterswood. The children, who are far better characterised than the Secret Seven, are conscious of their detective role and repeatedly look for clues, interview witnesses, track suspects and successfully solve the mystery ahead of their competitor, the hapless village policeman, Mr. Goon. Furthermore, Fatty, undoubtedly the lead detective of the series, is a Holmesian master of disguise, using his gift to play pranks on the unsuspecting Mr. Goon as well as to advance the Find-Outers' investigations. Although, like Blyton's other detective ensembles, the Find-Outers stop short of tackling the criminals themselves, calling on the kindly Inspector Jenks to round up the culprits, their investigative competency, independence and achievement eclipses that of their school story predecessors, and the resolution of each case provides child readers with a sense of empowerment that is somewhat lacking in earlier juvenile detective narratives.

Despite her commercial success and her immense popularity with child readers, from the mid-1950s Blyton faced increasing opposition from parents, teachers, librarians and literary critics. Initially, the main focus of their criticism was the poor literary quality of Blyton's work. The simplicity of language and repetitive nature of her plots were judged to be a hindrance to child readers' development. Many people, however, recognised the suitability of Blyton's work for reluctant readers and saw her stories as a steppingstone towards more sophisticated fiction. Yet concern for the child who read only Blyton may partially explain the reluctance of librarians to stock her books from the 1950s to the 1970s, though press claims of a widespread ban of Blyton's work in libraries were wildly exaggerated. Another reason for Blyton's exclusion from libraries was the vast catalogue of books she produced, which, if purchased in its entirety, would dominate the shelves at the expense of better-quality titles. In fact, the quantity of Blyton's work prompted rumours that Blyton did not write all her books, an accusation that she vehemently refuted.

Soon, however, criticisms extended from the literary quality of Blyton's work to the characterisation of her protagonists and the values she endorsed through them. While many objected to Blyton's portrayal of cruel and spiteful behaviour in her middle-class child characters, still more condemned the sexist, classist and racist attitudes inherent in her stories. Her *Noddy* series was at the heart of this controversy, particularly for its use of racial slurs. In the 1980s, in a climate of increasing political correctness, *Noddy* and other Blyton series underwent revisions. The debate over the suitability of Blyton's work for child readers diminished in the 1990s, signifying a turnaround in critical opinions towards Blyton, whose stories are now widely stocked in public libraries and are beginning, at last, to receive serious attention from literary critics.

Suggested Reading/Works Cited

McClaren, Duncan, *Looking for Enid: The Mysterious and Inventive Life of Enid Blyton* (London: Portobello Books, 2008).
Mullan, Bob, *The Enid Blyton Story* (London: Boxtree Limited, 1987).
Ray, Sheila G., *The Blyton Phenomenon: The Controversy Surrounding the World's Most Successful Children's Writer* (London: Andre Deutsch, 1983).
Rudd, David, *Enid Blyton and the Mystery of Children's Literature* (Basingstoke: Palgrave, 2000).
Stoney, Barbara, *Enid Blyton* (London, Sydney, Auckland, Toronto: Hodder and Stoughton, 1974).

CHAPTER 46

Edmund Crispin (Pseudonym of Robert Bruce Montgomery, 1921–1978), 1944: *The Case of the Gilded Fly*

Malcah Effron

Edmund Crispin first appeared with the publication of *The Case of the Gilded Fly* (1944), launching a nine-volume detective fiction series featuring Oxford Professor of English literature Gervase Fen as the amateur detective. Crispin is the pseudonym for Robert Bruce Montgomery, noted composer of film scores, such as for the popular British *Carry On* film series. Montgomery coined the pseudonym to reserve his given name for music compositions. The pseudonym assumed a life of its own, beginning with the initial popular assumption that it belonged to an Oxford don, in the same manner as Michael Innes was the pseudonym for Oxford professor J. I. M. Stewart. Furthermore, Montgomery edited and introduced critical collections of science fiction and detective fiction under the Crispin pseudonym. Most importantly, however, the pseudonym develops another dimension in its appearance within the texts, as the detective Fen often refers to Crispin as the author of the books or Crispin provides signed footnotes within the text. With this dialogue between

M. Effron (✉)
Massachusetts Institute of Technology, Cambridge, MA, USA

© The Author(s) 2020
E. Miskimmin (ed.), *100 British Crime Writers*, Crime Files,
https://doi.org/10.1057/978-1-137-31902-9_46

author and character, the novels create a sense of realism and distinguish the Edmund Crispin figure from the person Bruce Montgomery.

Robert Bruce Montgomery was born on 2 October 1921. He attended St. John's College, Oxford, where he read modern languages. He wrote his first detective novel when he should have been preparing for his exams. After finishing his degree, Montgomery taught at a public school in Shrewsbury, where produced detective novels at the rate of one a year, until 1951, at which point he took a twenty-year hiatus. Reasons for the hiatus included focus on film scores, ill health, increasing alcoholism and burn out. He completed *The Glimpses of the Moon* (1977), his last novel, three months after he married his secretary Ann Clements in 1977. Though his friends, including literati Kingsley Amis and Philip Larkin and queens of crime Agatha Christie and Dorothy L. Sayers, assumed he would die of alcoholism he died of heart failure during surgery related to osteoporosis on 15 September 1978.

The Crispin detective novels integrate a sense of farce with the intricate British Golden Age puzzle. Gervase Fen and his assistants and colleagues, who, despite disclaimers, are loosely based on Montgomery and his friends, integrate these conventions into their investigative methods. Within these erudite analyses of murders, there is always a comedic pursuit, for, as David Whittle claims, 'a Crispin novel would not be a Crispin novel if it did not finish with a chase of some sort'. Crispin published shorter pieces in the *Evening Standard*, *Beware of Trains* (1962) and the posthumous *Fen Country* (1979). These works are pithy, developing the clever puzzles of the novels rather than the caricatures that abound in his longer work. Because his detective texts revel in the complex puzzles and the intricacy of detective conventions, as Whittle suggests, Crispin's detective fiction can be summarised as 'never fashionable, in the sense of following contemporary trends [belonging] to an earlier era than the one in which they were written'.

Suggested Readings/Works Cited

Christie, David A., 'Edmund Crispin (Robert Bruce Montgomery)', in *Dictionary of Literary Biography, Volume 87: British Mystery and Thriller Writers Since 1940: First Series*, ed. by Bernard Benstock and Thomas F. Stanley (Detroit: Gale, 1989), pp. 28–35.

Routley, Erik, *The Puritan Pleasures of the Detective Story* (London: Gollancz, 1972).
Whittle, David, *Bruce Montgomery/Edmund Crispin: A Life in Music and Books* (Aldershot: Ashgate, 2007).

CHAPTER 47

Julian Symons (1912–1994), 1945: *The Immaterial Murder Case*, and 1972: *Bloody Murder: From the Detective Story to the Crime Novel* (critical work)

Christopher Routledge

Julian Gustave Symons was a prolific writer, critic, poet, historian and author of award-winning crime novels and stories. His crime fiction focuses on motivation and psychology rather than detection as such and his obituary in the *New York Times* quotes him expressing an interest in 'violence behind respectable faces, the civil servant planning how to kill Jews most efficiently, the judge speaking with passion about the need for capital punishment, the quiet obedient boy who kills for fun'. As a novelist and as a critic of the genre Symons was instrumental in establishing crime and detective fiction as a serious literary art form.

Symons was born in London, the son of a Jewish Russian immigrant and an English mother. He was educated privately at home, but because of a severe stammer was later sent to a school for children with low intelligence. Family financial circumstances meant that from their early teens

---

C. Routledge (✉)
Freelance Writer and Photographer, NW England, UK

© The Author(s) 2020
E. Miskimmin (ed.), *100 British Crime Writers*, Crime Files,
https://doi.org/10.1057/978-1-137-31902-9_47

209

Symons and his brother were essentially self-educated and Symons credited his brother, the biographer and anthologist A. J. A. Symons, who was twelve years his senior, with helping continue his education.

After leaving school at fourteen, Symons found a job as a clerk at an engineering firm, where he stayed until 1941. In 1937 he founded the poetry journal *Twentieth Century Verse* and edited it for two years, during which time he also published his first book, a collection of poetry entitled *Confusions About X* (1938). Symons was a conscientious objector in World War Two, but did eventually serve in the army for two years from 1942 to 1944.

Symons' first novel, *The Immaterial Murder Case*, was published in 1945 after his wife submitted a manuscript she found in a desk drawer to a publisher. Symons himself considered this novel a 'slapdash' piece of work, but it was bought by a publisher for £200. By then Symons was working as an advertising copywriter, but he continued to write books and he was able to become a full-time writer in 1947. His novels have a small but loyal following of readers attracted by complex, teasing plotting and characters driven by dark obsessions. Among his most highly praised novels are *The Broken Penny* (1953), *The Colour of Murder* (1957), *The Man Whose Dreams Came True* (1968) and *The Plot Against Roger Rider* (1973). His final novel, *A Sort of Virtue: A Political Crime Novel*, was published posthumously in 1996.

As a critic, Symons wrote books about Charles Dickens, Edgar Allan Poe, Dashiell Hammett, Arthur Conan Doyle and Agatha Christie, among others. He also wrote a biography of his brother, *A. J. A. Symons: His Life and Speculations* (1950). He published two books of his own poetry and wrote books on British history, and literary history. He edited collections including the selected works of Thomas Carlyle, Samuel Johnson, *Edgar Allan Poe Selected Tales* (1980) and *Verdict of Thirteen: A Detection Club Anthology* (1978). He was editor of the Penguin Mystery Series from 1974 to 1979, and later edited the *Penguin Classic Crime Omnibus* (1984).

Symons' most important book of criticism is his survey of crime and detective fiction entitled *Bloody Murder: From the Detective Story to the Crime Novel* (1972) (published as *Mortal Consequences* in the United States and revised in 1985 and 1992). This influential book is an impressively wide-ranging survey of the genre and remains among the best overviews of crime and detective writing. It was among the first works of criticism to focus on the genre's variants, in particular the difference between 'detective fiction' and 'crime fiction', the latter of which, Symons argues, offers more possibilities for social criticism and character development.

In the 1970s Symons taught at Amherst College in Massachusetts and retained links with the college thereafter. He was also a reviewer for the *Manchester Evening News*, *The Times* (London) and *Sunday Times*. In *The Sunday Times* in 1958 he published a controversial, but widely reprinted list of the '100 Best Crime Stories', beginning with William Godwin's *Caleb Williams* (1794) and ending, in 1957, with Ian Fleming's *From Russia With Love* and Mayer Levin's *Compulsion*.

Though never a bestselling novelist, Symons was widely admired for the quality and style of his work, and he won many awards and prizes. His 1957 novel *The Colour of Murder* won a Gold Dagger Award, presented by the Crime Writers' Association for best crime novel of the year; in 1961 he won an Edgar Award for Best Novel, for *The Progress of Crime* (1960). In 1982 he became a Grand Master of the Mystery Writers of America. He was the president of the Detection Club (1976–1985), a position he inherited from Agatha Christie, and was also chairman of the Crime Writers' Association. He was made a Fellow of the Royal Society of Literature in 1975.

The Julian Symons Papers are held at the University of Delaware.

FURTHER READING/WORKS CITED

Allen, Bonnie and John Walsdorf, *Julian Symons: A Bibliography. With Commentaries and a Personal Memoir by Julian Symons* (New Castle, DE: Oak Knoll Press, 1996).

Craig, Patricia, ed., *Julian Symons at 80: A Tribute* (New Castle, DE: Werner Shaw, 1992).

Symons, Julian, *Bloody Murder: From the Detective Story to the Crime Novel* (London: Viking, 1972).

PART III

Post-War and Cold War, 1946–1989

INTRODUCTION

This section begins with Michael Gilbert, whose first novel, *Close Quarters*, was published in 1947, and whose crime writing career serves as a useful introduction to some of the key features of this period, such as its marked diversity of genre. In the entry below, Christopher Routledge discusses Gilbert as a writer of thrillers, plays and clue-puzzler detective novels, but also of police procedurals and legal thrillers, demonstrating in one writer the potential variety that Haycraft hoped for in his imagined future of crime writing. In this era we find further examples of all of the above genres by some of their chief exponents, as well as examples of some very specific subgenres, such as the historical crime novel, or Dick Francis' horse-racing thrillers. There's also a growing oeuvre written specifically for younger readers, such as Antony Horowitz's 'Diamond Brothers' detective novels and his 'Alex Rider' juvenile spy series.

Despite the diversity and innovation in terms of genre in this period, there is still a place for the traditional mystery or puzzle story that dominated the previous era; some of its key exponents such as Agatha Christie continued to write long after the end of World War Two, and many writers who began their career in the latter half on the twentieth century, such as Ruth Rendell and P. D. James, utilised this older genre as the basis for their writing, adapting and developing it and introducing elements of the emerging realism and social complexity that we find throughout the crime fiction in this section. It is notable that both Rendell and

James utilise policemen as their fictional detectives, reflecting a trend in this era towards the police-procedural genre, and a stronger focus on professional rather than amateur investigators; only seven of the detective fiction writers in this part do not take a policeman or woman as at least one of their chief detectives. Although James' Adam Dalgliesh has elements of the gentleman-detective about him – echoes, perhaps, of Marsh's Alleyn or Allingham's Campion – the police-inspector character soon moves away from this, and in the ranks that include R. D. Winfield's Frost, Colin Dexter's Morse and Peter Robinson's Banks, we see a collection of generally troubled, flawed and morally conflicted human beings, career policemen who attempt to locate truths, social, legal and personal, by whatever means they can.

The diversity of this period extends also to format, with the emergence of the comic strip crime narrative such as the *Modesty Blaise* stories by Peter O'Donnell that ran in the *Evening Standard* from 1963–2001, and the development of the crime genre graphic novel such as those by Ian Rankin. The previous era saw crime writing in dramatic form with the stage plays of Christie and Sayers and the Paul Temple radio series of Francis Durbridge; in this era the scripted crime narrative continues and expands through the medium of television. This manifests itself in the adaptation of works by authors such as Colin Dexter, whose Inspector Morse novels generated the long-running television series, but perhaps more significantly through the work of authors such as Linda La Plante, who write specifically for the screen.

As the genres and formats diversify, so do the milieu. The two previous parts showed the largely polarised alternatives of London or the ubiquitous (and for the most part home-counties) country village as their setting. After World War Two we still see these, but urban writing is far less London-centric, and in many of the works discussed in this part, urban or rural, we see the beginnings of specifically regional writing, both exploring and celebrating definite regional identities. In her discussion of Reginald Hill, Malcha Effron discusses how he established and developed the 'Northern Crime' novel with his Dalziel and Pascoe series, a genre joined and sustained by many authors, such as Peter Robinson whose Banks books are set in what Greg Rees describes as a 'real and vivid' Yorkshire. The latter part of this period also sees the advent of specifically national writing by Welsh, Scottish and Northern Irish writers, particularly Scottish with the emergence of the 'Tartan Noir' movement, represented here by authors such as Val McDermid and Ian Rankin, for whom the city of Edinburgh is as intrinsic to the Rebus novels as the character himself.

The novels of Val McDermid also exemplify how much the representations of women in crime fiction have changed, especially with the advent of second-wave feminism. Just over a hundred years after Mary Elizabeth Braddon struggled with being accepted as a female writer and reader of crime fiction, P. D. James' *A Suitable Job for a Woman* (1972) deliberately establishes the role of women as a focus for discussion, and forms part of a wider discourse in both fiction and criticism on women as detectives, victims, and criminals within the genre. A more directly feminist agenda emerges towards the end of the twentieth century, represented here by writers such as McDermid and La Plante. It is worth noting another change in perspective established through McDermid's writing: Susan Massey's entry below also draws attention to the fact that 'McDermid was one of the first British authors to write serial detective fiction around a homosexual protagonist', Lindsay Gordon, who paves the way for later characters such as Stella Duffy's Saz Martin, discussed in the final part of this book.

The changes in this era are not only in attitudes to issues such as gender and sexuality. Michael Gilbert's career as a writer spans the entirely of the 'Post-War and Cold War' part, but, although only forty years lie between them, the world of Gilbert's Inspector Hazlerigg in his 1947 debut seems an unrecognisably different place to that of McDermid's Gordon, or Rankin's Rebus. Gilbert began writing after his return from serving in World War Two, and, like many of the writers in the early part of this part, his writing is directly informed by his wartime experiences and his early work belongs very much to the zeitgeist of the post-war forties and early fifties, as does that of several others. Peter O'Donnell, for example, drew on his wartime experience on the settings and events of his books, basing Modesty Blaise on a refugee child he encountered while serving with his mobile radio detachment. Ian Fleming, whose writing segues into the Cold War period, was an intelligence officer during the war and for a while after, a role that provided first-hand knowledge for the James Bond novels. As with the writing during and immediately after World War One, conflict and its concomitant literature raises the possibility of crime on an international level, with potential for the destruction of mankind rather than one individual victim. The identities of villains, victims and even crime-fighters become blurred still further in the world of Cold War spy fiction. Like Fleming, le Carré's work is informed by his time in British intelligence, although Steven Powell argues a 'level of pessimistic realism' in Le Carré's work that he sees as a counter to Fleming's more 'glamorous world of espionage'.

The prerequisite gadgets of spy fiction remind us of another significant influence on the crime writing of this period: the technological advances that both assist and hinder the endeavours of criminals and detectives alike. In four decades we move from operator-controlled landlines to mobile phones and from notebooks and paper archives to word processors and computer databases. At the very end of this era, in the late eighties, a technological innovation that would change the world forever loomed large – the impact of the internet on the content, style and production of crime fiction was phenomenal. Some authors update the worlds of their detectives according to technological progress: the last Miss Marple novel, *The Mirror Crack'd From Side to Side* (1962), sees the elderly detective in a world of supermarkets, housing estates and 'dish-washing machines', although neither she nor her creator ever had to contend with a mobile phone. Malcah Effron discusses the developing world of technology and communications in Dick Francis' novels, wryly observing that while the world of Sid Halley is updated with every modern innovation, the detective himself barely ages over the thirty years he is in print. There are, though, a number of writers in this era who eschew the modern world and its developments altogether as we see the emergence of another subgenre, that of the historical crime novel. Although there are earlier, isolated, examples of historical crime stories – Agatha Christie set her 1944 novel *Death Comes as the End* in ancient Egypt, for example – this form really begins with Ellis Peters, inceptor of the genre with her medieval monk-detective, Cadfael. Anne Perry's two Victorian detective series arguably take crime fiction back to its roots in nineteenth-century London, and her modern eye on the past arguably generates a discourse between the fiction of then and now. Lindsey Davis, best-known for her Roman private eye, Falco, is also represented below, and Heather Worthington considers the appeal of the historical crime novel in her assertion that Davis' novels reveal 'a common humanity' between the citizens of now and then.

A final and perhaps less-easily defined development of the genre in this era is also exemplified by Michael Gilbert; Christopher Routledge describes how, in his later novels, Gilbert's writing becomes darker, focusing on issues of sexual corruption, and is more shocking and vivid in its detailing of violence. This is not to say that the world itself became necessarily more corrupt or violent in the period, but there was arguably a move towards a more 'realistic' portrayal of the world and of crime and detection. Maybe it is no coincidence that many of the writers in this part such as Ruth Rendell, Frederick Forsyth and Bill James, to name but three, began their careers as journalists, recording the events of the twentieth century rather than constructing an imagined or contrived version of it to fit a plot (it is interesting to note that in the Golden Age many crime writers, including Sayers, Christie and Marsh, were also dramatists, writing and directing performed versions of the world, rather than reporting and reflecting on its realities as these later journalist-authors do). Much of the writing selected from the latter half of this era for inclusion in this list is undeniably psychologically darker than the writing of the previous parts. In considering the work of Ruth Rendell writing as Barbara Vine, Anne-Marie Beller describes how the reader often finds themselves 'cast adrift in a chillingly amoral and dangerous universe'. This focus on reader discomfort is interesting; as we move away from the neat resolution of puzzle mysteries, the exploration of humanity, morality and justice as focuses for crime writing becomes even more complex, and the reader is not always offered the comfort or resolution of a neat solution or a clear sense of who is 'right', legally or morally. As the twentieth century progresses, crimes of a different kind are written about and we see an increase in depictions of sexual violence and gun crime, also of trafficking, child abuse and terrorism. Concomitantly, it seems, the descriptions of these crimes become more direct and graphic; Susan Massey describes Val McDermid's use of violence in *The Mermaids Singing* as 'almost medieval in its barbarism'. This move towards a more brutal, dark and potentially realistic representation of crime foreshadows what is to come as the genre moves towards and into the twenty-first century. It becomes harder to interpret the processes of reading crime fiction as vicariously comforting and the stories themselves as a reassurance of the restored order that we can hope for in the hands of the detective. Instead, we are increasingly presented with investigators who operate in a world that is as fragmented, damaged and irreparable as they are.

Esme Miskimmin

CHAPTER 48

Michael Gilbert (1912–2006), 1947: *Close Quarters*

Christopher Routledge

A writer of many thrillers, plays and 'clue-puzzler' detective novels, most notably the novel *Smallbone Deceased* (1950), Gilbert was also a partner in the Lincoln's Inn law firm of Trower, Still and Keeling. His novels, which sold well on both sides of the Atlantic, often feature lawyers, but his influences were wide-ranging, from the hard-boiled stories of Dashiell Hammett, through Agatha Christie, to the spy fiction of Eric Ambler, as well as legal thrillers. His best-known series character is a policeman, Inspector Hazlerigg, who appears in several novels and short stories, including Gilbert's first, *Close Quarters* (1947) and *Smallbone Deceased*. Other popular series characters include the spies Daniel John Calder and Samuel Behrens. Gilbert was one of the most successful and prolific British crime writers of his generation, publishing over thirty novels and hundreds of short stories in a career lasting fifty years.

Michael Francis Gilbert was born in Billinghay, Lincolnshire. His father, Bernard Gilbert, was a novelist and poet, while his mother, Anne Cuthbert, was a journalist. He was educated at Blundell's School in Tiverton, Devon, and received his law degree (LLB) from the University

---

C. Routledge (✉)
Freelance Writer and Photographer, NW England, UK

© The Author(s) 2020
E. Miskimmin (ed.), *100 British Crime Writers*, Crime Files,
https://doi.org/10.1057/978-1-137-31902-9_48

of London in 1937, while he was working as a teacher at the Cathedral School, Salisbury. World War Two interrupted Gilbert's budding legal career. He served in North Africa with the Honourable Artillery Company, was taken as a prisoner of war to Italy, and after escape and recapture, was eventually released in the chaos of the Italian army's unilateral declaration of an armistice. He and two others, one of whom was Eric Newby, the travel writer, walked back to the Allied lines some five hundred miles to the south, where they took part in the Battle for Rome. Gilbert's novel *Death in Captivity* (1952) is set in a prisoner of war camp, but he also wrote about his personal experience in *The Long Journey Home* (1985).

Gilbert's clients as senior partner in Trower, Still and Keeling included the Sultan of Bahrain and the Conservative Party. In the 1950s he advised crime writer Raymond Chandler, who was in dispute with the British tax and immigration authorities, and they became friends. Chandler, who by then was becoming a hopeless drunk, wrote around one hundred letters to Gilbert, who reminisced in his essay 'Autumn in London': 'To go out with him in the evening was asking for trouble, but he could still be his delightful self at lunch'. Gilbert's experiences as a lawyer frequently informed his writing and many of his novels have a legal theme or courtroom setting, including *Death Has Deep Roots* (1951), *Flash Point* (1974) and the widely praised *Smallbone Deceased*, which H. R. F. Keating described as 'a classic of the genre'. Lawyers, such as Jonas Pickett, and policemen, such as Chief Inspector Hazlerigg, are among his most engaging characters.

Gilbert married Roberta Marsden in 1947, the same year that his first novel, *Close Quarters* was published. They had two sons and five daughters, one of whom, Harriet Gilbert, is a novelist and academic. Much of Gilbert's remarkable output of novels, stories and plays was produced for thirty years alongside his work as a lawyer. Famously, he did much of his writing in this period during his fifty-minute commute by train from his home in Kent to the centre of London.

Gilbert is known not only for the volume but also for the range of crime and detective stories he produced. While considered by many a proponent of the 'cosy' English style, he wrote police procedurals, espionage thrillers and legal thrillers, many of which take a very clear-eyed and topical approach to corruption and violence in institutions and establishment organisations. For example, *The Crack in the Teacup* (1965) involves a corruption plot in local government, and was published at a time when real-life corruption plots, in cities such as Newcastle upon Tyne, were coming to light. In his obituary of Gilbert H. R. F. Keating cites *The Night of the Twelfth* (1976) as his masterpiece of 'darker undercurrents ... and ugly reality, in the shape of sadism, sexual corruption, and sudden, shocking violence ....'.

Gilbert was never a well-known writer outside of mystery and crime writing circles, partly because he was reluctant to promote himself; in fact his byline often credits him as 'Michael Gilbert, British solicitor' rather than mentioning his writing. But his books sold steadily and were very well received by critics and an appreciative readership. He was a conscientious prose stylist and a careful plotter whose advice on writing to his daughter Harriet was 'For God's sake, don't use adverbs'.

He was elected to the Detection Club in 1949 and was a founder member of the Crime Writers' Association. In 1988 he was made a Grand Master of the Mystery Writers of America and received a Lifetime Achievement Award at the 1990 Bouchercon, which was held in London. He was made a Commander of the Order of the British Empire (CBE) in 1980 and became a Fellow of the Royal Society of Literature (FRSL) in 1999.

Suggested Reading/Works Cited

Adrian, Jack, 'Obituary: Michael Gilbert', *The Independent*, 10 February 2006.
Gilbert, Michael, 'Autumn in London', in *The World of Raymond Chandler*, ed. by Miriam Gross (London: Wiedenfeld and Nicholson, 1977), pp. 103–114.
Keating, H. R. F., 'Michael Gilbert' (obituary), *The Guardian*, 10 February, 2006.

CHAPTER 49

Ellis Peters (Pseudonym of Edith Mary Pargeter, also wrote as Jolyon Carr, 1913–1995), 1951: *Fallen into the Pit*

Suzanne Bray

Ellis Peters is best known as the creator of Brother Cadfael, the hero of a series of twenty novels and three short stories of historical detective fiction, based in twelfth-century Shrewsbury at the time of the civil war between King Stephen and his cousin the Empress Maud.

Ellis Peters was born Edith Mary Pargeter on September 28, 1913, in the village of Horsehay, near Telford, Shropshire, to Edmund Valentine Pargeter and his wife Edith, *née* Hordley. She was the youngest of their three children. Edmund Ellis (always known as Ellis), born in 1907, was named after his Welsh maternal grandmother, Emma Ellis. Margaret was born in 1911. They were not wealthy, but the family was musical and spent any spare money on books, which the children were encouraged to read. Edith attended Dawley Church of England Primary School in a nearby village and then won a scholarship to Coalbrookdale County High School for Girls. She was known at school as 'the girl who never stopped writing' and started her first novel at the age of twelve. Although Edith

S. Bray (✉)
Lille Catholic University, Lille, France

© The Author(s) 2020
E. Miskimmin (ed.), *100 British Crime Writers*, Crime Files,
https://doi.org/10.1057/978-1-137-31902-9_49

was good enough academically to go to university, she decided to become financially independent and earn her own living as soon as possible. She started work as a pharmacist's assistant at Dawley in 1933 and stayed there for the next seven years, gaining information about drugs and poisons which would come in useful later when she started writing detective fiction. Her first novel, *Hortensius, Friend of Nero*, was published in 1936, but did not sell well. However, she had more success with her next novels, two of which, *Murder in the Dispensary* (1938) and *Freedom for Two* (1939), published under the pseudonym Jolyon Carr, were first written as serial stories for a local magazine before being written up for publication in book form. These were her first attempt at crime fiction, although they are not classic detective novels, but rather sensational thrillers, concerned with rescuing damsels in distress.

When war broke out in 1939, Edith tried to join the WRAF, but found that she could not enlist because pharmacy was a reserved occupation. She therefore resigned from her job and applied to join the WRNS, listing her occupation as 'writer'. This time there was no problem and she was sent first to Portsmouth and then to Liverpool, where she spent most of the war working as a teleprinter operator in the Signals Office with nine other women, working shifts around the clock to monitor the war in and over the Atlantic. She had a good war, being promoted to Petty Officer and winning the British Empire Medal 'for meritorious service' in 1945, before hostilities actually ended. It was presented to her by the King on VE Day. The war also gave her plenty to write about and the free time to do it. Her first bestseller, *She Goes to War* (1942), the fictionalised correspondence of a teleprinter operator at the heart of the war effort, and a critically acclaimed trilogy, *The Eight Champion of Christendom* (1945–47), which presented the war as it happened from the point of view of a young soldier, gave her the financial autonomy she sought. As her father had died in 1940, after demobilisation Edith returned to Shropshire to live with her widowed mother, who died in 1956. She then bought a house in Madeley with her brother Ellis, where they lived together for the next thirty-five years.

Ellis Peters claimed to have 'approached the detective story almost inadvertently' through her 1951 novel *Fallen into the Pit*, which provides a transition between Second World War fiction and crime. This is the first book to feature her police detective George Felse and his son Dominic, who are faced with a murder-mystery rooted in the problems of displaced persons, former prisoners of war and soldiers returned from the front, ill-at-ease in their calm, native village after six years of travel and violence. Although it was first published by Edith Pargeter, *Fallen into the Pit* is now part of the Ellis Peters corpus. The pseudonym was first used for her second detective novel, *Death Mask* (1959), where a bereaved teenage, Crispin Almond, turns detective in order to find the truth about his father's death. The first name Ellis was borrowed from her brother and the surname Peters from Petra, the daughter of a Czech friend. From then on, the pseudonym was used for all Pargeter's crime novels.

The George and Dominic Felse series is mainly set in the fictional county of Midshire, which corresponds to Shropshire, and particularly in the area around the town of Comerford, more or less equivalent to the Upper Teme Valley. The novels exploit the author's deep attachment to the border country and the terrain is at the heart of the plots. Peters claimed in *Shropshire* (1990) that the county was 'simply in [her] blood' and that 'in the course of creation the blood gets into the ink'. One of the most successful novels, *Flight of a Witch* (1964) evokes an ancient, mystical landscape, the Hallowmount and its interaction with modern society. The sixth-formers in the local school, including Dominic Felse, see 'nothing incongruous about having one foot in the twentieth century and one in the roots of time', an attitude certainly shared by their creator.

Peters also used other settings she knew well. Together with her brother, she was an active member of the WEA (Workers' Educational Association) and worked with others to turn the eighteenth-century mansion Attingham Park into Shrophire Education Adult College. Sir George Trevelyan was the warden from its opening in 1948. Although Peters is careful to note that Follymead in *Black Is the Colour of My True Love's Heart* (1967) is not Attingham – Follymead is Gothic and Attingham neo-classical – there is a strong resemblance between the atmosphere and aims of the two establishments.

In the same way, Peters used her knowledge of Czechoslovakia for the setting of her 1966 novel *The Piper on the Mountain*. In 1938, she had felt betrayed by Chamberlain's willingness to sacrifice Czechoslovakia in the Munich agreement with Hitler and thought that Britain owed a debt to the Czech people. After making friends with several Czech airmen during the war, she and her brother made the most of the first opportunity to visit the country, for a summer school in 1947. She returned the following summer and stayed for three months. A book, *Coast of Bohemia* (1950), was the fruit of these visits. From then on Peters taught herself Czech and translated several classics of Czech literature into English. In 1968 she was awarded the gold medal and ribbon of the Czech Society for International Relations. In *Piper on the Mountain*, Peters shows her knowledge of the landscape and culture, but also plays with the conventions of the thriller at the time. Dominic Felse strongly suspects the Czechs of being up to no good and of hiding the reason for his friend Tossa's stepfather's death. However, the suspected spy turns out to be a musician, the Czech police are virtue personified and the tale is really one of the misuse of power and corruption in the British corridors of power. Two attempts to use her visit to India, at the invitation of friends from the Indian embassy in Prague, in the same way were less successful, particularly *Mourning Raga* (1969). This is mainly because the virtuous Indian Swami is rather too good to be true and the villains are hardly credible. Although the Indian setting is no easier to accept in *Death to the Landlords* (1972), the character of Patti Galloway is very convincing and helps to explain why some wealthy, middle-class young people were attracted to terrorist movements in the 1970s.

The strength and weakness of the Felse series is in its police family. George is a pleasant ordinary policeman, trying hard to do his job. He has no eccentricities and is rarely the central character, enabling Peters' strong supporting cast to take centre stage. His equally charming and upright wife, Bunty, only really comes to life in *The Grass Widow's Tale* (1968), when she helps bring justice to a young man who falsely thinks he is guilty of murder. Dominic's development from curious thirteen-year-old to Oxford graduate with a fiancée and a social conscience has more substance. The adolescent crush which motivates his first rebellion against paternal authority in *Death and the Joyful Woman* (1961), so as to clear his beloved from suspicion, is sensitively handled, winning his creator the Edgar Allan Poe Award from the Mystery Writers of America. Although they all have contemporary settings, both the Felse novels and the other one-off detective mysteries Peters was writing at the time have many cultural and historical elements. Music, artifacts and ancient buildings play an important part in the plot and the characters frequently have to face ghosts from the past in order to the unravel the mysteries of the present.

Peters was always more interested in good than in evil, in her crime fiction as well as her straight novels. In *Twentieth Century Crime and Mystery Writers* she says this about the detective novel: 'It is, it ought to be, it must be, a morality. If it strays from the side of the angels, provokes despair, wilfully destroys – without pressing need in the plot – the innocent and the good, takes pleasure in evil, that is the unforgiveable sin. I use the word deliberately and gravely'. However, Peters was not interested in the mere puzzle plot and always tried to create 'a cast of genuine, rounded, knowable characters, caught in conditions of stress ... and still try to preserve to the end the secret of which of these is a murderer'. Annoyed by the fact that detective fiction was not taken seriously by the literary establishment and 'allotted about one twentieth of the review space', she explained in an article called 'The Thriller is a Novel': '... the thriller is a paradox. It must be a mystery and it must be a novel. And it is virtually schizophrenia to aim at both. But for a dedicated author nothing less is conceivable'. The psychology of the characters is therefore always essential to the understanding of Peters' plots and the crime is not always the principal interest. Lonely people find companions and tormented people are set free from past terrors.

In 1977, at the age of 63, shortly before writing the final Felse novel, *Rainbow's End* (1978), Ellis Peters wrote a story, which she intended as a one-off, about the history of Shrewsbury Abbey, *A Morbid Taste for Bones* (1977). For this reason she created the character of Brother Cadfael ap Meilyr ap Dafydd, a monk of Shrewsbury Abbey who, like his creator, was at home on both sides of the English/Welsh border. Peters, although English, always claimed that she had 'a toehold over the border, by courtesy of one Welsh grandmother' and that she could feel 'the tension that Housman sensed between England and Wales'. Her publisher, lacking enthusiasm, only had it printed in a hardback edition for libraries. Peters had found the plot in the Cartulary of Shrewsbury Abbey, published by the National Library of Wales in 1975. Although she had not intended to create a series, she kept reading and found a second plot in the siege of Shrewsbury in 1138, a year after the events in her first Cadfael novel. From then on Brother Cadfael developed a life of his own and Peters continued for twenty novels and three short stories chronicling the life of Shrewsbury, season by season, through his eyes. Possibly encouraged by the phenomenal success of Umberto Eco's *The Name of the Rose* (1980; first English edn 1983), historical detective fiction became the fashion and all the Cadfael stories sold well, making their author a celebrity. The third novel, *Monk's Hood* (1980) won the English Crime Writers' Association's Silver Dagger award. Thirteen years later, she received a Diamond Dagger for the whole Cadfael series. This was presented in a formal ceremony in the House of Lords.

Although Ellis Peters considered that she was 'not very good at short stories', needing 'the elbow room of the novel' in order to create credible characters, her short story about Cadfael's call to monastic life, 'A Light on the Road to Woodstock', published in the collection *A Rare Benedictine* (1988), is a masterpiece. It charts Cadfael's last days as a crusader, his vocation and his first steps as a detective. Peters' history is always accurate. In her introduction to *The Cadfael Companion* she refers to the series as 'an amalgam of stark fact and derived fiction'. Her respect for this fact is considerable and she claims: 'The fictional element is derived always with due respect to the known, recorded and agreed facts of English and Welsh history in the twelfth century. I have not tampered with anything that is accepted as authentic ....'.

However, within this framework, Peters felt free 'to imagine, to name and to fit into the trellis of history' all the 'teeming thousands whose names are not recorded'. These common people, in her opinion, 'existed as surely as did the kings, then and in every age since'. Mixing proven fact and fictional might-have-been is a delicate process. Peters claimed that 'only when the authorities fight over details do I use my own judgment'. A good example of this may be seen in 'A Light on the Road to Woodstock', with its background of international tensions. It is set in November 1120, at the time of the wreck of the White Ship, which killed the king's son, his bride and many of their friends. Cadfael's progress is delayed by the official period of mourning declared for the whole country and this gives him the time to solve the mystery.

The Cadfael stories are not just murder mysteries. Some people read them for their historical content, others for the inevitable love story which Peters always combines with the crime and detection. Contemporary readers are often interested in the herbal remedies brewed in Cadfael's workshop. Several of the Cadfael novels have been adapted for television with Derek Jacobi in the title role.

Cadfael took up most of Ellis Peters' final years and she became increasingly frail. After her brother's death in 1984, she moved into a modern house next door to her cousin Mavis, whose husband Roy collaborated with her in producing her book on Shropshire and a further work about the border country, *Strongholds and Sanctuaries*, in 1993.

Her right leg was amputated at the knee when she was 82. She died on October 14, 1995 in her house in Madeley. There is a memorial to her in Shrewsbury Abbey.

SUGGESTED READING/WORKS CITED

Lewis, Margaret, *Edith Pargeter: Ellis Peters* (Bridgend: Seren, 1994).
Peters, Ellis, 'The Thriller Is a Novel', in *Techniques of Novel Writing*, ed. by A. S. Burack (Boston, MA: The Writer, Inc, 1973), pp. 213–218.
Reilly, John M., *Twentieth Century Crime and Mystery Writers* (London: St. Martin's press, 1980).
Talbot, Rob and Robin Whiteman, *Cadfael Country* (London: Little Brown, 1990).
Whiteman, Robin, *The Cadfael Companion* (London: Little Brown, 1991).

CHAPTER 50

Ian Fleming (1908–1964), 1953: *Casino Royale*

Christopher Routledge

Ian Fleming is the creator of the fictional spy James Bond, agent 007, who appeared in twelve bestselling novels and two short story collections between 1953 and 1966, and who features as the central character in a billion-dollar movie franchise spanning forty years. Bond is a famously overdrawn character, who smokes and drinks too much, exercises too little, and yet is irresistible to women, and able to withstand near super-human levels of physical punishment. He is most often deployed by the British secret service to investigate and prevent criminal acts of global significance. These are planned by agents of the Russian intelligence agency, SMERSH, or by ruthless criminal masterminds plotting world domination. The titles of Fleming's early novels in particular are as familiar as any in literature: *Casino Royale* (1953); *Live and Let Die* (1954); *Moonraker* (1955); *Diamonds Are Forever* (1956); *From Russia with Love* (1957) and *Dr. No* (1958). In addition to the Bond series, Fleming also wrote *Chitty Chitty Bang Bang* (first published in three volumes, 1964), a children's story about a flying car. In 2008 Fleming was

C. Routledge (✉)
Freelance Writer and Photographer, NW England, UK

© The Author(s) 2020
E. Miskimmin (ed.), *100 British Crime Writers*, Crime Files,
https://doi.org/10.1057/978-1-137-31902-9_50

listed by *The Times* (London) as one of the fifty greatest British writers since 1945.

Ian Lancaster Fleming was born in Mayfair, London, the son of Valentine Fleming and Evelyn St. Croix Rose Fleming. Fleming's father came from a wealthy landowning family and was Conservative MP for Henley from 1910 until 1917, when he was killed in action during World War One in Picardy, France. Fleming's mother inherited his fortune, but it was held in trust for her, with the stipulation that she would lose it if she married again. John Cork, author of *The James Bond Encyclopedia* suggests that Fleming's ruthless ambition was driven at least in part by his sense of being overshadowed by his father and his older brother Peter.

Like his brother Fleming attended Eton College, where he excelled at sports, but he did not complete his schooling there before moving to Sandhurst, the training college for British Army officers. Leaving Sandhurst before receiving his commission, he was sent abroad to study languages, first to Austria, then to Germany, where he studied at Munich University, and to Switzerland. Having failed to enter the Foreign Office as his mother had planned, Fleming took a job with the news agency Reuters and worked for a while in Moscow. After the death of his grandfather Robert Fleming in 1933, Ian Fleming became a stockbroker with Rowe and Pitman.

After his return to London, Fleming held stylish dinner parties at his flat in Belgravia, and developed a taste for Bridge and casual affairs. He had friends and contacts in journalism, the Foreign Office, the banks and in government, and entertained them all with his elegant wit and stylish parties. But by 1939 he was bored with the stock market and joined the Royal Navy as assistant to Rear Admiral John Henry Godfrey, Director of Naval Intelligence.

With his imagination, his willingness to take calculated risks, and his strong sense of loyalty, Fleming was ideal in the role of intelligence officer. Like his most famous fictional character, James Bond, he eventually rose to the rank of Commander. Fleming oversaw operations such as the evacuation of Dieppe in 1940, and managed commando intelligence missions behind German lines. His work with 30 Assault Unit, for which he was widely praised, as well as his intelligence work more generally, has an obvious connection with the Bond novels. Despite their melodramatic plots and fanciful conspiracies, it is Fleming's first-hand knowledge of spying that gives the books a sense of being grounded in reality.

50 IAN FLEMING (1908-1964), 1953: *CASINO ROYALE* 233

Fleming's personal life often had an effect on his professional direction. After the war Fleming continued to work for the intelligence service, but he was increasingly attracted to the island of Jamaica, which he had visited for conference in 1945. He built a house there, which he called Goldeneye, after an intelligence operation in which he was involved during World War Two. Fleming spent his winters on the Jamaica estate, travelling back to England to work as a journalist for the rest of the year. In 1952 Fleming married his long-term, and pregnant, mistress, Lady Anne Rothermere (Anne Charteris) at Goldeneye, in a ceremony witnessed by his close friend and neighbour Noël Coward. Goldeneye became their main home, and was the place where all Fleming's novels were written.

The James Bond series has its origins in English spy thrillers of the early twentieth century – books such as John Buchan's *The 39 Steps* (1915) – but with the additional tension provided by the Cold War, the possibility of global destruction, and, as Julian Symons suggests, a taste for glamour and excitement among readers in Britain's post-war austerity years. Bond, whose name comes from an American ornithologist, is famously picky about the tools he uses, from his Mont Blanc pen, to his 1933 Bentley and the Walther PPK automatic pistol he carries.

It was at Goldeneye in 1952 that Fleming began writing his first novel, *Casino Royale*, and it was published the following spring by Jonathan Cape. While this is the novel that introduced James Bond, Agent 007, to the world, initial sales were unspectacular. Symons speculates that this was in part because Bond's freedom to act provided an antithesis to the Welfare State and that in the United States, where no such contrast existed, Bond made less sense. But it seems more likely that it was Bond's pathological Britishness that made him less appealing to Americans.

Fleming built his narratives around the idea of a ferociously capable British spy standing alone against overwhelming odds. It was a narrative that British readers after World War Two will have recognised from the war years. When Bond does seek help, it is most often from the technologically and financially superior CIA, an American organisation which nonetheless relies on Bond's abilities even while it disowns him. David Seed elaborates on this reading in his essay on 'Spy Fiction' arguing in relation to Bond's rescue by an American agent in *Casino Royale* that: 'Although the Bond novels heavily emphasise the British identity of their hero, his activities are constantly supported by American agencies, financing, and know-how'.

As a hero, and as a representative of Britain's secret services, Bond also appealed to a sense in Cold War Britain that however vulnerable British society might seem to threats from larger nations and organisations lacking a sense of fair play, its institutions could also, in their own way, play dirty. Bond's 'double-oh' code number '007', indicates that he has a 'license to kill', which, in a culture where the police did not carry guns, gave him a lethal edge sanctioned by the regulating bureaucracy. In this respect, as in several others, Bond resembles the 'licensed' private eye of American hard-boiled detective fiction. Like the private eye, Bond is always at risk of having his license revoked or suspended.

At the beginning of his writing career in the 1950s, Fleming was encouraged and supported by Raymond Chandler, the anglophile creator of the series detective Philip Marlowe. They became friends, and in April 1956, having written a very favourable review of *Moonraker* (1955) for the *Sunday Times*, Chandler wrote to Fleming, who was considering killing off his creation after just three novels: 'I think you will have to make up your mind what kind of writer you are going to be. You could be almost anything except that I think you are a bit of a sadist!' There is something of Marlowe in Bond's fondness for alcohol and women, and something of the hard-boiled style in Fleming's minimalist descriptions, much admired by Chandler. Umberto Eco, in his essay 'Narrative Structures in Fleming' refers to him as a 'knight', a term also used to describe Marlowe. But the amoral British spy is much more rakish and decadent than the down at heel, honourable American detective. *Casino Royale*, with its extended game of Baccarat, its detailed cocktail recipes, and brand name checking, set a tone for the series that was as much to do with male fantasy as it was spying. The books have been criticised for their sexism and racism; Bond is frequently violent towards women. Yet the reasons for the eventual huge success of the books are their vivid characters, strong plotting and thrilling set pieces; the early Bond novels are exemplary thrillers.

Although Fleming's early books sold steadily, they were not bestsellers outside of Britain. *Casino Royale*, and *Live and Let Die* (1954) were written in quick succession, establishing the series, while *Moonraker* is the first of the novels not to involve SMERSH but a criminally insane industrialist, Hugo Drax. *Moonraker* is generally regarded as having established Fleming's reputation as a writer of real quality, and was widely praised by reviewers in Britain and the United States. However, it was not until President John F. Kennedy admitted in 1961 that *From Russia with Love* was one of his favourite books that James Bond became a huge success. Thereafter, and with each successful film adaptation, the popularity of the Bond stories grew.

The first Fleming novel to be made into a feature-length movie was *Dr. No* (1962) starring Sean Connery in the lead role. The film, like those that followed, was more light-hearted than the novel, a formula that helped sustain the franchise for over forty years. In 1961 Fleming sold the rights to all his Bond novels and stories, past and future, to Harry Salzman, who with fellow producer Albert R. 'Cubby' Broccoli, guided the movie franchise for most of its existence through the production company Eon.

At first Fleming was not happy with the choice of Connery, who was one of six actors screentested, but Connery played Bond in the first five films, and then returned in 1971 for the seventh, *Diamonds Are Forever*. There is an ongoing dispute among Bond fans over whether Connery or Roger Moore, who played Bond seven times, is best, but there is little doubt that these two actors presided over the franchise's heyday, even if subsequent films have made more at the box office. A further four actors have played Bond in the main franchise: George Lazenby once in *On Her Majesty's Secret Service* (1969), Timothy Dalton twice, Pierce Brosnan, four times, and Daniel Craig twice in 2006 and 2008. Craig's performances in *Casino Royale* (2006), *Quantum of Solace* (2008) and *Skyfall* (2012) are notably tougher and less humorous than earlier Bonds. Outside the Eon franchise Connery played Bond coming out of retirement in *Never Say Never Again* (1983) while David Niven also played an out of retirement Bond in the parody *Casino Royale* (1967).

The Bond novels are the most successful spy novels ever written, and are much copied and parodied. The novels and stories themselves have to some extent been overshadowed by the big budget movies they inspired, but they are among the best of their kind: well informed, dramatically forceful and written with a dry wit and descriptive economy. Fleming honed and developed his style, particularly in the course of the first six books.

By the late 1950s Fleming was wealthy enough to retire to Jamaica to write full-time. He also became enthused by golf, which he played as often as he could, but his interest in writing novels declined: by 1960 he had achieved his aim to write 'the spy story to end all spy stories'. Fleming was an enthusiastic traveller, a bibliophile with a large collection of first editions, and also involved himself in the production of the Bond movies, though he only lived long enough to see two of them. By the early 1960s Fleming's heavy drinking and smoking had begun to affect his health and in 1961 he suffered a heart attack from which he never fully recovered. He died at the age of 56, in Canterbury, England. His son Caspar died of a drug overdose in 1975 and his wife Anne died in 1981.

After his death, partly because of the success of the movie franchise which demanded new stories at regular intervals, other writers were hired by the Fleming estate to write James Bond stories. These included Kingsley Amis (*Colonel Sun*, 1968), John Gardner, Raymond Benson and Sebastian Faulks, whose book *Devil May Care* appeared in 2008 in tribute to the 100th anniversary of Fleming's birth. Jeffery Deaver's *Carte Blanche* was published in 2011, and the most recent Bond novel *Solo*, by William Boyd was published in 2013. There is also a series of 'Young Bond' novels, written by Charlie Higson. But Fleming's influence on the genre is also realised in the gritty realistic work of John le Carré, Len Deighton and others, whose stories emphasise the harsh cynicism and mundane nature of Cold War political narratives, and were to some extent a reaction against the fantasised depiction of spying in the work of Fleming and his imitators.

Suggested Reading/Works Cited

Cork, John, *The James Bond Encyclopedia* (London: Dorling Kindersley, 2007).
Eco, Umberto, 'Narrative Structures in Fleming', in *The Role of the Reader: Explorations in the Semiotics of Texts* (London: Hutchinson, 1987), pp. 144–172.
Lycett, Andrew, *Ian Fleming* (London: Orion, 2009).
Pearson, John, *The Life of Ian Fleming* (London: Aurum Press, 2003).
Seed, David, 'Spy Fiction', in *The Cambridge Companion to Crime Fiction*, ed. by Martin Priestman (Cambridge: Cambridge University Press, 2003), pp. 115–134.
'The 50 Greatest British Writers Since 1945', *The Times*, 5 January 2008. http://www.thetimes.co.uk/tto/arts/books/article2452094.ece.

CHAPTER 51

H. R. F. Keating (1926–2011), 1959: *Death and the Visiting Firemen*

Christopher Routledge

Journalist and crime fiction reviewer for *The Times* newspaper, Keating is the author of over fifty books, including the popular and acclaimed Inspector Ghote series of detective novels. Although a British-based writer, Keating is notable for having set his most successful work in India, Inspector Ghote being an officer of the Bombay (Mumbai) Police. Along with Julian Symons, Keating was an important crime and detective fiction book reviewer in the 1960s and 1970s; he is the author of books about Sherlock Holmes, Agatha Christie, and *How to Write Crime Fiction* (1986).

Henry Raymond Fitzwalter Keating – known as Harry – was born in St. Leonards on Sea, East Sussex and attended Merchant Taylor's School, London, before reading Modern Languages at Trinity College, Dublin. In 1953 he married Sheila Mitchell, with whom he had four children. In 1956 the couple moved to London, where Keating became a journalist with the *Daily Telegraph*. He later moved to *The Times*, where he was the crime fiction reviewer for fifteen years. Keating was encouraged to write

C. Routledge (✉)
Freelance Writer and Photographer, NW England, UK

© The Author(s) 2020
E. Miskimmin (ed.), *100 British Crime Writers*, Crime Files,
https://doi.org/10.1057/978-1-137-31902-9_51

and publish his stories by his wife, and his first published novel, the surreal *Death and the Visiting Firemen*, appeared in 1959.

Inspector Ghote first appeared in the 1964 novel *The Perfect Murder*, which won the Crime Writers' Association's (CWA) prestigious Gold Dagger Award in Britain and the Edgar Allan Poe Award in the United States. It was Keating's sixth published novel and those that came before were successful in Britain. In their *Good Reading Guide to Murder* (1990), Kenneth and Valerie MacLeish describe books like *Death and the Visiting Fireman* (set in a firefighting conference) and *Zen There Was Murder* (1960; set on a retreat for Zen Buddhists) as 'brilliant spoofs', but these books did not translate well to American audiences and were never published in the United States.

Keating began working on the Inspector Ghote books partly as a response to this sense of being 'too English'. In search of somewhere exotic as a setting for his next story Keating reports sitting down with an Atlas and picking India almost on a whim. *The Perfect Murder* was an almost immediate success on both sides of the Atlantic, and Ghote featured in a series of books published more or less annually for the next fifteen years. Ghote's bankability as a character is evident in the titles published in the 1960s and early 1970s: *Inspector Ghote's Good Crusade* (1966), *Inspector Ghote Caught in Meshes* (1967), *Inspector Ghote Hunts the Peacock* (1968) and so on. Keating's novels were also popular in India, but it is worth noting that he did not visit the country for the first time until ten years after the publication of the first Ghote novel. Until then his only experience of India was from research; after his visit he claimed to have found writing the books more difficult.

Julian Symons, who categorised Keating, in *Bloody Murder* (1985), as an 'entertainer' nevertheless thought highly of him as a writer, and believed he had been 'hampered' by Ghote, and prevented from developing in more interesting directions. Symons gives *The Murder of the Maharajah* (1980), a non-Ghote mystery which earned Keating his second Golden Dagger, as an example, and says that it 'shows what Keating can do when free of Ghote'.

After the late 1970s Keating wrote Ghote novels more intermittently, in between stand-alone novels and other series. In 1978 he published an apocalyptic science fiction novel, *A Long Walk to Wimbledon*, and between 1984 and 1986 he published three novels as Evelyn Hervey. From 2000 he pursued his Harriett Martens series about a female Detective Inspector in the British police force, and in 2008 returned to Inspector Ghote, with a prequel, *Inspector Ghote's First Case*, and, in 2009, *A Small Case for Inspector Ghote?* Keating's non-fiction has been similarly influential. In 1977 his book *Agatha Christie: First Lady of Crime* was the first book about Christie to appear after her death, while *Writing Crime Fiction* (1986) remains a perceptive and important guide to writing in the genre. In 1987 Keating published *Crime and Mystery: The 100 Best Books*, containing short critical pieces on the 100 books Keating thought were the best in the genre up to that point. In terms of influence Keating's list was equivalent to that drawn up by Symons for the *Times* thirty years earlier. Yet despite his success, Keating's work never made the transition from book to television or film in a significant way. Of Keating's fifty-plus novels, only one, *The Perfect Murder*, has so far been adapted for film (by Ismail Merchant, in 1998).

Besides his writing, Keating was always an active member of the crime and detective writing community: a Fellow of the Royal Society of Literature, he was Chairman of the Crime Writers' Association (1970–1971), The Society of Authors (1983–1984) and was President of the Detection Club (1985–2000). In 1996 he received the Crime Writers' Association Cartier Diamond Dagger in honour of his remarkable lifetime service to crime writing.

Suggested Reading/Works Cited

Keating, H. R. F., *Crime and Mystery: The Best 100 Books* (New York: Carroll & Graf, 1987).
Ripley, Mike, 'Obituary: H. R. F. Keating', *The Guardian*, 28 March 2011. http://www.guardian.co.uk/books/2011/mar/28/hrf-keating-obituary.
Salwak, Dale, ed., *Mystery Voices: Interviews with British Crime Writers— Catherine Aird, P. D. James, H. R. F. Keating, Ruth Rendell and Julian Symons* (San Bernadino, CA: Borgo Press, 1991).
Tamaya, Meera, *H. R. F. Keating: Post-Colonial Detection (A Critical Study)* (Bowling Green, OH: Bowling Green State University Popular Press, 1993).

CHAPTER 52

John le Carré (Pseudonym of David John Moore Cornwell, b. 1931), 1961: *A Call for the Dead*

Steven Powell

John le Carré is best known for his spy novels that have brought a level of pessimistic realism to spy fiction, serving as the perfect antithesis to the glamorous world of espionage portrayed in Ian Fleming's James Bond novels. Le Carré's most famous fictional creation is the British spy George Smiley. Smiley is a cunning, successful spy but is emotionally inadequate as a husband and is often cuckolded by his wife Ann. Smiley appears as a character in seven of le Carré's novels, including the celebrated Karla trilogy: *Tinker Tailor Soldier Spy* (1974), *The Honourable Schoolboy* (1977) and *Smiley's People* (1979).

David John Moore Cornwell was born to Ronald and Olive Glassy Cornwell in Poole, Dorset. Olive deserted the family when Cornwell was still an infant. Ronald Cornwell was a professional swindler and conman who funded his lavish lifestyle by setting up fictional companies and lines of credit. This led to him being in and out of prison for fraud and periodically being declared bankrupt. Although Ronald's crimes did pay for

S. Powell (✉)
University of Liverpool, Liverpool, UK

© The Author(s) 2020
E. Miskimmin (ed.), *100 British Crime Writers*, Crime Files,
https://doi.org/10.1057/978-1-137-31902-9_52

his son to attend Sherborne School in 1948, David was unhappy at there, and he once received a severe beating from his fellow pupils (an incident alluded to in his most autobiographical novel *A Perfect Spy*, 1986). He moved to Switzerland to study at Bern University before being drafted into the Army as part of his National Service.

Cornwell served in British Army Intelligence in Vienna from 1950 to 1952, and his duties included interrogating refugees who defected from the Czechoslovakian border. Many of his novels include thrilling, menacing and subtle interrogation scenes, which are almost completely devoid of violence. Cornwell studied modern languages at Lincoln College, Oxford from 1952 to 1954 until his father's bankruptcy forced him to leave prematurely. Cornwell married Alison Ann Veronica Sharp in 1954 and worked as a teacher at Millfield Junior School before returning to Oxford in 1955 and graduating with a first-class degree. Cornwell worked as Assistant Master at Eton from 1956 to 1958. During this time, he may have been recruited by MI5 and was possibly working for them while a freelance illustrator from 1958 to 1960. Cornwell worked for the Foreign Office in Bonn, West Germany from 1960 to 1963 and may have been employed or involved with the Intelligence service MI6. The novel, *A Small Town in Germany* (1968) is partially based on his experiences in West Germany. Cornwell has always been evasive about his time in British intelligence. The novelist Robert Harris is currently writing the authorised biography of Cornwell with the stipulation that it will not be published until after his death.

Cornwell's first two novels, *A Call for the Dead* (1961) and *A Murder of Quality* (1962) both feature Smiley in the leading role, yet neither made any critical or commercial impact. Cornwell adopted the pseudonym John le Carré for the publication of his first novel on account that it was traditional for any employee of the Foreign Office to use a pseudonym when publishing their work. For years Cornwell insisted that he took the name after seeing it on the front window of a London shoe shop. He later admitted that he invented this story, and the pseudonym came from nowhere, although he stated he liked the name John le Carré for its evocative combination of English and European ancestry. Cornwell was transferred by the Foreign Office to Hamburg in 1963 and began writing his breakthrough novel *The Spy Who Came in from the Cold* (1963). This novel contained a level of realism and pessimism which was absent from his first two books. The story concerns a disgruntled British spy Alec Leamus who is assigned one last mission – to entrap an East

German spy – before Alec 'comes in from the cold', or retires from active service. Leamus, however, discovers he is part of a much wider and more complex conspiracy than he realised.

Cornwell stated that one of his biggest literary influences was drafting reports for the foreign office, which required clinical precision and constant rewriting. The novel took Cornwell around five months to write, and the surprise ending only came to him halfway through the drafting stage. *The Spy Who Came in from the Cold* was a major critical and commercial success. In his following novel, *The Looking Glass War* (1965), Cornwell portrayed spies who struggled to adapt from the 'Hot war' of World War Two to the Cold War of restrictions and bureaucracy. Cornwell sent all of his early novels to the Foreign Office before publication so that the manuscript could be double-checked to ensure that it did not contain any information that might constitute a breach of security.

Cornwell resigned from the foreign office in 1965, having given instructions to his accountant that he should be informed if his assets ever totalled £20,000 or more. The success of *The Spy Who Came in from the Cold*, which remained at the top of the American bestseller lists for fourteen consecutive months, brought Cornwell considerable wealth. Before the breakdown of his first marriage, Cornwell had several extra-marital affairs. *The Naïve and Sentimental Lover* (1971) is Cornwell's only novel not set in the world of espionage, although the complexity of the relationships and the ongoing deceit does in itself suggest a secret world. In it he fictionalised his unusual triangular relationship with the novelist James Kennaway and Kennaway's wife Susan. Similarly, Kennaway dramatised the three-way relationship in his novel *Some Gorgeous Accident* (1967). *The Naïve and Sentimental Lover* was a critical and commercial failure, and Cornwell's father tried to sue him over a thinly veiled portrayal of a professional conman who is the father of the leading character. Cornwell married his second wife, Valerie Jane Eustace in 1971.

Cornwell's next novel, *Tinker Tailor Soldier Spy*, re-established his reputation: the book is regarded as one of the best spy novels ever written. Cornwell returned George Smiley to the leading role by subtly rewriting Smiley's back-story, so that his advanced age is not an issue, and making his colleague Peter Guillam more of a protégé than a contemporary as he is in the earlier novels. In the novel, Smiley is called out of retirement to find the mole in British Intelligence, the traitor whom Cornwell strongly based on the real-life British Intelligence Officer Kim Philby of the 'Cambridge Five' spy ring.

Smiley would continue his battle against Karla, his nemesis in Russian Intelligence, in Cornwell's next two novels. Cornwell spent eighteen months travelling through south-east Asia researching the war-torn setting for *The Honourable Schoolboy*. His novel on the Israeli–Palestinian conflict *The Little Drummer Girl* (1983) was intended to be one of the first works of fiction to portray the political situation from the Palestinian as well as the Israeli viewpoint. Cornwell had several meetings with the former leader of the Palestinian Liberation Organisation, Yasser Arafat, while researching the novels and also met senior figures in the Israeli Intelligence service Mossad. Cornwell's most critically acclaimed novel *A Perfect Spy* (1986) is also his most autobiographical. The novel tells the life-story of Magnus Pym who is recruited into British Intelligence in post-war Germany and rises to the most senior levels, but throughout his career Pym is acting as a double agent. *A Perfect Spy* is perhaps the greatest achievement in Cornwell's career. The American novelist Philip Roth described it as 'the best English novel since the war'.

Cornwell visited the Soviet Union to research his novel *The Russia House* (1989). He had been lobbying to visit the country for years and the new policies of glasnost and perestroika finally made it possible. With the fall of the Berlin Wall and the end of the Cold War, Cornwell turned his writing to more varied subjects: *The Night Manager* (1993) concerns the international arms trade, and *The Tailor of Panama* (1996), the future of the Panama Canal. *The Mission Song* (2006) loosely revolves around Western-backed mercenaries plotting to overthrow an African dictatorship, in a thinly disguised account of the ill-fated Simon Mann/Mark Thatcher plot to overthrow the government of Equatorial Guinea. Cornwell's novels have always contained a level of cynicism towards the United States and frustration at how during the Cold War, British Intelligence was forced to become a junior partner to the CIA in the global battle against communism. In the later novels, the anti-Americanism became more overt. *Absolute Friends* (2003) is a critique of the political 'Special Relationship' between the United States and the United Kingdom. *A Most Wanted Man* (2008) explores the controversial practice of extraordinary rendition. Cornwell was a vocal critic of the George Bush administration and the War in Iraq. He expressed his views in an article for the *Times*, simply titled, 'The United States Has Gone Mad'. Many of his novels, including *A Delicate Truth* (2013), have been adapted for film, television and radio.

Suggested Reading/Works Cited

Barley, Tony, *Taking Sides: The Fiction of John Le Carré* (Milton Keynes: Open University, 1986).
Bloom, Harold, *John Le Carré* (New York: Chelsea House, 1987).
Bruccoli, Matthew J. and Judith Baugman, *Conversations with John Le Carré* (Jackson: University of Mississippi, 2004).
Homberger, Eric, *John Le Carré* (London: Methuen, 1986).
Monaghan, David, *The Novels of John Le Carré: The Art of Survival* (Oxford: Blackwell, 1985).

CHAPTER 53

Dick Francis (1920–2010), 1962: *Dead Cert*

Malcah Effron

Unlike many of his crime writer colleagues, Dick Francis' series develops not around a common detective but around a common theme, namely the world of horse-racing. In his forty-plus racing thrillers, he focuses on various elements of the world of horse-racing. These novels combine Francis' in-depth familiarity from his experiences as a champion jump jockey with thorough research into the specialty explored in each novel. Three of his novels, *Blood Sport* (1967), *In the Frame* (1976) and *Twice Shy* (1981), were adapted to film in 1989, by Deirdre Friel and Harvey Hart.

Francis, who by the end of his career was riding for the Queen Mother, first began riding at age five and showing horses at twelve. He decided to be a jockey when he was fifteen. In World War Two, he served in the Royal Air Force and returned to be a jockey after the war. Because of his height, he became a steeplechase jockey and excelled to be named champion jockey for the 1953–54 season. He retired from riding aged thirty-six.

At this point, he turned to writing to earn a living, beginning as a journalist for the *Sunday Express* and then writing his autobiography, *The Sport of Queens* (1957) before embarking on a long career as a crime

---

M. Effron (✉)
Massachusetts Institute of Technology, Cambridge, MA, USA

© The Author(s) 2020
E. Miskimmin (ed.), *100 British Crime Writers*, Crime Files,
https://doi.org/10.1057/978-1-137-31902-9_53

fiction writer. His first novel, *Dead Cert* (1962), initiates the horse-racing theme carried through all of his novels, where a jockey turns amateur detective to solve the murder of another jockey. As the Francis library developed, the novels move away from the exclusive domain of jockeys, incorporating a variety of trades and specialties, including all aspects of horse ownership, training and racing, as well as careers that might initially seem tangential to racing including, but not limited to, photography, acting, flying, ballooning, law and cookery. Francis prides himself on his accuracy in portraying each of these specialties with correct details. Until her death in 2000, his wife Mary served as his primary research assistant, ensuring his record for accuracy. Thus, his wife's death can perhaps explain, both professionally as well as personally, the six-year publishing hiatus between 2000 and 2006, the first gap of this length since he began his career as a novelist. After *Under Orders* (2006), the first novel Francis published after his wife's death, his youngest son Felix Francis began co-authoring his novels. Felix had previously only contributed as a researcher for his father's novels, but beginning with *Dead Heat* (2007), Felix's name also appears on the covers. Though Dick Francis died in February 2010, the final Dick and Felix Francis novel, *Crossfire* appeared later in 2010.

While horse-racing is the theme that binds the Francis oeuvre together, the novels also have several themes that pervade his work. Several critics have articulated how Francis' novels explore the complicated relationships between parents and children, and particularly between fathers and sons. Many of Francis' heroes begin either orphaned or estranged from their parents, which Elaine Wagner argues becomes the origin for measuring the morality of his characters: '[t]he ability or lack of ability to deal with the denial of parental affection frequently forms the characters' personality and differentiates the Francis hero from the Francis villain'. Characters who can overcome the effects of abandonment to pursue their careers successfully become the heroes, whereas characters who are stunted by parental abandonment become villains in their continual pursuit of their parents' attention. As Gina Macdonald suggests, the conflicts between heroes and villains in Francis' novels can be summarised as 'contrasts between the competent and the incompetent', which she takes as a sign of Francis' ability to blend the conventions of the hard-boiled American crime fiction and the puzzle-oriented British detective tradition. Rachel Shaffer similarly understands the main dynamics of the Francis style to revolve around the balanced behaviour of the abandoned outsider who still conforms to society's moral values, as she proposes that '[t]he six-gun mystique of a Francis hero is loaded not with bullets but with the kind of personality traits that enable him to comply with modern limitations on violent actions and still emerge victorious'. As such, good is defined in Francis' novels as overcoming negative personal experiences to maintain a sense of equality and fair play in relation to family and society.

In addition to familial plots as developed through the theme of parent–child relationships, Francis' novels also all develop a love interest. Francis uses first-person narratives through the eyes of his male detectives. He has claimed that he writes male protagonists because he does not believe himself capable of writing acceptable female protagonists, but in every story he provides his male protagonist with a female love interest. Especially as the protagonist typically ends each novel engaged to his love interest, Francis' novels can be understood not only to explore family relations along bloodlines but also in relation to constructed families. Often, these constructed families have more stable constructions than familial ones, indicating a support for like minds and like morals rather than for genetic bonds. In this regard, Macdonald's assessment that Francis' covert political message that '[t]he future belongs to the competent' appears also in the love narratives that develop alongside his thrilling tales of criminal investigation.

While all of Francis' novels are held together by themes rather than by characters, two characters make repeated appearances in Francis' work, Sid Halley and Kit Fielding, but they do not reappear in the same manner as each other. Kit Fielding appears in two consecutive novels, *Break In* (1985) and *Bolt* (1986). In this regard, his reappearance can be considered as the conclusion of the story begun in the first novel. In this sense, Fielding can be considered a serial character. He continues to appear until his story is told completely, and his reappearance allows his story to be developed more fully and finished more conclusively. With the second novel, the Fielding narrative progresses beyond the happy engagement on short acquaintance that typically concludes Francis' novels.

If Fielding's novels can be considered serial, Sid Halley's novels are more episodic, as he appears in *Odds Against* (1965), *Whip Hand* (1979), *Come to Grief* (1995) and *Under Orders* (2006). While each of these novels continues the narrative of Halley's life, they do not have the same serial structure as the Fielding novels because they do not provide a continual narrative nor do they provide the back-story for the intervening years. Of all Francis' detectives, Halley provides the best base for a series detective, as after his initial amateur function in *Odds Against*, he sets up as a professional detective, allowing Francis to reuse him without needing to concoct absurd scenarios for the repeated presence of the amateur detective. This repetition also suggests that Sid Halley, the crippled jockey turned detective, repeatedly interested Francis. This interest might arise from Halley's crippled left hand, as Francis traces the changes in views of disability and in technology of prostheses over forty years by returning to Halley with updated developments. While Halley's accessories, including his use of mobile phones and the internet, progress in real time, the character does not age in real time as he is only thirty-eight over thirty years after his initial appearance. Nevertheless, Halley's reappearance with his supporting characters, such as his ex-father-in-law, create a reassuring sense of stability in the continuity of Francis' work, and perhaps this comfort and stability is the reason why he returned to Halley for the first novel after his wife died and the last novel he published exclusively under his own name. Sid Halley also was televised in 1979 in John Mackenzie's 'The Dick Francis Thriller: The Racing Game', which nominally was a serialisation of *Odds Against*.

Though all his novels after the final Sid Halley novel have been co-authored with his son Felix, a former physics teacher, the novels have not shifted in style. They still maintain their feel of rigorously researched and carefully written thriller plots that maintain their ties to the world of horse-racing. The novels read seamlessly, leaving no stylistic indication of a shift between father and father-and-son. It remains to be seen whether the son will continue the father's series on his own.

Francis' skill as a crime novelist has been repeatedly recognised by his profession. He won the Edgar Award for Best Novel three times (1970, 1981, and 1996), and his 1996 novel, *Come to Grief*, was also nominated for the Shamus Award for Best Novel. He was awarded the Crime Writers' Association's Cartier Diamond Dagger in 1989 and was made a Mystery Writers of America Grand Master in 1996. Outside the crime fiction guilds, Francis' writing has also been recognised with the award of an Honorary Doctorate of Letters from Tufts University in 1991 and with a CBE in the Queen's Birthday Honours list in 2000.

Suggested Reading/Works Cited

Francis, Dick, *The Sport of Queens: The Autobiography of Dick Francis* (London: Michael Joseph, 1957).

Macdonald, Gina, 'Dick Francis' in *British Mystery and Thriller Writers Since 1940: First Series*, ed. by Bernard Benstock and Thomas F. Stanley (Detroit: Gale, 1989), pp. 136–155.

Schaffer, Rachel, 'Dick Francis's Six-Gun Mystique', *Clues: A Journal of Detection*, 21.2 (2000), 17–26.

Sudgen, Stephen, *A Dick Francis Companion: Characters, Horses, Plots, Settings and Themes* (Jefferson: McFarland, 2008).

Wagner, Elaine, 'The Theme of Paternal Rejection in the Novels of Dick Francis', *Clues: A Journal of Detection*, 18.1 (1997), 7–13.

CHAPTER 54

P. D. James (1920–2014), 1962: *Cover Her Face*

Delphine Cingal

P. D. James, the Baroness James of Holland Park, OBE, FRSA (Fellow of the Royal Society of Arts), FRSL (Fellow of the Royal Society of Literature), was best known for her sensitive intellectual police detective, Adam Dalgliesh, who appears in fourteen novels. James' amateur detective Cordelia Gray appears in only two novels, but is perhaps equally well known due to her place in discussions of women's roles in the detection of crime (deliberately invoked by James in the title of the first Cordelia Gray novel: *An Unsuitable Job for a Woman*, 1972). James also wrote three non-series novels, the last of which, *Death Comes to Pemberley* (2011), was a murder-mystery sequel to Jane Austen's *Pride and Prejudice*. Her non-fiction oeuvre covered articles, essays and books, including her 2009 critical work, a personal history of the genre: *Talking About Detective Fiction*, and her autobiography, *Time to be Earnest: A Fragment of Autobiography*, published in 1999.

Phyllis Dorothy James was born in Oxford, the eldest of three children. Her father, Sidney James was a revenue officer and James admitted that she was somewhat afraid of him. He was very clever, but cold. On the

---

D. Cingal (✉)
Paris 2-Panthéon-Assas University, Paris, France

© The Author(s) 2020
E. Miskimmin (ed.), *100 British Crime Writers*, Crime Files,
https://doi.org/10.1057/978-1-137-31902-9_54

253

other hand, her mother, Amelia Hone James, was a warm and romantic woman. The family tended to move a lot: from London to Ludlow, and then to Cambridge, a city that James loves and used as a background for *An Unsuitable Job for a Woman*. James was educated at the British School and the National School in Ludlow and then at the Cambridge Girls High School (where there was a teacher named Dalgliesh). Her family could not afford to pay for a College or University education, and did not deem it necessary for a woman to have such an education anyway, so she had to start working when she was sixteen. This was to have a bearing on her work, since several of her female characters, such as Cordelia Gray, face the same predicament.

For some time, James worked for the Inland Revenue like her father, a job that she disliked. She then became the assistant of a theatre director at the Cambridge Festival Theatre. This might have been more congenial to her, except that she was mainly dealing with administrative and financial issues. During World War Two, James worked as a Red Cross Nurse and in 1941 she married Dr. Connor Bantry White who was serving in the Royal Army Medical Corps, and who she had met while he was a medical student. They had two daughters, Clare, born in 1942, and Jane, born in 1944. James' husband returned from the war with severe mental health problems and was frequently admitted to psychiatric institutions for the rest of his life. James helped to nurse him, as well as supporting the family financially, until his death in 1964. James worked at Paddington Hospital while studying for qualifications in hospital administration, and between 1949 and 1968 she was the administrator for several psychiatric units for the NHS in London. Both the medical milieu and the knowledge of civil service administration and institutions have been utilised in her writing: *A Mind to Murder* (1963) details Dalgliesh's investigation into the murder of an employee at a psychiatric clinic, and *Shroud for a Nightingale* (1971) concerns the murder of two student nurses at Nightingale house, a hospital nursing school. The final Dalgliesh novel, *The Private Patient* (2008) is set in a plastic surgery clinic. In 1968 James changed jobs to work as an administrator in the Home Office, in both the police and criminal policy departments, until her retirement in 1979 and again her work was arguably a source of inspiration for her writing such as in *Death of an Expert Witness* (1977), in which a forensic biologist is murdered. Within the Home Office, she championed the Children's Act, a legislation giving adopted children the right to learn the identities of their natural parents, which was also to influence her for the writing of her non-serial novel, *Innocent Blood* (1980).

The first Dalgliesh novel, *Cover Her Face* (1962) was written, as with all of James' novels until her retirement, while she was working full-time and (until they grew up) looking after her daughters. In an interview with Emma Brockes she describes how she achieved this by rising early and writing for two hours every day before work. In the same interview she explains that she chose 'P. D. James' not with the intention of concealing her gender, but because it would look 'enigmatic'. She discussed her choice of detective fiction as a genre in several interviews, commenting to Brockes that it was 'a kind of instinct', having read so many classical detective stories in her youth, and arguing that 'The novel is a way in which the writer's own enthusiasms, interests, compulsions, maybe even neuroses, are rearranged in a form that he or she hopes will be compelling and attractive to the reader'. She staunchly defended the potentially formulaic or structured nature of the detective story, citing this as part of its creative appeal. In an interview with Lynn Kaczmarek she compares the structural aesthetic of a detective story to the sonnet form: 'I love the structure, that's part of it, producing order out of chaos. I am fascinated by structure in novels, and also of course, in poetry. I love a sonnet which is very structured, with only 14 lines and a strict rhyming sequence. And I find that structure is supporting and liberating of my creative imagination. I do like a book which has a shape, I think, a beginning, a middle and an end. I like a strong narrative thrust to a book [...]. And I like the difficulty of a challenge (I hate using that overworked word), of holding the tension between all the necessary elements of the story, the plot, the setting, the characterization and the scene and holding them all in unity'. James' appreciation of poetry is also an attribute of her detective: Adam Dalgliesh is a published poet, an aspect of his characterisation that contributes to its complexity.

Adam Dalgliesh is a very guarded person, and is largely solitary in his private life following the death of his wife and son in childbirth, and having no family other than an aunt, introduced in *Unnatural Causes* (1967) and whose death (of natural causes) leads to Dalgliesh's presence in Norfolk for the events of *Devices and Desires* (1989). The relationships he forms in the novels, even with his colleagues, seem tentative and distant, although there are 'love interests'; in *The Skull Beneath the Skin* (1982), the second Cordelia Gray novel, Gray seems to harbour romantic, if undeveloped and unfulfilled, emotions towards Dalgliesh, who she meets in *An Unsuitable Job for a Woman*. He develops an understanding with Deborah Riscoe in *Cover Her Face*, but she ends their relationship at the end of *Unatural Causes* due to his fear of emotional commitment. In *Death in Holy Orders* (2001), however, he meets English lecturer Emma Lavenham, and eventually marries her at the end of *The Private Patient*.

Dalgliesh's main interactions otherwise are with his police colleagues. He works his way up the Metropolitan Police hierarchy, beginning his career as a Detective Chief Inspector, then becoming a Superintendent in *A Mind to Murder*, Chief Superintendent in *Shroud for a Nightingale* and Commander in *The Black Tower* (1975). In *A Taste for Death* (1986) he creates a team in charge of highly sensitive cases, such as those with a political basis. Dalgliesh has various partners including Detective Sergeant Martin, Detective Sergeant Masterson and Detective Chief Inspector Massingham, but perhaps his most significant professional relationship is with Detective Inspector Kate Miskin, who arguably has a very similar personality to Dalgliesh's, but who provides a foil to his character through James' construction of her back-story: Miskin grew up in difficult circumstances and was brought up by a grandmother on a troubled south London council estate. Miskin's awareness, and often resentment, of these social differences is intrinsic to her characterisation, and it is interesting that, through her, James gives us another female character who has had to fight for her position in the world.

In 1972, James published her first Cordelia Gray novel, *An Unsuitable Job for a Woman*, in which Adam Dalgliesh is only a secondary character at the end of the novel, when he finds himself checkmated by Gray and unable to bring the criminal to justice. At the beginning of this novel, Gray inherits the detective agency she was working for from her boss and partner who committed suicide and finds herself hampered not just by debt, but by people's perceptions of a young woman doing the job she does. She is also, perhaps, hindered by the same emotional complexities or sensibilities that hinder Dalgliesh in his work as a policeman. Being an amateur, however, Gray has more freedom to act on these feelings: In *An Unsuitable Job for a Woman*, she ends up feeling too close to the victim and then to his mother, finally becoming a party to concealing a revenge killing that she feels is justified. Gray appeared briefly in several novels such as *The Black Tower* or *A Taste for Death* before having another novel to herself: *The Skull Beneath the Skin*. As with many of James' works, *The Skull Beneath the Skin* pushes the boundaries of genre-writing through its poeticism and utilisation of a much older 'literary' text. It is based around a performance of Webster's *The Duchess of Malfi*, and James makes use of the Jacobean domestic tragedy in many ways, from direct quotation in the death threats received by the victim to more complex usage of theme and motif.

Both Dalgliesh and Gray novels have been adapted for film or television, with varying degrees of success. The first ten Dalgliesh novels were dramatised by Anglia TV between 1985 and 1997 as 'The Adam Dalgliesh Chronicles' with Roy Marsden in the title role (although James suggested that perhaps he is not how she envisaged her creation). Martin Shaw has since played Dalgliesh for the BBC in *Death in Holy Orders* and *The Murder Room* (broadcast in 2003). *An Unsuitable Job for a Woman* was made into a film in 1982 (directed by Chris Petit) with Pippa Guard in the role of Cordelia Gray, and the book was also used as the basis for four feature-length television episodes between 1997 and 1999 in which the lead role was taken by Helen Baxendale.

James' Anglicanism was a significant part of her life: she was Vice-president of the Prayer Book Society and member of the Liturgy Commission of the Church of England. While James' faith did not directly impact on her crime novels, except perhaps a little in terms of settings and details – *Death in Holy Orders* is set in an Anglican theological college, for example – it could be seen to be influential in its style or aesthetics. In her essay 'As it Was in the Beginning: the shaping of a writer' (her contribution to the collection *Why I Am Still an Anglican: Essays and Conversations*, 2006) she talks about the roots of her faith as being in her childhood, and the impact of the powerful language of the Church, its services and texts, on 'someone who was already dimly aware that she would one day become a novelist': 'those marvellous prayers, at once so beautifully constructed, so simple and yet so pregnant with meaning, entered early into my consciousness to become part of my religious and literary heritage and to help make me a writer'. This inspiration is evident in the language and lyricism of James' writing and also forms a link with Dorothy L. Sayers, a writer James cited as a favourite and whom she wrote much, and who also drew on her Anglican upbringing in her work.

P. D. James received many awards and accolades, both within and without the literary world. The most significant of these include being made an Officer of the Order of the British Empire (OBE) in 1983 and, in 1991, becoming a Conservative life peer, Baroness James of Holland Park. She holds seven honorary doctorates and four honorary fellowships, and her literary awards include (but are no means limited to): the Creasey Award for Best First Novel (*Cover Her Face*, 1962); the Crime Writers' Association (CWA) Cartier Diamond Dagger (1987); the CWA Macallan Silver Dagger for Fiction for *Shroud for a Nightingale* (1971), *the Black Tower* (1975), and *A Taste For Death* (1986); the Deo Gloria Award for *The Children of Men* (1992); and the Grandmaster Award from the Mystery Writers of America (1999). James was President of the Society of Authors between 1984 and 1986 and held this post again from 1997 to 2013.

Suggested Reading/Works Cited

Brockes, Emma, 'Murder, She Wrote: Interview with P. D. James', *The Guardian*, 3 March 2001. http://www.theguardian.com/books/2001/mar/03/crime.pdjames.

Harrington, Louise, 'P. D. James (1920–)', in *A Companion to Crime Fiction*, ed. by Charles J. Rzepka and Lee Horsley (Chichester: Wiley-Blackwell, 2010), pp. 495–502.

James, P. D., 'As It Was in the Beginning: The Shaping of a Writer', in *Why I Am Still an Anglican: Essays and Conversations*, ed. by Caroline Chartres (London: Continuum, 2006), pp. 16–26.

———, *Talking About Detective Fiction* (London: Faber and Faber, 2009).

———, *Time to Be Earnest: A Fragment of Autobiography* (London: Faber and Faber, 1999).

Kaczmarek, Lynne, 'Interview with P. D. James', *Mystery News*, February/March (2006), [pp. unknown].

Macdonald, Andrew F., 'P. D. James', in *Dictionary of Literary Biography, Volume 276: British Mystery and Thriller Writers Since 1960*, ed. by Gina Macdonald (Detroit, MI: Thomson Gale; 2003), pp. 217–228.

Rowland, Susan, *From Agatha Christie to Ruth Rendell: British Woman Writers in Detective and Crime Fiction* (Basingstoke: Palgrave Macmillan, 2000).

CHAPTER 55

Simon Nash (Pseudonym of Raymond Chapman, 1924–2013), 1962: *Dead of a Counterplot*

Christopher Routledge

Simon Nash was the pseudonym of Raymond Chapman, university teacher, Emeritus Professor of English at the University of London and non-stipendiary priest in the Anglican diocese of Southwark. The name was formed from the maiden names of his two grandmothers. He wrote the first of his five detective novels, *Dead of a Counterplot* to submit to a competition arranged by the publisher Collins which hoped to find a new writer to carry on the established tradition of dons and detective fiction which includes Michael Innes. The novel did not win the competition but it was picked up by Geoffrey Bles and published in 1962.

Over the following four years Chapman wrote four more novels as Simon Nash, before the demands of an academic career overtook his novel writing. All five of the Simon Nash novels feature Adam Ludlow, an academic and literary scholar who gets drawn into murder situations and solves them by a mixture of deduction and applying apparently irrelevant special knowledge. Ludlow's skill as a literary critic becomes demonstrably

---

C. Routledge (✉)
Freelance Writer and Photographer, NW England, UK

© The Author(s) 2020
E. Miskimmin (ed.), *100 British Crime Writers*, Crime Files,
https://doi.org/10.1057/978-1-137-31902-9_55

'useful' in reading clues and understanding character traits and motives. His method follows the traditional style of an amateur detective who solves the mystery but keeps amicable relations with the police officer investigating it.

While Chapman did not have a long career writing as Simon Nash he did have some impact as a writer of stories that are archetypes of the academic-as-detective subgenre. Most notably *Killed by Scandal* (1962), a tale of murder and intrigue in an amateur dramatics society, is among the ninety crime and detective novels named by Jacques Barzun and Wendell Hertig Taylor in their influential *Catalogue of Crime* (first published in 1971). *Killed by Scandal* was also republished by Garland in 1983 as one of the 'Fifty Classics of Crime Fiction 1960–75'. The other three Simon Nash novels are *Death Over Deep Water* (1964), *Dead Woman's Ditch* (1964) and *Unhallowed Murder* (1966). All five novels were republished in the United States by Harper Row in 1985.

Among Chapman's many other books are *The Victorian Debate; English Literature and Society 1832–1901* (1968), *Linguistics and Literature* (1973), *The Language of English Literature* (1982), *The Language of Thomas Hardy* (1990), and *Forms of Speech in Victorian Fiction* (1994). He also wrote several books on Anglican liturgy.

CHAPTER 56

Peter O'Donnell (1920–2010), 1963: *Modesty Blaise* (comic strip)

Esme Miskimmin

Peter O'Donnell was a writer of comic strips, novels and short stories and is best known for the character Modesty Blaise, unbeatable all-action heroine, retired criminal and occasional field-operator for British intelligence. Modesty Blaise, her sidekick Willie Garvin, and other recurring characters from the series appeared in the comic strips of the same name in *The Evening Standard* from 1963 to 2001 and in eleven novels and two collections of short stories between 1965 and 1996. O'Donnell also wrote historical romance novels under the name of Madeleine Brent.

Born in Lewisham, where his father was a crime reporter on the *Empire News*, O'Donnell started writing while still at school, selling his first story, 'The Lucky Break' to *The Scout* and then joining the Amalgamated Press in 1937 to work on various children's comics. From 1938 and throughout World War Two he served as an NCO in the Royal Signal Corps in a mobile radio detachment, travelling into what was then Persia (now Iran), Syria, Egypt, Italy and Greece, all places that serve as backgrounds to the Blaise stories. More importantly, it was in Persia in 1942 that he had an encounter that gave him the inspiration for Modesty Blaise

---

E. Miskimmin (✉)
University of Liverpool, Liverpool, UK

© The Author(s) 2020
E. Miskimmin (ed.), *100 British Crime Writers*, Crime Files,
https://doi.org/10.1057/978-1-137-31902-9_56

herself. In 'Girl Walking: The Real Modesty Blaise', O'Donnell gives an account of the incident. His unit occasionally ran into refugees from the Balkan States, and one day they gave some food to a young girl, 'a small figure [...] wearing a thin sunbleached shirt that fell to just below her knees'. O'Donnell describes how 'the little girl was very much in charge of herself, clearly used to being alone, wary but not afraid, and with no expectation of help from anybody', and how he 'could see that the thing hanging from her neck like a pendant was a short piece of wood with a long nail bound tightly to it with thin wire, the nail projecting a good two inches from the makeshift haft. It was a weapon, a crude weapon - and I felt chilled as I wondered what might have brought home to her the need for some way of defending herself'. O'Donnell drew on this encounter for his character's back-story, revealed and developed as the series and books progress: a child-refugee in the Balkans, Modesty Blaise learns to fend for herself and defend herself, carrying the same weapon that O'Donnell saw around the real child's neck in 1942. Blaise becomes a beautiful, self-assured and powerful woman, both physically and emotionally, but O'Donnell also writes counter-characteristics in his heroine; at the end of a mission she sometimes has a 'little weep' on the shoulder of Willie Garvin, one of the few individuals allowed to see her softer side. When not involved in a caper she is often portrayed as 'urchin' or gamine in appearance, with an appealing grin and hair tied back, often in a 'sunbleached' ribbon: an echo, perhaps, of the child who inspired the character.

In 1940, O'Donnell married Constance Green with whom he later had two daughters, and on his return from the war he started writing scripts for various newspapers, such as *The Daily Mirror* ('Belinda', 'Garth' and 'Romeo Brown', the latter being his first collaboration with illustrator Jim Holdaway, who drew the 'Modesty Blaise' strips until his death in 1970), *The Daily Herald* ('For Better or Worse'), and *The Daily Sketch* ('Tug Transom', 'Eve'). In 1962 he was invited to create a new comic strip for the *Daily Express* and came up with the idea for Modesty Blaise. Blaise's criminal background was not considered suitable for a family paper, however, and the *Express* rejected it. Charles Wintour of the *London Evening Standard* took it up and it ran daily for the next thirty-eight years. Arguably, O'Donnell aims to negate this potentially problematic nature of Blaise's criminality through establishing the very strict 'code of honour' that The Network operated on (no drugs, no trafficking; in fact they assist various police forces to combat these crimes) and through Modesty Blaise's own sense of morality and need to champion the underdog and protect innocence (a quality she values as she is herself without it).

More problematic to a modern readership of the Blaise strips might be the titillatory nature of the illustrations: Modesty is often semi-clad or naked, and her body is often the focus for the male gaze within the story. In both comic and novel, however, her many and varied sexual encounters are not presented in a judgemental way, and she is afforded the same sexual freedom as her male counterparts. In both comics and prose stories Blaise is shown by O'Donnell to have an awareness and control of her sexuality that might characterise a much more modern heroine, as does her intelligence and ability to take care of herself through her limitless command of weaponry and martial arts. In her platonic partnership with Willie Garvin she is the boss: he calls her 'Princess' and obeys her orders, and both characters are contemptuous of men who have problems with female authority.

O'Donnell's prose villains arguably have their basis in the comic strip roots of the stories: they are often grotesques, mutations of humanity with either physical deformities or mental and moral kinks that are almost cartoon-like at times, such as Delicata in *A Taste for Death* (1969), who stands 'over six and a half feet tall' with 'shoulders almost as wide as the door, and very square, with a huge round head perched upon them […]. His massive trunk was an unnaturally long oblong from which short legs projected [and] the hands hung almost to the knees'. In many cases the criminals' plans, which range from stealing archaeological treasures from the desert (*A Taste for Death*), to a bizarre secret slave-plantation of the rich and famous (*Last Day in Limbo*, 1976), often become bound up with a personal vendetta against Blaise and Garvin. The locations for the final show-downs between them are remote, challenging, environments which call on the duo's survival skills and ingenuity, and the fast-paced plots usually involve a significant body-count by the end, with the villains getting the comeuppance they deserve.

In addition to the comic strips and books, O'Donnell also wrote the screenplay for a film of Modesty Blaise, but almost none of his work was actually used in the 1966 film directed by Joseph Losey with Monica Vitti in the title role. The film did well, but it bears little resemblance to anything of O'Donnell's creating, and was described by Dirk Bogarde (who played Gabriel, the villain) as 'a comedy of the absurd gone mad'.

O'Donnell wrote the last ever caper of Blaise and Garvin in the short story 'The Cobra Trap', published in a collection of short stories by the same name in 1996, and Modesty Blaise made her last comic strip appearance in 2001 when O'Donnell retired from full-time writing. Collections of the comic strips have been reprinted by Titan books since 2004 (O'Donnell wrote the introductions to these up until his death), and over the last decade the Souvenir Press have republished the novels and short stories, suggesting that Modesty Blaise remains as popular as ever.

SUGGESTED READING/WORKS CITED

Drew, Bernard A., 'He Nails 'Em with Modesty: Peter O'Donnell's Femme Fatale Uses Everything to Fight Evil Forces', *Armchair Detective: A Quarterly Journal Devoted to the Appreciation of Mystery, Detective, and Suspense Fiction*, 20.1 (1987), 26–30.

Holland, Steve, 'Peter O'Donnell: Obituary', *The Guardian*, 5 March 2006.

O'Donnell, Peter, 'Girl Walking: The Real Modesty Blaise', *Crimetime* Online, 2005. http://www.crimetime.co.uk/features/modestyblaise.php.

The Official Modesty Blaise Website. http://www.modestyblaiseltd.com/.

CHAPTER 57

Joyce Porter (Also wrote as Deborah Joyce and Deborah Bryan, 1924–1999), 1964: *Dover One*

Heather Worthington

Biographical detail of Joyce Porter is limited. She was born in Marple, Cheshire, and educated at the High School for Girls, Macclesfield, and King's College London. She served in the Women's Royal Air Force as a Flight Officer between 1949 and 1963; there is then a long information gap until her death in 1999. But while personal details of her life are obscure, possibly intentionally, her career as a crime writer is mapped out by the nineteen novels and at least fifteen short stories she produced from 1964 to 1980. She also wrote romantic novels under the pseudonyms Deborah Joyce and Deborah Bryan. Her books were written with the intention of providing entertainment for the reader while earning as much money as possible. With this in mind, she created three memorable serial characters: a police detective, an amateur private eye and a secret agent.

These varied protagonists allowed Porter to parody the formulaic police procedural, the amateur detective/private eye novel and the spy thriller. Porter's 'James Bond' equivalent is the incompetent Eddie

H. Worthington (✉)
Cardiff University, Cardiff, UK

© The Author(s) 2020
E. Miskimmin (ed.), *100 British Crime Writers*, Crime Files,
https://doi.org/10.1057/978-1-137-31902-9_57

265

Brown, whose missions in dangerous foreign climes are hampered by his ineptitude and his irresistibility to predatory females. Even disguised as a woman, in *Neither a Candle nor a Pitchfork* (1969), Brown is the object of desire for a lesbian Russian government official. He appeared in four novels, the last of which is *Only with a Bargepole* (1971).

Porter's amateur detective is the Honourable Constance Ethel Morrison-Burke (the Hon. Con), whose domestic arrangements strongly suggest lesbian leanings. The Hon. Con is perhaps a tired stereotype of lesbianism, parodically masculine in her representation, but this is alleviated by a rather touching naivety about matters sexual. Humour in the five Hon. Con novels is mainly to be found in the protagonist's dogged pursuit of clues and incorrect deductions, and in her relationships with her housemate, the devoted Miss Jones, and Detective Sergeant Fenner.

The most successful of Porter's series characters is Detective Inspector Dover, obese, incompetent, idle, unhygienic and deeply unattractive, in contrast to his hard-working, intelligent, and handsome assistant, Detective Sergeant MacGregor. *Dover One* (1964) sets in place the pattern for the subsequent nine Dover novels and the short stories, and also offers a template for the Hon. Con and Miss Jones in its representation of the female Colonel Bing and her companion, Miss McLintock. While Dover wanders around upsetting all and sundry, MacGregor carries out the real legwork. Yet, surprisingly, it is Dover who apparently serendipitously finally discovers the solution to the crime (*Dover Three*, 1965).

Police, detective, criminal and victim are equally unattractive in much of Porter's fiction, and while this contributes to the humour, her satirical take on society can at times be uncomfortable, as in the misandrist *The Unkindest Cut of All* (1967), which features cannibalism and castration. While the gender politics, indeed politics generally, are deeply incorrect, Porter's texts manage to some degree to maintain their humour, if rather repetitively; as Julian Symons notes in *Bloody Murder* (1985), for the comedy detective, the 'law of diminishing returns operates most powerfully'. Nonetheless, Porter's Inspector Dover appeared in the BBC television series 'Detective' (1964–9; 1968) and has been introduced to a new, twenty-first-century audience through Paul Mendelson's adaptations of the novels for BBC Radio 4 (2005–present).

SUGGESTED READING/WORKS CITED

Reilly, John M., ed., *Twentieth-Century Crime and Mystery Writers* (London and New York: Macmillan, 1980).

Winn, Dilys, *Murder Inc.: The Mystery Reader's Companion*, rev. edn (New York: Workman Pub. Inc., 1984).

CHAPTER 58

Ruth Rendell (Also wrote as Barbara Vine, 1930–2015), 1964: *From Doon with Death*

Anne-Marie Beller

Although best known for her Chief Inspector Wexford series, Ruth Rendell wrote over sixty novels, including fourteen under the name of Barbara Vine, and her work has been translated into twenty-five languages. She also published several collections of short stories and a handful of non-fiction works reflecting other interests. Rendell's achievements were immense: she won countless honours, including numerous Edgar Awards from the Mystery Writers of America, and Silver, Gold, and Cartier Daggers from the Crime Writers' Association. In 1996 she was awarded a CBE, and the following year created a Labour life peer. As Baroness Rendell of Babergh, she was an active member of the House of Lords. Rendell was also a Fellow of the Royal Society of Literature, and remains one of the best-known writers of British crime fiction.

Rendell was born Ruth Barbara Grasemann on 17 February 1930 in Leyton, East London. Her father Arthur Grasemann and her Swedish mother, Ebba, were both school teachers. Their marriage was volatile, which seems to have led to an unhappy childhood for Rendell, something she preferred not to discuss in interviews. Ebba Grasemann died

A.-M. Beller (✉)
Loughborough University, Loughborough, UK

© The Author(s) 2020
E. Miskimmin (ed.), *100 British Crime Writers*, Crime Files,
https://doi.org/10.1057/978-1-137-31902-9_58

relatively young, having suffered with multiple sclerosis for many years before the condition was finally diagnosed. Rendell attended Loughton High School in Essex, leaving at eighteen to work as a feature writer for the local newspaper.

She joined the *Chigwell Times* as a junior reporter in 1948 and later progressed to sub-editor. At the age of twenty, she married her colleague and sometime boss on the newspaper, Don Rendell, whom she had met, somewhat ironically in view of her later career, at an inquest. Their son, and only child, Simon, was born in 1952. Rendell resigned her position at the newspaper the following year. In fact, she narrowly avoided being dismissed after reporting on a local tennis club event which she did not actually attend. Her copy therefore omitted the vital detail that the after-dinner speaker had collapsed and died during his speech.

Rendell had begun to write fiction when she was fifteen and during her twenties she wrote a number of novels, largely in secret. Those she did submit to publishers were rejected, until *From Doon with Death* was accepted by John Long and published in 1964. In some senses, Rendell became a crime writer by default. The first novel, featuring her popular detective Inspector Reg Wexford, was originally conceived as a very different kind of book and only rewritten as a detective story when the initial manuscript was rejected. In its new form, *From Doon with Death* was an immediate hit and Rendell realised that her policeman detective would have a longer life than she had anticipated. She subsequently developed the character beyond his original form as a generic convention, making him more liberal, literate and generally more interesting. Rendell admitted in interviews that Wexford possesses many of her own traits, as well as aspects of Arthur Grasemann: 'I realised that I had put an enormous amount of me - and to some extent my father - into him, but it may be that women creating a detective always put their fathers into them'. Rendell continued to produce Wexford novels regularly and their popularity never waned. The books also spawned a successful television series, with George Baker as Wexford and Christopher Ravenscroft as his assistant, Inspector Mike Burden. Twenty-three feature-length episodes were filmed between 1987 and 2000. In 2009 *The Monster in the Box*, the twenty-second novel in the Wexford series, was published and was rumoured to be the last. These rumours, together with persistent speculation that Wexford would be 'killed off', proved erroneous, and Rendell brought Wexford out of retirement to advise the police in two more cases (*The Vault*, 2011, and *No Man's Nightingale*, 2013).

In many respects the relationship between Wexford and Burden follows the traditional conventions of the detective and sidekick. Wexford embodies Rendell's own liberal sympathies, whereas Mike Burden is much more conservative, providing not only an alternative viewpoint (and effective foil) to his superior officer, but also operating as the voice of 'the moral majority'. Though the Chief Inspector's broadly liberal and progressive views were admitted by his author to be her own, Wexford is never a mere mouthpiece for a political agenda or reducible to an abstract expression of ideology; he is a credible and fallible human being. In *Simisola* (1994), for instance, Wexford is forced to confront the possibility of his own internalised racism, despite his previously complacent belief in his enlightened outlook, when he makes a mistake over the identification of a young African woman. One of the many strengths of Rendell's social commentary was her refusal to turn a blind eye to those uncomfortable aspects of modern life and our own complicity in them. In a clinical, almost forensic, manner, she dissected the deeper processes by which we are all implicated in oppressive social practices.

Rendell was a socialist and a working Labour peer in the House of Lords. She was committed to, and campaigned on behalf of, a range of social issues such as racial discrimination within the Arts, public libraries, domestic violence and female genital mutilation. These varied political and social concerns often find expression in her novels. For instance, she explores environmentalism and the extremes of political activism in *Road Rage* (1997); domestic violence (as well as paedophilia and vigilantism) in *Harm Done* (1999); and racism in *Simisola*.

Unlike other writers working within the genre, Rendell did not feel compelled to carry out practical research, for instance through meeting with people who have been convicted of the sort of crimes she writes about. Her inspiration, she claimed, came from imagination and, sometimes, through her reading of psychology books and conversations with her son, Simon, a psychiatric social worker. Throughout her oeuvre, Rendell's interest in psychology is evident. From the beginning of her career, she made a deliberate break from the 'golden age' detective novel through her emphasis on *why* a crime is committed, rather than simply *who* committed it. There are sometimes explicit references to Freud and psychoanalysis in her fiction, such as in *An Unkindness of Ravens* (1985), but generally there is in all her novels a fascination with the more bizarre aspects of human psychology, and the dark impulses that lie at the heart of violent action. Reflecting this interest, Rendell published *The Reason*

Why: An Anthology of the Murderous Mind in 1995, an edited collection of fictional and non-fictional writings that purport to illuminate the aberrations of the human psyche.

After the success of *From Doon With Death* (1964) one might have expected Rendell to take advantage of the popularity of her detective by immediately writing another novel featuring Wexford. Instead, she published *To Fear a Painted Devil* (1995), a more unsettling kind of crime thriller, devoid of the comforting presence of Kingsmarkham's benevolent policeman. Instead, it is left to the doctor, Max Greenleaf, to unravel the solution to a mysterious death, and he constitutes a rare example of an amateur detective in Rendell's work.

Rendell continued to alternate her Wexford titles with non-series novels, a practice that allowed her the freedom to explore subject matter not easily treatable within the more traditional structure of the Kingsmarkham books. These stand-alone novels tend to transcend the conventions of the detective fiction genre, often encompassing broader issues and themes beyond the interest of a central crime. Indeed, frequently, the murder or crime may seem incidental or marginal to the novel as a whole. This is the key difference from the Wexford books, which are more firmly grounded in the conventions of the police-procedural or detective novel, although they are never formulaic, and refuse to slavishly follow established patterns. The last Wexford-free Rendell title, *Dark Corners* (2015) continued the detailed exploration of human behaviour and its peculiarities found in her work as a whole.

The Wexford series is set in Sussex, but as she lived in the capital herself, it is unsurprising that a large number of Rendell's non-series novels took London as their setting. Nevertheless, Rendell had an extraordinary ability to render the city both recognisably familiar and, at the same time, unsettlingly strange. In novels such as *King Solomon's Carpet* (1991; set largely in the London underground) and *The Keys to the Street* (1996; among the haunts of homeless people around Covent Garden and its environs) she successfully shows her readers an alternative London, a hidden world that is both convincing and compelling.

In 1986, Rendell published her first 'Barbara Vine' novel, *A Dark-Adapted Eye*. An appended letter addressed to the reader, explained that the new name was as much a part of the author's personality as that under which she had hitherto published: 'For a long time I have wanted Barbara to have a voice as well as Ruth. It would be a softer voice, speaking at a slower pace, more sensitive perhaps, and more intuitive'. The Vine books are perhaps best described as novels of psychological suspense. They have in common a preoccupation with the past and explore in unhurried detail its persistent influence on the present. For example, in *The Blood Doctor* (2002), the narrator investigates the secrets of his great-grandfather, Lord Henry of Nanther, a physician to Queen Victoria. Through this process of uncovering the past, and the themes of blood, heredity, and power that emerge, Vine explores different aspects of the issue of inheritance, against the backdrop of House of Lords reform. In other Vine novels, the past that is explored may be a more recent one: for instance, in *No Night Is Too Long* (1994), multiple narrative voices gradually reveal the circumstances of a crime committed two years previously by Tim Cornish.

The distinction between the Barbara Vine novels and those written under Rendell's real name is frequently overstated. For instance, it is often claimed that the Vine novels enter darker, more disturbing territory. However, this had already become a trend in Rendell's work before the publication of *A Dark-Adapted Eye* in 1986. In fact, it is noteworthy that the 'Rendell' novel published for that year, *Live Flesh*, places the reader in much the same challenging, and often uncomfortable, position as the subsequent Vine novels, suggesting a continuity in her literary vision, as well as a shift into new types of narrative experiments. The narrator of *Live Flesh*, Victor Jenner, is a convicted rapist who becomes obsessed with the girlfriend of the policeman he shot and left paralysed. The reader is thus forced into uncomfortable proximity to the thought processes of a pathological mind, a technique that is continued in the Vine novels, which are invariably written from the criminal's first-person perspective.

Perhaps a more defensible difference between the Wexford series and the stand-alone Rendell and Vine books, relates to the reader's frequent sense of disorientation, of being cast adrift in a chillingly amoral and dangerous universe. For while all her books deal with the darker, disconcerting aspects of human behaviour, the comforting presence of the solid and benign Reg Wexford provides a moral centre and point of identification for the reader. It is also true to say that the Vine novels explore the psychological aspects of criminality and aberrant behaviour in greater depth and more leisurely, incremental detail than the Wexford novels, possibly in part because they are freed from the requirements of the puzzle-type, police detective plot.

Perhaps as part of her wider philosophy of individual responsibility, Rendell's novels reject a determinist world-view. All her novels, to varying degrees, explore the processes by which aberrant human behaviour is produced, and Rendell refuses to endorse a doctrine which posits a murderer as purely, inexplicably evil. In *The Brimstone Wedding* (1995), the protagonist Jenny states: 'I don't believe in fate. I don't believe in destiny or patterns in life but in chance and that what happens is what you do yourself'. Similarly, in *Live Flesh*, David Fleetwood concludes that everything that has happened has been the result of chance: 'All accidents. [....] There's no answer to it, no pattern'. In a related way, the novels written as Barbara Vine resist traditional 'closure' in their resolutions. As Susan Rowland has noted, 'Vine novels leave some aspect of the crime as indecipherable, usually connoting something unknowable, even sublime, about human characters at the extremity of passion'.

Rendell was widowed in 1999. She and Don Rendell had separated in 1975, only to remarry a few years later (another episode in her life that Rendell was reluctant to discuss in interviews). Rendell continued to live in London and divide her time between writing and her parliamentary work until her death in May 2015.

Suggested Reading/Works Cited

Brooks, Libby, 'The Profile: Ruth Rendell. Dark Lady of Whodunnits', *The Guardian*, 3 August 2002. http://www.guardian.co.uk/books/2002/aug/03/featuresreviews.guardianreview9.

Horsley, Lee, *Twentieth-Century Crime Fiction* (Oxford and New York: Oxford University Press, 2005).

Macdonald, Marianne, 'Her Dark Materials' [Interview with Ruth Rendell], *The Telegraph*, 11 April 2005. http://www.telegraph.co.uk/culture/donotmigrate/3640185/Her-dark-materials.html.

Rowland, Susan, *From Agatha Christie to Ruth Rendell: British Women Writers in Detective and Crime Fiction* (Basingstoke: Palgrave Macmillan, 2001).

Russett, Margaret, 'Three Faces of Ruth Rendell: Feminism, Popular Fiction, and the Question of Genre', in *Genre Matters: Essays in Theory and Criticism*, ed. by Gariin Dowd, Jeremy Strong, and Lesley Stevenson (Bristol: Intellect Books, 2006), pp. 135–154.

CHAPTER 59

Catherine Aird (Pseudonym of Kinn Hamilton McIntosh, b. 1930), 1966: *The Religious Body*

Jasmine Simeone

Catherine Aird is best known for some twenty novels featuring Inspector C. D. Sloan, several volumes of short stories and local histories relating to villages on the outskirts of Canterbury, Kent. Aird was educated at Waverley School and Greenhead High School Huddersfield before moving with her parents to Kent in 1946. She worked for many years as a doctor's receptionist for her father in the community where she still lives. This continuity gives her insights into human life and medical details, which she draws on in her crime writing.

Aird's series detective is Detective Inspector Christopher Dennis ('Seedy') Sloan, head of the Criminal Investigation Department, Berebury, county town of fictional Calleshire. DI Sloan first appeared in *The Religious Body* (1966) and is known for growing roses and for his dry sense of humour. His understanding wife Margaret allows him to tend his garden when not dealing with murders and mysteries. He has to contend with a slow-witted, speed-loving assistant, Detective Constable Crosby, glum Inspector 'Happy' Harry Harpe, of Berebury Traffic Division and the older, rather reactionary superior Superintendent Leeyes who

J. Simeone (✉)
The Dorothy L. Sayers Society, Essex, UK

provides humour and frustration during investigations. Sloan's penchant for literary allusion betrays his author's own wide reading habits and perspicacious and witty style. Plots and characters are finely worked and believable, owing more to 'Golden Age' detection than contemporary trends. Aird has succeeded in giving imaginary Calleshire a charm and verisimilitude, which owes as much to occasional inclusion of historical characters and contemporary references as to realistically described places. *A Most Contagious Game* (1967), which does not feature Sloan, is also set in Calleshire.

Aird was awarded the Diamond Dagger in 2015 for an outstanding lifetime's contribution to crime fiction, by which point she had written over twenty novels and several collections of short stories. Information for this profile was kindly provided by Catherine Aird in interviews conducted by Jasmine Simeone in 2009.

SUGGESTED READING/WORKS CITED

Barnes, Melvyn, *Murder in Print: A Guide to Two Centuries of Crime Fiction* (London: Barn Owl, 1986).

Herbert, Rosemary, *Whodunit? A Who's Who in Crime & Mystery Writing* (Oxford: Oxford University Press, 2003).

Salwak, Dale, ed., *Mystery Voices: Interviews with British Crime Writers— Catherine Aird, P. D. James, H. R. F. Keating, Ruth Rendell and Julian Symons* (San Bernadino, CA: Borgo Press, 1991).

CHAPTER 60

Reginald Hill (Also wrote as Patrick Ruell, Dick Morland and Charles Underhill, 1936–2012), 1970: *A Clubbable Woman*

Malcah Effron

From his first novel, *A Clubbable Woman* (1970), which introduced his longest-running series characters Dalziel (Dee-ell) and Pascoe, Reginald Hill developed the place of Northern England in the contemporary crime novel.

Born in Hartlepool in 1936 to Reginald and Isabel Hill, his family later moved to County Cumberland, now Cumbria, in the Lake District, which is the setting of his second novel, *Fell of Dark* (1971). He completed his national service in the British Army Border Regiment between 1955 and 1957, after which he attended St. Catherine's College, Oxford, where he earned a B. A. with honours in 1960, the same year that he married his wife Patricia Ruell. After university, Hill taught at a school in Essex, and five years later he accepted a job at the Doncaster College of Education in Yorkshire. While teaching in Doncaster, Hill began publishing professionally, achieving success as a writer so that after a decade and

M. Effron (✉)
Massachusetts Institute of Technology, Cambridge, MA, USA

nineteen novels, he retired from teaching and became a full-time writer in 1981. He produced nearly forty novels, which include twenty-four Dalziel and Pascoe novels, five Joe Sixsmith novels, ten thrillers published under his own name, eight adventure novels published under the name Patrick Ruell, two science fiction novels published under the name Dick Morland, and two historical novels published under the pseudonym Charles Underhill. Additionally, he contributed to critical exploration of the crime genre, critiquing what he saw as a non-literary focus in crime fiction studies: 'But unless we are careful, the sociological century of such studies, the concern with crime novels merely as a phenomenon of popular culture, may serve only to drive the genre deeper into a critical ghetto'. With his promotion of the literary value of crime novels and the breadth of his publications both in terms of the types of novels he published and the forms he used for his series characters, Reginald Hill identified himself as a literary writer of crime fiction, which distinguishes the innovative elements of Hill's writing styles.

Reginald Hill's literary experimentation extended not only to the variety of genres he wrote in but also to the variety of narrative styles he employed in his series. Though known mostly as the author of the Dalziel and Pascoe series, he did not begin as a series writer, publishing his first stand-alone novel after his first series novel. In fact, unlike writers like Sue Grafton and Janet Evanovich, who chose their first novels' titles to facilitate the sale of their books as a clearly defined series, Hill acknowledged that he did not create his first detective protagonists, Detective Superintendent Andy Dalziel and Detective Sergeant Peter Pascoe, as series characters. Furthermore, Hill wrote frankly about the potential pitfalls writing a series: 'I was aware from the start that with the pleasure of recognition and the interest of long-term development, which are the advantages of series characters, come the dangers of overfamiliarity and stagnation'. Hill's diverse production can in some sense be traced to the desire to avoid such dangers.

Hill ensured that he did not stagnate by writing a non-Dalziel and Pascoe between each Dalziel and Pascoe novel. As such, his first standalone novel, *Fell of Dark*, appeared after his first Dalziel and Pascoe novel, shifting in the crime genre from the detective novel to the thriller by changing the narrative focus from a third-person account of the police's investigation to a first-person account of the prime suspect's attempts to clear himself. The pattern of writing stand-alone stories in between the Dalziel and Pascoe novels is only slightly compromised by the Joe

Sixsmith series, as the new detective figure appears between Dalziel and Pascoe novels through the mid-1990s, but with the interspersion of two series, Hill continued to produce Dalziel and Pascoe only every other novel. He continued this pattern, publishing *The Woodcutter* (2010) after his last Dalziel and Pascoe novel, *Midnight Fugue* (2009).

Hill's literary experimentation was not confined to his work outside of the Dalziel and Pascoe series; in fact, his longest and most prominent detective series in itself indicates Hill's range. Over the twenty-four novels and three decades of Dalziel and Pascoe, Hill played with a variety of forms. His first few novels seem to adhere to the traditional British whodunit, providing a strange murder with a limited cast of suspects in a specific social setting, such as the rugby club in *A Clubbable Woman* and the college in *An Advancement of Learning* (1971). In other novels, however, he clearly shifts the form, indicating the new style in the titles of the novels, such as *Child's Play* (1986), which is described on the title page as 'a tragic-comedy in three acts of violence with a prologue and an epilogue', although Hill does not place the acts of the play in chronological order, and *A Cure for All Diseases* (2008), subtitled 'a novel in six volumes'. Hill similarly takes the structure from non-novelistic narratives in *Midnight Fugue*, using the movements of a fugue to structure the sections of the novel. The titles thus become the first signal to Hill's innovative approach to the basic structure of the classical detective form.

In the previous cases, the titles of the narrative signal the stylistic experimentation contained within each novel, but Hill did not always designate his narrative approach within his title. In several novels, like *Under World* (1988) and *Pictures of Perfection* (1994), the narrative opens with a scene repeated at the conclusion, often setting up either Dalziel or Pascoe in a scenario that seemingly implies their immanent death, with Pascoe trapped in a fallen mine in *Under World* and Dalziel, Pascoe, and their colleague Sergeant Wield are set up to be shot in *Pictures of Perfection*. Other works weave different narrative trajectories through the novels, providing multiple perspectives on the narrative and allowing Hill to experiment with different forms of narration. He often combines the epistolary form with third-person omniscient narrative. For instance, *Bones and Silence* (1990), which was nominated for an Edgar Award, intersperses the main narrative with anonymous letters from a suicide, and in *Death's Jest-Book* (2002) the murderer from *An Advancement of Learning*, Franny Roote, writes letters to Pascoe that appear in the text. *A Cure for All Diseases* (2008) has epistolary inserts, as well, in the form of e-mails from one of the witnesses to her sister, and this new medium for written communication allows Hill to play with spelling and grammar beyond the incorporation of regional dialect that fills his novels. Additionally, in this novel, he allows Dalziel a first-person narrative through the medium of Dictaphone playback. These different narrative devices indicate how Hill experiments with form to bring the detective novel beyond the plot-driven formulae with which it is traditionally associated.

While Hill's literary experimentation created an array of narrative styles and novelistic forms across his writings, he consistently employed literary allusion throughout his narratives. From *Fell of Dark*, whose title comes from a Gerard Manly Hopkins poem, Hill frequently uses epigrams for his novels and his chapters, drawing them from literary sources as diverse as the medieval York mystery play cycles (*Bones and Silence*), the Renaissance's Francis Bacon (*An Advancement of Learning*) nineteenth-century writers such as Thomas Lovell Beddoes (*Death's Jest-Book*), Emily Dickinson (*Good Morning, Midnight* [2004]), and Jane Austen (*A Cure for All Diseases*), and twentieth-century poets like Hopkins, mentioned previously, and Stevie Smith. Hill's breadth of literary allusion clearly reflects that he read English at Oxford, and his self-professed status as a Janeite, or devotee of Jane Austen, can be understood to provide the motive behind the parallels to Austen's novels of manners in his writing, particularly in *Pictures of Perfection*, which James Hurt calls his 'Austen novel'. Hurt sees these allusions as taking on more structural importance in the latter decades of Hill's production, but consistently throughout his writing, Hill showed an open engagement with the literary, though his production has only been catalogued in terms of genre fiction.

Hill's longest and best-known series features Andy Dalziel, a detective superintendent with the Mid-Yorkshire Criminal Investigative Division (CID), and Peter Pascoe, who progresses from detective sergeant to detective chief inspector (DCI). The series introduces a variety of other recurrent characters, notably Detective Sergeant Edgar Wield, and Detective Constables Dennis Seymour, Hat Bowler, Shirley Novello, and Adolphus Hector. These figures allow Hill to introduce different social issues into his novels, including issues of gender and sexuality, as Shirley Novello, as a woman, challenges the still patriarchal police hierarchy of Mid-Yorkshire and Wield, as a homosexual, challenges the homophobic, yet supposedly egalitarian, world of the police. The large cast of series characters allowed Hill the opportunity to address different social issues, but his principal detectives, Dalziel and Pascoe, offer both sides of the social spectrum on most issues that he chooses to investigate, interrogating both liberal and conservative social and political policies within characters that seem figureheads for each side and neither side simultaneously.

Dalziel at first seems the model for conservative policies. Described as larger-than-life in terms of both his size and his social power, the detective superintendent speaks in a local dialect, is unabashedly not politically correct and refuses to change to meet the new standards, he becomes the face of local policing, using what Hunt describes as an 'old-fashioned, personal, intuitive approach'. Faced with the progress of the twentieth and twenty-first centuries, he appears the dinosaur that Pascoe initially perceives, except for his complete inability to become extinct. As Ellie Pascoe, Peter's wife, remarks in response to the news that Dalziel is in a coma in *The Death of Dalziel* (initially published as *Death Comes for the Fat Man*, 2007), 'Humans went [...] But Dalziel, when he went, it would be like losing a mountain. Every time you saw the space where it had been, you'd be reminded that nothing was forever'. Nevertheless, the superficial character of the old-fashioned, sedentary Yorkshireman gives way to tolerance and a keen understanding of human nature, as is seen when he acknowledges that he has always known that DS Wield is homosexual when he comes out after eight novels in *Child's Play*. As such, he presents a progressive face of the 'old-fashioned, personal, intuitive approach', indicating its value in a changing social climate.

As a graduate entrant into the police force, Peter Pascoe represents the opposite end of the spectrum from Dalziel. With a degree in sociology, he is meant to represent a liberal form of police officer, acutely aware of the stigma associated with the police by the university-educated, as his university friends have abandoned him, and even his wife Ellie constantly creates problems for him with her outspoken liberal activities in many of the novels. Because of his education, his political correctness and savvy, Hunt categorises Pascoe as using a 'modern, systematic, "scientific" approach'. While Pascoe's educated and open-minded pose indicates him as the figurehead of liberality, he is frequently confronted with his own close-mindedness, particularly in confronting his own prejudices. While this is occasionally attributed to a shell hardened by police work, Pascoe's conservative tempering of his wife's liberal stances enables him to support and illustrate the functioning of the police. With the Dalziel and Pascoe team, Hill created protagonists that both support and critique the social systems and their shifting policies over four decades.

Hill's other serial character, Joe Sixsmith, was introduced in the short story 'Bring Back the Cat,' in which the black factory-worker turned private detective, Joe Sixsmith, brings Hill away from his well-known Yorkshire setting, focusing instead on industrialised urban spaces instead of village and rural life. Hill emphasises that his Luton is wholly fictional, as he has never been to the real Luton, deviating from the Dalziel and Pascoe series by writing about a cultural region with which he is not familiar. This setting gives a breadth of social exploration beyond that cultivated in the Dalziel and Pascoe series. Moreover, Sixsmith allows Hill freer play with the means of investigation, particularly as Sixsmith follows neither the intuitive approach of Dalziel nor the scientific approach of Pascoe, but instead has his own style that his lawyer friend Cheryl Butcher calls serendipitous. As is repeated in multiple novels, when Butcher tells him he has serendipity, Sixsmith asks if it can be treated on the NHS. Following lines through multiple neighbourhoods and classes in the Luton area and one adventure to Wales, Sixsmith muddles his way through, trying to earn the maximum amount with the minimum of danger, while maintaining his moral integrity. With comedic series characters like his religious Aunt Mirabelle, choir master Reverend Percy Potempkin, taxi driver Merv Golightly, and in-out girlfriend, nurse Beryl Boddington, in addition to Butcher, who works at the job centre, the series explores the deteriorating situations of industrial communities through the comedy of the mean streets of Hill's Luton.

In his work, Hill used crime as a means of exploring different social situations in contemporary Britain. The crimes take him from the rugby club to the senior common room to the bottom of a mineshaft, always placing the situations in light of the current economic and political situations. The issues he takes up engage with society from regional and national perspectives in an increasingly global society, as Peter Ling notes, using regional and national differences to create intrigue both in terms of the investigation and in terms of the establishment of the crime. But as Sabine Vanacker observes, regardless of their reach socially, economically and politically, all the mysteries unravel into issues of family dynamics. His writing thus literally brings home the consequences of the social issues he explores through the medium of criminal investigation. His success in dealing with these issues in an innovative and exciting fashion is not only documented by his sales, for which he often thanked readers in his acknowledgements, interviews and critical material, but also in his receipt of the Crime Writers' Association's Golden Dagger Award for the Dalziel and Pascoe series (1990) and the coveted Cartier Diamond Dagger Lifetime Achievement Award (1995). Ultimately, Hill did as he claimed he desired, to 'tell powerful stories powerfully'.

SUGGESTED READING/WORKS CITED

Hill, Reginald, 'Looking for a Programme', in *Colloquium on Crime: Eleven Renowned Mystery Writers Discuss Their Work*, ed. by Robin W. Winks (New York: Charles Scribner's Sons, 1986), pp. 149–166.
Hurt, James, 'Reginald (Charles) Hill', in *Dictionary of Literary Biography, Volume 276: British Mystery and Thriller Writers Since 1960*, ed. by Gina MacDonald (Detroit: Thomson Gale, 2003), pp. 199–207.
Ling, Peter J., 'Identity, Allusions, and Agency in Reginald Hill's *Good Morning, Midnight*', *Clues: A Journal of Detection*, 24:4 (2006), 59–71.
'Reginald Hill', on Contemporary Authors Online, Literature Resource Center. http://go.galegroup.com/ps/i.do?&id=GALE%7CH1000045593&v=2.1&u=imcpl_indy&it=r&p=LitRC&sw=w.
Vanacker, Sabine, 'The Family Plot in Recent Novels by P. D. James and Reginald Hill', *Critical Survey*, 20:1 (2008), 17–28.

CHAPTER 61

Frederick Forsyth (b. 1938), 1971: *The Day of the Jackal*

Christopher Routledge

Frederick Forsyth is a British thriller writer whose first novel, *The Day of the Jackal* (1971), became an international bestseller. Like Forsyth's later novels, it blends well-researched set pieces based on real events, real technical details, and real people, with fictional plotlines. This combination of real and imaginary gives Forsyth's books an air of documentary authority, especially when delivered in his characteristically plot-driven style. Forsyth is also well known for his right-wing political views, in particular his opposition to Britain's membership of the European Union, and his advocacy of constitutional monarchy.

Forsyth was born in Ashford, Kent, and educated at Tonbridge School, and the University of Granada, Spain. In 1956 he joined the Royal Air Force, and trained as a pilot, before leaving in 1958 to begin a career as a journalist. Forsyth was a talented linguist, and after three years working for a British local newspaper, he joined Reuters, where in the early 1960s, he reported from France, Germany and Eastern Europe. He joined the BBC in1965, and became the corporation's correspondent in Biafra, during the country's war with Nigeria. In 1968, Forsyth left the

---

C. Routledge (✉)
Freelance Writer and Photographer, NW England, UK

© The Author(s) 2020
E. Miskimmin (ed.), *100 British Crime Writers*, Crime Files,
https://doi.org/10.1057/978-1-137-31902-9_61

BBC following allegations that he had falsified parts of his reports from the country, and had become overtly sympathetic to the Biafran cause. He later returned to the country as a freelance reporter, and Biafra became the subject of his first non-fiction book, *The Biafra Story* (1969).

Biafra existed as an independent state for only a few years in the late 1960s, all of them consumed by war, and Forsyth's life behind the lines was difficult and precarious. He returned to the UK weighing only eight stone, according to an interview he gave for the *Observer* in 2002. Needing money, Forsyth wrote *The Day of the Jackal* (1971), a fast-paced thriller about a plot to assassinate the French President, Charles de Gaulle, and it was bought in 1970, along with his next two books, by publisher Harold Harris, at Hutchinson.

Forsyth himself is realistic and self-effacing about his abilities as a writer, likening his work to 'painting by numbers', but detailed research, combined with his ability to create believable plots and conspiracies, more than make up for any literary limitations. Forsyth cleverly weaves fictional material with events his readers recognise from the actual news headlines to make his stories seem real. Famously, for example, *The Day of the Jackal* begins with a detailed description of an actual (failed) attempt to kill Charles de Gaulle.

The Day of the Jackal became a bestseller – as of 2013 it has sold at least 10 million copies – and was a defining popular novel for the 1970s, representing as it does an era of military coups, assassinations, terrorism and conspiracy theories. Besides its popularity, the novel's realism has made it a controversial book, and perhaps even the inspiration for real assassinations, including the murder of Israeli Prime Minister Yitzhak Rabin, in 1995, and an attempted killing of United States President George W. Bush, in 2005. Ilich Ramírez Sánchez, a Venezuelan assassin, arrested in 1994 for killing two French agents, even became known in the media as 'Carlos the Jackal'.

By 1973, when *The Day of the Jackal* became a film, Forsyth's novel was a worldwide hit, but in 1970 Forsyth struggled to find a publisher who would take it seriously, because, he was told he had 'broken all the rules'. The central character was a particular problem from a publisher's point of view, being so unlikable. Interviewed by the *Daily Telegraph* in 2011 Forsyth commented: 'I was very surprised when readers said they loved [the Jackal]. He was the ruddy killer'. Within a few months of appearing in Britain, the novel was published in the United States, and won the Edgar Award for best novel from the Mystery Writers of America in 1972.

Forsyth's second novel, *The Odessa File* (1972) addresses another newsworthy theme of its era: the pursuit of German ex-Nazis on the run from the international authorities. In *The Dogs of War* (1974), he wrote about the relationship between Third World governments and the corporations by which they are manipulated and exploited. Set in Africa, this third novel draws heavily on Forsyth's experiences in Biafra, and contains a great deal of detail about the way mercenaries operate.

Much of Forsyth's research for his books has involved visiting war zones, and spending time in the countries in which the novels are set. Blending the roles of journalist and novelist, his novels are often topical and politically relevant: *The Fist of God* (1994) was about the first Gulf War, in 1990–1991, while *The Afghan* (2006) considers the contemporary issues of al-Qaeda and the Guantanamo Bay detention camp. Like many journalists, Forsyth has often found himself in dangerous and potentially compromising situations. He was an acquaintance of rebels plotting to overthrow the president of Equatorial Guinea, in 1973, and has been criticised for paying them for information. While researching his novel about drug cartels, *The Cobra* (2010), he found himself involved in fighting between factions in the West African state of Guinea-Bissau.

In his forty-year career Forsyth has written fifteen novels, several works of non-fiction, and numerous short stories. With his emphasis on action, and settings that include expensive restaurants, airports and hotels, no doubt Forsyth's success owed something to the popularity of Ian Fleming's James Bond series. But Forsyth took the espionage crime thriller in an entirely different and more realistic direction, followed by writers such as Jack Higgins, and more recently Andy McNab. While Fleming's stories are self-evident fantasies built on a foundation of Cold War paranoia, the realism of Forsyth's work makes such paranoia seem all the more justified. Where Fleming's villains seek global power, Forsyth's have more pragmatic, but no less lethal, ambitions.

The detailed plotting and technical accuracy of Forsyth's stories have won him many fans, and, as Charles Cumming argues somewhat contentiously in *The Guardian* in June 2011, made him the originator of a whole new class of thriller. Forsyth has continued to write novels, not least because in 1990 he was swindled out of £2.2 million by his investment adviser, and needed to make a living. But since the 1990s, Forsyth has made a name for himself as a conservative and often controversial political commentator on television and radio. He has also continued to work as a journalist for the *Daily Express* and other newspapers. He was awarded a CBE in 1997.

SUGGESTED READING/WORKS CITED

Brown, Helen, 'Interview with Frederick Forsyth', *The Telegraph*, 20 May 2011. http://www.telegraph.co.uk/culture/books/authorinterviews/8524091/Frederick-Forsyth-I-had-expected-women-to-hate-him.-But-no....html.

Cumming, Charles, 'Interview with Frederick Forsyth', *The Guardian*, 3 June 2011. http://www.guardian.co.uk/commentisfree/2011/jun/03/day-jackal-frederick-forsyth.

The Official Frederick Forsyth Webpage. http://www.booksattransworld.co.uk/frederickforsyth/.

CHAPTER 62

Robert Barnard (1936–2013), 1974: *Death of an Old Goat*

Stephen Knight

Born on 23 November 1936 in Burnham-on-Crouch, Essex, Robert Barnard studied English at Balliol College Oxford, lectured at the University of New England, Armidale, Australia 1961–6, moved to Bergen, Norway, 1966–76, where he took a Ph.D. in 1972, and then became Professor at Tromsö, 1976–83, when he retired early to write full-time.

His first novel was *Death of an Old Goat* (1974), set in Armidale, and by 2010 he had published 29 other mysteries, all involving a mix of witty satire and some social considerations, including two series, one starring Perry Trethowan, beginning with *Death by Sheer Torture* (1981: in the USA just *Sheer Torture*), and a more up-to-date series focused on Charlie Peace, black police detective, starting with *Death and the Chaste Apprentice* (1989). He has also published three lighter novels as 'Bernard Bastable'. There are two crime short-story collections, an academic critique of Dickens (his Ph.D.) and a study of Agatha Christie, *A Talent to Deceive* (1974). He was awarded the British Crime Writers Diamond Dagger in 2003 for lifetime achievement, and was a regular and very successful speaker at crime fiction conferences and gatherings.

S. Knight (✉)
University of Melbourne, Melbourne, VIC, Australia

Barnard's work is rich with thematic variety, literary power and edgy wit, often playing with generic patterns, and frequently returning to social concerns—he described his politics as 'pretty left wing'. His first novel satirised, with equal impact, academic pomposity and Australian self-confidence. Just as ironically, the killer of the 'old goat', a pompous English academic visitor, is only later caught by accident. From the start Barnard's novels question, or sometimes just mock, the criminographical modes they skilfully develop.

With *A Little Local Murder* (1976) Barnard returned to Britain, and this and *Mother's Boys* (1981) typify his often dark condition-of-England crime writing: families are at odds, social change leaves many behind. The first novel can be over-witty, but the second deals powerfully with a brutal mother and the crimes she generates, including her own murder – Americans would call it a crime novel.

Barnard branched out with Perry Trethowan, police superintendent of good family who rises to royal bodyguard. London's social life interweaves with ironies about contemporary radicalism, but the novel reverts to playfulness. *Posthumous Papers* (1979) perhaps revealingly focuses on a writer whose fame was always a hoax: murder is the outcome but the criminal gets away with it. This game-playing (or confessional) Barnard voice seems contradicted by his turn towards serious recent historicism. In *Out of the Blackout* (1985) a man traces his neuroses and his mysterious family back to wartime London. A fine psychothriller, this mix of familial jealousies and fantasies shapes a convincing miniature of British life over twenty years. A later period is handled with similar energy in *A Scandal in Belgravia* (1991), about the tragedy of a gay politician in the Suez period: all is worked out skilfully, with a remarkable, and morally revealing, final surprise. Three novels published as 'Bernard Bastable' deploy a lighter historicism. *To Die like a Gentleman* (1993) is a condensed story mostly told in letters and diary entries, but not without some darknesses; two subsequent novels are told in person by Mozart, surviving into the nineteenth century only to teach piano to the future Queen Victoria.

A lively and supple writer, with varied themes and settings, Barnard seems not to have achieved as much as his best work promises. When he tackled in 1989 the timely topic of a black police inspector in his 'Charlie Peace' series, he made his stories wry and suggestive rather than incisive and assertive like American contemporaries. Barnard often seemed unable to elude his own academicism in his crime writing and his finest achievement may well be his excellent study of Christie.

SUGGESTED READING/WORKS CITED

Barnard, Robert, *Contemporary Authors, New Revision Series*, Vol. 20, ed. by Linda Metzger and Deborah A. Straub (Detroit: Gale, 1987), pp. 36–40 (including interview with Jean W. Ross).

Breen, Jon L., 'Robert Barnard', in *Mystery and Suspense Writers*, 2 vols, ed. by Robin W. Winks (New York: Charles Scribner's Sons, 1998), vol. 1, pp. 31–40.

Campbell, Mark, 'Robert Barnard', in *British Crime Writing: An Encyclopedia*, 2 vols, ed. by Barry Forshaw (Westport CT: Greenwood, 2009), vol. 2, pp. 47–48.

Ford, Susan Allen, 'Stately Homes of England: Robert Barnard's Country House Mysteries', *Clues: A Journal of Detection*, 23:4 (Summer 2005), 3–14.

CHAPTER 63

Simon Brett (b. 1945), 1975: *Cast, in Order of Disappearance*

Jasmine Simeone

Television and radio writer, producer, playwright and prolific mystery writer, Simon Anthony Lee Brett has written the Charles Paris and Fethering mysteries, as well as the much-loved television series *After Henry* (1985–1989), radio series *No Commitments* (1992–2007), *Smelling of Roses* (2000–2003), and the best seller, *How to Be a Little Sod* (1991), adapted for television with Rik Mayall as the voice of the baby. His crime novel *A Shock to the System* (1984), became a feature film starring Michael Caine.

Brett was educated at the Beacon School, Banstead, at Homefield boys' preparatory school, Sutton, and at Dulwich College. An interest in both history and drama led him to gain a scholarship to Wadham College, Oxford, initially to read History but graduating with a first-class honours degree in English in 1967. While there he became involved with OUDS (Oxford University Dramatic Society) with whom he expanded his repertoire as an amateur actor, playing several roles such as Edgar in *King Lear*, Costard in *Love's Labour's Lost* and Leontes in *The Winter's Tale*.

J. Simeone (✉)
Dorothy L. Sayers Society, Essex, UK

At this period he also wrote, directed and performed in revues, in 1966/7 with the Oxford University late night show on the Edinburgh Festival Fringe, the second year of which resulted in a year's contract as Trainee Light Entertainment Producer for BBC Radio, a post which he took following seven weeks as Father Christmas in a local department store. Brett produced a variety of programmes including quiz and sketch shows, panel games and anthologies, such as *Frank Muir Goes Into...* (*1973–1992*), for which he wrote over a hundred scripts. He also produced the first radio episode of Douglas Adams' *Hitch-Hiker's Guide to the Galaxy* (1978). Most significantly to his role as crime writer he was also largely responsible, with Ian Carmichael, for introducing the Lord Peter Wimsey stories of Dorothy L. Sayers to radio, which gave him the idea of creating his own actor-detective, Charles Paris. His first Charles Paris novel, *Cast, in Order of Disappearance*, was published by Gollancz in 1975, to be followed by eighteen other stories in the series, including *The Cinderella Killer* (2014).

In a research interview (2010) with Jasmine Simeone, Brett commented that, 'My writing the first Charles Paris novel did arise directly out of my producing adaptations of the Lord Peter Wimsey books for Radio 4. At that stage in my life (age twenty-eight), I had written four very properly unpublished novels, but always been a bit scared of crime fiction. I thought a writer needed a computer-like brain to tease out the plots. I discovered [...] that though plot was important, character and dialogue were at least as important – and I thought I might have skill in doing those. That encouraged me to have a go at my first crime novel and, because on the Wimsey series I was working with a lot of middle-aged actors, it seemed an interesting idea to make my investigator an actor'. Charles Paris is quite unlike the suave Lord Peter Wimsey, however; Paris has a disastrous marriage that he is constantly attempting to resurrect, as he does not cope well on his own and he frequently tends towards the inebriated. This somewhat dysfunctional personal life ensures he lands only minor roles, giving him the opportunity to witness the events that he pieces together to solve crimes.

In 1977, Brett moved from the BBC to London Weekend Television, but found the whole TV process much slower and less interesting than his work in radio. Writing began to take up more of his time and two years later he decided to make the break and devote himself entirely to his literary career. He says now, however, that: 'I find writing in different media works well for me, on the "a change is as good as a rest" principle. Writing a book is a wonderful private experience, but it can be very isolating. Working in different media also brings a welcome variation of pace into my professional life. Embarking on a book is a commitment to some months of concentration, whereas writing a radio script or a short story can sometimes be fitted into a week or a fortnight'.

Alongside the later Charles Paris books came the novels about Mrs Pargeter, a rich widow who has useful detective instincts and the money to allow her to visit places where the rich are pampered and suspicious deaths occur. The six-book series began with *A Nice Class of Corpse* (1986) and concluded with *Mrs Pargeter's Point of Honour* (1999). Brett's books are uniformly 'Golden Age' in character, and though technically 'cosy', there is no doubt about the horror of the finding of the corpse. The outrageous Melita Pargeter is not as successful a character as Charles Paris or as Carol and Jude in the Fethering mysteries, but as with those books, Brett is far more interested in the living characters and their interplay, than in the effects of the horror of the death. Brett's style is gently witty, but never at the expense of his characters that he always treats with affection.

Since 2000, the Fethering Mysteries have appeared, each one with an alliterative title, such as *Death on the Downs* (2001) and *Blood at the Bookies* (2008), and featuring the unlikely pair of detectives, Carol and Jude, next door neighbours in the village of Fethering. Each character has a hidden past, Carol the very upright Civil Servant, and Jude the more New Age Hippy, and different abilities and strengths, more being revealed with each book in the series. These women are portrayed sympathetically and realistically as is Fethering, an archetypical Sussex south coast village, the realism of which is enhanced by reference to existing places. The characters here are all entirely believable and Brett avoids the cardboard-cut-out nature of many supporting characters in detective stories by using deft strokes to describe each and set them in context of the two women's lives, usually with some reference to their past, such as old friends, past lovers, a son and daughter-in-law and Ted the publican who has a history with the women.

On embarking on the first of a new series of detective stories, Brett wrote, 'My new series, which began with *Blotto, Twinks and the Ex-King's Daughter* (2009), is an unashamed attempt to write comic romps set between the two World Wars. It's the world of the Golden Age detective story, with a liberal sprinkling of Bulldog Drummond and Fu-Manchu. It's a world of impossibly optimistic investigators and double-dyed villains'. By 2015, the Blotto and Twinks series ran to six novels with *Blotto, Twinks and the Heir to the Tsar* being published in 2015.

Brett has also written individual crime novels out of series, such as *Dead Romantic* (1985), and is responsible for editing occasional anthologies. After a lifetime of radio and TV work, he has contributed to the television series *Rosemary and Thyme* (2003–2007), a humorous look at detection from the gardening perspective. He says, 'Perhaps my background in radio is part of the reason why my books seem to adapt well for performance. I have always realised the importance of dialogue, and enjoy writing it. I'm not very good at physical description; I would much rather define a character by the way they speak and behave than by what they look like. And I do "hear voices" (people sometimes look at me rather oddly when I say this); once I know how a character speaks, I know everything about their personality. I also – maybe my radio training again – when I'm reading a book, skip over the author's descriptions and form my own mental images of the characters'.

Brett's humorous stage thrillers: *Murder In Play* (1994) and *Silhouette* (1998) are produced by amateur companies, five of Brett's pantomimes have been performed at The Theatre, Chipping Norton, Oxfordshire and he usually writes a short play for each annual Arundel Festival, Sussex.

Simon Brett is interested in promoting writers and writing. He has been Chair of the Crime Writers' Association (1986–7), the Society of Authors (1995–7), and the Public Lending Right Advisory Committee (2003–2008). He is also on the committee of the Royal Literary Fund, and Patron to both the West Sussex Writers' Club and the Chichester Literary Society. Between 2001 and 2015 he was President of the Detection Club before handing the role on to Martin Edwards.

Suggested Reading/Works Cited

Alderson, Martha, 'Death at the Stage Door: Anne Morice's Theresa Crichton and Simon Brett's Charles Paris', *Clues*, 4:2 (1983), 21–29.

Bargainnier, Earl F., 'Simon Brett', in *Twelve Englishmen of Mystery*, ed. by Earl F. Bargainnier (Bowling Green, OH: Bowling Green Popular Press, 1984), pp. 305–325.

Steiner, T. R., 'Simon Brett', in *Dictionary of Literary Bibliography, Volume 276: British Mystery and Thriller Writers Since 1960*, ed. by Gina Macdonald (Detroit, MI: Thomson Gale, 2003), pp. 52–66.

Sykes, Jerry, 'Simon Brett', *Mystery Scene*, 56 (1997), 33–37.

The Official Simon Brett Website. http://simonbrett.com/.

CHAPTER 64

Colin Dexter (1930–2017), 1975: *Last Bus to Woodstock*

Susan Massey

Colin Dexter was the creator of the iconic Inspector Morse, one of the most popular characters in post-war British crime fiction. Dexter wrote thirteen Morse novels and the character attained the status of national institution, both through Dexter's work itself, but also thanks to the highly successful ITV television series, which featured John Thaw in the title role.

Dexter was born in Stamford, Lincolnshire. Educated at Stamford School, Dexter spent his National Service with the Royal Corps of Signals before reading Classics at Christ's College, Cambridge. He graduated in 1953 and embarked upon a career teaching Greek and Latin, during which time he also authored three textbooks, aimed at students intending to apply to Oxbridge. In 1956 Dexter married Dorothy Cooper and the couple had two children. Although happy in teaching, Dexter was forced to leave the profession in 1966 because of problems with his hearing. He relocated to Oxford, taking a job as Assistant Secretary to the Oxford Delegacy of Local Examinations and remained in this post until his retirement in 1988. It was while on a family holiday to North Wales in 1972

S. Massey (✉)
University of St Andrews, St Andrews, Scotland, UK

© The Author(s) 2020
E. Miskimmin (ed.), *100 British Crime Writers*, Crime Files,
https://doi.org/10.1057/978-1-137-31902-9_64

that Dexter's life took a turn for the unexpected. Seeking distraction from the poor weather, Dexter turned to detective fiction. However, the calibre of the novels he read was so poor that he was inspired to try to do better. The text Dexter began would form the basis of *Last Bus to Woodstock* (1975), the first Inspector Morse novel.

The setting for Dexter's Morse novels is the university city of Oxford. Novels set within an academic environment are not a new development in the genre. Such collegiate backgrounds were particularly popular in the 1930s, with Dorothy L. Sayers' *Gaudy Night* (1935), featuring Lord Peter Wimsey, being a classic example of the subgenre. Other authors who have situated their fiction within the cloistered spaces of academia include Michael Innes, Margaret Yorke, Veronica Stallwood, Michelle Spring and Ruth Dudley Edwards. Dexter does more, however, than simply employ Oxford and its colleges as a backdrop for his fiction; rather, he integrates city and protagonist to such an extent that it becomes impossible to imagine one without the other. Dexter's choice of location also plays an important role in constructing Morse's character, which is forged as oppositional to the Oxford establishment. During the series, Dexter reveals that Morse was himself a scholarship student at the university but was sent down before he could complete his degree. The exact circumstances are never explained by Dexter, but the incident leaves Morse with a sizable chip on his shoulder and renders him as an outsider in an environment to which he otherwise possesses the intellectual acumen to belong.

When the reader is first introduced to Morse, in *Last Bus to Woodstock*, he is a middle-aged bachelor whose passions include opera, cryptic crossword puzzles, real ale and his beloved Lancia. Dexter admitted that there was a degree of autobiography in his characterisation of Morse, attributing many of his own tastes and predilections to his protagonist. However, Morse also possesses many traits that Dexter would probably have been less keen to ascribe to himself. Defined by a sense of egotism that is almost boundless – by his own admission, he is 'blessed with the best brain in Oxford' – Morse is arrogant and condescending. He is also almost comically vain, as is well illustrated when he becomes annoyed after the wind destroys the careful comb-over he has constructed to hide his bald spot. Although a detective of enormous skill, Morse is not over-enamoured with the more tedious, bureaucratic aspects of police work. Rather than wasting his own considerable gifts on tasks seemingly beneath his dignity (such as police reports), he prefers delegating to his long-suffering sergeant, Lewis.

Functioning as a foil to the cerebral Morse, Lewis is a stable, sensible family man, a solid police officer who may lack flair and imagination when compared to the idiosyncratic and unorthodox Morse, but who compensates for it with his strong work ethic. As a sidekick, Lewis bears the brunt of his boss' frequent temper tantrums and is also the regular target of Morse's lectures on the correct usage of the English language. Although Lewis, therefore, exposes some of the more unpalatable aspects of Morse's character, it is also through him that the reader is able to see Morse as more than simply a cantankerous and pedantic misanthrope. Despite Morse's poor treatment of his junior officer, the affable Lewis is generous towards his boss tolerating his flaws and recognising that Morse's gruff demeanour belies a more sympathetic interior. Morse is, as Lewis recognises, 'arrogant, ungracious, vulnerable, lovable'. Lewis' own domestic contentment emphasises his superior's loneliness. In the absence of a sustaining private life, it is Morse's relationship with Lewis that forms the emotional centre of the novels. Although the bond between the two men is largely unspoken – in keeping with the demands of stiff upper lip British masculinity neither man is comfortable articulating his feelings – it is based upon genuine affection and, as a sign of such, Morse shares the closely guarded secret of his first name with Lewis in 1996's *Death is Now My Neighbour*. Christened 'Endeavour' by his Quaker parents (who, we are told, named their children after virtues), Dexter's earlier refusal to disclose Morse's name contributed greatly to his character's enigma and presented his reader's with a mystery more complex than those found in the texts themselves. When the secret was finally revealed there was such interest from the public that the story made it into the British national press.

Given Morse's middle-class proclivities and the fact that the series is based in Oxford, one of the bastions of English tradition and privilege, it is perhaps unsurprising that Dexter's texts are characterised by a sensibility that puts the reader in mind of classic 'Golden Age' crime fiction. As a novelist, Dexter did not use his fiction to explore social or political issues – his texts neither analyse nor critique the environment in which they are set. Instead, they hark back to an earlier era, redeploying the clue-puzzle format successfully used by writers such as Christie and Sayers. That brain-teasers are integral to the novels is obvious from the name of Dexter's protagonist. 'Morse', of course, evokes Morse code, but Dexter stated that he chose the name as a tribute to Sir Jeremy Morse, a chairman of Lloyds Bank and a renowned crossword setter. The character of Lewis is also named after another crossword expert, Mrs. B. Lewis, the pseudonym of Dorothy Taylor. The action in the texts themselves is largely cerebral. This is most obvious in *The Wench is Dead*, in which Morse investigates a murder committed in the nineteenth century from his bed in the Radcliffe Hospital, where he is being treated for a perforated ulcer. Having stumbled upon a publication detailing the crime in the hospital library, Morse sets his mind to solving what he considers to be a historical miscarriage of justice, using Lewis as a proxy to do his legwork. In many ways this is the essence of Morse's method, which privileges careful, logical thought over irrational hunches or gut instinct.

In the late 1980s Central Television commissioned a series based on the Morse novels, hoping to emulate the success the BBC had enjoyed with its adaptations of Agatha Christie's Miss Marple novels, which starred Joan Hickson. Featuring John Thaw as Morse and Kevin Whately as Lewis, the first episodes of the *Inspector Morse* television series were broadcast on ITV in January 1987. The show was an immediate hit, attaining viewing figures of eighteen million. Colin Dexter was thrilled with the programme, whose success boosted sales of the novels on which they were based. From the series' inception, Dexter was closely involved – the first episodes were direct adaptations of his texts and when demand for the character out-stripped the supply of Dexter's original material, he then turned his hand to inventing plot scenarios, which were expanded and scripted by other writers. One of the episodes plotted by Dexter, 'The Wolvercote Tongue' (1988), was later rewritten and published as a Morse novel – *The Jewel That Was Ours* (1991).

However, despite the close involvement of Morse's creator in the development of the television series, there are some major differences between the world of Dexter's creation and its screen version. The most obvious of these is the character of Lewis. In the novels, Lewis is older than Morse and is a Welshman. Yet on screen he is many years Morse's junior and hails from the north of England. Such was the influence of the television show that is it this Lewis, Kevin Whatley's Lewis, that endures as 'authentic', replacing the textual version not only in the public imagination but, gradually, in Dexter's novels themselves. As Dexter continued to write, his texts became more synchronised with the television series; thus, not only did Lewis become younger, but Morse's Lancia was seamlessly replaced by the red Jaguar Mark 2 he drove on screen.

There are, however, unresolved inconsistencies in the depiction of Morse. In the novels, Morse is frequently represented as a lecherous old man. He displays a seedy relish when it comes to interviewing attractive women and, as he ages, and spends more time in hospital, he becomes a randy scourge of the nursing profession, cheerfully making the most of his increasing physical incapacity to harass the women who are supposed to be looking after him (see, for example, *The Wench is Dead*). On occasions he is crude and coarse in both behaviour and language and, although he is a man of good taste in many respects – his passion for Wagner and A. E. Housman, for example – he also has a marked tendency towards the low-brow, taking *The Mirror* with his *Times*. The Morse that appears on television is a much more sanitised version of Dexter's original character. He lacks the outright sexism displayed by his textual precursor (although he does take exception to the presence of a female pathologist, Dr. Grayling Russell, arguing that it is an unsuitable job for a woman) and, although still keen for female companionship, John Thaw's Morse is more resigned to a life of melancholy bachelorhood. The television series emphasises the English gentleman side of Morse's character, downplaying the vulgarity frequently found in the novels. In *The Silent World of Nicolas Quinn* Dexter writes '[f]or half an hour he [Morse] let his thoughts run wild and free, like randy rabbits in orgiastic intercourse'. It is difficult to imagine such a simile being used of John Thaw's more dignified screen Morse.

Thirty-three episodes of *Inspector Morse* were broadcast and, over the years, many leading lights of the British entertainment industry honed their craft on the programme, including the Oscar-winning directors Danny Boyle and Anthony Minghella. However, despite Morse's popularity, Dexter never intended to keep the character alive indefinitely. Unlike many other series protagonists, Dexter consciously chose to age his protagonist in a realistic fashion. Thus, in the novels, the older Morse gets, the more physically frail he becomes. He is hospitalised several times during the series and develops diabetes, exacerbated by his drinking, in *Death is Now My Neighbour*. Neglectful of his health, Morse finally dies from complications arising from his diabetes in *The Remorseful Day* (1999). Taking its title from an A. E. Housman poem, the novel was quickly adapted for television and the final Morse episode aired, to huge viewing figures and widespread media coverage, in 2000.

After the death of Morse, Colin Dexter did not return to writing crime fiction. However, his most famous character continues to be influential. In 2006, Granada Television produced the pilot episode of a spin-off programme, *Lewis*, which featured Kevin Whately's character in the leading role and Lawrence Fox in the sergeant's role, providing a different version of the intellectual foil to Lewis more dogged investigator. Dexter was not directly involved (although he cameoed in several episodes), but the series returns to the familiar environment of Oxford and the spectre of Morse is constantly present. While never as enigmatic as Morse, Dexter always represented Lewis as a perfectly proficient detective. The partnership between Morse and Lewis may have been unequal but Lewis was not an incompetent sidekick in the mode of a character like Christie's Captain Hastings. Hence, it does not stretch the realms of plausibility to let him carry a television show of his own. Since 2012 there have also been a number of series of *Endeavour*, based around the early police career of the young Morse, played by Shaun Evans, which Dexter also made a Cameo appearance in.

In terms of fiction, Morse has also had a significant legacy. In recent years, British reading tastes have embraced detective fiction emanating from mainland Europe. Writers such as Henning Mankell, Arnaldur Indriðason, Fred Vargas, Andrea Camilleri and Petros Markaris have all found receptive audiences in the UK. While these authors may not themselves have been directly influenced by Dexter's work, the basic prototype of their detectives owes much to the model popularised by Dexter. Despite their geographical heterogeneity, the protagonists of these various authors share a similar blueprint, tending to be work-obsessed middle-aged men with melancholic dispositions, minimal social skills, addictive personalities and quirky hobbies. While Dexter obviously did not invent this model – the above definition can easily be applied to Sherlock Holmes – he successfully adapted it for the police-procedural format and his fiction has been instrumental in shaping the palate of British crime fiction fans. The fact that Mankell's Kurt Wallander has recently been marketed as a successor to Morse – insert inevitable 'Inspector Norse' pun here – underlines the lasting importance of both Dexter and his detective to the genre.

In 1980 Dexter was elected a member of the Detection Club. He has twice been the recipient of the Crime Writers' Association Silver Dagger – for *Service of All the Dead* (1979) and *The Dead of Jericho* (1981) – and has also won the Gold Dagger on two occasions – for *The Wench is Dead*

(1989) and *The Way Through the Woods* (1992). He was awarded the Cartier Diamond Dagger for lifetime achievement in 1997 and, in 2000, was made an Officer of the Order of the British Empire for services to literature. In 1990 the character of Morse was named as the most famous British detective by the Crime Writer's Association.

Suggested Reading/Works Cited

Edmonds, Joanne, 'Creation, Adaptation, and Re-Creation: The Lives of Colin Dexter's Characters', in *It's a Print!: Detective Fiction from Page to Screen*, ed. by William Reynolds and Elizabeth A. Trembley (Bowling Green, OH: Bowling Green Popular Press, 1994), pp. 129–143.

Greene, Douglas G., 'Colin Dexter', in *Mystery and Suspense Writers: The Literature of Crime, Detection, and Espionage*, ed. by Robin W. Winks (New York: Charles Scribner's Sons, 1998).

Millar, Peter, 'Dexter, Colin', in *British Crime Writing: An Encyclopedia*, ed. by Barry Forshaw (Oxford: Greenwood World Publishing, 2009).

CHAPTER 65

John Mortimer (1923–2009), 1975: First Broadcast of *Rumpole of the Bailey* Television Series

Diana Powell

Best known for his character Horace Rumpole, the grumpy, henpecked husband but formidable lawyer in the *Rumpole of the Bailey* series, Mortimer was a prolific author of novels, screen and stage plays, and television and radio scripts, with many of his stories gaining an audience in more than one medium.

John Clifford Mortimer was born in 1923. His father was a successful divorce barrister who was blinded in an accident in 1936. Mortimer attended Harrow and studied law at Oxford before becoming a barrister, specialising, like his father, in divorce cases. During World War Two, Mortimer worked as a fourth assistant director and then script writer for the Crown Film Unit because 'you can't divorce people in war: it doesn't look good'. Due to the limited opportunities in screenwriting following the war, Mortimer returned to his 'day job' of divorce lawyer and began writing novels in his spare time. As a lawyer, Mortimer handled

---

D. Powell (✉)
University of Liverpool, Liverpool, UK

© The Author(s) 2020
E. Miskimmin (ed.), *100 British Crime Writers*, Crime Files,
https://doi.org/10.1057/978-1-137-31902-9_65

several famous censorship cases, including defending the publisher of *Lady Chatterley's Lover* in 1960 against obscenity charges.

Mortimer's father was a towering figure in his life, and he plundered their relationship most famously in *A Voyage Round My Father* (1963 radio, 1970 play, 1971 novel, 1969 and 1982 television), but Mortimer also drew heavily on his memories of his father to create his most famous character, Rumpole, including his dishevelled dress, his quoting of Shakespeare (jarring and nonsensical) and his references to Sherlock Holmes. Mortimer has described Rumpole as 'Sherlockian' and explained that when Rumpole pretends to die in the episode 'Rumpole and The Last Resort' (1983), it is based on Doyle's 'The Dying Detective' (1913). Mortimer also employed his father's, and his own, understanding of the law and the courtroom as entertaining as well as morally inferior to common sense. Mortimer claimed that his work as an advocate aided his writing, helping him to write in a clear way that would 'arrest' the reader's attention and keep it.

The character of Rumpole first appeared in 'Rumpole of the Bailey' (1975) on BBC television's *Play for Today*. The unsuccessful lawyer in Mortimer's *The Dock Brief* (1957) can be seen as a forerunner to the underachieving Rumpole, who loves cheap cigars, claret and is always dressed shabbily. Rumpole is unscrupulous in taking on cases and in his interpretation of the law. Although his view of the law is flexible, his opinion of his domineering wife Hilda is absolute: 'She who must be obeyed'. Regardless of his courtroom triumphs, Hilda re-establishes Rumpole's downtrodden position, both through her nagging and through her comparisons of her husband's career as a junior barrister to her father's as a judge. The Rumpole series continued on ITV from 1978 to 1992.

Mortimer's other notable achievements include the screenplays for the adaptations of Henry James' *The Turn of the Screw* as *The Innocents* (1961 with Truman Capote and William Archibald); the ITV drama *Brideshead Revisited* (1981); and the television adaptation of his novel *Paradise Postponed* (1985) and its sequel *Titmuss Regained* (1991). He was a consultant on the American television series *Boston Legal* in 2004.

Mortimer had an unstable marriage to fellow writer Penelope (Fletcher) Mortimer (1949–1971), which provided inspiration for both authors' writing, and he married Penelope Gollop in 1972. Mortimer rose to Queen's Counsel in 1966, received a CBE in 1986 and was knighted in 1998.

SUGGESTED READING/WORKS CITED

Grove, Valerie, *A Voyage Around John Mortimer* (London: Viking, 2008).
Herbert, Rosemary, 'The Art of Fiction: John Mortimer No. 106', *Paris Review*, Winter 1988, p. 109. http://www.theparisreview.org/interviews/2466/the-art-of-fiction-no-106-john-mortimer.
Mortimer, John, *Clinging to the Wreckage: A Part of Life* (London: Weidenfield & Nicholson, 1982).
———, *Murderers and Other Friends: Another Part of Life* (New York: Viking, 1994).

CHAPTER 66

John Harvey (b. 1938), 1976: *Amphetamines and Pearls*

Delphine Cingal

Best known for the Charlie Resnick series of detective stories, Harvey has also written for radio and television and writes poetry (he founded and, between 1977 and 1999, directed, Slow Dancer, a publishing company specialised in poetry). He also writes 'Western' genre novels under several pseudonyms such as John McLaglen, William S. Brady and J. D. Sandon, to name but a few.

Harvey was born in London. He first taught English and Drama in high schools in Heanor, in Andover and in Stevenage before writing his first novel, *Avenging Angel* in 1975 in order to help a pulp fiction writer friend of his meet with the demands of his publisher. This was followed immediately by *Angel Alone* in 1976, the year that his first crime novel, *Amphetamines and Pearls*, featuring detective Scott Mitchell was also published. The Scott Mitchell series takes the American hard-boiled style of private eye investigation and places them in a British milieu, perhaps a result of Harvey's enjoyment of American crime writing; he cites Elmore Leonard as his main inspiration.

D. Cingal (✉)
Paris 2-Panthéon-Assas University, Paris, France

In 1980, he started teaching part-time Film and American Literature at the University of Nottingham, but gave up teaching altogether in 1986 to become a full-time, prolific writer. The first Resnick novel, *Lonely Hearts* (1989) gained Harvey a place in the Times list of the Hundred Best Crime Novels of the Last Century (1989). This success made his publisher Tony Lacey ask him to write a series of novels with the same character. A collection of Resnick short stories, *Now's the Time* (1999), and eleven novels followed, although there was a ten-year gap between *Last Rites* (1998) and the most recent, *Cold in Hand* (2008). Charles Resnick, of Polish descent, works for the Nottingham police force, loves jazz and named his four cats after famous jazzmen: Bud, Pepper, Miles and Dizzy. The deep influence of jazz can be felt both on Resnick and on his inventor since John Harvey is a great jazz fan, which is obvious from his poetry, especially his 1999 *Bluer Than This* collection, with poems on Chet Baker and Thelonious Monk.

After Harvey stopped writing his Resnick series, Resnick appeared as a guest character in Harvey's Frank Elder trilogy. Frank Elder, a retired Nottinghamshire policeman, moves to Cornwall (Harvey's own home at the time of writing this series) on the breakdown of his marriage. In *Flesh and Blood* (2005), he is asked by detective Maureen Prior to investigate the kidnapping of a girl and the brutal murder of another. At the same time, he tries to protect his teenage daughter from the dark side of the world. His ex-wife and daughter feature strongly in all three novels; in the last novel of the trilogy, *Darkness and Light* (2007) he goes back home at his ex's request, to investigate the disappearance of her friend's sister. This is also an opportunity for him to try and help his daughter Katherine get over the events of *Flesh and Blood*.

Harvey received the French Crime Writers' Association award for the best foreign novel, *Off Minor* in 1997, the Sherlock Award for *Last Rites* in 1998, the French Grand Prix du Roman Noir Etranger for *Cold Light* in 2000, the CWA Silver Dagger for *Flesh and Blood* in 2004, the Prix du Polar Européen for *Ash and Bones* in 2007 and the Crime Writers' Association Cartier Diamond Dagger for his lifetime's achievement in 2007. In 2008, he was the International Guest of Honour at the American Bouchercon Convention. In 2009, Harvey became *doctor honoris causa* at the University of Nottingham for his work with them and for his depiction of Nottingham in his Charlie Resnick series. He has published over a hundred books and lives in London with his partner and their daughter.

SUGGESTED READING/WORKS CITED

Silet, Charles L. P., 'Nottingham Noir: An Interview with John Harvey', *Armchair Detective: A Quarterly Journal Devoted to the Appreciation of Mystery, Detective and Suspense Fiction*, 29:3 (1996), 272–279.

The Official John Harvey Website (with access to interviews in various publications). http://mellotone.co.uk/.

CHAPTER 67

Antonia Fraser (b. 1932), 1977: *Quiet as a Nun*

Suzanne Bray

Although Lady Antonia Fraser is principally known as a historian and biographer, she has also written a highly acclaimed series of detective novels and short stories featuring Jemima Shore, as well as occasional television plays and short stories with a detective theme.

Antonia Margaret Caroline Pakenham was born on 27 August 1932, the daughter of Frank Pakenham, the 7th Earl of Longford, and his wife Elizabeth, nee Harman. She was educated at the Dragon School, Oxford, and St. Mary's Convent, Ascot. She converted to Roman Catholicism in her teens, along with her parents and most of the rest of her family. She read history at Lady Margaret Hall, Oxford. Her marriage to the Conservative MP Sir Hugh Fraser lasted from 1956 until it was dissolved in 1977. She then married the playwright Harold Pinter (1930–2008) in 1980. She has three sons and three daughters from her first marriage and numerous grandchildren. Before becoming a full-time writer, Fraser worked as an assistant to George Weidenfeld at the publishers Weidenfeld & Nicolson. They later published her works.

S. Bray (✉)
Lille Catholic University, Lille, France

© The Author(s) 2020
E. Miskimmin (ed.), *100 British Crime Writers*, Crime Files,
https://doi.org/10.1057/978-1-137-31902-9_67

Her first detective novel, *Quiet as a Nun*, appeared in 1977. Her amateur detective, Jemima Shore, is intelligent, highly literate and entertaining. Although capable of logical deduction, she relies a lot on her intuitions and has a dangerous habit of jumping into bed with attractive male suspects during her investigations. The Jemima Shore mysteries nearly all take place in settings Fraser knows well: a convent school (*Quiet as a Nun* and the short story 'Jemima Shore's First Case'), the Scottish Highlands (*Tartan Tragedy* 1978), Oxford University (*Oxford Blood* 1985), and the theatre (*Cool Repentance* 1982). Some of her knowledge of the world of broadcasting, invaluable as background for the Jemima Shore novels, came from Sir Hugh Fraser's appearances on television talk shows and the radio programme *My Word*. The vivid portrayals of exclusive groups such as politicians, actors, aristocrats, minor royals or Scottish highlanders add to the charm of her fast-moving stories. Critics have praised Fraser for her sophisticated, sometimes tongue-in-cheek, dialogue and characterisation, as well as for her ability to investigate the subtleties of human behaviour.

Quiet as a Nun was adapted for television in 1978 for ITV's *Armchair Theatre* series. Maria Aitken, a personal friend of Fraser's, starred as Jemima Shore and the adaptation was praised for its sinister atmosphere. The short story 'Have a Nice Death' (1983) was also adapted for television the following year and Fraser wrote the TV mystery play *Mister Clay*, *Mister Clay*, a tale of murder and intrigue in a boys' school, for the *Time for Murder* series in 1985. She has also written several mystery stories for inclusion in anthologies.

The Lady Antonia Fraser Archive in the British Library contains the author's uncatalogued papers. Nineteen boxes of materials are listed.

SUGGESTED READING/WORKS CITED

Dougary, Ginny, 'Lady Antonia Fraser's Life Less Ordinary', *The Times*, 5 July 2008. http://women.timesonline.co.uk/tol/life_and_style/women/article42 41665.ece.

Fraser, Antonia, *Must You Go? My Life with Harold Pinter* (London: Weidenfeld & Nicolson, 2010).

CHAPTER 68

Anne Perry (Pseudonym of Juliet Hulme, b. 1938), 1979: *The Cater Street Hangman*

Delphine Cingal

Anne Perry is a prolific author of historical detective fiction, mostly set either during the Victorian era or during World War One. She has two ongoing serial Victorian detectives; Thomas Pitt, who first appeared in *The Cater Street Hangman* (1979), and William Monk, whose first case was in *The Face of a Stranger* (1990) and who and had featured in thirty and twenty-one novels respectively by 2015. She also wrote 'The World War One' series of books (2003–2007), and, since 2003, the ongoing 'Christmas Stories', the thirteenth of which *A Christmas Escape* was published in 2015. She has also written several stand-alone novels, including *The Sheen on the Silk* (2010) as well as innumerable short stories in her own collections and in volumes with other authors, and a series of 'time-shift' stories for young adults.

Perry was born as Juliet Marion Hulme in Blackheath, London. Her father was Dr. Henry Hulme, an English physicist who was to head the British hydrogen bomb programme. Hulme suffered from tuberculosis and when she was six, she almost died. Two years later she was sent to live with a foster family in the Bahamas where the weather was more

D. Cingal (✉)
Paris 2-Panthéon-Assas University, Paris, France

© The Author(s) 2020
E. Miskimmin (ed.), *100 British Crime Writers*, Crime Files,
https://doi.org/10.1057/978-1-137-31902-9_68

congenial. Her own family then moved to a private island off the coast of New Zealand (her father was now the Rector of Canterbury University College in New Zealand), and Hulme joined them. She therefore never really attended school on a regular basis, but her mother had taught her to read and write when she was four. She did attend school between the ages of ten and thirteen before coming down with tuberculosis once more and she was removed from school again from then on. Her parents went on teaching her at home.

In 1954, she became very close friends with Pauline Parker whom she had met at school. The two girls shared a passion for writing and for movies, and developed a very intense friendship. When Hulme's parents separated, Hulme was due to be sent to South Africa to live with a relative. Pauline Parker wished to go with her friend and, when her mother would not agree to this project, both girls battered her to death. It was a brutal murder and it was discussed at length in the press, and has been given a great deal of coverage since. Found guilty of murder, Hulme and Parker were then detained 'at her Majesty's pleasure' in separate prisons, since they were too young to be sentenced to death. Hulme was sent to Mt. Eden women's prison in Auckland. Both were released and given new identities five years later and have never met again.

Until 1994 it was not known that the writer Anne Perry was in fact Juliet Hulme. In this year, however, Kate Winslet portrayed Juliet Hulme in Peter Jackson's movie *Heavenly Creatures*. This drew attention to the case once more and Anne Perry was forced into admitting that she was in fact Juliet Hulme. Initially, Perry talked little of the case, mainly denying that her relationship with Parker had been sexual, as both the trial and the 1994 film had depicted them. In 2005 she acceded to discussing the case on the *Trisha Goddard Show*. Although ongoing interest is inevitable, Perry's own website makes no mention of the murder or her past identity, focusing entirely on herself and writing as Anne Perry. This said, Perry is very much concerned with ideas of guilt and redemption in her work, and these concepts are intrinsic to the character of William Monk, through whom she manages to show how people can actually change and redeem themselves through their actions, as Monk disassociates himself from her former life. On her website she writes: 'I began the Monk series in order to explore a different, darker character, and to raise questions about responsibility, particularly that of a person for acts he cannot remember. How much of a person's identity is bound up in memory?

All our reactions, decisions, etc. spring from what we know, have experienced. We are in so many ways the sum of all we have been!', a statement that may or may not be interpreted biographically.

After her release from prison, Hulme became Anne Perry (Perry being her stepfather's surname), finished her education and took on various jobs as a salesperson, flight attendant and insurance underwriter. She lived for five years in the late 1960s in the United States where she joined the Church of the Latter-Day Saints, a church that she is still a member of, and then moved to Portmahomack, a remote village in Scotland with her mother. In 2009, Dana Linkiewicz shot a documentary about Anne Perry's life, entitled *Anne Perry Interiors*. It mostly deals with the burden of guilt on Anne Perry's present life and on her writing.

In 1979, Perry published *The Cater Street Hangman*, the first novel in which the characters of Thomas Pitt and his future wife, Charlotte Ellison, appear. In 1881, Thomas Pitt, a London policeman, is called to investigate the brutal murders of several young women, among whom is Charlotte's eldest sister, Sarah. This novel met with immediate success. It had been meant as a stand-alone story but soon became the first of a series. Each of the novels depicts a different part of London (hence the geographical locations within the titles), a different set of people, a different background and a different issue for the Victorians (*Bethlehem Road*, 1990, tackles the issue of suffragettes, for example, and Irish Home Rule is dealt with in *Ashworth Hall*, 1997). Many secondary characters are recurring and help Pitt and his wife fit into each different milieu: Emily, Charlotte's sister, is at first married to a viscount and, after his death, to a famous politician; Emily's aunt by marriage, Vespasia Cumming-Gould, is a very distinguished elderly lady with very progressive ideas, Gracie Phipps, the Pitts' maid, helps care for their two children Jemima and Daniel. *The Cater Street Hangman* was somewhat freely adapted for Yorkshire Television by Ardent Productions in 1998, with Eoin McCarthy and Keeley Hawes as Thomas and Charlotte, and broadcast on A&E, ITV Britain and on Turner Classic Movies in America.

The William Monk series is also set in nineteenth-century London, but about thirty years prior to the Pitt stories. The first novel, *The Face of a Stranger* opens with Monk in a hospital bed after a carriage accident, with complete amnesia. In order to retain his job as a policeman he must conceal his memory loss, simultaneously being both himself and not, a device which raises the issues of identity that recur in Perry's writing. During the case he meets Hester Latterly, an intelligent and logical woman who was a Crimean war nurse, and who guesses his secret and helps conceal it. Despite the antagonism between them, they eventually marry: *The Twisted Root* (1999) is their first investigation as a married couple. Monk begins as a police officer, but in the second book in the series *A Dangerous Mourning* (1991), Monk is fired from the police force for insubordination and becomes a private investigator, mostly financed by Lady Callandra Daviott. He returns to the force in the form of the Thames River Police in *The Shifting Tide* (2004); the move from official law-enforcer, to amateur, and back, reinforces the complexities of guilt and innocence and the role of the individual in establishing and judging these matters in the Monk books.

Both Victorian series have been used occasionally, since 2003, for Anne Perry's annual Christmas novel. They often centre on the secondary characters from the series, for example: Lady Vespasia Cumming-Gould, in her youth, features in *A Christmas Journey* (2003), Grandmama Ellison appears in *A Christmas Guest* (2005), and Dominic Corde, Sarah Ellison's widower, is in *A Christmas Secret* (2006), to name but a few.

Perry's historical fiction is predominantly set in the Victorian era, but she is also the author of what she calls the 'First World War Quintet', five novels taking place during World War One, featuring the Reavley brothers and sisters, Hannah, Judith, Joseph and Matthew, living in Cambridgeshire until the World War One changes their lives. In each novel, the mystery, the family and the war become intrinsically bound, overlapping personal and national intrigues and tragedies. Perry has also written about Revolutionary France (*The One Thing More*, 2000, and *A Dish Taken Cold*, 2001) and about the Byzantine Empire *(The Sheen on the Silk)*. More recently, Perry has written novels for young adults, 'The Timepiece Series', beginning with *Tudor Rose* (2011). Each features the word 'Rose' in the title, an allusion to the heroine, Rosie Sands, who is transported back to different periods in history in each novel, such as Tudor England, World War One, the American slave trade, and the English Civil War in *A Rose Between Two Thorns*, (2012).

Suggested Reading/Works Cited

Korte, Barbara, 'Anne Perry: World War I as Period Mystery', *Clues: A Journal of Detection*, 28:1 (2010), 79–89.

Rye, Marilyn, 'Anne Perry', in *Dictionary of Literary Biography, Volume 276: British Mystery and Thriller Writers Since 1960*, ed. by Gina Macdonald (Detroit, MI: Thomson Gale, 2003), pp. 269–283.

The Official Anne Perry Website. http://www.anneperry.co.uk/.

CHAPTER 69

Dorothy Simpson (b. 1933), 1981: *The Night She Died* (First 'Inspector Thanet' Novel)

Christine R. Simpson

Born in Wales, Dorothy Simpson studied at Bristol University. She taught English and French at two grammar schools in Kent before marrying in 1961 and having three children. Later she became a Marriage Guidance Counsellor. She embarked on her writing career while convalescing from a long illness. *Harbingers of Fear*, a novel of suspense, was well-received when it was published in 1977, but her lasting success is the series featuring Detective Inspector Luke Thanet, who first appeared in *The Night She Died* (1981). Although each novel deals with the investigation of a suspicious death by Thanet and his Sergeant, Mike Lineham, the books are not straightforward police procedurals. They are partly psychological, whydunits, as well as whodunits. The two policemen are seen doing their job, but also shown in their family backgrounds. Over the years, relationships with their wives, problems of children growing up, and friction caused by difficult elderly relatives are developed. Sometimes a family problem is mirrored in an element of the case in progress, which helps its solution, such as in *Six Feet Under* (1982). Thanet finds it difficult to adjust to his wife's determination to become a probation officer,

C. R. Simpson (✉)
The Dorothy L. Sayers Society, Essex, UK

© The Author(s) 2020
E. Miskimmin (ed.), *100 British Crime Writers*, Crime Files,
https://doi.org/10.1057/978-1-137-31902-9_69

321

as it sometimes leads to a conflict of interest over possible suspects (such as in *Element of Doubt*, 1987 and *Wake The Dead*, 1992).

The plots are well-contrived with puzzle elements and clever twists, such as *Puppet for a Corpse*. The majority of deaths are not premeditated, and are the result of dark family secrets or long-past sexual relationships (*Dead By Morning*, 1982; *Suspicious Death*, 1988; *No Laughing Matter*, 1993). A number of the victims have had illegitimate babies in their teens, which provides a motive for killing (*Close Her Eyes*, 1984). *Doomed to Die* (1991) is a good example of Simpson's ability to portray such family turmoil. A decent, conscientious and compassionate man, Thanet's investigative method is to establish the victim's background and relationships. He creates theoretical scenarios in which particular suspects might have committed the crime, then tests them against the evidence. Often a solution is hovering at the back of his mind, until it comes to him in a sudden moment of revelation. Lineham envies his intuitive powers and tries to emulate them.

The novels are set in Kent. Its scenery, architecture and the imaginary villages and town of Sturrenden, are lovingly described by the author, who lives in the county. Her writing is clear and elegant, whether describing the countryside or the interiors of houses where characters live. The portrayal of major characters is convincing, but many secondary ones are also brought to life, with credible backgrounds and distinct personalities. The award of the Crime Writers' Association Silver Dagger to her in 1985 for *Last Seen Alive* was a well-merited recognition of her excellence in creating credible, entertaining fiction.

SUGGESTED READING/WORKS CITED

Reynolds, William, 'Second Best, but Not Second-Rate: Dorothy Simpson's Luke Thanet Series', *Clues: A Journal of Detection*, 19:1 (1998), 39–46.

CHAPTER 70

Linda La Plante (b. 1943), 1983: First Broadcast of *Widows* Television Series

Anne-Marie Beller

Screenwriter, producer, novelist and former actor, Lynda La Plante is best known for her highly acclaimed series *Prime Suspect*, which secured numerous awards including six BAFTAs, the Royal Television Society Writer's Award, the British Broadcasting Award, the Edgar Allen Poe Writer's Award, the prestigious TV Spielfilm Award and an EMMY. La Plante's crime novels are all bestsellers, but her greatest achievements have been as a screenwriter and she is often seen as a female pioneer in the British television industry. La Plante is an honorary member of the British Film Institute and has been awarded the Dennis Potter Writer's Award by the British Academy of Film and Television Arts (2001). In 2008 she was awarded a CBE for her contribution to literature, drama and charity. Though her work covers a number of genres, La Plante has most consistently produced crime dramas and novels.

La Plante was born Lynda Titchmarsh in Merseyside; her father was a successful salesman and her mother a housewife. She grew up in Crosby, a suburb of Liverpool, as the middle child of three. Another sister, Dale, was killed in a road accident, aged five, months before La Plante's own

---

A.-M. Beller (✉)
Loughborough University, Loughborough, UK

© The Author(s) 2020
E. Miskimmin (ed.), *100 British Crime Writers*, Crime Files,
https://doi.org/10.1057/978-1-137-31902-9_70

birth. At sixteen, La Plante enrolled at the Royal Academy of Dramatic Art (RADA). Her subsequent stage career included stints with the Royal Shakespeare Company and the National Theatre, and it was following an audition for Laurence Olivier, who apparently found the name Titchmarsh amusing, that La Plante adopted the stage name Lynda Marchal. During the 1970s and 80s she appeared in a succession of prime-time television dramas, including *The Sweeney*, *The Professionals*, *The Gentle Touch* and *Bergerac*. The paucity of interesting roles available to women in television shows, and La Plante's frustration with the endemic stereotyping which meant women were confined to minor roles as wives, girlfriends and prostitutes, were key factors in persuading her to write her own scripts. While playing a prostitute on *The Gentle Touch*, La Plante sent four plot suggestions to the production team. None were accepted, but the fact that someone had written an enthusiastic comment on one encouraged La Plante to develop it into a full-length script. The outline in question concerned a group of women who carried out an armed robbery and this ultimately developed into *Widows*, a hugely popular success which provided the breakthrough into screenwriting that La Plante looked for.

In the early 1980s, female senior executives in television were still a rarity, and the realm of prime-time evening drama remained particularly male-dominated. Two women who had managed to reach influential positions within the industry shared La Plante's views regarding the dearth of interesting roles for women, and they proved to be crucial in bringing *Widows* to production. Verity Lambert, head of drama at Thames Television, and Lynda Agran, Euston Films' director of development, were both keen to produce more drama focused on women. Consequently, when La Plante approached Euston Films with the proposal for *Widows* (then provisionally entitled *The Women*) her idea was timely. As a crime narrative centred around four women, with men in secondary or supporting roles, *Widows* was revolutionary for crime dramas of the time. The six-hour-long episodes begin with a failed robbery, during which three men are killed, with a fourth unidentified man escaping. The widows of the robbers, led by Dolly Rawlins, decide to attempt the men's next planned job themselves. Beset by complications, including the obsessive investigation of DCI Resnick and the discovery that Harry Rawlins, Dolly's husband, is still alive, the women successfully execute the robbery and escape to Rio. As Julia Hallam has argued, '*Widows* foregrounds the women's ability to operate in the public realm as professionals', and it also engages with ideas of the performativity of gender in interesting and prescient ways. The success of the series led to a second being commissioned, *Widows 2*, and ten years later in 1995, La Plante productions and Cinema Verity (Lambert's production company) produced the final instalment of the *Widows* story, *She's Out*, for Carlton TV. La Plante's subsequent work for television has displayed an ongoing interest in representing strong, independent women although, in the dramas which follow *Widows* (such as *Prime Suspect*, *The Governor*, and *The Commander*), her female protagonists have tended to be on the side of investigating and punishing crime rather than committing it.

The first series of *Prime Suspect* (commissioned and produced by Granada) was shown as a two-part four-hour mini-series in April 1991. Its success was phenomenal, garnering a host of awards for La Plante (as creator and writer), the producers, and its star Helen Mirren. Deborah Jermyn has argued that *Prime Suspect* is a 'transitional text in the history of TV crime drama, for its simultaneous intervention into the genre's sexual politics and representation of 'realism'. Through its depiction of Detective Chief Inspector Jane Tennison, consummately played by Mirren, the drama engages implicitly with contemporaneous discourses on Equal Opportunities legislation, exploring the obstacles faced by career-minded women within the misogynistic environment of the Metropolitan Police Force.

La Plante accounts for the realism in her dramas by emphasising the first-hand research she undertakes. She has famously interviewed murderers and prostitutes, shadowed police officers, visited brothels and attended post-mortems in her bid to deliver accurate and realistic representations in her writing. Having obtained the commission for *Prime Suspect*, La Plante contacted Scotland Yard and requested to interview a senior female officer. There were only four women of sufficiently high rank at the time, including DCI Jackie Malton who agreed to meet with La Plante. Malton's input provided valuable information about police procedure and also contributed to the development of aspects of Tennison's character.

In the first *Prime Suspect* the examination of institutionalised police misogyny and corruption is given equal weighting with the more conventional narrative of murder and investigation. DCI Tennison, who despite her rank has been consistently marginalised and passed over in favour of male colleagues, is grudgingly handed a murder case after the lead officer, DCI Shefford dies. Tennison is forced to confront the overt hostility and lack of cooperation of her team, while struggling simultaneously to prevent her personal life from falling apart. La Plante skilfully evokes the chauvinism of the exclusively male environment Tennison attempts to negotiate, not only through the casual sexism of the primary male characters, such as Sergeant Bill Otley, but also through a commentary on male violence – a recurring concern in La Plante's work. Significantly, the death of DCI John Shefford, is commemorated by a boxing benefit. The scenes at the boxing match operate to re-emphasise the 'macho' culture of the environment that Tennison has invaded. They also serve to evoke parallels between the legitimised male violence exhibited by the police officers in the boxing ring and the unlawful violence against women represented by the crime under investigation.

La Plante provided the storyline for *Prime Suspect 2* (1992), which was written by Alan Cubitt and explores institutionalised racism in the police force. *Prime Suspect 3* (1993), written once more by La Plante herself, deals with the challenging subjects of paedophilia and male prostitution. These sequels consolidated the success of the first mini-series, but La Plante left *Prime Suspect* with Granada after the third series, frustrated at her lack of influence on the development and direction of the drama. Since 1994 La Plante has run her own production company, allowing her to retain more control over her creativity, and she has also moved into film production, launching Cougar films with Sophie Balhetchet. Following her defection, four more series of La Plante's most successful drama were produced without her involvement, concluding with *Prime Suspect 7: The Final Act* in 2006. An American adaptation is scheduled to premiere on NBC during 2011–2012, with Maria Bello taking on Mirren's iconic role.

Of La Plante's numerous television dramas since *Prime Suspect*, her most successful projects have largely been within the crime genre. *Trial and Retribution* (1997–2009) continued the popular format of the police procedural, but also incorporated more formally experimental techniques, such as the innovative use of the split screen to produce multiple perspectives simultaneously. Other successful crime dramas followed, including *Killer Net* (1997), *Supply and Demand* (1998) and *Mind Games* (2001). *The Commander* (2003–2008), starring Amanda Burton in the eponymous role, revisits aspects of *Prime Suspect* in its focus on a high-ranking female police officer. The latest crime series, *Above Suspicion*, is based on La Plante's Anna Travis novels and premiered on ITV1 in 2009. The initial two-part drama (based on the first book) attracted over 8 million viewers and several further series were commissioned, including *The Red Dahlia* (2010), *Deadly Intent* (2011) and *Silent Scream* (2012).

La Plante first turned her attention to writing novels after *Widows 2*, when she was struggling to persuade TV executives to produce her post-Falklands war drama, *Civvies*. She published three novels before *Prime Suspect* aired in 1991 – *The Legacy* (1987), its sequel *The Talisman* (1989), and *Bella Mafia* (1991). The latter revisited the idea of a group of widows, this time setting the narrative within the underworld of the Sicilian Mafiosa. Her next novel, *Entwined* (1993), is based around a set of characters who survived the holocaust. In *Cold Shoulder* (1994), *Cold Blood* (1996), and *Cold Heart* (1998), her trilogy about an American cop, Lorraine Page, who is ejected from the police force after shooting a boy while drunk on the job, La Plante takes her nascent interest in female dysfunctional behaviour to its logical extreme. After the death of her partner, Page descends into a bleak spiral of prostitution, chronic alcoholism, violence and homelessness. When she survives an attack by a serial killer preying on prostitutes, Page unwittingly becomes the police's only witness. Agreeing to become a paid informant for her previous commanding officer, Page sets about investigating the murders and, in the process, overcomes her alcoholism. By the end of *Cold Shoulder*, Page has established herself as a private investigator, setting up the premise for the subsequent two novels.

Sleeping Cruelty (2000) and *Royal Flush* (2002) are both thrillers, revolving around betrayal and criminal intrigue. In 2004, La Plante published the first novel featuring her character Anna Travis, *Above Suspicion*. This series has been successful, both in its novel form and in the subsequent television adaptations. It returns to the focus on police procedure familiar from *Prime Suspect* and *Trial and Retribution*, following the young and ambitious rookie detective Anna Travis (played by Kelly Reilly), as she fast-tracks her way through the ranks of the Metropolitan police force. By 2015, the books published in the series were *The Red Dahlia* (2006), *Clean Cut* (2007), *Deadly Intent* (2008), *Silent Scream* (2009), *Blind Fury* (2010), *Blood Line* (2011), *Backlash* (2012) and *Wrongful Death* (2013).

Although her novels have consistently become bestsellers, La Plante has failed to secure the critical recognition enjoyed by other British contemporary female crime writers such as Ruth Rendell or P. D. James. Critics have often suggested that La Plante's screenwriting is superior to her novels, partly because she benefits from the collaborative process, which allows for input by production teams. La Plante has repeatedly signalled her indifference to critical opinion, stressing that she writes for the public and that her readers and viewers are the only judges of her work that matter. The enduring popularity of her drama has established La Plante as one of the most successful female television screenwriters and her achievements as a producer of her own work are significant.

SUGGESTED READING/WORKS CITED

Brunsdon, Charlotte, 'Structure of Anxiety: Recent British Television Crime Fiction', *Screen*, 39:3 (1998), 223–243.

Hallam, Julia, *Lynda La Plante: The Television Series* (Manchester: Manchester University Press, 2005).

Jermyn, Deborah, 'Women with a Mission: Lynda La Plante, DCI Tennison and the Reconfiguration of TV Crime Drama', *International Journal of Cultural Studies*, 6.1 (2003), 46–63.

CHAPTER 71

R. D. Wingfield (1928–2007), 1984: *Frost at Christmas*

Steven Powell

Wingfield's creation, the laconic chain-smoking Detective Inspector William 'Jack' Frost has proved immensely popular in the medium of novels, radio and television.

Rodney David Wingfield was born in Hackney, East London and educated at the Copper's Company School. During World War Two he was evacuated to Frome, Somerset. He married Phyllis Patten in 1952, and the marriage lasted until her death in 2004. Wingfield worked as an office clerk for the Petrofina oil company at Epsom and wrote radio plays, his greatest passion as a writer, in his spare time. In 1968, the BBC accepted his play *Compensating Error* and commissioned two more. He was soon writing full time. Wingfield excelled in radio. His work was noted for its plot twists and clever endings, and he had an intuitive understanding of the demands of the format. His success caught the attention of the publisher Macmillan who offered him a £50 'non-returnable' advance for a crime novel. His effort, *Frost at Christmas*, introduced his now-iconic detective and ran to 250,000 words. It was promptly rejected. However, Wingfield's agent saw potential in the novel

---

S. Powell (✉)
University of Liverpool, Liverpool, UK

© The Author(s) 2020
E. Miskimmin (ed.), *100 British Crime Writers*, Crime Files,
https://doi.org/10.1057/978-1-137-31902-9_71

and set it aside for several years. It was finally published in Canada in 1984. Wingfield, however, became attached to the character from his rejected novel, and created a radio play *Three Days of Frost* (1977), in which Frost was played by Leslie Sands. Wingfield abandoned radio in the late 1980s as the Frost novels grew in popularity. The actor David Jason read a Frost novel on holiday and was so impressed he made enquiries as to the film rights. The resulting television series, which had the umbrella title *A Touch of Frost*, starred Jason in the title role and proved immensely popular running to a total of forty-two episodes. Wingfield, however, was less enthusiastic. He claimed never to have watched the show beyond the pilot episode and was ambivalent about Jason's performance. Much of the coarse, black humour that made Frost so distinctive in the novels was toned down on television and the chain-smoking was cut altogether.

Wingfield was a private man who lived quietly in Basildon, Essex, and usually declined interviews. There are very few known photographs of him. A photograph of the actor Kenneth Williams, who appeared in one Wingfield's radio series, was once mistakenly printed as the author's photo. He occasionally appeared sullen, as when discussing the television series *A Touch of Frost*, but in his obituary of the author, Mike Ripley claims Wingfield was well regarded by his neighbours, who were apparently unaware he was a writer, as 'a thoughtful and generous man who liked cats and dogs'. He died of cancer in 2007. Wingfield's sixth and final Frost novel, *A Killing Frost*, was published posthumously (2008) and two more Frost novels *First Frost* (2011) and *Fatal Frost* (2012) were written by James Gurbett and Henry Sutton under the pseudonym James Henry.

SUGGESTED READING/WORKS CITED

Mike Ripley, 'Obituary: R. D. Wingfield', *The Guardian*, 4 August 2007. http://www.guardian.co.uk/news/2007/aug/04/guardianobituaries.obituaries.
'Obituary: R. D. Wingfield', *The Telegraph*, 8 August 2007. http://www.telegraph.co.uk/news/obituaries/1559701/R-D-Wingfield.html.

CHAPTER 72

Bill James (Pseudonym of James Tucker, also Writes as David Craig, b. 1929), 1985: *You'd Better Believe It* (First 'Harpur and Iles' Novel)

Catherine Phelps

Born and educated in Cardiff where he still lives, James is a prolific writer who has been published for over five decades. He has spoken of how he draws on his Non-Conformist Chapel upbringing and its 'elevated, pompous, pulpit language' yet his early career as a journalist also informs the pithy dialogue and caustic, bleak humour of his work. James taught English Literature and Creative Writing at University of Wales Institute, Cardiff, and wrote the well-received critical study *The Novels of Anthony Powell* (1976). Although his narratives are peppered with literary allusions and quotations, academia and literary pretensions are frequently satirised.

James started writing spy thrillers in the 1960s under the pseudonym David Craig, one of which, *Whose Little Girl Are You?* (1974), was filmed as *The Squeeze* (1977). However, it is for his Harpur and Iles series that he is most well known. Superficially police procedurals, they owe much to

---

C. Phelps (✉)
Cardiff University, Cardiff, UK

© The Author(s) 2020
E. Miskimmin (ed.), *100 British Crime Writers*, Crime Files,
https://doi.org/10.1057/978-1-137-31902-9_72

the hard-boiled P. I. novel. Boundaries between police and criminals are blurred; both Colin Harpur and his superior, Desmond Iles, frequently operate in the interstices between right and wrong. Bill James has praised George V. Higgins' *The Friends of Eddie Coyle* (1972) for its sympathetic portrayal of a police informant. This sympathy for those who inhabit the margins of the law has found its way into James' work; it could be argued that Harpur's most fruitful and enduring relationship is with his grass, Jack Lamb.

James uses an anytown setting in both his early Craig incarnation and throughout the Harpur and Iles series. The first, *You'd Better Believe It* (1985), describes Harpur's home town as an 'artistically null English town' but, for the informed reader, there are visible traces of James' native Cardiff. *You'd Better Believe It* depicts a New Orleans style funeral, a custom carried on today in Cardiff's Butetown, for instance. Many characters are either named after local places or have some connection with Wales. The BBC Wales production of *Protection* (1988) as *Harpur and Iles* (1997) made these connections overt by filming in Cardiff.

James revitalised pseudonym of David Craig to return to writing spy thrillers and for a new crime series set in the revitalised, post-devolution, Cardiff Bay, the first of which was *The Tattooed Detective* (1998). He has said that the regeneration of the area now makes it possible for organised crime to be set in the Welsh capital as the increase in money flowing through the city opens up further possibility for corruption. However, naming a black, Welsh-speaking detective Glyndwr Jenkins and placing him near the devolved Welsh Senedd surely speaks of a new cultural confidence in Welsh crime fiction.

SUGGESTED READING/WORKS CITED

Brockway, Anthony, 'An Interview with Bill James', *The Wolf Man Knew My Father: Notes from the Margins of Welsh Popular Culture*. http://www.babylonwales.verywierd.com/.

Earwaker, Julian and Kathleen Becker, *Scene of the Crime: A Guide to the Landscapes of British Detective Fiction* (London: Aurum Press, 2002).

CHAPTER 73

Anthony Horowitz (b. 1956), 1986: *The Falcon's Malteser* (First 'Diamond Brothers' Novel)

Lucy Andrew

Anthony Horowitz is a successful children's author and screenwriter with a significant crime output. He is best known for his teenage spy thriller series, *Alex Rider* (2000–2011). He was born in 1956 in Stanmore, Middlesex, into a wealthy family, and his early life was fraught with troubles. As a young boy he was overweight and he despised his boarding school, Orley Farm, which was presided over by a cruel headmaster. He later moved to Rugby school and went on to read English and Art History at the University of York. His father, a millionaire businessman, died when Horowitz was twenty-two, taking with him the codes of the Swiss bank accounts that held his fortune. The money was never recovered. Horowitz met his wife, television producer Jill Green, while working as a copywriter for McCann Erickson. They married in Hong Kong in 1988 and their first son, Nicholas Mark, was born in 1989, followed by Cassian James in 1991.

L. Andrew (✉)
University of Chester, Chester, UK

From the age of eight, Horowitz intended to become an author, a dream that was realised with the publication of *The Sinister Secret of Frederick K. Bower*, a comic adventure story for children, in 1978. Horowitz's early fiction for children often contained fantasy and supernatural elements, as in his second novel, *Misha, the Magician and the Mysterious Amulet* (1981), the *Pentagram* series (1983–1989), which provided some of the inspiration for his more successful *Power of Five* series (2005–2012), and his two *Groosham Grange* books (1988 and 1999), the first of which won the Lancashire Children's Book Award in 1989. Yet his writing for children was not limited to fantasy. He also wrote stories about legendary heroes Robin Hood (*The Hooded Man*, with Richard Carpenter, 1986), and William Tell (*New Adventures of William Tell*, 1987), and his novel *Granny* (1994), whose wicked title character was based on his own equally unpleasant maternal grandmother, was shortlisted for the 1994 Children's Book Award. This was followed by a body-swap fantasy *The Switch* (1996), an historical adventure story, *The Devil and His Boy* (1998), and a collection of short horror stories, *Horowitz Horror* (1999).

Although Horowitz's status as a popular children's author was not firmly established until the release of his *Alex Rider* series in 2000, he began to enjoy some success with his first venture into the juvenile detective genre in 1986. *The Falcon's Malteser* was the first title in his *Diamond Brothers* series, which parodied the American hard-boiled detective genre through its focus upon hapless private investigator Tim Diamond and his younger brother, Nick. Thirty-year-old Tim Diamond, whose real name, Herbert Timothy Simple, is far more fitting to his character, is charged with looking after his thirteen-year-old brother, Nick, when their negligent parents moved to Australia. After a brief and disastrous stint in the police force, Tim establishes himself as a private detective in a dilapidated flat in Fulham that doubles for the brothers' home. It is the narrator of the story, Nick, who is the real detective talent while Tim, childlike and cowardly, often falls victim to his younger brother's wit and constantly relies upon Nick to extricate him from precarious situations. The second *Diamond Brothers* novel, *Public Enemy Number Two* was published in 1987, followed by *South by South East* in 1991. The initial titles were successful enough to prompt a film adaptation of *The Falcon's Malteser*, renamed *Just Ask for Diamond*, in 1990, for which Horowitz wrote the screenplay. Horowitz also wrote and directed a six-part miniseries entitled *The Diamond Brothers* for ITV in 1991. This series was based on the third *Diamond Brothers* novel, *South by South East*, and Dursley McLinden and Colin Dale, who had played Tim and Nick in the earlier film, were again cast as the two brothers. After the initial success of his *Alex Rider* series, Horowitz released three new *Diamond Brothers* novellas: *The French Confection*, *The Blurred Man* and *I Know What You Did Last Wednesday* (all 2003). His latest *Diamond Brothers* instalment, *The Greek Who Stole Christmas*, was published in 2007.

Horowitz's popularity as a children's writer increased dramatically with the release of his *Alex Rider* series. Influenced by a love of James Bond developed early in life, Horowitz first introduced reluctant teenage spy Alex Rider in *Stormbreaker* (2000). Alex is a fourteen-year-old orphan living in London, whose world is turned upside down when his guardian and only living relative, his uncle Ian Rider, dies in suspicious circumstances. Cursed with youthful curiosity, Alex soon discovers that his uncle was an MI6 agent, killed in the line of duty, and realises that Ian had been secretly training him to enter the same profession. Alex has acquired many skills from his uncle, such as driving, pick-pocketing and fluency in French, German and Spanish. He is also a qualified diver and holds a black belt in karate. MI6 are quick to exploit Alex's skills as they use blackmail and bureaucracy to force him to undertake missions that only a teenager could accomplish. *Stormbreaker* was shortlisted for the Children's Book Award in 2000 and other books in the series followed in quick succession. The *Alex Rider* series' popularity with young readers was confirmed as *Skeleton Key* (2002), the third book in series, won the Red House Children's Book Award, voted for entirely by children, in 2003. Horowitz also won the British Book Awards' Children's Book of the Year award for *Ark Angel* (2005), the sixth book in the series, in 2006 and the Bookseller Association/Neilson Author of the Year Award in 2007, while the seventh *Alex Rider* instalment, *Snakehead* (2007), was shortlisted for the Booktrust Teenage Prize in 2008. *Scorpia Rising* was published in 2011 with an ending that suggested that it might be the last in the series, but there were more books to follow, starting with *Russian Roulette* in 2013. Critics have not only credited the *Alex Rider* series with popularising the spy thriller genre for children, a trend which has continued with series such as Charlie Higson's *Young Bond* (2005-2008), but also with encouraging reading among reluctant groups, particularly boys. As a consequence of its popularity, the series has been adapted in various formats. All nine titles in the series are available in audiobook form and the first four novels have been adapted as graphic novels. A film version of *Stormbreaker*, for which Horowitz wrote the screenplay, was released in 2006.

Despite the dominance of Horowitz's *Alex Rider* series, his crime writing is not confined to his children's books. His first book for adults, *The Killing Joke* (2004), a black comedy about a man determined to trace offensive jokes back to their sources, is set in a murky, criminal world. His play, *Mindgame* (2000), explores the psychology of a serial killer who has, ostensibly, broken out of a hospital for the criminally insane. Horowitz's greatest success as an adult crime writer, however, has been achieved through his television screenplays. In addition to writing for popular crime series *Murder Most Horrid*, *Agatha Christie's Poirot*, and *Midsomer Murders*, he has created a number of original crime and detective series, including his immensely popular World War Two detective drama, *Foyle's War* (2002–2015), *Murder in Mind* (2001–2003), the less successful *Crime Traveller* (1997), which ran for only eight episodes, and, most recently, his five-part mini-series, *Collision* (2009) and *Injustice* (2011). Horowitz continues to write adult crime fiction; he has published two original Sherlock Holmes novels, *The House of Silk* (2011) and *Moriarty* (2014), commissioned by the Conan Doyle Estate, and a new James Bond novel *Trigger Mortis* (2015). Horowitz was awarded an OBE for series to literature in 2014.

CHAPTER 74

Val McDermid (b. 1955), 1987: *Report for Murder*

Susan Massey

Best known for her compelling psychological thrillers, Val McDermid is one of the UK's most popular contemporary female crime writers. Her novels have sold over ten million copies worldwide and have been praised for their taut, atmospheric content and unflinchingly realistic depictions of violence. A self-professed feminist, McDermid's work is also characterised by a strong sense of social awareness, shaped by her own experiences growing up in a former mining community.

Val McDermid was born in Kirkcaldy, an industrial town on the east coast of Scotland. From a young age, McDermid was an avid reader and her precocity was further underlined when she was selected to be part of an experimental scheme at Kirkcaldy High School. Along with a small group of equally gifted contemporaries, including the former British Prime Minister Gordon Brown, McDermid's education was geared exclusively towards the goal of gaining entry to university. The intensive scheme bore fruit and, at the age of seventeen, McDermid was offered a place to read English at St. Hilda's College, Oxford, becoming not only one of the youngest undergraduates ever admitted but also the first to

S. Massey (✉)
University of St Andrews, St Andrews, Scotland, UK

© The Author(s) 2020
E. Miskimmin (Ed.), *100 British Crime Writers*, Crime Files,
https://doi.org/10.1057/978-1-137-31902-9_74

be accepted from a Scottish state school. After graduating, McDermid, keen to avoid a structured 'nine to five' existence and also keen to write, became a journalist. She spent two years training in Devon, on the *Plymouth and South Devon Times*, and was named National Trainee Journalist of the Year in 1977. Her prize was to interview Prince Charles and McDermid, a proud Scot even from a young age, wore a kilt for the occasion. For her first proper posting McDermid returned north of the border, taking a job with Glasgow's *Daily Record*, before relocating, a few years later, to the Manchester-based *Sunday People*, where she was eventually made Northern Bureau Chief.

It was while she was still based in Devon that McDermid first turned her hand to creative writing, producing a novel that then failed to find a publisher. However, following the advice of an actor friend, McDermid rewrote the text as a screenplay and the result, *Like a Happy Ending* (1981), was commissioned by the director of the Plymouth Theatre Company. After this success, McDermid attempted to write a second play but, realising her talent and interest lay elsewhere, she instead began a crime novel. Heavily influenced by the work of feminist crime writers from America, such as Marcia Muller, Sara Paretsky and Sue Grafton, McDermid started *Report for Murder* in 1984 and it was published by The Women's Press in 1987. In 1991, McDermid became a full-time author and, by 2015 she had written over thirty novels, two books of short stories, a children's book, *My Granny Is a Pirate* (2012), and four works of non-fiction, including *A Suitable Job for a Woman* (1994), which investigates the world of the real-life female private eye, and *Forensics, The Anatomy of Crime* (2014). McDermid is a frequent reviewer for the national press and also appears regularly on the radio. She currently divides her time between Manchester and Alnmouth, Northumberland and shares custody of her son, Cameron, with her former partner. In 2006, McDermid married the American publisher Kelly Smith.

In 1995, McDermid won the Crime Writer's Association's Gold Dagger for Best Novel of the Year for *The Mermaids Singing*. She was also the recipient of the 2010 CWA Cartier Diamond Dagger, which honours outstanding achievement in the field of crime writing. McDermid's other accolades include the LA Times Book of the Year Award (2000), the Stonewall Writer of the Year Award (2007), and an honorary fellowship at her *alma mater*, St. Hilda's College, Oxford. She has also been named an Icon of Scotland and has been inducted into the GLBT Hall of Fame.

McDermid's early novels feature the protagonist Lindsay Gordon, a freelance journalist who hails from Scotland. First introduced in *Report for Murder*, Gordon is a feminist lesbian whose politics are firmly left of centre. There is an aspect of self-portraiture in McDermid's representation of Gordon and the novels benefit from an air of authenticity, thanks to the fact that McDermid was able to draw upon her own journalistic background while writing the series. The character of Gordon seems to be one that is especially close to McDermid's heart – when speaking of the impetus behind Gordon's creation, McDermid stated that she envisioned her heroine serving as something of role model; the kind of which she herself lacked when growing up young and lesbian in provincial Scotland. McDermid was one of the first British authors to write serial detective fiction around a homosexual protagonist and the Gordon novels proved popular with lesbian readers; although, as far as reaching a wider audience goes, McDermid herself has recognised that the novels made little impact when originally published and they remain the least financially successful of all her series. Despite this, McDermid's fondness for Gordon goes some way to explaining why she returned to the character in 2003, after an eight-year absence, for the novel *Hostage to Murder*, despite having moved on by then to more lucrative fictional territory.

While the Gordon series is notable for its marginalised protagonist, the texts themselves are initially quite conventional in terms of plot and action. *Report for Murder* reads like a standard 'whodunit', with Gordon striving to catch a killer after a body is discovered locked in a cupboard at an exclusive girl's school. However, as the series evolves, McDermid's storytelling becomes more complex and nuanced, and issues such as women's activism, political scandal and trade unionism are all addressed. McDermid has spoken of the early development of her own political consciousness, thanks to the influence of her grandfather, who was a trade union organiser, and this tendency to use her fiction as a site to explore social injustice is a recurring hallmark of her work.

In 1992, McDermid introduced a new serial protagonist, the private investigator Kate Brannigan. Over the next seven years, the prolific McDermid authored six Brannigan novels, beginning with *Dead Beat* and ending with *Star Struck* (1998). In terms of attitude, the feisty and anti-authoritarian Brannigan has much in common with Lindsay Gordon. However, McDermid, eager to avoid limiting her audience, chose to make Brannigan heterosexual, much to the initial disappointment of her devoted lesbian fan base. Throughout the series, Brannigan is represented as being in a long-term relationship with her partner, Richard Barclay. However, she retains her much-valued independence by living in a house adjoining that of Richard, rather than committing to full-time cohabitation. Brannigan has been described as the British V. I. Warshawski and the wise-cracking, hard-drinking and, occasionally, law-breaking character does owe a certain debt to the kind of heroines featured in the work of State-side female crime writers. However, rather than just replicating the oeuvre of an author such as Paretsky, McDermid successfully redeploys the paradigm of the female investigator, making it work within a specifically British context. Like Paretsky, she adds depth to the hard-boiled archetype by refusing to characterise Brannigan as an invulnerable tough girl. Instead, Brannigan is grounded in her community and benefits from a close network of female friendship. These friendships come to the fore in the fifth novel in the series, *Blue Genes* (1996), which explores the clandestine world of unlicensed fertility treatment through the experiences of Brannigan's best friend, Alexis, and her partner, Christine.

While the Brannigan series was more successful than McDermid's Lindsay Gordon novels, it was not until she created the characters of Dr. Tony Hill and Detective Inspector Carol Jordan that McDermid became a bestseller. Hill, a clinical psychologist and criminal profiler, and Jordan, a workaholic career copper, make their first appearance in *The Mermaids Singing* (1995). Set in the fictional northern town of Bradfield, the novel follows Hill and Jordan as they attempt to apprehend a serial predator who has been killing men in spectacularly vicious style. The text is notable because of McDermid's unconventional choice of killer and use of violence that is almost mediaeval in its barbarism; but it is the characterisation of Dr. Hill that really makes the novel stand out. Cutting a nerdish and socially isolated figure, Hill is already an atypical hero, but McDermid compounds his unlikely position at the heart of the narrative by rendering him impotent. As if this were not enough, his sexual neurosis makes him vulnerable to the very killer he is seeking and, as the novel progresses, a twisted bond emerges between Hill and the murderer. Gradually, it becomes clear that while Dr. Hill's ability to share mental proximity with those who perpetrate acts of great evil is the key to his success as a profiler, it also exacts a huge toll on his own psychological well-being. McDermid's technique of splitting the narrative between the perspective of Dr. Hill and that of his quarry creates extra tension by allowing the reader access to the dark spaces that Hill himself must inhabit in order to be successful.

The damaged and vulnerable Dr. Hill is counterbalanced by the character of Carol Jordan, who appears, at least superficially, tougher and more in control than her male colleague. By virtue of making her way through the male-dominated ranks of the police force, Jordan has acquired a hard outer shell and a steely determination to succeed. By reversing traditional gender roles in this way, McDermid creates a usual and compelling dynamic between her two leading characters that builds into a relationship of mutual trust and co-dependency that transcends the purely professional. As the series develops, there is, needless to say, an element of sexual attraction between Hill and Jordan and although she occasionally teases her readers, McDermid has spoken of her desire to keep the relationship platonic.

By 2015 there were nine books in the Hill and Jordan series, with a range of elaborate scenarios to the duo's crime-fighting prowess. In *The Last Temptation* (2002), Carol goes undercover in Berlin and, after a brutal personal attack, she is joined by Hill to solve a mystery that has its roots in Nazi atrocities committed during World War Two. *The Torment of Others* (2004) sees them back in Britain searching for a copy-cat killer, while *Beneath the Bleeding* (2007) uses the spectre of terrorism to cover up a crime that has more mundane origins. *Fever of the Bone* (2009) deals with a child-killer who uses a social networking site to target potential victims. While McDermid's plotting remains intricate and the characters continue to sustain interest, these later novels lack the disturbing power of *The Mermaids Singing*, and its follow-up, *The Wire in the Blood* (1997). These novels best showcase McDermid's ability to write genuinely shocking, risk-taking fiction, not just because of the violence employed in *The Mermaids Singing*, but also because of McDermid's willingness, in *The Wire in the Blood*, to kill off a leading character early in the novel.

McDermid has gained some unwanted media attention because of the brutality of her fiction. While McDermid, who is herself afraid of the sight of blood, sees nothing salacious in the depiction of violence in her texts, others have not been so convinced. In 2007, a furore arose after comments made by Ian Rankin on the graphic nature of crime writing by lesbian authors were widely reported. While McDermid was not angry with Rankin specifically – the two are close friends and together they form the vanguard of the contemporary 'Tartan Noir' resurgence in Scottish crime fiction – she was dismayed by the way the incident was covered in the media. McDermid, naturally enough, rejects any link between her sexuality and the way in which she chooses to represent violence. She sees herself as writing in a realistic and honest manner. While this might be debatable – McDermid is, after all, a novelist with books to sell – the attacks on McDermid do seem heavy-handed when her work is compared to the casual brutality found in the texts of James Ellroy or David Peace.

McDermid's work was brought to a wider audience in 2002 when ITV commissioned a television series based on the Hill and Jordan novels. Screened under the title *The Wire in the Blood*, the programme featured Robson Green as Tony Hill and Hermione Norris as Carol Jordan. When Norris left the series she was replaced by Simone Lahbib as Alex Fielding, a character written specifically for the television show. *The Wire in the Blood* attracted respectable ratings and ran until 2009, when, after six series, it was not recommissioned. Although McDermid was not directly involved in the programme, she was a vocal fan of the adaptation, lavishing particular praise on Green's portrayal of Dr. Hill. She was delighted to be given a small speaking role in one of the earliest episodes.

In addition to her series fiction, McDermid has written a number of stand-alone novels. In 1999, she published the critically acclaimed *A Place of Execution*, which tells the story of a child who goes missing in an isolated English community in 1963. Told in two parts, one set in the year of crime and the other decades later, the novel is one of McDermid's best. She followed it with *Killing the Shadows* (2000), in which, with a self-referential master stroke, a serial killer stalks crime novelists. McDermid's most recent books all have a strong historical element. *The Distant Echo* (2003) is set in St. Andrews and, like *A Place of Execution*, it focuses on a murder whose consequences span two different time periods. *The Grave Tattoo* (2006) followed in this trend of connecting the past with the present. In it, McDermid's heroine, a literary scholar, reveals evidence that connects the notorious mutineer Fletcher Christian with William Wordsworth and is almost murdered as a result. 2008s *A Darker Domain* takes as its subject the more recent past, telling of a kidnapping that occurs against the vivid backdrop of the Miner's Strike. The novel is heavy on social commentary and this slight polemicising occurs at the expense of narrative pace. However, the text does introduce another potential series protagonist in the form of Detective Inspector Karen Pirie, a cold case investigator, whose first appearance was in *The Skeleton Road* (2014).

Suggested Reading/Works Cited

Markowitz, Judith A., *The Gay Detective Novel: Lesbian and Gay Main Characters and Themes in Mystery Fiction* (Jefferson, NC: McFarland & Co, 2004).

McCaw, Neil, 'Beyond Gender and Sexuality: The Serial Killers of Val McDermid', in *Murdering Miss Marple: Essays on Gender and Sexuality in the New Golden Age of Women's Crime Fiction*, ed. by Julie H. Kim (Jefferson, NC: McFarland, 2012), pp. 191–210.

Plain, Gill, *Twentieth-Century Crime Fiction: Gender, Sexuality and the Body* (Edinburgh: Edinburgh University Press, 2001).

The Official Val McDermid Website. www.valmcdermid.com.

Walton, Priscilla and Manina Jones, *Detective Agency: Rewriting the Hard-Boiled Tradition* (Berkeley and London: University of California Press, 1999).

CHAPTER 75

Ian Rankin (Also writes as Jack Harvey, b. 1960), 1987: *Knots and Crosses* (First 'Rebus' Novel)

Christopher Routledge

Rankin is the creator of the cynical and embittered Edinburgh police detective John Rebus, who by 2015 had appeared in twenty highly regarded and popular novels that made Rankin the bestselling British crime writer. Rebus first appeared in *Knots and Crosses* (1987), a novel that established the dark, hard-boiled tone of the series, which is as much in the Gothic tradition of Robert Louis Stevenson's *The Strange Case of Dr. Jekyll and Mr. Hyde* as it is specifically crime fiction. Rebus' dislike of authority, his suspicion of motives, and his willingness to bend the rules for the sake of enforcing a wider principle, make him a compelling detective hero, but Rankin's ambition as a novelist is evident in the way he interweaves the landscape of Edinburgh, and Scotland itself, with Rebus' thoughts and emotional states. Rankin has won many awards, including, in 2005, the Crime Writers' Association Cartier Diamond Dagger lifetime achievement award. In the late 1990s American crime writer James Ellroy paid tribute to Rankin, calling him 'the king of Tartan Noir'.

C. Routledge (✉)
Freelance Writer and Photographer, NW England, UK

© The Author(s) 2020
E. Miskimmin (ed.), *100 British Crime Writers*, Crime Files,
https://doi.org/10.1057/978-1-137-31902-9_75

Ian Rankin was born in Cardenden, a coalmining village in Fife, Scotland, the son of a grocer. He attended Beath High School, Cowdenbeath, and combined a developing interest in books with a love of comics, and Punk Rock. As a teenager he enjoyed reading thrillers by Frederick Forsyth and Alistair MacLean, but he also wrote poetry and short stories. Rankin lists grape picker, swineherd, taxman, alcohol researcher and hi-fi journalist as his former jobs; he was also, briefly, the vocalist for a punk band called the Dancing Pigs. He studied American literature at Edinburgh University and graduated with a first-class degree before starting a Ph.D. thesis about Scottish literature.

By the time he began working on his Ph.D., however, Rankin's attention was already divided. He had been writing fiction as an undergraduate and used some of the grant-funded time when he should have been researching the novels of Muriel Spark to write three novels, one of which remains unpublished. *The Flood*, was published in 1986, and, as Rankin acknowledges, is written in a style that reflects his developing voice as a writer. In August 2010, in an interview for the *Daily Telegraph*, he admitted that '[...] it's like the writing of a PhD student [...] There's words in it I don't understand'. Rankin found his voice in his second published novel, the first in the Rebus series, *Knots and Crosses* (1987).

Knots and Crosses introduces Detective Sergeant (later Detective Inspector) John Rebus. He is in many ways an archetypal tough detective hero, capable of taking punishment and willing to stand up to hardened criminals even at the risk of his own safety. He is a heavy-drinking, cynical police detective with a deep and longstanding lack of respect for authority, and an obsessive approach to his work. He is troubled by the violence and corruption he sees around him, and the failure of the 'system' to engage with suffering at a human level. He is also a complex, difficult, even unpleasant, man, whose personal life hovers at the edge of his professional experiences: murder victims remind him of his daughter; cases of neglect and family breakdown remind him of his own failures as a father and husband; his brother's criminality intrudes on his ability to perform his duties as a detective.

Rankin has said that in early drafts of *Knots and Crosses*, Rebus did not survive, and in many ways this first book in the series is different from those that follow. The Edinburgh of *Knots and Crosses* is much more an invention than in later novels – police stations and other locations are fictionalised – and this is significant because the reality of Edinburgh itself, as a means to explore Scottish identity, is a central part of those later novels. Indeed, Rankin has become identified so closely with Edinburgh that, as with Hammett in San Francisco, walking tours are organised to visit locations in the Rebus novels. The Oxford Bar, where the detective does a lot of his drinking, is a particular focal point for Rebus tourists. In *Rebus's Scotland: A Personal Journey* (2005, new edition 2012) Rankin explores the significance of the Scottish setting to his own life, and Rebus' creation and development.

Rankin's interest in writing beyond the crime fiction genre meant that at first he was surprised and annoyed to see *Knots and Crosses* on the crime fiction shelves in bookshops. He told J. Kingston Pierce, in an interview for *January Magazine* 'it went onto the Mystery shelves in bookstores, I was appalled! I thought, here I am doing a Ph.D., and I'm going to be a professor of English... and *I've written a whodunit*'. Rankin has since become something of a defender of crime and detective fiction, arguing that crime novels talk about the same things as 'literary' novels and that the best crime fiction is literature.

The second Rebus novel, *Hide and Seek*, did not arrive until 1991, though Rankin produced two novels in between: *Watchman*, and *Westwind*, in 1988 and 1990 respectively. *Watchman* is a spy novel, set against the troubled background of Belfast in the 1980s; *Westwind*, which Rankin admits was not a success, was, in his own words 'my attempt at a big conspiracy-theory novel'. *Hide and Seek* saw further development of Rebus as a character, investigating the death of a junkie and in the process uncovering the unsavoury lives of some of Edinburgh's elite. Rebus' troubled personal life, the social and political aspects of police operations, and the 'Jekyll and Hyde' identity of Edinburgh itself, emerge in this novel as the major tropes of the series as a whole. This was followed by *Tooth and Nail* (originally titled *Wolfman*) in 1992.

During the late 1980s and early 1990s Rankin and his wife Miranda lived in London, and then, from 1990, in the Dordogne, France, returning to Edinburgh in 1996. This was his most prolific period. Partly because of his isolation in rural France, Rankin published nine novels and a collection of stories between 1992 and 1997. Three of these, *Witch Hunt* (1993), *Bleeding Hearts* (1994), and *Blood Hunt* (1995), are thrillers, written under the name Jack Harvey, a combination of the name of his first son, and his wife's birth surname.

In 1991 Rankin won the Chandler-Fulbright award, and in 1994 he was awarded the Crime Writers' Association Macallan Short Story Dagger for 'A Deep Hole'; he won a second Short Story Dagger in 1996 for

'Herbert in Motion'. He continued to write Rebus books, which were by then developing into complex, powerful novels. Where the early books had been tough, tightly paced police procedurals with a realistic edge, novels such as *Mortal Causes* (1994), in which the Edinburgh Festival is marred by gangland killings and the threat of terrorism, are altogether more confident and effective in their treatment of contemporary moral and political issues.

Black and Blue (1997), Rankin's fifteenth book, and the eighth in the Rebus series, is a landmark novel in several ways. Returning to Edinburgh, Rankin was a mid-list author with unspectacular sales. Despite the quality of his work, and the pace at which he produced it, he was almost dropped by his publishers. Then, in 1997, *Black and Blue* won the Crime Writers' Association Macallan Gold Dagger Award, becoming the first of Rankin's novels to achieve widespread popularity. It was also his most ambitious novel up to that date. *Black and Blue*, which takes its title from a Rolling Stones album, finds Rebus looking back in his spare time to the real unsolved 'Bible John' serial killings, which took place in Glasgow in the late 1960s. The novel uses songs and song titles extensively to indicate Rebus' mood, and marks a significant development in Rebus as a character, embroiling him in multiple plots, and moving him to a different police station, increasing his sense of isolation and persecution. Rebus, who is himself under investigation, pursues several cases, travelling as far afield as Shetland to investigate a series of killings by 'Johnny Bible'. Parts of the novel are presented from the point of view of 'Bible John' as he goes after the 'upstart' trading on his notoriety, and taking credit for his crimes.

In *Black and Blue* Rebus' marginal position becomes more significant than in earlier books, allowing greater complexity in its examination of Scottish society and institutions. Later books, such as *Fleshmarket Close* (2004), and *The Naming of the Dead* (2006), are more explicit still in their social criticism, but do not sacrifice the detective plot, or the development of Rebus as a character, to the exploration of wider themes.

The success of *Black and Blue* brought Rankin and Rebus to a much wider and more diverse audience. The novel appears on high school reading lists, and ten of the books have been adapted for television, beginning in 2000, with John Hannah playing an inappropriately young and healthy Rebus. More awards and nominations followed, including a Gold Dagger Award nomination in 1999 for *Dead Souls* (1999). In 2002 Rankin was included in the Queen's Golden Jubilee Birthday Honours

List, and was awarded an OBE. Other awards include, in 2005, the Crime Writers' Association Cartier Diamond Dagger award for lifetime achievement. He has won the British Book Awards Crime Novel of the Year award twice, in 2005 for *Fleshmarket Close* (2004) and in 2007 for *The Naming of the Dead* (2006). He has also won awards in France and Germany.

The Rebus series follows the career of its central character from the age of 41 in 1987 to his return from enforced retirement (*Exit Music*, 2007) in *Standing in Another Man's Grave* (2012, also the third novel to feature Inspector Malcolm Fox). Despite his misanthropy, Rebus must work with colleagues, in particular Siobhan Clarke, who becomes increasingly important after her first appearance in *The Black Book* (1993). Clarke is a methodical, practical sidekick to the more instinctive, even chaotic, Rebus. She is a key character in several of Rankin's most successful books, including *Resurrection Men* (2002), for which he won the 2004 Edgar, the most prestigious award for crime and mystery writers in the United States. In that novel Rebus is sent back to police training college as punishment for an act of insubordination, and Clarke, newly promoted to Detective Sergeant, is left to handle his caseload, including the release from prison of gangster and longtime Rebus adversary, 'Big Ger' Cafferty.

In later novels, including *Fleshmarket Close* (2004), which deals with human trafficking and illegal immigration, the relationship between Rebus and Clarke grows increasingly close, so that in *The Naming of the Dead*, they are isolated together against the forces of both the establishment and the criminal community. *The Naming of the Dead*, which centres on the G8 meeting at Gleneagles in 2005, and the protests that grew around it, explores the relationships between the establishment and the population at large, between the 1960s 'hippy' generation, and their children. The global political significance of the G8 is set against the local politicking that sees poverty and crime on the streets and gangsters fighting for control.

When, in 2005, Rankin was told he had been awarded the CWA Cartier Diamond Dagger, he said with characteristic modesty that he thought it should really go to Inspector Rebus because 'all I've done is sit at a desk in a well-heated room, drinking coffee and eating chocolate'. In the Rebus series Rankin created not only one of the most popular of all detective series characters, but an extended examination of Scottish culture, politics, and the detective novel itself. Rebus' obsessive pursuit of justice, often in the face of a police service that seems more obstructive than encouraging, concludes, at the end of his long career, with a lack of resolution. Rebus' efforts, however personally damaging they may have been, have done nothing to resolve the underlying corruption he has fought all along.

Despite the length of the series, Rankin claims to have moved on relatively easily, to work on opera libretti, graphic novels, and new novels, including *Doors Open* (2008), and *The Complaints* (2009). The latter is the first novel to feature Inspector Malcolm Fox, whose department, Edinburgh's Police Complaints and Conduct Office, investigates the police themselves. In *Standing in Another Man's Grave* he finds himself investigating Rebus on his return from retirement. Rebus and Fox are pitted against each other once more in Rankin's most recent novels, including *Even Dogs in the Wild* (2015).

Since the year 2000 Rankin has also made regular television appearances, on the BBC2 arts programme, Newsnight Review, and as the presenter of documentaries, on subjects such as Edinburgh, Jekyll and Hyde and 'Evil'. His graphic novel, *Dark Entries*, which features an occult detective, was published in 2009.

Rankin and his wife Miranda have two sons, the younger of whom, Kit, has Angelman's Syndrome, suffering severe learning difficulties and speech problems; Rankin is a campaigner for the rights of people with special needs. He holds honorary doctorates and fellowships from numerous universities, and has held a Hawthornden Fellowship. In 2009 he was presented with the inaugural Edinburgh Award for his 'outstanding contribution to the cultural and social landscape of Edinburgh' and in 2015 he was elected a Fellow of the Royal Society of Edinburgh.

SUGGESTED READING/WORKS CITED

Moore, Clayton, 'An Interview with Ian Rankin', *Bookslut*, April 2005. http://www.bookslut.com/features/2005_04_005009.php.

Pierce, J. Kingston, 'January Interviews Ian Rankin: The Accidental Crime Writer'. http://januarymagazine.com/profiles/ianrankin.html.

Plain, Gill, *Ian Rankin's Black and Blue* (London & New York: Continuum, 2002).

Rankin, Ian, Tricia Malley, and Ross Gillespie, *Rebus's Scotland: A Personal Journey* (London: Orion, 2005).

Roberts, Laura, 'Ian Rankin Says His First Novel Used Language He No Longer Understands', *The Daily Telegraph*, 15 August 2010. http://www.telegraph.

co.uk/culture/books/booknews/7946625/Ian-Rankin-says-his-first-novel-used-language-he-no-longer-understands.html.
The Official Ian Rankin Website. http://ianrankin.net.

CHAPTER 76

Peter Robinson (b. 1950), 1987: *Gallows View*

Greg Rees

Peter Robinson is an English writer most famous for his series of novels featuring Detective Inspector Alan Banks of West Yorkshire Police. Robinson was born and raised in West Yorkshire, and the picturesque (though sometimes bleak) Yorkshire terrain is integral to the Banks novels: as Robinson himself states, a 'sense of place has always been important in my work'. He studied English Literature at Leeds University, gaining his M. A. from Windsor University, Toronto, and his Ph.D. from the University of York. Robinson now resides in Canada with his wife, Sheila, and combines his writing career with lecturing on crime writing at various colleges in the Toronto area.

The first Inspector Banks novel, *Gallows View* (1987), introduced Banks as an experienced policeman who has become desperate for a change of scenery, both professionally and for his wife and children. Still relatively young and having recently left the ranks of the Metropolitan Police in London, Banks brings his jaded yet often optimistic world view to the small market town of Eastvale in the Yorkshire dales, an area with a crime rate belying its outwardly sleepy aura. Over the course of the series, Banks integrates into his new environment perfectly, developing good relationships with almost all of his colleagues, often winning them over

G. Rees (✉)
Cardiff University, Cardiff, UK

© The Author(s) 2020
E. Miskimmin (ed.), *100 British Crime Writers*, Crime Files,
https://doi.org/10.1057/978-1-137-31902-9_76

353

from positions of initial distrust or indifference, as seen with his erstwhile sergeant, Jim Hatchley. The bane of Banks' professional life is Jeremiah 'Jimmy' Riddle, some-time Chief Constable and the one real thorn in Banks' side.

Although his police work is usually phenomenally successful, Banks' personal life is far more flawed, and we see the gradual breakdown of his marriage and several other relationships over the years. In this, Banks mirrors those other great detectives who, for one reason or another, fail to maintain success in their private lives. In Banks, Peter Robinson has created a uniquely interesting character; an old-fashioned copper imbued with the ability to change and progress, to modernise alongside modern policing. Banks is an erudite, intelligent bruiser with a love for beer and classical music; his outsider's eyes conjure a Yorkshire every bit as real and vivid as Sherlock Holmes' London or Morse's Oxford.

In his Banks books, Robinson has proved unafraid to tackle sensitive subjects, such as neo-Nazism in *Dead Right* (1997) and establishment child abuse in *The Summer That Never Was* (2003). He is also highly skilled in creating an accurate sense of the past, such as his portrayal of the 1960s music scene and its negative sides in *Piece of My Heart* (2006). In 2011–2012, the series was adapted by ITV into *DCI Banks*, a well-constructed though largely miscast version of several Banks stories.

In addition to the Banks novels, of which there are now over twenty, Robinson has also written a number of short stories, many in the crime genre (the first collection of his short stories was published as *Not Safe After Dark* in 2004), as well as the stand-alone novels *Caedmon's Song* (1990), *No Cure For Love* (1995) and *Before the* Poison (2011) He has won numerous awards for the Banks series and his short stories, including several Arthur Ellis Awards and the *Dagger in The Library* award from the UK Crime Writers' Association in 2002.

Further Reading/Works Cited

Foster, Jordan, 'An Introspective Inspector', *Publishers Weekly*, 254:56 (2007), 32.

Robinson, Peter, 'Introduction', in *Not Safe After Dark* (London: Pan Books, 2007), pp. xv–xviv.

CHAPTER 77

Lindsey Davis (b. 1949), 1989: *The Silver Pigs*

Heather Worthington

Lindsey Davis began her literary career writing historical romances; an unpublished book was the runner up for the Georgette Heyer Historical Novel prize (1985). She was inspired by this near success to leave her employment as a Civil Servant and embark on writing full time. Initially, she wrote romantic fiction for magazines, but finally came up with the idea of a city-based private eye with a difference. Her detective would work not in a modern metropolitan city but in Rome and its Empire circa 70AD and she would incorporate an element of humour into the narrative and its protagonist, the all-too-human Marcus Didius Falco. Her early interest in romance is still evident in her crime fiction, where Falco and his personal life are generally more important than the crimes he solves, but the Falco novels are based in sound historical research.

Davis was educated at King Edward's Girls' High School, Birmingham and read English Literature at Oxford. What she calls her 'classical education' included the study of Latin, and one of her classics teachers, Elys Varney, ran an archaeological society that visited Roman sites on which Davis sometimes worked as a volunteer. The presence of the Romans in Britain is a recurring theme in the Falco novels; Falco returns to Britannia in *A Body in the Bath House* (2001) and *The Jupiter Myth* (2002). Davis

H. Worthington (✉)
Cardiff University, Cardiff, UK

© The Author(s) 2020
E. Miskimmin (ed.), *100 British Crime Writers*, Crime Files,
https://doi.org/10.1057/978-1-137-31902-9_77

finds the past in relation to the present intriguing, especially on the human rather than historical level. She admires the Romans' skill in engineering, efficient bureaucracy and literary satire, all of which feature strongly in the Falco novels. Unlike other writers of Roman historical crime fiction, such as the American Steven Saylor, Davis does not use the format deliberately to comment on present-day politics. Rather, her narratives suggest the common humanity between the Romans and ourselves.

The crimes with which Falco deals are frequently the consequence of corruption, personal or political; the criminals come both from aristocratic and common backgrounds, but the lower-class criminals are usually in the pay of or are being manipulated by those in power. Falco is an ex-legionnaire of the plebeian class, which causes him problems in his personal life as his beloved, Helena Justina, is a senator's daughter and hence a patrician. Cross-class marriages are fraught with difficulty and Falco and Helena instead live together with their two children in an arrangement recognised and approved by Helena's parents, a situation whose possibility is verified by historical information about marriage in the period. The relationship between Falco and Helena grows increasingly important in the novels, from their first meeting in Britannia in *The Silver Pigs* (1989) to *Nemesis* (2010), which opens with the death of their recently born son. Helena is not merely Falco's lover but often assists him in his investigations; she is highly intelligent and independent, indeed, a prototype feminist, while her social connections are often useful to Falco. Over the series her two brothers are also drawn into Falco's orbit and occasionally work with him.

The novels also chart Falco's rise through the ranks of Roman society from plebeian to equestrian, made possible by his occasional employment by the Emperor Vespasian. While the concept of Falco as a detective is clearly anachronistic, locating him as an informer gives him historical credibility: Roman informers came from across the social classes, from senators to plebeians, as Davis demonstrates in *The Accusers* (2003). Davis' interest in revealing the commonalities between Roman and modern Western society has resulted in cases for Falco that coincidentally explore, for example, the world of estate agency (*Venus in Copper*, 1991), vanity publishing (*Ode to a Banker*, 2000), and package holidays (*See Delphi and Die*, 2005). Other aspects of Roman life that can be related to the modern day are academia (*Alexandria*, 2009) and bureaucracy and taxes (*Two for the Lions*, 1998), although as the title of the latter suggests, it is also concerned with gladiators and the Roman circus. Davis also takes advantage of crime fiction's prolific subgenres, attempting a foray into the police procedural in *Time to Depart* (1995).

Davis undertakes meticulous research into the Roman way of life, the food, clothing, culture, social structures, architecture and art. The city of Rome and the Roman Empire in the time of Vespasian are carefully mapped and actual events from the period are carefully located in the timeline of the texts. Making Falco and his birth family plebeian allows Davis to construct an accurate, if fictional, representation of the daily life of the ordinary Roman, rather than the famous figures of history and the wealthy whose lives, manners and morals are more likely to be recorded for posterity. Real people feature; the Emperor, Vespasian, his sons Domitian and Titus, and *The Iron Hand of Mars* (1992) is loosely based on events in the incomplete *Historiae* of Tacitus. In *The Silver Pigs* (1989), the murder of the beautiful Sosia Camillina draws on fact. Sosia is stabbed with an inky pen by Domitian; the contemporary Roman historian Seutonius' account of the life of Domitian records that the Emperor's son was in the habit of stabbing flies with his pen.

The Falco books are enormously popular. Davis has been awarded the Authors' Club Best First Novel prize (1989), the Crime Writers' Association Dagger in the Library Award (1995), the Crime Writers' Association Ellis Peters Historical Dagger (1999), the Sherlock Award for the Best Comic Detective (2000) and the Premio de Honor de Novela Histórica (2009) by the city of Zaragoza. Her books are translated into many languages and the early books have been dramatised for BBC Radio Four. Davis has also written several short stories, some with a Roman inflection, published in various anthologies. Her factual account of Emperor Vespasian's love affair with his mistress, Antonia Caenis, *The Course of Honour* (1997) demonstrates the close relationship between fact and fiction in her historical writing. More recently she has also turned her attention to Britain rather than Rome, writing a novel set in the English Civil War, *Rebels and Traitors* (2009), described as 'epic' by Hilary Mantel, although her next stand-alone novel *Master and God* (2012) returned to ancient Rome as the scene of the action, and this is also the setting for her new series of detective novels featuring detective Flavia Albia. Albia is the British-born, adopted, daughter of Falco and at the time of the first novel, *The Ides of April* (2013), she is a 28-year-old widower. By 2015 there were three books and one novella, *The Spook Who Spoke Again* (2015), in the ongoing series.

This is cleverly written crime fiction that catches the period of its setting but peoples it with characters with whom the reader can identify. Davis makes Rome, its Empire and its history accessible to a wide audience; the Falco novels educate without teaching and enlighten the reader while engaging their interest with wit and excellent plotting. Davis is writing in a long tradition of historical crime fiction, much of which uses history simplistically and as little more than a backdrop to the activities of the detective. For Lindsey Davis, the accurate representation of Ancient Rome is integral to her detective stories and she makes the city and its Roman inhabitants recognisable, indeed familiar, to modern readers.

SUGGESTED READING/WORKS CITED

Browne, Ray B., Lawrence A. Kreiser Jnr, and Robin Winks, eds, *The Detective as Historian: History and Art in Crime Fiction* (Bowling Green, OH: Bowling Green University Popular Press, 2000).

Davis, Lindsey, 'Falco the Ambulance Chaser?', 2004. http://www.twbookmark.com/authorslounge/articles/2004/march/article18516.html.

——, 'Well How Did This Happen?', *Texas Classics in Action*, Summer 1997. http://www.txclassics.org/exrpts9.html.

Howard, David, 'Lindsey Davis', *Book and Magazine Collector*, 183 (1999), 24–33.

The Official Lindsey Davis Website. http://www.lindseydavis.co.uk.

PART IV

To the Millennium and Beyond, 1990–2015

In the sections of this book on Victorian and Edwardian fiction and the Golden Age, I discuss how these eras tend to have popularly perceived or stereotyped identities in terms of their crime writing. The various entries demonstrate repeatedly that those identities can be challenged and reviewed in many ways, but they remain largely clear and coherent despite history's refusal to be 'neat and tidy', as Haycraft puts it. This final part is different: we do not have the luxury of a retrospective on an apparently begun-and-ended period in time. The cut-off date of 2015 is as arbitrary and brutal as the other temporal impositions in this collection: we had to stop somewhere, and it made a neat one hundred and 60 years since the publication of Caroline Clive's *Paul Ferroll*. During the time it has taken to produce and edit all of the entries, existing authors have continued to write, new authors have continued to emerge and crime fiction has continued to evolve as a genre, making it impossible to pin down a definitive sense of 'now'. The increasing diversity noted in the previous era continues here: we find puzzle stories, police procedurals, historical crime fiction, psychothrillers and Welsh Noir, to name but a few of the forms represented. We also see the development of the genre in new directions, such as the emerging trend for crime fiction for a teen or young adult readership in the *Point Crime* series contributed to by Malcolm Rose, or the hybrid science fiction / detective stories of Justin Richards.

Despite the diversity of writers and genres represented below, however, there are some recurring features that we can identify that, in future reconsiderations, may become defining elements of this period. As with all of the crime fiction that has come before, these are inevitably linked to the times in which the works are written. In the final entry of the book, the '100th crime writer', Gerard Brennan, refers to Declan Burke's description of crime fiction as 'the second draft of history', and I would argue that no previous period of crime wring engages so directly with the world around it. In the entries in this final part we see reflected many of the social and political concerns of the last thirty years, including – in no particular order – terrorism, the power of the media and social media, immigration and cultural diversity, mental health, the Iraq conflicts and devolution. These are addressed in terms of both their personal and social impact and the fictive action is often generated by a conflict between these two elements of life. In his foreword, Stephen Knight observes that the modern crime novel 'thrives in energetic variations of current sociopersonal conflict'. His identification of conflict as a culture in which to 'grow' crime fiction is evidenced repeatedly in the entries below, where many writers are discussed in terms of their response to social change and unrest.

Although most of these social and political focuses are represented within fictional stories, there is also a distinct trend for referencing or utilising actual events, people and places: Minette Walters' 2007 *The Chameleon's Shadow*, for example, explores the individual and communal impact of the events of 9/11. Heather Worthington discusses the ways in which Walters' work presents the intrinsic links between the social, familial and individual in relation to crime, often with real-life events as the basis for her work. This is also seen in the writing of Alison Taylor, whose own experiences in bringing to light cases of the abuse of children in care are drawn on in her writing, particularly in *In Guilty Night* (1996), and that of Lindsay Ashford, who drew on her job collecting data on Wolverhampton's sex workers for her first novel *Frozen* (2003). Women's roles and rights continue to be the subject for discussion by writers such as Stella Duffy, whose work Susan Massey describes as being 'characterised by a strong feminist sensibility', Dreda Say Mitchell, and Ashford whose work Catherine Phelps argues is 'informed by the concerns of second-wave feminism'.

These fusions of fact and fiction clearly demonstrate the continuation of the more 'journalistic' nature of modern crime writing, and it is worth mentioning the emergence of another, increasingly popular, sub-genre – that of 'true crime'. These books are not strictly within the remit of this collection, but there are examples to be found here, such as John Williams' 1994 *Bloody Valentine*, which is an account of the 1988 murder of Lynette White in Cardiff and which, Catherine Phelps argues, 'sets the tone for Williams' future work'. Linked to this, perhaps, is a phenomenon that I noted in my introduction to the previous part: the darker and more disturbing nature of the crimes, and the very much more realistic, graphic portrayal of these deeds and their impact on the victim, the wider community and the investigator. This unease can be compounded by a movement towards crime writing in which there is no 'investigator' as such; below we see a range of professional and private detectives, but we also see stories, such as some of those by Stuart Neville, in which they simply do not appear and in which no sense of order or resolution can be brought about through the efforts of one individual.

It could be argued that this more socially reflective writing is, in part, a product of its Millennial context. As with any significant temporal marker when things are perceived to be simultaneously ending and beginning, there is a desire to 'take stock' and to assess and respond to that specific point in time, but another aspect of this 'fin du millénaire' writing is arguably an impulse to review and reconsider what has come before. 'The past' is arguably revealed as a strong and growing theme of Millennial crime writing in several ways. Most obviously, we see the perpetuation of the generic past through the continued presence of more traditional forms of crime writing, such as D. M. Greenwood's clerical mysteries that reveal the tenacity of the Golden Age puzzler. Ian Ousby once observed that 'the Golden Age was a long time a-dying', and it is certainly not dead yet. As Suzanne Bray points out, however, Greenwood's works have a humourous twist, which perhaps shows their self-consciousness of form and their readership's awareness of this. Similarly, Christine Simpson discusses how Martin Edwards' writing 'follows the Golden Age pattern' to a degree, but her discussion of the 'chilling' circumstances of his first novel reveals the lack of the 'cosiness' found in the original genre, and demonstrates how older conventions are tempered by newer sensibilities.

The thematic presence of the past can also been seen through the sustained popularity of the historical crime story: Susanna Gregory writes both the Mediaeval and Restoration pasts in her various series, drawing on historical fact in the process, and C. J. Sansom reconstructs the England of Henry VIII in his Shardlake books. Sansom also exemplifies the more subtle and complex retrospective tendency of crime writing in this period in his novel *Dominion* (2012), which, as Martin Lightening argues 'deconstructs and rewrites the past' in its imagining of a world in which Britain and its Allies lost World War Two. This complex and simultaneous exploration of past and present is to be found in many other works explored in this part; the importance of geographical and temporal pasts to Dreda Say Mitchell's writing is always evident and Martin Edward's second series of crime novels feature a cold-case unit, and so the revisiting and 'investigating' of the past becomes the vehicle for the plots in the present. Similarly, Martina Cole's novels take London as their setting, but individual books are set at different times in London's past, from the early 1900s to the present day, and some of her 'pasts' are therefore only just so, as is the case with Denise Mina's novels set in 1980s Glasgow, and Minette Walters' temporally-complex exploration of the Stephen Lawrence case in *The Shape of Snakes*, which was written in 2000, but uses the backdrop of 1978 to explore events that occurred in 1993.

National pasts dominate the writings of three of the final five authors in the list; the late-twentieth and early twenty-first centuries saw the emergence of Northern-Irish crime writing, represented here by four writers described by Stephen Knight in his foreword as 'the edgy best' of N. I. crime fiction, and a growing movement to discuss and define this genre, through texts such as Declan Burke's edited volume *Down These Green Streets* (2011). In the entries below, Gerard Brennan and Steven Powell return repeatedly to the intrinsic and complicated role of the Troubles as a focus for the writings of Adrian McKinty, Brian McGilloway and Stuart Neville, exemplifying the complex relationship between past and present in the crime writing of this period, but also establishing its focuses on potential futures, as Brennan posits a time when the Troubles 'are not the first thing a reader thinks of when they find out a writer is from Northern Ireland'.

Brennan is the final writer discussed in this volume, and at this book's inception he was at the very beginning of his career: his first novella *The Point* was published in 2011. The entry is slightly different to the previous ninety-nine, in as much that it takes the form of an interview between Brennan and myself. In it, we discuss the complex issues of 'Britishness' as mentioned in the general introduction, which Brennan characterises as 'a can of angry worms', and the interview itself is both retrospective and forward-looking as I ask him to consider the canon of work that comes before him in this collection, and the future of crime fiction, particularly in Northern Ireland. His responses include many of the issues covered above in relation to the political and social focuses of contemporary crime writing, and he articulates his belief that crime writers should continue to focus on communities and their problems and to generate serious thought about this in their readerships.

We return, therefore, to the questions posed in the general introduction about the functions of crime writing and our impulses to read about this dark side to human nature. In 1941, Haycraft saw detective fiction as safeguarding, through its form and narrative content, society's 'known, just and logical rules'; crime fiction was a literature that upheld the tenets of civilised society. Over time, this certainty seems to have disappeared: there is no one society represented in the genre, no one set of tenets to be upheld. The idea of reading crime fiction for vicarious reassurance seems to be fading, and, although there are still resolutions of sorts to be had, these are less absolute and less satisfying and often brought about by people who, like us, don't have the moral high ground to judge and be certain. Returning to Stephen Knight's arguments above, though, these 'variations of sociopersonal conflict' seem to mean that the genre 'thrives' as never before, as writers continue to produce more diverse, brilliant, challenging and endlessly-evolving fiction about crime. It is now the highest-selling genre in Britain, which would suggest that reading about crime for leisure – or pleasure – is still a very popular pastime. But maybe the role of crime fiction now is in recording, commenting on, and 'investigating' humanity, rather than providing solutions to its problems and reassurances to its fears.

Esme Miskimmin

WORKS CITED

Burke, Declan, ed., *Down These Green Streets: Irish Crime Writing in the 21st Century*, (Dublin: Liberties Press, 2011).
Haycraft, Howard, *Murder for Pleasure: The Life and Times of the Detective Story*, (1941; repr. London: Peter Davies, 1942).
Ousby, Ian, *The Crime and Mystery Book: A Reader's Companion*, (London: Thames and Hudson, 1997).

CHAPTER 78

Martin Edwards (b. 1955), 1991: *All the Lonely People*

Christine R. Simpson

A solicitor by profession, Kenneth Martin Edwards was born in Cheshire where he attended grammar school before reading law at Balliol College, Oxford. After obtaining his degree and qualifying as a solicitor in 1980, he joined a firm in Liverpool and became a partner. His prolific writing career began in 1983 with legal works, but it was not until 1991 that his first novel, *All the Lonely People*, appeared. This introduces his amateur detective, Harry Devlin, a Liverpool solicitor dealing with the defence of petty criminals. Devlin's first private investigation is to discover the murderer of his estranged wife, whom he is suspected of killing. This leads him to unsavoury places and people, and even into serious danger. The plot is gripping, with plenty of twists and sardonic humour – the pattern for the other seven novels in the Devlin series. Often the solution of one crime leads to the uncovering of another, as in *Suspicious Minds* (1992) and *Yesterday's Papers* (1994). Like his character, Edwards is a devotee of classic crime writers. *The Devil in Disguise* (1998) follows the 'Golden Age' pattern of victims and suspects belonging to a closed community, but with a difference: it is by no means 'cosy'. It opens with a chilling scene,

C. R. Simpson (✉)
The Dorothy L. Sayers Society, Essex, UK

seemingly unrelated to the main plot, which keeps the reader guessing until the last chapter.

In 2004, after a break of several years from the Liverpool scene, Edwards wrote the first of a second original and highly atmospheric series set in the Lake District. *The Coffin Trail* introduces two main characters whose lives become intertwined after Daniel Kind decides to abandon his academic life at Oxford, as well as a lucrative television career, to settle in a dilapidated cottage there. A historian, he believes that research into the past requires the same skills as crime detection. Investigating an old murder linked to his own home, he meets Detective Chief Inspector Hannah Scarlett, head of the police Cold Case Unit, who is reviewing the same case. The development of their relationship adds interest to the succeeding plots, especially as Kind's interest in old books involves him with Scarlett's partner, owner of a second-hand bookshop. All of the novels in the series cleverly link crimes from the past and present, with more than a few unexpected twists to the plot. Clues even come from the cottage garden (*The Cipher Garden*, 2006). As in the Liverpool series, much depends on relationships between the characters involved in each case, and especially their pasts.

Apart from the series novels, *Take My Breath Away* (2002) shows Edwards' skill in writing a novel of psychological suspense, while *Dancing for the Hangman* (2008) is a brilliant fictional reconstruction of the Crippen case. He has also written three volumes of short stories; 'The Bookbinder's Apprentice' (in *Where Do You Find Your Ideas? and Other Stories*, 2001), won a Crime Writers' Association award in 2008 and 'Acknowledgements' won the CWA Margery Allingham Prize in 2014. Edwards has edited many anthologies and contributed critical articles to many books, magazines and websites, as well as writing a full-length exploration of Golden Age crime fiction, *The Golden Age of Murder* (2015). He was appointed both Vice Chair of the CWA, and President of the Detection Club in 2015.

SUGGESTED READING/WORKS CITED

Herbert, Rosemary, 'Martin Edwards', in *Whodunit? A Who's Who in Crime and Mystery Writing* (Oxford: Oxford University Press, 2003), p. 60.
The Official Marin Edwards Website. http://www.martinedwardsbooks.com/martinbooks.htm.

CHAPTER 79

D. M. Greenwood (b. 1939), 1991: *Clerical Errors*

Suzanne Bray

Best known as the creator of the clerical detective Theodora Braithwaite. Born in Halifax, Yorkshire, Diane Greenwood spent much of her youth in Norfolk. She graduated from St. Anne's College, Oxford, in 1962 and taught classics for two years before studying theology at King's College, London, from 1964 to 1966. She then returned to teaching in a wide variety of establishments: a teacher training college, a difficult comprehensive, a traditional grammar school and a prestigious girls' independent school. In 1983 she completed her Ph.D. at the University of Birmingham on *The Relation of Religious Experience to Teaching Religion in Schools* and found a job as an ecclesiastical civil servant for the Diocese of Rochester with responsibility for church schools. She was appointed Director of Education for the diocese in 1997 and retired in 2000. Lionel Comfit's description in *A Grave Disturbance* (1998) of 'the old boot who ran the diocesan education department, a woman of advanced years not known for falling in with the wishes of others' is generally supposed to be a tongue-in-cheek allusion to the way her colleagues perceived Greenwood.

S. Bray (✉)
Lille Catholic University, Lille, France

© The Author(s) 2020
E. Miskimmin (ed.), *100 British Crime Writers*, Crime Files,
https://doi.org/10.1057/978-1-137-31902-9_79

Greenwood, who found writing a form of relaxation in her busy professional life, chose to write detective fiction as she thought it was the genre most likely to get published. The Reverend Theodora Braithwaite, characterised as one of the first women to be ordained deacon in the Church of England, first appeared in *Clerical Errors* (1991) and continued her exploits of detection through nine novels until *Foolish Ways* (1999). She is a devout, tolerant, usually relaxed and pastorally astute priest on the Anglo-Catholic wing of the Church, who gets on well with most people. She has a simple lifestyle and enjoys academic research: she is writing the definitive biography of the (fictional) tractarian Thomas Henry Newcome. Greenwood claims that Theodora's character was based on that of her former classics mistress at Norwich High School, Eileen Smith. Greenwood has also said that one of her main themes was the 'tension between what the clergy say and what they actually do'. As a result, the novels are highly satirical and often humorous as they expose the eccentricities and shortcomings of the Church of England in the 1990s.

Most of the crimes take place in settings the author knows well, which can often add to their humourous dimension: a famous girls' school and a rough comprehensive (*Holy Terrors* 1994), an Anglican place of pilgrimage (*Every Deadly Sin* 1995), rural Norfolk (*Unholy Ghosts* 1991) and a seaside holiday camp, based on one in Bognor where Greenwood once attended a memorable, cold and chaotic conference (*Foolish Ways*). The most significant setting for many is Ecclesia Place (*Mortal Spoils*, 1996), a thinly disguised parody of Church House, where incompetence and misogyny are is used to generate humour, but also become the basis for crime, highlighting the complexities of crime writing and the balance of entertainment and necessarily dark subject matter.

Suggested Reading/Works Cited

Bray, Suzanne, 'A New Generation of Anglican Crime Writers', in *Questions of Identity in Detective Fiction*, ed. by Linda Martz and Anita Higgie (Newcastle: Cambridge Scholars Publishing, 2007), pp. 77–94.

Grosset, Philip, 'Theodora Brathwaite', Clerical Detectives Website. http://www.detecs.org/braithwaite.html.

Tory Historian, 'A Clerical Detective', *The Conservative History Journal*, 6 November 2008. http://conservativehistory.blogspot.com/2008/11/clerical-detective.html.

CHAPTER 80

Patricia Hall (Pseudonym of Maureen O'Connor, b. 1940), 1991: *The Poison Pool*

Steven Powell

Patricia Hall was born in Bradford, where her father was a Latin teacher and later headmaster at a boy's grammar school. Hall herself attended grammar school and, as she had discovered a love of reading and telling stories early in life, resolved at the age of thirteen to be a journalist. After she 'talked [her] way onto the *Yorkshire Post* in Leeds', Hall read English at the University of Birmingham where she met her future husband with whom she had two children. She gained a traineeship at the then *Manchester Guardian* and, returning to the newspaper later in her career, launched the *Guardian's* education section and edited it for sixteen years.

Hall's first novel, *The Poison Pool*, was published in 1991 and was followed by *The Coldness of Killers* (1992). However it would be her third novel, *Death by Election* (1993), which would begin the series that would define her contribution to the genre. Set in the fictional town of Bradfield, based on Hall's native Bradford, the novel features the unlikely pairing of reporter Laura Ackroyd and DCI Michael Thackeray. The title is a play on words as a local by-election sparks a media circus, which unravels a slew of political and sexual scandals and murder. Ackroyd and

S. Powell (✉)
University of Liverpool, Liverpool, UK

© The Author(s) 2020
E. Miskimmin (ed.), *100 British Crime Writers*, Crime Files,
https://doi.org/10.1057/978-1-137-31902-9_80

Thackeray find their work overlaps, sometimes with tense results, as they investigate criminal cases. They become romantically involved and eventually end up living together. Hall's Bradfield evokes the rich cultural history and setting of Yorkshire as vividly as Reginald Hill's novels. It is a city where the traditional manufacturing economy has collapsed and community tensions run high amidst high levels of predominantly Muslim immigration. Hall has proved herself a skilled and prolific writer, producing a novel a year since her debut in 1991. Notable additions among the titles in the Ackroyd and Thackeray series include *In the Bleak Midwinter* (1995), which explores corruption relating to land deals and has a cast of characters that includes real estate agents, anti-land development campaigners and New Age travellers, and *Deep Freeze* (2001), which features another case rooted in contemporary social and political issues as the murder of a thirteen-year-old girl outside an abortion clinic possibly ties to the visit of a controversial American evangelist. *By Death Divided* (2008) portrays the complications that arise when police and intelligence work overlap, as a case involving domestic abuse and murder has potential connections to Islamic extremism.

Hall began a new series featuring photographer Kate O' Donnell in 2011. In the first novel, *Dead* Beat, set in 1963, O'Donnell travels from her home city of Liverpool to 'Swinging London' on secondment to a fashion photographer's studio. The grisly murder of a teenage prostitute exposes O'Donnell to the darker side of London life. The story is partly inspired by Hall's own experiences of moving to London in the 1960s from the north of England and working for the *Evening Standard*. By 2015, there were three more novels in the ongoing Kate O'Donnell series: *Death Trap* (2012), *Dressed to Kill* (2013), *Blood Brothers* (2014), all focusing on Kate's experiences in the 1960s London scene, especially its darker side, and developing Kate's fiery relationship with DS Harry Barnard of the Vice Squad.

Suggested Reading/Works Cited

The Official Patricia Hall Website. http://www.patriciahall.co.uk/index.html.

CHAPTER 81

Martina Cole (b. 1959), 1992: *Dangerous Lady*

Esme Miskimmin

Martina Cole has published over twenty crime novels set in the ganglands of east London, all of which have made it to number one in *The Times* bestsellers booklist. Four of her books, *Dangerous Lady* (1992), *The Jump* (1995), *The Runaway* (1997) and *The Take* (2005), have been made into major television dramas, and three, *Two Women* (1999), *The Graft* (2004) and *Dangerous Lady* have been adapted for the stage.

Cole grew up in Aveley, Essex, the youngest of five in an Irish Catholic family. Her council-estate upbringing is something that she often discusses in interviews, seeing it as significant to an understanding of herself and her writing. Cole was expelled from a convent school at 15 (apparently for reading Harold Robbin's *The Carpetbaggers*), got married at 16, divorced at 17, and had her first child, Christopher, at 18. She describes the various low-wage jobs that she did to support herself and her son, but she also describes how she always wrote, and had actually completed the manuscript for *Dangerous Lady* by the time she was twenty, but didn't do anything with it until a decade later when it was accepted enthusiastically by her agents, Darley Anderson.

E. Miskimmin (✉)
University of Liverpool, Liverpool, UK

© The Author(s) 2020
E. Miskimmin (ed.), *100 British Crime Writers*, Crime Files,
https://doi.org/10.1057/978-1-137-31902-9_81

371

Cole's books are largely set in the Essex badlands or urban London in various time periods ranging from the early 1900s to the present day and are gritty portrayals of life, filled with petty crime, almost constant, often sexual, violence and the fragmented lives and families who live in this world. Cole's novels are realistic in terms of setting, referencing genuine places as well as fictional ones, and she writes the dialect with the accuracy of someone who is familiar with it. Many of the female figures she portrays from this background are downtrodden, beaten by their lives and their environment, but Cole also writes some very strong women, and most of her novels have a forceful female protagonist, such as the 17-year-old Maura Ryan, anti-heroine of *Dangerous Lady*, or DCI Kate Burrows, one of the few recurring figures for Cole, whose novels are chiefly stand-alones and linked by setting rather than character (Burrows appears in *The Ladykiller*, 1993, *Broken*, 2000, and *Hard Girls*, 2009).

Cole's writing draws heavily on sensory descriptions which are very evocative of the milieu she describes, such as the 'slum stench' of the Ryan household in 1950s Notting Hill, or the smell of Holloway prison as it hits Susan Dalston in *Two Women*, combining 'overcooked cabbage' with 'sweat and cheap soap and deodorant'. Cole's vivid descriptions, pacey dialogue and unceasing brutality make for compelling, if often uncomfortable, reading, and contribute to her works' adaptability to dramatic form. The most successful screen version of Cole's work has been the award-winning *The Take*, made for Sky 1 in 2009 and starring Tom Hardy as Freddie Jackson.

In recent interviews, Cole has suggested that her rheumatoid arthritis, which she has suffered from for over thirty years, may hinder her writing in the future, but for now she continues to add to an impressive list of bestselling crime novels.

Suggested Reading/Works Cited

Cadwaladr, Carole, 'The Booker Prize Money Wouldn't Even Keep Me in Cigarettes: Interview with Martina Cole', *The Observer*, 31 May 2009. http://www.theguardian.com/lifeandstyle/2009/may/31/martina-cole-books.

Ross, Deborah, 'Martina Cole: I Know I Don't Write Literature', *The Independent*, 15 October 2011. http://www.independent.co.uk/news/people/profiles/martina-cole-i-know-i-dont-write-literature-2369460.html.

The Official Martina Cole Website. http://www.martinacole.co.uk/index.html.

CHAPTER 82

Minette Walters (b. 1949), 1992: *The Ice House*

Heather Worthington

Minette Walters' novels do not conform to the familiar crime fiction pattern which places the detective at the centre of the narrative and where the criminal's role is as much to drive the plot as to commit the crime; technically, her books are more properly thrillers in the mode of Patricia Highsmith or Barbara Vine (pseudonym of Ruth Rendell). Stephen Knight considers Walters to be the inheritor of what he calls the 'British psychothriller tradition', that is crime fiction that concerns itself with the psychology of those individuals who commit crimes. Central to Walters' work are the roles of the family and of society in creating the criminal, and the issue of justice. Her first-hand knowledge and understanding of criminals and criminality come from her long service as a prison visitor, and she maintains that the problems of many of those she has visited can be attributed to a lack of education and the absence of a strong nuclear family.

Perhaps because of the psychological and social aspects of her fiction, Walters' novels are not only enormously popular with her readers but have attracted serious critical attention. Unusually in crime writing, Walters

H. Worthington (✉)
Cardiff University, Cardiff, UK

© The Author(s) 2020
E. Miskimmin (Ed.), *100 British Crime Writers*, Crime Files,
https://doi.org/10.1057/978-1-137-31902-9_82

has refused the lure of the series and her novels are all stand-alone texts that bear no relation to each other apart from an often bleak appraisal of contemporary British society. It is precisely in her narratives' dialogue with the present or very recent past reality, their use of fact within the fiction, that their appeal to both a popular and an academic audience lies.

Walters was born in Bishop's Stortford, Hertfordshire. Her father was an Army Captain, and the first ten years of Walters' life were spent in various British Army bases. After the death of her father in 1960, Walters attended the Abbey School in Berkshire before gaining a Foundation Scholarship at the Godolphin School, Salisbury. On completing her secondary education, she spent a gap year working on a kibbutz in Israel and in a home for delinquent boys in Jerusalem. On her return to Britain, she studied French at Durham University, graduating in 1971. Prior to her marriage in 1978, Walters effectively served her apprenticeship in writing, working for IPC Magazines as a subeditor on a romantic fiction magazine, penning articles, short stories and novelettes. Subsequently she went freelance, writing for women's magazines. Writing, she says, is appallingly hard work, and writers require a thick skin in order to survive the criticism that comes their way; equally, the praise is a delight. She calls the whole project of authorship 'one long ego trip'.

While her children were young, Walters ceased writing. She was, however, active in other areas, working as a School Governor and standing as a candidate in a political election. She declares herself to be politically left of centre, and her socialist leanings are evident in her work and in her prison visiting. In 1987 Walters returned to writing, embarking on a full-length novel. Her interest in the psychology of crime and her passionate engagement with social issues made crime fiction a logical choice of genre, and she completed *The Ice House* in 1989. It was a further two years before it found a publisher, but after its publication by Macmillan in 1992 the novel won the Crime Writers' Association John Creasey Award for best first novel. Within six months *The Ice House* had gone into translation with eleven foreign publishers. Her books continue to be published across the world; *The Sculptress* (1993) won the Edgar Allan Poe Award in America, *The Shape of Snakes* (2000) was awarded the Danish Pelle Rosenkrantz Prize.

By 2015 she had written sixteen novels and three novellas (*The Tinderbox*, 1999, *Chickenfeed*, 2006, and *A Dreadful Murder*, 2013), the latter two being Walters' contribution to the 'Quick Reads' initiative aimed at encouraging developing readers and adult learners in their reading. She also writes short stories including 'English Autumn, American Fall' (1999) and is a regular contributor to newspapers and magazines. Walters is very aware of her female crime writing predecessors; while rejecting the tendency of the Golden Age crime fiction authors such as Dorothy L. Sayers, Ngaio Marsh, Margery Allingham or Agatha Christie to use a serial detective and to focus their attention on middle- or upper-class society, her writing is part of that tradition in which crime reveals the often unpleasant reality behind society's façade of respectability. For Walters, society is absolutely central to her work; although each of her novels revolves around a single protagonist, it is the place of that protagonist within the community and equally the role of the community, whether local or global, in the creation of the criminal that forms the core of the narrative. There has been a gradual development in Walters' novels from a close focus on the family to a broader exploration of a localised community in, for example *The Shape of Snakes* (2000) or *Acid Row* (2001) and, more recently, in *Disordered Minds* (2003), *The Devil's Feather* (2005) and *The Chameleon's Shadow* (2007), an examination of the secondary impact on the individual and the community of the events of 9/11 and the wars in Africa and Iraq.

Despite Walters' recognition of global as well as local issues, her fiction returns always to small communities in its analysis of the effects of crime and the making of the criminal. Hampshire, Wiltshire and Dorset, counties known to Walters, are favourite settings. These counties abound in small villages and country houses, affording exactly the microcosmic social arenas which best demonstrate the effects of crime. Walters' novels are also concerned with contemporary social and political issues, from inadequate social services to corrupt police and from feminism to racism, paedophilia to prejudice, but the issues are not foregrounded. Instead, they emerge naturally in the course of the narrative. A strong and recurring theme in Walters' work is the effect of the past on the present. *The Shape of Snakes* exemplifies this and is typical of Walters' weaving together of social issues, psychology, family relationships and crime.

As in much of Walters' work, real events inspire or are incorporated into the fiction. *The Shape of Snakes* was in part a response to the Stephen Lawrence case of 1993 and its aftermath, and the crime at the novel's centre takes place against the backdrop of 'the winter of discontent'; 1978, when Britain was in the grip of mass strikes by private and public sector workers. The case is retrospectively explored by the protagonist, Mrs Ranelagh, or 'M', who had discovered the body of Annie, a black woman who suffers from Tourette's syndrome and alcoholism and whose colour is unacceptable to her London neighbours. 'M' is convinced that it is not a road accident but murder, but her attempts to prove this at the time of Annie's death, in combination with other factors, result in 'M' being considered to be mentally unstable.

Twenty years later, 'M' returns to the neighbourhood where the death occurred and tries to persuade her old neighbours to rethink their statements made at the time. Her lack of success and the attitude of the police suggest that the contemporary society and its policing bodies are not only racist but misogynist and corrupt. Gradually, the reader realises that 'M' is not the reliable narrator/investigator he or she might have expected. Various forms of 'factual' documentation inserted into the narrative, letters, medical reports and so on – a recurring feature of Walters' novels – reveals that 'M' has a long history of mental problems and has been in psychotherapy for many years. Finally, it becomes clear that 'M' is no more mad than Annie; both are victims of society, victimised because they did not conform to social 'norms': in the case of 'M', normative motherhood and proper wifely obedience. *The Shape of Snakes* explores, through crime, social issues of race and gender at both the individual and communal level.

Many of Walters' novels have female protagonists or are female focused; where the protagonist is male, as in *The Echo* (1997) *Fox Evil* (2002), *Disordered Minds* (2003) and *The Chameleon's Shadow* (2007), male–female relationships play a significant role. Family is important, particularly in terms of children. The effects of childhood neglect or actual abuse are explored to various degrees in *The Ice House* (1992), *The Sculptress* (1993), *The Scold's Bridle* (1994), *Acid Row* (2001) and *Fox Evil*. *Acid Row* is set in the context of the contemporary hysteria about paedophilia, but also incorporates issues of race, street violence, urban deprivation and gender. Her extensive use of other modes of writing in her novels strengthens the illusion of a real world in the fiction: facsimiles of newspaper reports, medical records, letters, official and personal, witness statements, court and police records and, more recently email exchanges, all add verisimilitude to her accounts.

Walters has received multiple awards for her fiction and has been twice shortlisted for the Crime Writers' Association Golden Dagger Award (*The Dark Room*, 1995 and *Acid Row*). Her first five novels were adapted for television by the BBC (1996–99).

Suggested Reading/Works Cited

Forselius, Tilda Maria, 'The Impenetrable M and the Mysteries of Narration: Narrative in Minette Walters's *The Shape of Snakes*', *CLUES: A Journal of Detection*, 24:2 (2006), 47–61.

Hadley, Mary and Sarah D. Fogle, eds, *Minette Walters and the Meaning of Justice: Essays on the Crime Novels* (Jefferson, NC and London: McFarland, 2008).

Knight, Stephen, *Crime Fiction Since 1800: Detection, Death, Diversity*, rev. ed. (Basingstoke: Palgrave Macmillan, 2010).

The Official Minette Walters Website. http://www.minettewalters.co.uk.

CHAPTER 83

Malcolm Rose (b. 1953), 1993: *The Smoking Gun* (First contribution to the *Point Crime* Series)

Lucy Andrew

Malcolm Rose is the author of over thirty crime novels and thrillers for young adults, and whose background as a researcher and lecturer in Chemistry informs much of his work. He published his first novel, *Rift*, in 1985 and relinquished his lecturing post at the Open University in 1996 to pursue a full-time writing career. His thrillers have been praised for their treatment of hard-hitting issues, such as racism, bullying, drug use, medical ethics and biological warfare. Rose won the Angus Book Award in 1997 for *Tunnel Vision* and in 2001 for *Plague*, which also won the Lancashire Children's Book of the Year Award. *Transplant* (2003) and *Kiss of Death* (2006) were later shortlisted for this award.

Though Rose's thrillers often feature crime content, it was his contribution to the *Point Crime* series that established him as a writer of the newly evolving young adult crime genre. While pre-teen crime fiction centres around solving a mystery, teenage crime narratives focus more closely upon the perpetration and impact of serious crime, particularly

L. Andrew (✉)
University of Chester, Chester, UK

© The Author(s) 2020
E. Miskimmin (ed.), *100 British Crime Writers*, Crime Files,
https://doi.org/10.1057/978-1-137-31902-9_83

379

murder. Rose's original *Point Crime* novels, *The Smoking Gun* (1993), *Concrete Evidence* (1995) and *The Alibi* (1996), all feature quasi-detective young protagonists who investigate the murder of a relative. From 1997 to 2000, Rose produced the *Lawless & Tilley* series for *Point Crime*, which follows young police detectives Brett Lawless and Clare Tilley as they hunt down blackmailers, kidnappers and murderers. The police-procedural novel for young adults was pioneered by another *Point Crime* series, David Belbin's *The Beat* (1993–2000), which featured a police team from Nottingham. Rose's series, however, established its originality through the introduction of forensic science as a key investigative tool within the narrative.

Rose's most innovative crime series, however, is *Traces* (2005 to the present). Like *Lawless & Tilley*, this series focuses upon forensic science and maintains the procedural format commonly found in adult crime fiction. Yet *Traces* is set in a futuristic, parallel universe, under an oppressive state regime, where sixteen-year-old Luke Harding has qualified as the youngest ever Forensic Investigator and works alongside a robot sidekick called Malc. Through *Traces*, Rose contributes to two major developments within the crime genre for young readers: the professionalisation of the young detective protagonist, through the introduction of a young character as an official investigator; and the hybridisation of the genre, in this case by imbuing the crime narrative with fantasy elements.

Traces has been well received by critics. In 2006 the first book in the series, *Framed!*, was selected by the United States Board on Books for Young People (USBBY) and the Children's Book Council as an 'Outstanding International Book' and by the International Reading Association as 'Best International Book'. Rose's new crime series, *Jordan Stryker: Bionic Agent* and *Jordan Stryker: Cyber Terror* (2010 to the present) builds on the successful formula established in *Traces*, again creating a hybrid crime narrative featuring a professional young detective hero, this time through the introduction of a teenage secret agent protagonist with superhuman abilities.

Suggested Reading/Works Cited

The Official Malcolm Rose Website. http://www.malcolmrose.co.uk.

CHAPTER 84

Veronica Stallwood (Has also written as Kate Ivory, b. 1939), 1993: *Death and the Oxford Box* (First novel in the 'Kate Ivory' Series)

Megan Hoffman

Veronica Stallwood is best known for her series of crime novels featuring historical romance writer and amateur sleuth Kate Ivory, all set in Oxford, England. Before Stallwood began writing crime fiction, she published two contemporary romances, *Wildfire Love* (1988) and *Imperfect Harmony* (1989), under the pseudonym Kate Ivory, the name she would later give to the protagonist of her detective series. Stallwood has also produced two non-series suspense novels, *Deathspell* (1992) and *The Rainbow Sign* (1999), under her own name.

Stallwood was born in South London and attended boarding school while her mother and father, who was a Foreign Office employee, lived in the Middle East. At the age of ten, Stallwood joined her parents abroad, first in Athens and then in Beirut, where she was educated at a convent school. Stallwood later completed secretarial college and worked at various jobs including technical translation and public relations until she married in her early twenties. After nine years of marriage, Stallwood

M. Hoffman (✉)
Independent Scholar, Southsea, UK

© The Author(s) 2020
E. Miskimmin (ed.), *100 British Crime Writers*, Crime Files,
https://doi.org/10.1057/978-1-137-31902-9_84

divorced and returned to England from Belgium with her two children. Her fluency in French helped her to obtain a position at a publishing company that was opening a European headquarters in Oxford. Stallwood would later work at Oxford University's Bodleian Library and New College Library.

In the 1980s, Stallwood saw an advertisement in *Cosmopolitan* magazine for a novel-writing course and decided that she wanted to write in her spare time. She soon produced the two novels written as Kate Ivory, and then in 1992, Stallwood published the suspense novel *Deathspell* under her own name. A year later, Stallwood's first crime novel, *Death and the Oxford Box* (1993), was released.

The Kate Ivory series is notable for its evocative use of Oxford settings, which has resulted in frequent comparisons with Colin Dexter's Inspector Morse novels. Besides drawing on her knowledge of Oxford for the series, Stallwood has also used her own experience as a librarian for the plot of *Oxford Exit* (1994), in which Kate Ivory takes on a temporary job at the Bodleian Library in order to uncover a suspected ring of book thieves. Stallwood's observant, independent amateur detective often stumbles upon cases through research for her romance novels or is persuaded to investigate by friends who are reluctant to consult the police. Stallwood concluded the Kate Ivory series in 2011 with the fourteenth novel, *Oxford Ransom*.

In her spare time, Stallwood gives lectures about writing and runs creative writing workshops in schools. She has also taught adult education courses in creative writing for the Workers' Educational Association (WEA).

Suggested Reading/Works Cited

Becker, Kathleen and Julian Earwaker, *Scene of the Crime: A Guide to the Landscapes of British Detective Fiction* (London: Aurum Press, 2002).
Heising, Willetta L., *Detecting Women 2: A Reader's Guide and Checklist for Mystery Series Written by Women* (Dearborn, MI: Purple Moon Press, 1996).
Kramer, John E., *Academe in Mystery and Detective Fiction: An Annotated Bibliography* (Lanham, MD: Scarecrow Press, 2000).

CHAPTER 85

Stella Duffy (b. 1963), 1994: *Calendar Girl*

Susan Massey

Although now carving out a successful career for herself as an author of literary fiction (two of her most recent novels were long-listed for the Orange Prize and *Theodora: Actress, Empress, Whore* (2010) offers a fictionalised account of the life of one of the most powerful women in Ancient Rome, the wife of the Emperor Justinian I), Stella Duffy remains an important figure in contemporary crime writing, thanks to her series featuring the lesbian private investigator Saz Martin.

Duffy was born in London but spent her formative years in Tokoroa, a small town in New Zealand, before returning to the UK in 1986. She is the author of twelve novels and is a prolific short story writer. In addition to her fiction, Duffy has also written extensively for radio and theatre and is a successful performer, particularly of improvisational comedy. In 2002, Duffy was awarded the Crime Writers' Association's Short Story Dagger for 'Martha Grace', taken from the anthology *Tart Noir*, which she co-edited with Lauren Henderson. The term 'Tart Noir' was coined by Henderson and Sparkle Hayter to describe crime writing featuring 'independent-minded female sleuths who are tough enough to take on thugs and corrupt cops, tender enough to be moved by tough, tender

S. Massey (✉)
University of St Andrews, St Andrews, Scotland, UK

© The Author(s) 2020
E. Miskimmin (ed.), *100 British Crime Writers*, Crime Files,
https://doi.org/10.1057/978-1-137-31902-9_85

383

men (or women, as the case may be)'. Characterised by a strong feminist sensibility, typical 'Tart Noir' heroines are fiercely autonomous and unapologetically sexual, without taking themselves too seriously.

Saz Martin fits this definition nicely. Yet Saz was not originally intended to be the protagonist of Duffy's first foray into the crime genre. Instead, Saz's role in *Calendar Girl* (1994) is essentially a plot device to reveal more about the mysterious 'Woman with the Kelly McGillis body'. However, Saz proved to be a popular and compelling character and took centre stage in four further novels – *Wavewalker* (1996), *Beneath the Blonde* (1997), *Fresh Flesh* (1999) and *Mouth of Babes* (2005). The series is just as concerned with Saz's love life as it is with her career as a self-employed investigator and it follows Saz as she achieves domestic bliss with her lover, Molly. In *Fresh Flesh*, a novel about reproductive rights and the emotional damage that often lurks behind the façade of the supposedly 'respectable' nuclear family, Molly becomes pregnant through IVF. However, despite her impending motherhood, Saz is still compelled by her job, and her own penchant towards masochism, to become embroiled in violence and danger. Throughout the series, Saz's body is a site of trauma, suffering not only burns and beatings but also the rigours of Saz's own brutal exercise regime. While Saz is tough-talking and, on occasions, macho, she is not just a feminised version of the hard-boiled PI figure. Instead, Saz's characterisation emphasises her physical and emotional vulnerability and she is also presented as being rooted in a supportive lesbian community, with an active network of friends, sources and informants.

Suggested Reading/Works Cited

'Not Writing But Blogging': Stella Duffy's Website. http://stelladuffy.wordpress.com/.

Plain, Gill, *Twentieth-Century Crime Fiction: Gender, Sexuality and the Body* (Edinburgh: Edinburgh University Press, 2001).

'Tart City' Website. http://www.tartcity.com/.

CHAPTER 86

Alison Taylor (Birth Date Unknown), 1995: *Simeon's Bride*

Catherine Phelps

Alison Taylor was brought up in Cheshire and Derbyshire but had family roots in North Wales. In 1965 she returned to Anglesey where she lives with her family. After studying architecture, Taylor pursued a career in probation and social work. When working for Gwynedd council in the 1980s, she raised concerns regarding the abuse of children in care. As these went unheeded, Taylor took her concerns to the media, losing her job in the process. It took over ten years for her to be vindicated by a subsequent government inquiry whose report uncovered high levels of abuse and which praised Taylor for her courage and persistence in bringing the matter to light. Unsurprisingly, her crime fiction draws heavily on this experience. Nonetheless, Taylor's novels also contain allusions to her other interests which include Beethoven and eighteenth-century Welsh poetry.

Taylor writes police procedurals set in Bangor, North Wales. Despite the mostly masculine make-up of the team, Taylor's male characters are curiously feminised; gender roles are often reversed in her world. Rather than detection through masculine ratiocination, cases are led by intuition

C. Phelps (✉)
Cardiff University, Cardiff, UK

© The Author(s) 2020
E. Miskimmin (ed.), *100 British Crime Writers*, Crime Files,
https://doi.org/10.1057/978-1-137-31902-9_86

and clues are garnered through gossip gathered at kitchen tables over cups of tea. The team bicker neurotically, none more so than the central figure of the series, Michael McKenna. McKenna cuts a lonely figure, marginalised by his Irish Catholic background despite being a native of Bangor and a fluent Welsh speaker.

Taylor's first novel was the gothic *Simeon's Bride* (1995). Police procedural and ghost story combine in an investigation into the discovery of a woman's body hanging from a tree deep in woods near Bangor. (This has since been translated and published in Welsh as *Corff yn y Goedwig* [*Body in the Forest*].) Malign motherhood and child abuse are central to the plot. However, it is her second novel, *In Guilty Night* (1996), which is overt in fictionalising her past experiences. Set in a children's home, it demonises social workers and those in care of the vulnerable.

All of Taylor's novels are rooted in their North Welsh setting and culture; *In Guilty Night* deploys the sixteenth-century practice of 'sin-eating', for instance. *The House of Women* (1998) centres on the forgery of a mediaeval document and makes explicit reference to Iolo Morganwg, the eighteenth-century antiquarian responsible for the publication of ancient Welsh texts, who nonetheless was also responsible for the forgery of some of those newly discovered works. Even when the action is moved to the Pennines, as in *Unsafe Convictions* (1999), much is made of the police team's nationality. However, her novel, *Child's Play* (2001), centres on a private girl's school; although set in Bangor, this is arguably her most 'English' novel as Welsh characters and culture are pushed to the margins and, as such, this is arguably her least successful of the series.

SUGGESTED READING/WORKS CITED

Phelps, Catherine, 'Re-shaping Crime Fiction in Simeon's Bride', *Assuming Gender*, 1:1 (2010), 62–70.

CHAPTER 87

Christopher Brookmyre (b. 1968), 1996: *Quite Ugly One Morning*

Christopher Routledge

Christopher Brookmyre is a Scottish crime writer whose comic novels provide a sardonic and sometimes snarling commentary on popular culture and modern life. This is particularly acute in the detective novels set in Scotland, in which Brookmyre satirises the influence of business practices in organisations such as the National Health Service. Brookmyre is known for his fast-paced plotting, dark humour and unusual book titles, many of which are based on popular phrases, clichés and sayings such as *Quite Ugly One Morning* (1996) and *All Fun and Games Until Somebody Loses an Eye* (2005). Brookmyre's American counterparts in terms of style are Elmore Leonard and, as he has admitted himself, Carl Hiaasen.

Brookmyre was born in Glasgow on 6 September 1968 and attended Glasgow University, graduating in 1989 with an M. A. in English Literature and Theatre Studies. He began his professional writing career as a journalist for newspapers and magazines such as *The Scotsman*, the *Edinburgh Evening News* and *Screen International*. His first novel, *Quite Ugly One Morning* became an immediate success, winning that year's Critics First Blood Award for the best first crime novel of the year. *Quite Ugly*

C. Routledge (✉)
Freelance Writer and Photographer, NW England, UK

© The Author(s) 2020
E. Miskimmin (Ed.), *100 British Crime Writers*, Crime Files,
https://doi.org/10.1057/978-1-137-31902-9_87

387

One Morning introduced Jack Parlabane, an investigative journalist with a rebellious attitude, who features in several of Brookmyre's novels. Parlabane's reckless attitude to his own safety and disregard for protocol and social convention makes for high speed and action-packed plotting, a characteristic of Brookmyre's writing in general. Parlabane instinctively distrusts the rich and powerful and sees conspiracies everywhere, pursuing his investigations by breaking and entering, illegal bugging, computer hacking and phone tapping, which he justifies on the basis that more acceptable – and legal – methods would not work.

Brookmyre's social commentary tends to focus on corruption and greed in public institutions and in business. *Quite Ugly One Morning* involves the discovery of corruption among managers of an NHS trust, one of the local bodies set up by the Tory governments of the 1980s and 1990s to bring the 'free market' to healthcare in the United Kingdom. Other novels, such as *Country of the Blind* (1997) critique the security services, while the 2000 Sherlock Award-winning *Boiling a Frog*, involves corruption in the then-new Scottish Parliament. Brookmyre's satire is broadly left wing, but the novels are more generally suspicious of 'The Establishment'; general targets include the media, English politicians, big business, the Catholic Church and those who choose to operate within these institutions. Another frequent target is parochialism and the pettiness that follows from it. This is perhaps best represented by the character of Gavin Hutchinson in *One Fine Day in the Middle of the Night* (1999) who, despite financial and personal success, still harbours resentment over playground rivalries.

Not all of Brookmyre's novels are set in Scotland and not all of them are detective novels as such. *Not the End of the World* (1998) features press photographer Steff Kennedy in the 'Parlabane' role; it is set in Los Angeles and pokes fun at the religious right. Later books, such as *A Big Boy Did It and Ran Away* (2001) stray into the territory of the crime caper. Its central character Simon Darcourt, terrorist and assassin, reappears in *A Snowball in Hell* (2008). *Pandaemonium* (2009), which takes its title from Milton's *Paradise Lost*, was described by Patrick Ness in *The Guardian* as 'a book in which vengeful demons meet horny teenagers in a remote location' but also as one with 'vivid plotting, detailed characterisations and vigorously sincere debates over the nature of heaven and hell, all coupled with profanity, sex, and cheerful slaughter'.

While Brookmyre's novels often have a sharp political edge, they are also entertaining and funny with a comic style that depends on exaggerated characters, elaborate conspiracies and situations that sometimes slip into the unreal. His later work has become more speculative and fantastical. Apart from the opening of a portal into hell in *Pandaemonium*, Jack Parlabane appears as a ghost in *Attack of the Unsinkable Rubber Ducks* (2008). Yet while Brookmyre is primarily a writer of novels driven by strong plotting and gaudily drawn characters, he is also notable for his sharp eye and verbal humour. In *A Big Boy Did It and Ran Away*, for example, is the following observation: 'Living in Aberdeen had taught him the difference between the parochial and the truly insular. The parochial was defined by a naïve, even innocent ignorance of the world beyond its borders. The truly insular knew fine there was a world outside, they just didnae fuckin' like it, and had nae fuckin' need for it!'

In 2006 Brookmyre won the Bollinger Everyman Wodehouse Prize for *All Fun and Games Until Somebody Loses an Eye* (2005), which was also shortlisted in 2007 for the Theakston's Old Peculier Crime Novel of the Year. He was shortlisted again for the Theakston's Old Peculier Crime Novel of the Year for *A Tale Etched in Blood and Hard Black Pencil* in 2008, while *A Snowball in Hell* was shortlisted for the 2009 Bollinger Everyman Wodehouse Prize.

SUGGESTED READING/WORKS CITED

Christopher Brookmyre at Contemporary Writers. http://www.contemporarywriters.com/authors/?p=auth02D4J064212627313.
The Official Christopher Brookmyre Website. http://www.brookmyre.co.uk/.

CHAPTER 88

Susanna Gregory (Pseudonym of Elizabeth Cruwys, b. 1958), 1996: *A Plague on Both Your Houses*

Steven Powell

Susanna Gregory is a Marine Biologist and historical novelist. Raised in Bristol, Gregory attended the University of Lancaster and then worked as police officer in Leeds. She obtained her Ph.D. at the University of Cambridge and has enjoyed a career in academe.

It would be her experiences at Cambridge, which she describes as 'one of the most magical, magnificent and murderous places anywhere', and her experience of academe which would be the inspiration for her first novel, *A Plague on Both Your Houses* (1996), set in 1348 at the dawn of the seemingly unstoppable destruction of the 'Black Death'. This became first in the series of 'the Chronicles of Matthew Bartholomew' and introduced Cambridge physician Matthew Bartholomew, a scientist in an age of religion and superstition. As the series progresses, Bartholomew finds that his position as master of College of Michaelmas at the University puts him at the centre of intrigue and plotting. In *An Order for Death* (2002) Bartholomew investigates the murder of a friar at a time of heightened

S. Powell (✉)
University of Liverpool, Liverpool, UK

religious tension. *The Devil's Disciples* (2008) finds Cambridge terrified over the arrival of a mysterious sorcerer. The novels are notable for their portrayal of the emerging University, and share some similarities with Ellis Peters' 'Cadfael' series.

With her husband, Beau Riffenburgh, Gregory has written eight novels under the joint pseudonym Simon Beaufort. These feature Sir Geoffrey Mappestone, the fictional son of the English landowner Godric, who began Goodrich's castle in the eleventh century. As there was almost no historical detail available on Godric, Gregory and Riffenburgh had free rein to invent the family and place Mappestone at the centre of a turbulent period of history. The first novel, *Murder in the Holy City* (1998), takes place in 1100 shortly after the Fall of Jerusalem. Sir Geoffrey, a reluctant warrior in the First Crusade, is ordered to investigate the murder of a knight. There are two other stand-alone novels written under the Beaufort pseudonym. *The Nimrod Murders* (2011), concerns the murder of an assistant biologist on the eve of the 1907 Nimrod expedition to the Antarctic. The murder is investigated by the geologist and Antarctic explorer Raymond Priestley. *The Murder House* (2013) is a contemporary novel featuring PC Helen Anderson, the first-person narrator who finds herself drawn into a complex and dark series of events.

Gregory's most recent series is set in Restoration England and features Thomas Chaloner, a detective and former Parliamentarian spy. The first novel of the series, *A Conspiracy of Violence* (2006), begins with Chaloner uncertain of his future after the death of Oliver Cromwell and the collapse of the Commonwealth. Chaloner's backstory is every bit as compelling as the Restoration setting, as he has fought for the New Model Army during the Civil War and served as a spy afterwards in the Netherlands, Spain and France. The character is fictional but, like Mappestone, is based on a historical family. Chaloner is the imagined nephew of Thomas and James Chaloner, who signed the death warrant of Charles I, and the grandson of Thomas Chaloner, a noted naturalist and favourite of James I.

Gregory's skill as a writer is in vividly bringing to life her period settings, suffusing the novels with scholarly details without ever seeming to be overly self-conscious in writing historical fiction. Her characters are plausible people, who despite carrying the common prejudices of their era, can still evoke sympathy from the contemporary reader.

Suggested Reading/Works Cited

Betts, Charlotte, 'Susanna Gregory—Guest Author'. http://www.charlottebetts.com/.

Profile: Historical Fiction Writer Liz Cruwys. http://www.cam.ac.uk/for-staff/features/profile-historical-fiction-writer-liz-cruwys.

The Official Susanna Gregory Website. http://www.susannagregory.com/.

CHAPTER 89

Denise Mina (b. 1966), 1998: *Garnethill*

Esme Miskimmin

Novelist, film-maker and writer of comics and plays, Denise Mina began her crime writing career in 1998 with her *Garnethill* trilogy and is now well known for her Paddy Meehan series (2005–2007) and her novels featuring Detective Inspector Alex Morrow (2009–present). Mina was born in Glasgow and despite moving around the world as a child as a result of her father's job returned to the city as a Law student in her twenties and still lives there with her partner and children. Mina is often associated with the 'Tartan Noir' group of Scottish crime writers, a term coined by James Ellroy to describe Ian Rankin's writing and which now extends to a group of writers whose work perhaps has its roots more in the American hard-boiled or noir genres than in any British 'murder-mystery'; often police-orientated, the stories are brutally stark in their events and approach, complex in their perspectives and moralities and darkly humorous on occasion. They are also very much located within a realistic and recognisable Scotland, and this is also true of Mina: the Glasgow she constructs is a real space, from the bleak social and economic landscape of the 1980s, the setting for the Paddy Meehan novels, to the post-regeneration Glasgow which serves in part as a background for the Morrow novels.

E. Miskimmin (✉)
University of Liverpool, Liverpool, UK

© The Author(s) 2020
E. Miskimmin (ed.), *100 British Crime Writers*, Crime Files,
https://doi.org/10.1057/978-1-137-31902-9_89

Mina began a PhD in Law and Psychiatry to study 'differential ascription to male and female offenders', but, in her words, 'misused her grant to write [her] first novel' (*Garnethill*, winner of the 1998 John Creasy Dagger for Best First Crime Novel). The focuses of the PhD, though, perhaps reveal the political and social agendas of Mina's writing which are apparent throughout and which are delivered to the reader through Mina's often disconcerting and uncompromising style. Whether a first or third person, Mina's stories often involve shifting, multiple points-of-view and narrators who are often uncertain or unreliable. The novels are often graphic in their descriptions of violence – both of action and emotion – but there is also much that is implicit or merely hinted at, leaving the reader to make discoveries or construct details for themselves. This is sometimes a unsettling process, such as in recent short story for the OxCrimes collection of short stories, 'The Calm Before', in which the reader finds themselves presented with events from the perspective of the criminal, a device that Mina returns to more than once and is reminiscent of the much earlier female noir writer, Dorothy B. Hughes in her novel *In a Lonely Place* (1947).

All of Mina's serial investigators are female, although only one is a professional detective, and to an extent, there is a gender agenda in all of the novels: women as victims and survivors (*Garnethill*'s Maureen O'Donnell is an ex-psychiatric patient and survivor of sexual abuse, who starts the first novel as a murder suspect); women working in a man's world (Paddy Meehan is a reporter with Irish Catholic roots, working for the 'Scottish Daily News' in 1980s Glasgow) and women balancing the two, sometimes deeply disparate, worlds of work and family (Alex Morrow investigates some brutal crimes in her capacity as police detective, but the novels also focus on her personal life as daughter, wife and mother – she is mourning the loss of a child in the first novel, *Still Midnight*, 2009, and is heavily pregnant throughout the investigations in *The End of the Wasp Season*, 2010).

In addition to her crime fiction, Denise Mina also writes graphic novels: she wrote the 13-episode story 'Empathy is the Enemy' in the *Hellblazer* comic series (2006, illustrated by Leonardo Manco and Andrea Mutti) and has adapted Stieg Larsson's 'Millennium' Trilogy for graphic novel form (2012–2013, illustrated by Leonardo Manco and Andrea Mutti). The darkness of these two series is in keeping with Mina's own oeuvre, but the comic form also reinforces her alternative approaches to the processes of storytelling: in *The New York Times* she comments on how comics engage her interest in 'other forms of narrative' and adapting *The Girl with the Dragon Tattoo* allowed her to explore this further. Mina's own work has been the subject of adaptation: the first Paddy Meehan Novel, *The Field of Blood* (2005) was filmed for the BBC in 2011, and the second, *The Dead Hour* (2006) in 2013, with Jayd Johnson in the role of Meehan.

Suggested Reading/Works Cited

Clanfield, Peter, 'Denise Mina, Ian Rankin, Paul Johnston, and the Architectural Crime Novel', *Clues: A Journal of Detection*, 26:2 (2008), 79–91.

Smith, Dinita, 'Denise Mina and the Rise of Scottish Detective Fiction', *The New York Times*, 22 July 2006. http://www.nytimes.com/2006/07/22/arts/22mina.html?_r=0.

The Official Denise Mina Website. http://www.denisemina.com/.

CHAPTER 90

Alexander McCall Smith (b. 1948), 1999: *The No. 1 Ladies' Detective Agency*

Susan Massey

Having enjoyed a distinguished career in the fields of medical law and bioethics, Alexander McCall Smith became one of the more unlikely figures in contemporary crime fiction when he published *The No. 1 Ladies' Detective Agency* (1999), the first novel in a series featuring an equally unlikely protagonist, Mma Precious Ramotswe.

McCall Smith was born in Bulawayo, in what was then the British colony of Southern Rhodesia and is now Zimbabwe. The youngest son of a public prosecutor, he was educated at the prestigious Christian Brothers College, before leaving Africa at the age of seventeen to study law at the University of Edinburgh. After attaining an LLB and a Ph.D., McCall Smith took a teaching post at Queen's University, Belfast. However, he soon returned to Africa; working first in Swaziland before moving to Botswana, where he helped to establish the Faculty of Law at the country's national university. In 1984, McCall Smith moved back to Scotland, becoming Professor of Medical Law at the University of Edinburgh, a position he held until 2005. In addition to his teaching commitments, McCall Smith has also acted as an advisor to both UNESCO and the

S. Massey (✉)
University of St Andrews, St Andrews, Scotland, UK

© The Author(s) 2020
E. Miskimmin (Ed.), *100 British Crime Writers*, Crime Files,
https://doi.org/10.1057/978-1-137-31902-9_90

399

British government and has a considerable bibliography of academic publications. He received a CBE for service to literature in 2007 and holds honorary doctorates from nine universities in Europe and North America.

Running in tandem with his scientific pursuits is McCall Smith's lifelong interest in the literary world. He wrote his first book at the age of eight and began writing children's fiction while still employed at Queen's. In 1998, a visit to Botswana provided the inspiration for his first foray into adult fiction, *The No. 1 Ladies' Detective Agency*. By 2015, McCall Smith had published seventeen novels in the ongoing series featuring the 'traditionally built' amateur sleuth Precious Ramotswe, a woman characterised by her positive outlook on life, her strong moral code and her resolute belief in the soothing powers of red bush tea. For the most part, the world which McCall Smith portrays in his fiction is idyllic. The novels are charmingly naïve in tone and content; crime is small-scale and, with her blend of old-fashioned values and warm empathy, Precious is an engaging heroine. Although McCall Smith has been accused of being overly simplistic in his representation of Africa, his work has enjoyed tremendous international success. The series has been translated into many languages and has been adapted for both television and radio.

Precious is not McCall Smith's only serial protagonist. He gently mocks the world of academia in the Professor Von Igelfeld series and has also created an Edinburgh-based detective in the form of Isabel Dalhousie, the philosopher–heroine of *The Sunday Philosophy Club (2004)*, the first book in another long-running series. McCall Smith has also published the episodic *44 Scotland Street* series, which tracks a revolving cast of characters in and around Edinburgh.

Suggested Reading/Works Cited

O'Donoghue, Heather, 'Smith, Alexander McCall', in *British Crime Writing: An Encyclopedia*, ed. by Barry Forshaw (Oxford: Greenwood World Publishing, 2009).

The Official Alexander McCall Smith Website. http://www.alexandermccall smith.co.uk.

CHAPTER 91

John Williams (b. 1961), 1999: *Five Pubs, Two Bars and a Nightclub*

Catherine Phelps

John Williams was born and grew up in Cardiff. After a variety of jobs which included working in an anarchist printshop and writing for a punk fanzine, he moved to London where he worked as a journalist. His career as a novelist and editor began when still living in London but, as he explains in his introduction to the short story anthology, *Wales Half Welsh*, his 'Welshness started creeping up' on him and he made the decision to return to Cardiff. He currently lives in Cardiff with his writer/musician wife, Charlotte Greig, and their children.

Williams writes in a variety of genres: travel writing, true crime, crime fiction and biography. His first book, *Into the Badlands* (1991), recounts his travels across America to interview native crime writers. These are essays firmly focused on the grittier aspects of America. However, Williams' true crime account of the infamous Lynette White murder in Cardiff's docklands, *Bloody Valentine* (1994), set the tone for Williams' future work. *Bloody Valentine* follows the so-called Cardiff Three's fight to clear their name after their wrongful imprisonment for the murder. Williams spent time with the Cardiff Three and their families

C. Phelps (✉)
Cardiff University, Cardiff, UK

© The Author(s) 2020
E. Miskimmin (ed.), *100 British Crime Writers*, Crime Files,
https://doi.org/10.1057/978-1-137-31902-9_91

in Butetown, the council estate and site of the demolished Tiger Bay. This much-vilified area stands in direct contrast to its neighbour, the regenerated Cardiff Bay. As the title of his edited short story anthology suggests, Williams sees himself writing in the tradition of Colin MacInnes. Williams' work, like MacInnes' examines the ordinariness of those who inhabit a marginalised netherworld and attempts to demystify them.

On his return home, Williams went on to write the Cardiff-set crime fiction for which he is best known: *Five Pubs, Two Bars and a Nightclub* (1999); *Cardiff Dead* (2000); *The Prince of Wales* (2003) and *Temperance Town* (2004). The first three are also published in one collection, *The Cardiff Trilogy* (2006). These are more urban thrillers than conventional crime fiction as very little detection seems to take place. Featuring a large cast of characters, each Cardiff novels focuses on a particular individual's story. For instance, *The Prince of Wales* centres on a female pimp, Bobby Ranger, and her search for her father. Williams' Cardiff is one which is recognisable and familiar to the native reader, as are his characters, many of whom are barely disguised personas of the people he spent time with when researching *Bloody Valentine*.

Williams has since turned from crime fiction to write biographies. However, these share similar thematic connections to his other work. *Michael X* (2008) tells the story of the Trinidadian conman, black power figure and possible victim of a miscarriage of justice, Michael de Freitas. His 2010 biography, *Miss Shirley Bassey* returns to Tiger Bay to uncover the impoverished beginnings of Cardiff's most famous daughter.

Suggested Reading/Works Cited

Brockway, Anthony, 'An Interview with John Williams', *The Wolfman Knew My Father*. http://homepage.ntlworld.com/elizabeth.ercocklly/johnw.htm.
Williams, John, 'Introduction', in *Wales Half Welsh*, ed. by John Williams (London: Bloomsbury, 2004), pp. 1–12.

CHAPTER 92

Malcolm Pryce (b. 1960), 2001: *Aberystwyth Mon Amour*

Catherine Phelps

Born near the England/Wales border in Shrewsbury, Pryce moved to Aberystwyth at the age of nine. After studying German at Warwick and Freiburg, Pryce worked as an aluminium salesman, copywriter and deckhand before travelling through East Asia. While working for an ad agency in Singapore, he was inspired to write a novel about the criminal classes of Aberystwyth and took a berth on a cargo ship bound for South America in order to start work on what became *Aberystwyth Mon Amour* (2001). Ill-health brought Pryce back to Britain where he wrote his Aberystwyth novels, although Oxford is his current home.

The insertion of 'Aberystwyth' into the titles of canonical works immediately alerts the reader to the playful nature of the series. Pryce's novels are ludic parodies that derive their comedy by marrying the hard-boiled novel with an exaggerated Welsh culture. His central investigative figure is private eye, Louie Knight, a name that reverberates with the echo of Raymond Chandler's homage to mediaeval chivalry, Philip Marlowe. Like Chandler's P. I., Louie is hard-drinking and hard-bitten, and operates in the grey area of the law. Still, Knight is not the solitary investigative figure

---

C. Phelps (✉)
Cardiff University, Cardiff, UK

© The Author(s) 2020
E. Miskimmin (ed.), *100 British Crime Writers*, Crime Files,
https://doi.org/10.1057/978-1-137-31902-9_92

of hard-boiled crime fiction but is partnered with a schoolgirl sidekick, Calamity Jane, reminding us of a crime fiction progenitor, the Western. Despite their geographic distance from one another, Pryce overlays West Wales with the lawless Wild West.

Pryce's Aberystwyth is one that is caricatured to the point of absurdity, especially its Welsh cultural identity. The opening paragraph of *Aberystwyth Mon Amour* is indicative of the tone throughout the series, with its references to the 'Druids', 'hanging around at Sospan's ice-cream stall, preening themselves in their sharp Swansea suits and teardrop aviator shades'. Much comedy is derived through cartoon images of Welsh culture. Because of this, the novels have received a mixed reception in Wales. However, this overlooks the fact that Pryce, as in Jasper Fforde's Thursday Next series, imagines an independent and self-sufficient, albeit anachronistic, Welsh state. And Pryce does explore forgotten aspects of Welsh history such as the Ukrainian town, Hughesovka, founded by the Welsh industrialist, John Hughes, in the late nineteenth century. Pryce uses Hughesovka as a setting in the fifth of the series, *From Aberystwyth with Love* (2009). Conversely, it could be argued that Pryce pokes fun at Welsh stereotypes in order to undermine them. The sweeping away of the old Aberystwyth at the finish of the first novel to reveal a regenerated, European-style Aberystwyth seems to suggest this. Nevertheless, this Aberystwyth is one which is devoid of any Welsh identity and it is the old druidic Wales that Pryce returns to in *Last Tango in Aberystwyth* (2003) and the subsequent books of the series.

Suggested Reading/Works Cited

Phelps, Catherine, 'Minstrelsy in Malcolm Pryce's *Aberystwyth Mon Amour*', in *Almanac 15: Yearbook of Welsh Writing in English*, ed. by Katie Gramich (Cardigan: Parthian, 2011), pp. 47–69.
The Official Malcolm Pryce Website. http://www.malcolmpryce.com.

CHAPTER 93

Lindsay Ashford (b. 1959), 2003: *Frozen*

Catherine Phelps

One of the first women to graduate from Queens' College Cambridge with a degree in criminology, Lindsay Ashford went on to work as a local reporter for the BBC in her native Wolverhampton. Following a long career as a freelance journalist, a creative writing course led her to crime fiction. Now living in Borth, West Wales, Ashford is known for her Megan Rhys series, which features a forensic psychologist of Welsh–Indian heritage. Her short stories have also been published by Honno, an independent press that publishes work by women writing from Wales, and for whom she edited the short story crime collection *Written in Blood* (2009).

Much of Ashford's work is informed by the concerns of second-wave feminism, such as male violence towards women and women's struggle for parity within the workplace. The first title in the series, *Frozen* (2003) sets the tone for much of Ashford's work. Drawing on her experiences collecting data on Wolverhampton's sex workers for a charity, this novel centres on an investigation into the serial murders of prostitutes in the Midlands. In an interview, Ashford describes how: '[…] the things I saw and heard while doing the research were incredible. I got to tour the red light district of the town with the local vice squad, interviewing prostitutes

C. Phelps (✉)
Cardiff University, Cardiff, UK

© The Author(s) 2020
E. Miskimmin (ed.), *100 British Crime Writers*, Crime Files,
https://doi.org/10.1057/978-1-137-31902-9_93

405

soliciting on street corners. When I'd finished I had more than a collection of statistics; I had the stories of these women's lives'. These stories also found their way into *The Rubber Woman* (2007), part of the Quick Read series designed to reintroduce adults to reading; this also focused on a serial killer of prostitutes but this time in a Cardiff setting. *Strange Blood* (2005) explored a similar theme of violent crime against women.

Ashford's move to Borth may have influenced her choice of Megan Rhys' hybrid nationality; the area also provides the setting for her third novel *Death Studies* (2006). Borth briefly featured in the two prior novels as a place of refuge and recuperation for her heroine and her sister Ceri. Originally Indian–Italian–Welsh in *Frozen*, Megan Rhys' nationality is simplified in the later books to Indian–Welsh. It is in *Death Studies* that Megan's Welsh background is more fully explored and once again Borth is a bolt-hole for those fleeing male violence. In *Death Studies*, however, this refuge is threatened by those from outside the area.

A mother of four children, Ashford also explores themes of motherhood, fertility and missing fathers; *The Killer Inside* (2008) ended with Rhys' unexpected pregnancy in a novel that, perhaps unsuccessfully, moves away from crimes against women and seeks to explore the reasons behind male criminality.

Suggested Reading/Works Cited

Ashford, Lindsay, 'The Worst Day of my Life'. http://www.honno.co.uk/interview-lindsay-ashford.php.

CHAPTER 94

Adrian McKinty (b. 1968), 2003: *Dead I May Well Be*

Gerard Brennan

Adrian McKinty grew up in Carrickfergus in Northern Ireland. He graduated from Oxford University in 1993 and then moved to New York City. He worked a number of jobs, from barman to librarian, before locating to Denver Colorado in 2000 where he worked as a high school English teacher. In 2008 he relocated again to St Kilda, Melbourne, Australia. Obviously a writer with itchy feet, it's no surprise that his work has been set in many corners of the world, such as New York, Mexico, Cuba and Ireland.

McKinty's most notable works come in the form of two unrelated trilogies. The 'Dead' trilogy follows the grim and brutal adventures of Michael Forsythe, a young man who left Northern Ireland to hook up with a criminal fraternity in New York. There are shades of Whitey Bulger in the Darkey White antagonist of *Dead I Well May Be* (2003), the first book in the series. As the body count mounts throughout the series, Forsythe becomes more powerful in his role as a reluctant gangster, losing friends and even a foot in the process. McKinty has been criticised for the level of violence portrayed in these books, but such is the world he writes about.

G. Brennan (✉)
Queen's University, Belfast, UK

© The Author(s) 2020
E. Miskimmin (ed.), *100 British Crime Writers*, Crime Files,
https://doi.org/10.1057/978-1-137-31902-9_94

His 'Troubles' trilogy, beginning with *The Cold Cold Ground* (2012), set in the early 1980s and featuring Detective Sean Duffy, contains his most political work to date. With echoes of Eoin McNamee and David Peace, McKinty strips away the romanticism of the Troubles and shows it for the dirty, violent war it really was. Revelling in conspiracies and betrayals, McKinty holds up the dark period in Northern Irish history to reveal a time and place that was rotten to the core. This trilogy may well become essential reading for anybody who wants to take an alternative approach to learning about Northern Ireland's tragic past.

McKinty wrote a third trilogy, aimed at young adults. The 'Lighthouse' trilogy is a series of science fiction novels that are closely tied to McKinty's home town, Carrickfergus. His stand-alone novels for adults, such as *Hidden River* (2005), *Fifty Grand* (2009) *Falling Glass* (2011) and *The Sun is God* (2014) are hard-hitting crime fiction narratives. *Fifty Grand* won the Spinetingler Award for Best Novel in 2010 and Audible.com selected *Falling Glass* as the Best Mystery or Thriller of 2011.

Frank McCourt described McKinty as 'a cross between Mickey Spillane and Damon Runyan, the toughest, the best', and as McCourt suggests, McKinty has carved himself a reputation as a 'tough guy' author and that fits very well with his gritty and fearless style. But there is also an intelligent and lyrical quality to his work that does not always get the credit it deserves. As Eoin McNamee writes in his review of *The Cold Cold Ground* for The Guardian, 'What makes McKinty a cut above the rest is the quality of his prose. His driven, spat-out sentences are more accessible than James Ellroy's edge-of-reason staccato, and he can be lyric'. His novels are not simply plotted high-octane thrillers, but something much more impacting and memorable.

SUGGESTED READING/WORKS CITED

Connolly, John and Declan Burke, eds, *Books to Die For: The World's Greatest Mystery Writers on the World's Greatest Mystery Novels* (London: Hodder and Stoughton, 2012).
Crime Scene NI Website. http://crimesceneni.blogspot.com/search/label/Adrian%20McKinty.
McKinty, Adrian, 'Odd Men Out', in *Down These Green Streets: Irish Crime Writing in the 21st Century*, ed. by Declan Burke (Dublin: Liberties Press, 2011), pp. 96–105.

McNamee, Eoin, 'Review of *The Cold Cold Ground* by Adrian McKinty', *The Guardian*, 6 January 2012. http://www.theguardian.com/books/2012/jan/06/cold-cold-gound-adrian-mckinty-review.

CHAPTER 95

Justin Richards (b. 1961), 2003: *The Paranormal Puppet Show* (First Novel in the 'The Invisible Detective' Series)

Lucy Andrew

Justin Richards is best known as a science fiction and fantasy writer for children. He works as Creative Consultant for BBC Books' *Doctor Who* series, for which he has written over twenty titles, along with a number of *Doctor Who* audio plays and reference books. Before he began writing for children he worked as a software designer for fourteen years and later as a technical writer, a magazine editor and contributor and a screenwriter.

Although Richards' work contains elements of time travel, science fiction and fantasy, his texts often focus upon pseudo-detective characters who attempt to solve mysteries, defeat criminals and restore order. Texts such as the *Department of Unclassified Artefacts* series (2006–10), *The Chaos Code* (2007) and the *Time Runners* series (2007–8) fit this pattern. In contrast, Richards' *Invisible Detective* series (2003–2005), while blending several genres, is more firmly rooted in the detective tradition. Inspired in part by his childhood enjoyment of Blyton's *Famous Five* and *Find-Outers* series and Agatha Christie's crime output, Richards'

L. Andrew (✉)
University of Chester, Chester, UK

© The Author(s) 2020
E. Miskimmin (ed.), *100 British Crime Writers*, Crime Files,
https://doi.org/10.1057/978-1-137-31902-9_95

411

Invisible Detective series heralds the creation of an innovative hybrid detective form.

The series' main protagonist, Arthur Drake, exists simultaneously as a child in 1930s London and as his grandson of the same name in present-day London. In the 1930s, Art and his friends create fictional detective Brandon Lake, known as 'the Invisible Detective' because of his elusive nature. Disguised as Brandon Lake, Art holds a weekly consulting session in which members of the public hire him to investigate suspicious occurrences in the local area. The mysteries that Art and his friends encounter in the 1930s resurface for the present-day Arthur and his grandad, the original Art, who is now in a nursing home. The series' greatest innovation is its rejection of the modernist 'knowingness' of early detective fiction in favour of a postmodern mystery formula which is characterised by its lack of resolution and explanation. *The Invisible Detective* books play on the reader's desire for explanation by creating a mystery that spans the entire series – namely, the link between the Invisible Detective in the past and the present. Although some pieces of the puzzle fall into place, the anticipated explanation of the texts' core mystery never arrives and, consequently, the series remains structurally open-ended and incomplete.

Richards' most recent crime narratives follow the contemporary trend for child spies and secret agents, as popularised in Anthony Horowitz's *Alex Rider* series and Charlie Higson's *Young Bond* books. Richards currently co-writes the *Rich and Jade* books with Jack Higgins, a series for teenagers which focuses on the children of a secret agent as they become embroiled in their father's dangerous criminal world and begin to play a decisive role in his missions. Richards has also written the *Agent Alfie* books (2008–2009), a comedic series for young readers which follow the adventures of Alfie, a postman's son, who is mistakenly admitted to a school for young spies.

Suggested Reading/Works Cited

The Official Justin Richards Website. http://justinrichardswriter.com.

CHAPTER 96

C. J. Sansom (b. 1952), 2003: *Dissolution*

Martin Lightening

C. J. Sansom had always wanted to write novels but he felt he might not have the time or the energy until he retired. When he was forty-eight his father died and left him a small inheritance which allowed him time to try. *Dissolution* (2003), set in the reign of Henry VIII introduced Sansom's hunchback detective, lawyer Mathew Shardlake, and became the first of an ongoing series of bestselling historical crime novels. Their success has caused Shardlake to be dubbed 'the Tudor Morse'.

Christopher John Sansom was born in Edinburgh into a comfortably conservative family, went to private school and then to Birmingham University. While there is a political awakening which had begun in his teens began to blossom. After his B. A. in history, and then his PhD, *British Labour Party's Policy Towards South Africa Between the Wars*, he felt himself to be something of a radical independent socialist. Spurning academia, he took a variety of jobs but eventually decided to retrain as a solicitor. Subsequently he practised in Sussex, often working for disadvantaged clients through the legal aid system.

His knowledge of the law and his love of the modern crime novels, especially those of P. D. James and Ruth Rendell, combined with his interest in Tudor history, gave him the idea for his first murder–mystery

M. Lightening (✉)
Freelance Cameraman and Writer, Manchester, UK

© The Author(s) 2020
E. Miskimmin (ed.), *100 British Crime Writers*, Crime Files,
https://doi.org/10.1057/978-1-137-31902-9_96

novel. *Dissolution* is set during the period of the dissolution of the monasteries; Mathew Shardlake is sent by Cromwell to investigate the gruesome murder of one of Henry VIII's commissioners at a monastery in Sussex. P. D. James' testimonial describes *Dissolution* as 'Remarkable [...]. The sights, the voices, the very smell of this turbulent age seem to rise from the page'. It was nominated for the 2003 Crime Writers' Association John Creasey Memorial Dagger for first books by a previously unpublished author. Each following Shardlake novel draws closely on events during Henry VIII's reign with accurate detail. *Dark Fire* (2004) finds Shardlake on another secret mission for Cromwell. This novel won the 2005 Ellis Peters Historical Dagger awarded by the CWA. *Sovereign* (2006), sees political intrigue and murder set in York around Henry VIII's spectacular Progress to the North. In *Revelation* (2008) a serial killer is enacting the dark prophecies of the book of Revelation. *Heartstone* (2010) brings Shardlake and his assistant Barak to Portsmouth where they are caught up with Henry VIII's preparations to fight off the French invasion fleet of 1545. *Lamentation* (2014), is set in the following year in the court of the dying king.

In 2003, fearing a Tudor crime novel might not be successful, Sansom also wrote a second, *Winter in Madrid*, set in Spain during and after the Spanish Civil War, although the publication of this was delayed until 2006 due to the success of the Shardlake novels, at which point it became a bestseller. Sansom's plotting is intricate and each novel is vivid in its historical details: the *New York Times* testimonial comment that 'History never seemed so real' is reflective of how most of his readers regard Sansom's Tudor novels. His stand-alone novel, *Dominion* (2012), focuses on another period again, but this time Sansom deliberately deconstructs and rewrites the past by imagining a Britain that has lost World War Two. Although this premise proved controversial for some, Sansom was applauded by others for another imaginative take on history.

Suggested Reading/Works Cited

Crown, Sarah, 'A Life in Books: C. J. Sansom'. http://www.guardian.co.uk/culture/2010/nov/15/cj-sansom-interview.

CHAPTER 97

Dreda Say Mitchell (Pseudonym of Louise Emma Joseph, b. 1965), 2004: *Running Hot*

Esme Miskimmin

Writer, journalist, broadcaster and campaigner, Dreda Say Mitchell's *Running Hot* was awarded the CWA John Creasey Dagger for the Best First Crime Novel. It was one of two standalone novels that Mitchell wrote before beginning the 'Gangland Girl' series of books for which she is probably best known (*Geezer Girls*, 2009, *Gangster Girl*, 2010, and *Hit Girls*, 2011). These were followed by the D.I. Rio Wray series – co-written with her partner Tony Mason – of which two novels had been published by 2015 (*Vendetta*, 2014, and *Death Trap*, 2015).

Mitchell was born in East London, the fourth child of Grenadian parents who came to England in the 1960s. She still lives there, having graduated from SOAS University of London with a degree in African Studies and an M.A. in Education from the London Metropolitan University, and having spent over two decades working in teaching and wider education, focusing on children from BAME and working-class backgrounds. Her crime writing is intrinsically bound to the area of London in which she has spent her life: in an interview with Laura Hardman she describes it as 'the bedrock of the types of stories [she] writes', adding

E. Miskimmin (✉)
University of Liverpool, Liverpool, UK

© The Author(s) 2020
E. Miskimmin (ed.), *100 British Crime Writers*, Crime Files,
https://doi.org/10.1057/978-1-137-31902-9_97

that the people she grew up with 'provide a great springboard for [her] characters'. A recurring theme of Mitchell's work is the tension between a desire to leave in search of a 'better' life and an inescapable bond to one's place of origin. *Running Hot* is the story of 'Schoolboy' Campbell, who has seven days to escape his current life in the criminal underworld, but who seems to be drawn back with every step he takes to get away. Similarly, in the 'Gangland Girl' series, each novel sees the female protagonists unable to free themselves from the criminal events of the past; in *Gangster Girl*, Daisy's respectable adult existence as a lawyer is torn apart by the return of the mother who abandoned her, and who still operates in the same moral hinterland as her 'long-dead gangster father, Frankie Sullivan'. Mitchell repeatedly reinforces the inescapability of Daisy's origins in her characterisation, even in the 'dollop of cockney heritage' that is 'rolling' in her 'upmarket London accent'.

Daisy Sullivan's heritage is often shown to be empowering, however: it gives her an edge in terms of understanding and behaviour, and the complexities of her social identity drive the narrative. Strong women are recurrent in Mitchell's writing, and once again they have a basis in her East London roots: in the Hardman interview, she says 'I grew up with strong women, both in the Caribbean community and in East London. It just seems to me that in both of these communities women are very often the backbone. [...] I also wasn't very interested in writing about women as "victims".'

Mitchell's fiction also challenges racial stereotypes: she says in an interview with Yvonne Roberts that she 'wrote [*Running* Hot] because [she] was sick of plots in which the young black guy dies in the end'. D. I. Rio Wray makes her first appearance in *Vendetta* as an unnamed woman at the crime scene: 'decked out in gold heels that matched her moon-shaped earrings, miniskirt, jeans jacket over a sparkling boob-tube top', with a 'glistening brown legs' and a 'mini finger-combed 'fro'. Mistaken by the uniformed policeman for a prostitute, she shows him her 'bling' in the form of her Metropolitan Police badge: 'I'm black, dressed like this, so I must be a working girl. Is that it?' Mitchell has also written about assumptions made on the basis of race and gender in her non-fiction work, such as in her piece for *The Guardian*, 'Yes, *Daily Mail* – black and Asian women can be qualified to talk', and wider issues of race, class and gender are often the focus of Mitchell's non-fiction writing and campaigning. She has appeared on many television and radio current affairs programmes, including *Question Time*, *Newsnight* and *Woman's Hour*, and her level of expertise and engagement with social and cultural issues has afforded her the same respect and recognition as a campaigner that she receives as a writer.

SUGGESTED READING/WORKS CITED

Hardman, Laura, 'Interview with Dreda Say Mitchell', *Shots: Crime and Thriller Ezine* (2010). http://www.shotsmag.co.uk/interview_view.aspx?interview_id=18.

Mitchell, Dreda Say, 'Yes, *Daily Mail*—Black and Asian Women Can Be Qualified to Talk', *The Guardian*, 24 March 2014. https://www.theguardian.com/commentisfree/2014/mar/24/daily-mail-black-asian-women-credentials-challenged.

Official Website: 'Dreda Say Mitchell, MBE: Best-Selling Crime Author'. https://dredamitchell.com/.

Roberts, Yvonne, 'Ms Grit', *Ready, Steady, Go!: Women in* Prison, Summer 2017. https://www.womeninprison.org.uk/perch/resources/articles/dreda-say-mitchell.pdf.

CHAPTER 98

Brian McGilloway (b. 1974), 2007: *Borderlands*

Gerard Brennan

In an article on the 'Writing.ie' website, Brian McGilloway observes: 'James Lee Burke argues that it is the writer's obligation to "tell the truth about the period he lives in and to expose those who exploit their fellow man." It's no surprise then that the past decade in Ireland has seen an explosion in crime writing'. Author of the Inspector Benedict Devlin mysteries and the DS Lucy Black novels, Brian McGilloway has penned police procedurals that examine both the *Garda Síochána* and the Police Service of Northern Ireland. He writes as he lives, with one foot on each side of the border. Born in Derry, Northern Ireland, and living in Inspector Devlin's hometown, Lifford, a County Donegal town in the Republic, McGilloway is in a unique position to look at the island of Ireland as a whole, and he takes full advantage of it.

McGilloway attended Queen's University in Belfast and went on to become the head of English Literature at St Columb's College in Derry before embarking on his literary career. He is not the first acclaimed literary figure to be associated with St Columb's College. Brian Friel, Seamus Heaney, Seamus Deane and Sean O'Reilly were all past pupils

---

G. Brennan (✉)
Queen's University, Belfast, UK

© The Author(s) 2020
E. Miskimmin (ed.), *100 British Crime Writers*, Crime Files,
https://doi.org/10.1057/978-1-137-31902-9_98

419

of the respected Derry school. Although it is still relatively early days in the Derry crime fiction writer's career, he is well on the way to reaching the dizzy heights of his predecessors. The first Inspector Devlin mystery, *Borderlands* (2007), was shortlisted for a Crime Writers' Association Dagger award for best debut novel, and his achievements continue to mount. His career began with the Macmillan imprint, Macmillan New Writing; renowned for taking chances on brand-new authors. In McGilloway's case, it was a chance that paid back in spades. He is reputedly the most successful author to have come from their stable, and the first to see his debut released in the US.

Gallows Lane (2008), the second in the Inspector Devlin series, was published to even further acclaim. Steeped in the politics of interdepartmental policing, it was a more ambitious novel than its predecessor and all the more powerful for it. *Gallows Lane* was shortlisted for the Theakston's Old Peculiar Crime Novel of the Year award in 2010. Inspector Devlin, McGilloway's most established character, is from a different mould than most of the detectives in contemporary crime fiction. He does not have a drinking problem and is not a brooding loose cannon with a self-destructive streak. In fact, Devlin is a devoted family man who seems quite happy with his stable home life and for the most part he plays by the rules at work. Devlin's everyday family life lends a realism that gives McGilloway's fiction all the more impact. Unlike the fabled lone wolves of police-procedural fiction, Inspector Devlin has everything to live for and everything to lose.

Inspector Devlin has appeared in three more novels: *Bleed a River Deep* (2009), *The Rising* (2010) and *The Nameless Dead* (2012). Each novel displays an empathic insight into contemporary life in Ireland. McGilloway's sense of a scarred society and the kind of justice craved by a country so recently at the mercy of paramilitary forces is ever-present and deftly handled. While he has a keen eye for politics, his work constantly looks towards the future rather than dwelling on the past. To begin with, McGilloway avoided writing about the Police Service of Northern Ireland as he started work on *Borderlands* at a time when the security forces were going through radical changes. Trying to get to grips with an organisation that was still evolving to become more inclusive of the Catholic community in Northern Ireland would have thrown up too many problems and had the potential to distract from the tale McGilloway wanted to spin. By 2011, however, McGilloway had written and published *Little Girl Lost*, the first novel to feature DS Lucy Black of the PSNI. Writing from the point of view of a very different character in a very different situation to Inspector Devlin, McGilloway planted the seed for a series that continues to flourish.

SUGGESTED READING/WORKS CITED

Connolly, John and Declan Burke, eds, *Books to Die For: The World's Greatest Mystery Writers on the World's Greatest Mystery Novels* (London: Hodder and Stoughton, 2012).

Crime Scene NI Website. http://crimesceneni.blogspot.com/search/label/Brian%20McGilloway.

McGilloway, Brian, 'Walking the Tightrope: The Border in Irish Fiction', in *Down These Green Streets: Irish Crime Writing in the 21st Century*, ed. by Declan Burke (Dublin: Liberties Press, 2011), pp. 302–313.

'Writing.ie: The Home of Irish Writing Online' Website. http://www.writing.ie/resources/the-nameless-dead-brian-mcgilloway/.

CHAPTER 99

Stuart Neville (b. 1972), 2010: *The Twelve*

Steven Powell

One of the most promising talents to have emerged in British crime writing in recent years, Stuart Neville's four novels have mostly focused on the complicated legacy of the Troubles since the signing of the Good Friday Agreement. Stuart Neville was born in Armagh 'within a few days of Bloody Sunday' and has worked in a variety of professions 'a musician, a composer, a teacher, a salesman, a film extra, a baker'. Neville's writing career began when he submitted a short story 'The Last Dance' to the online magazine *ThugLit.com* in 2008. Following its publication, Neville was contacted by renowned American literary agent Nat Sobel who wanted him to produce a novel.

Neville's debut novel *The Twelve* (2010), published as *The Ghosts of Belfast* in the US, follows former Republican paramilitary killer Gerry Fegan. Released from prison and left without work as a consequence of the peace process, an alcoholic Fegan is haunted by the souls of his twelve murder victims who literally follow him everywhere. To exorcise his demons, Fegan decides to kill some of his former associates who were jointly responsible for his twelve victim's deaths. He chooses terrorists turned politicians, unreformed gangsters and a hypocritical priest as his

S. Powell (✉)
University of Liverpool, Liverpool, UK

© The Author(s) 2020
E. Miskimmin (ed.), *100 British Crime Writers*, Crime Files,
https://doi.org/10.1057/978-1-137-31902-9_99

423

targets. For every person he kills, one of the souls haunting him disappears. *The Twelve* was followed by *Collusion* (2011), which sees the return of Gerry Fegan and examines the controversial subject of British Intelligence's relationship with paramilitaries on both sides. *Stolen Souls* (2012) looks at the changing ethnic demographics of Northern Ireland from the dark subject of sex trafficking from Eastern Europe.

Ratlines (2013) is a work of historical fiction, and Neville's most critically praised work to date. Taking as its subject Ireland's controversial role in World War Two and its aftermath, *Ratlines* is set in early 1963 as the Republic was preparing for the visit of President John F. Kennedy. The murder of a German businessman living in Ireland sparks fears that the Irish government's comfortable relationship with former high-ranking Nazi's could be exposed. Albert Ryan is a Directorate of Intelligence officer assigned to the case. Ostracised in Irish society for serving with the British army during the war, Ryan is torn between his duty and his hatred for the Nazis in hiding on Irish soil. *Ratlines* contains two barbed portraits of historical figures: Otto Skorzeny, 'Hitler's favourite commando' once dubbed 'the most dangerous man in Europe', features as an ageing playboy-type living off the myth of his wartime adventures. Minister for Justice and later Taoiseach Charles Haughey is brazenly depicted as venal and boorish, interested in nothing but self-advancement.

Neville's skill as a writer is that he is able to portray all sides of the Northern Ireland conflict with a degree of sympathy, while not shying away from the bigotry and violence that still persists since the end of 'the Troubles'. He has identified James Ellroy as his favourite author, and the influence of Ellroy's Underworld USA trilogy can be seen in the complex connectivity. Neville weaves between the British government, Intelligence services, Republican and Loyalist paramilitaries and the communities of Northern Ireland in his novels.

SUGGESTED READING/WORKS CITED

Nolan, Tom, 'Stuart Neville', *Mystery Scene*, 117 (2010), 38–39.
The Book Depository Blog 'Stuart Neville'. http://www.bookdepository.co.uk/int erview/with/author/stuart-neville.

CHAPTER 100

Gerard Brennan (b. 1979), 2011: *The Point*

Esme Miskimmin

Gerard Brennan is a crime writer from Dundrum, Northern Ireland. His short stories have appeared in a number of anthologies, including *The Mammoth Book of Best British Crime Volume 9* (2012). His first novella, *The Point* was published in 2011 and the second novel in this series, *Breaking Point* was published in 2014, as was the novel *Undercover*, featuring detective Cormac Kelly. Other work in print by 2015 included *Wee Rockets* (2012) and *Wee Danny* (2013). Realism is intrinsic to Brennan's writing: his locations are recognisable, his language is direct and often violent and his characters are believable in their construction, but perhaps more importantly in their ambiguous morality which can make his work disconcerting and exciting at the same time. In *The Point*, for example, set in the world of Belfast gangsters, the reader finds themselves wanting to invest in the romance of a burgeoning relationship between a criminal and a terrifyingly in control, out-of-control, femme fatale. None of the novel's characters has a straight moral compass, and this complexity is compounded by the book's shifting points of view that allow the reader vicarious access to their thoughts and motivations.

Brennan is a significant figure in the establishing of a specific canon of Northern Irish Crime writing, editing volumes such as *Requiems for*

E. Miskimmin (✉)
University of Liverpool, Liverpool, UK

the Departed, a collection of crime fiction based on Irish myths, and which won the 2011 Spinetingler Award for best anthology, as well as contributing to critical volumes on the subject, such as his essay 'The Truth Commissioners' in *Down these Green Streets* (2011), in which he discusses how the complexities of the post-Troubles era created 'a hotbed of inspiration for the new breed of Northern Irish crime fiction writer'. His website, 'Crime Scene NI' is a significant resource for those interested in the genre. Below, he responds to some questions about crime writing in general, and Northern Irish crime writing in particular, and assesses his position as the newest writer in this list that spans 160 years:

You're number 100 in this book— the newest author in a list that begins with Caroline Clive way back in 1855. Did you have any sense of joining a canon of writers when you started writing 'crime fiction', and does an awareness of what has come before have any bearing on how / what you write?

Yes and yes. As with any profession, I feel that a writer should serve a form of apprenticeship. A big part of that is to become familiar with those who have more experience. Each crime writer who has come before has the potential to teach a novice something, so long as they're willing to learn. For my part, I read and read and read, both inside and outside the genre (mostly inside, if I'm honest) and try to take a little from each book beyond enjoyment. Even the writers who aren't my cup of tea can teach or motivate.

Is there anyone on the list whose writing you enjoy, or would say has influenced you in any way?

I've read more of the writers featured in Section 4 of the list (1990–2015) than any of the others, so I suppose it's fair to say that most of my British influences come from contemporary crime fiction. I am especially indebted to Brian McGilloway, Adrian McKinty and Stuart Neville, first and foremost for the hours of pleasure their work has provided, but also because they prove time and again that writing about Northern Ireland is no longer uncool. Ian Sansom, a gifted writer and critic who was also my tutor on the creative writing M. A. at Queen's University Belfast, was once told by his editor that the two most boring words in publishing were Northern and Ireland. I feel as if the new generation of NI crime fiction writers have shaken that misconception.

Writers such as Val McDermid, Ian Rankin and Peter Robinson, I believe, have shaped the genre and although they are mere spring chickens compared to many on the list, I feel as if they are the godparents of the current crop of scribes.

The process of compiling this list was often collaborative, and sometimes quite tricky. Is there anyone you would add to the list: and if so – who would you take out?

I don't think I'd remove anybody from this list. Of the writers I've read, they all deserve their spot. And as for those I haven't read; well, I'm in no position to question their achievements. Come back to me when I've worked my way through all 100. But there are writers I would add if the list were to be expanded to 105. I think Ian Sansom's new series, 'The County Guides', will inevitably make waves and breathe new life into the cosy. Colin Bateman should be included. The prolific and successful author of the 'Mystery Man' series juggles humour and mayhem with enviable ease. Brian Moore has often been described as a crime fiction master, though probably not by himself. Of the latest crop of NI writers (I'll always be biased towards my own clique) I'd tip my hat to Claire McGowan (*The Lost*, 2013) and Anthony Quinn (*Disappeared*, 2012).

How do you feel about the labels 'British crime writer', and more specifically 'Northern Irish crime writer' and how do you see yourself in relation to them?

Now here's a can of angry worms…. My Catholic conditioning instinctually kicks in when the word 'British' is bandied about. I try to keep a handle on such silliness, but I think it'll be a few years before I accept the label without any guilt. However, I've been more than happy to have my work featured in Maxim Jakubowski's *Mammoth Book of Best British Crime* three times, I'm on *this* list and I have a British passport. I guess that's progress.

On the other hand, I have absolutely no problem being described as a Northern Irish crime fiction writer. I embrace it, in fact. If nothing else, it's a fair indicator of the content, and thanks to my contemporaries, the quality of a book that falls into this category. I believe that Northern Irish crime fiction is quite different to Irish crime fiction in terms of humour and style, and that difference is something that should be promoted.

In your essay 'The Truth Commissioners', you talk about 'post-Troubles' crime fiction, and your hope that Northern Irish crime writing (which currently seems intrinsically linked to the Troubles) will one day be discussed without the 'post-Troubles' tag. Do you think that crime writing (wherever it is from) is largely contextual? Do you think that some authors (Rankin, Pryce, for example) deliberately promote / sustain this as a genre feature?

Yes, crime writing is contextual. And writers tend to promote/sustain this in order to give the reader (and the publisher) what they expect. You generally know what you're getting from American, Scandinavian or British crime fiction. And that's not really a bad thing. If you want a good burger, you find an American diner. Pizza? Go to a nice Italian place. Shepherd's pie...? I think you can see where I'm going here. The point is, these filters are useful to a reader. It can also be useful for a writer, although, the real trailblazers will find a way to play with context.

I would still like to see the post-Troubles tag dropped. That's not to say that books about the Troubles and the period immediately after should be ignored. I intend to write my own novel set in our dark past at some point in my career. However, I envisage a time when men in balaclavas are not the first thing a reader thinks of when they find out a writer is from Northern Ireland.

A forward-looking perspective seems intrinsic to your approach. Where do you see the future of crime writing?

Yes, I'm concerned about what's around the corner for our society. To borrow a buzz-phrase from the politicians bumbling about in my neck of the woods, I'm interested in 'bread and butter' issues first and foremost. Social deprivation, lack of education, and justice, for a select few. These are the societal problems that fuel my imagination. Crime fiction has always been a powerful lens with which to scrutinise the social order. I want to see more and more new writers using their talent to highlight their community's problems and get their readers thinking about them.

Irish crime writer, Declan Burke, believes that 'if journalism is the first draft of history, crime fiction is its second'.

SUGGESTED READING/WORKS CITED

Brennan, Gerard, 'The Truth Commissioners', in *Down These Green Streets: Irish Crime Writing in the 21st Century*, ed. by Declan Burke (Dublin: Liberties Press, 2011), pp. 201–210.

Burke, Declan, 'Crime Fiction: The Second Draft of History', 11 April 2009, 'Crime Always Pays' Website. http://crimealwayspays.blogspot.com/2009/04/crime-fiction-second-draft-of-history.html.

Gerard Brennan's Crime Scene NI website. http://crimesceneni.blogspot.co.uk/.

Index

A
Academic (donnish) murder-mysteries, 97, 185–187, 259–260, 290, 298
Aird, Catherine, 275, 276
Allingham, Margery, 97, 99, 104, 107, 139–144, 158, 169, 172, 214, 366, 375
Ambler, Eric, 100, 101, 175–178, 219
American crime writing, xv, xvi, 101, 233, 248, 309, 334, 345, 387, 395
Ashford, Lindsay, 360, 405–406
Auden, W.H., xvii, 179

B
Bailey, H.C., 97, 103–106
Barnard, Robert, 289, 290
Bentley, E.C., 5, 6, 71, 83–86, 103, 104
Berkeley, Anthony, 98, 99, 135–138, 156
Blake, Nicholas, x, xv, xvi, xvii, xviii, xix, 99, 179–181

Blyton, Enid, 197–203, 411
Bobin, John William, 5, 89, 90
Braddon, Mary Elizabeth, 3, 13, 15, 19–24, 215
Bramah, Ernest, ix, 87, 88
Brennan, Gerard, 360, 362, 425–428
Brett, Simon, 293–296
Brookmyre, Christopher, 387–389
Brooks, Edwy Searles, 5, 79, 80
Buchan, John, 1, 5, 86, 91–95, 100, 233

C
Chesterton, G.K., 1, 2, 5, 67, 71–76, 83–85, 103, 156
Childers, Erskine, 1, 5, 53–55, 100
Children's crime fiction, 5, 8, 79, 80, 90, 92, 197–203, 213, 333–336, 379, 380, 411, 412
Christie, Agatha, xvii, xviii, 24, 59–61, 84, 97, 98, 100, 101, 103, 107–113, 116, 130, 158, 166, 169, 172, 189, 206, 210, 211, 213, 214, 216, 217, 219, 237,

© The Editor(s) (if applicable) and The Author(s), under exclusive licence to Springer Nature Limited 2020
E. Miskimmin (ed.), *100 British Crime Writers*, Crime Files,
https://doi.org/10.1057/978-1-137-31902-9

239, 289, 291, 299, 300, 302, 375, 411
Clive, Caroline, 1–3, 6–8, 10, 359
Cold War fiction, 144, 177, 213–217, 233, 234, 236, 243, 244, 287
Cole, G.D.H., 121, 122
Cole, Margaret, 121, 122
Cole, Martina, 362, 371, 372
Collins, Wilkie, 3, 9–13, 20, 42, 187
Comic strips, 214, 261–264
Creasey, John, 101, 189, 190
Crime drama, 6, 12, 193–196, 306, 307, 323–328, 336
Crispin, Edmund, 97, 98, 187, 205, 206
Crofts, Freeman Wills, ix, 67, 103, 115–117, 122

D
Davis, Lindsey, 216, 355–358
Dexter, Colin, 101, 214, 297–302, 382
Dickens, Charles, xvii, 10, 68, 210, 289
Doyle, Arthur Conan, viii, 1, 2, 4, 27–33, 63, 65, 73, 75, 107, 186, 210, 306
Duffy, Stella, 215, 360, 383, 384
du Maurier, Daphne, 101, 183, 184
Durbridge, Francis, 193–196, 214

E
Edwards, Martin, 296, 361, 365, 366

F
Feminist crime writing, 3, 215, 337, 338, 356, 360, 405
Ferrars, Elizabeth, 99, 161, 162
Fleming, Ian, 53, 211, 215, 216, 231–236, 241, 287

Forensic crime fiction, 1, 65, 66, 380, 405
Forsyth, Frederick, 217, 285–287, 346
Francis, Dick, 213, 216, 247–250
Fraser, Antonia, 313, 314
Freeman, R. Austin, 1, 3–5, 63–69, 97, 103, 122

G
Gilbert, Michael, viii, 213, 215, 216, 219–221
Golden Age crime fiction, xv, xix, 6, 11, 60, 61, 84, 97–102, 104, 107, 110, 116, 123, 125, 129, 130, 135, 136, 141, 142, 144, 154, 155, 156, 158, 162, 166–169, 171, 172, 181, 206, 217, 271, 276, 295, 299, 359, 361, 365, 366, 375
Graphic novels, 108, 214, 335, 350, 396
Greene, Graham, viii, 53, 101, 147–150
Greenwood, D.M., 361, 367, 368
Gregory, Susanna, 361, 391, 392

H
Hall, Patricia, 369, 370
Harvey, John, 309, 310
Haycraft, Howard, xv, xvii, 2–6, 84, 98–102, 180, 181, 185, 187, 213, 359, 363
Heyer, Georgette, 165, 166
Hill, Reginald, 101, 214, 277–283, 370
Historical crime fiction, 213, 216, 223–229, 315–319, 355–358, 359, 361, 391–393, 413, 414, 424
Hornung, E.W., xi, 3, 47, 48, 64

INDEX 431

Horowitz, Anthony, 213, 333–336, 412

I
Innes, Michael, 97, 185–187, 205, 259, 298

J
James, Bill, 217, 331, 332
James, P.D., 213–215, 253–258, 327, 413, 414

K
Keating H.R.F., xviii, 220, 221, 237–239
Knox, Ronald, 98

L
La Plante, Linda, 214, 215, 323–328
le Carré, John, 144, 175, 215, 216, 236, 241–245

M
MacDonald, Philip, 133, 134
Marsh, Ngaio, 97, 99, 101, 107, 158, 166, 169–173, 214, 217, 375
McCall Smith, Alexander, 399, 400
McDermid, Val, 214, 215, 217, 337–342, 426
McGilloway, Brian, 362, 419–421, 426
McKinty, Adrian, 362, 407, 408, 426
McNeile, H.C., 101, 119
Mina, Denise, ix, 362, 395–397
Mitchell, Dreda Say, 360, 362, 415–417
Mitchell, Gladys, 98, 101, 153–156
Morrison, Arthur, 3, 30, 41, 42, 64

Mortimer, John, 305, 306

N
Nash, Simon, 97, 187, 259, 260
Neville, Stuart, 361, 362, 423, 424, 426
Northern Irish crime writing, x, 214, 362, 363, 407, 408, 419–421, 423, 424, 425–428

O
O'Donnell, Peter, 214, 215, 261–264
Oppenheim, E. Phillips, 1, 5, 45, 46, 100
Orczy, Baroness, x, 3, 49–51, 59

P
Perry, Anne, 216, 315–318
Peters, Ellis, 216, 223–228, 357, 392
Pirkis, C.L., 3, 37, 38
Poe, Edgar Allan, 2, 30, 31, 67, 73–75, 134, 210
Police procedurals, 101, 190, 213, 214, 220, 265, 272, 302, 321, 326, 331, 348, 357, 359, 380, 385, 386, 419, 420
Porter, Joyce, 265, 266
Private detectives, 62, 73, 101, 116, 130, 178, 180, 216, 234, 265, 282, 309, 318, 327, 334, 339, 355, 361, 365, 385, 403
Pryce, Malcolm, 403, 404
Puzzle stories, x, 5, 59, 61, 97, 122, 125, 126, 135, 137, 206, 213, 217, 219, 227, 248, 273, 299, 359, 361

R
Rankin, Ian, 101, 214, 215, 341, 345–350, 395, 426

Regional crime fiction, 214
Rendell, Ruth, 213, 214, 217, 269–274, 327, 373, 413
Richards, Justin, 359, 411, 412
Robinson, Peter, 214, 353, 354, 426
Rohmer, Sax, 81, 82
Rose, Malcolm, 359, 379, 380

S
Sansom, C.J., 361, 413, 414
Sapper, 101, 119, 120
Sayers, Dorothy L., xvii, 57, 59, 61, 67, 69, 72, 84, 86, 97–99, 103, 104, 107, 113, 123–128, 138, 140, 158, 166, 168, 169, 171, 172, 206, 214, 217, 257, 294, 298, 299, 375
Scottish crime writing, xix, 214, 341, 347, 348, 387, 388, 395
Sensation fiction, viii, 6, 8–11, 13, 19–25, 101, 183, 224
Serialised fiction, 4, 11, 20, 21, 30, 82, 92, 93, 139, 193
Simpson, Dorothy, 321, 322
Sims, George, 35, 36
Snow, C.P., 98, 167, 168
Sporting crime stories, 247–251
Spy fiction, 1, 5, 45, 46, 53, 55, 74, 91, 93, 100, 101, 110, 111, 149, 175, 213, 215, 216, 219, 231–236, 241–244, 265, 331–333, 347
Stallwood, Veronica, 298, 381, 382

Symons, Julian, xviii, 53, 54, 75, 76, 102, 122, 134, 172, 209–211, 233, 237–239, 266

T
Tartan Noir, 214, 341, 345, 395
Tart Noir, 3, 383, 384
Taylor, Alison, 360, 385, 386
Teen crime fiction, 90, 333, 335, 359, 379, 380, 412
Tey, Josephine, 97, 99, 157, 158
Thriller fiction, xv, 1, 5, 53, 57, 59, 60, 68, 69, 81, 83, 86, 91, 100, 101, 110, 143, 148, 149, 175–177, 189, 193, 194, 196, 213, 219, 220, 224, 226, 227, 233, 234, 247, 250, 265, 272, 278, 285, 287, 290, 296, 327, 331–335, 337, 346, 347, 359, 373, 379, 402, 408
True crime, 136, 360, 401

W
Wallace, Edgar, 5, 57–61, 100
Walters, Minette, 360, 362, 373–376
Welsh crime writing, 214, 331, 332, 359, 385, 386, 401–404, 406
Wentworth, Patricia, 129, 130
Williams, John, 361, 401, 402
Wingfield, R.D., 101, 329, 330
Wood, Mrs Henry, 3, 4, 13–16

CPI Antony Rowe
Eastbourne, UK
November 16, 2020